The Sands of Time

"I love you, Hawke," Shawnalese proclaimed softly. "You're my everything."

Whispering her name, he crushed her in his arms, pulled her against him, his lips hot and eager. "Say that to me when you're a woman," he said huskily, before his moist lips claimed hers.

"Somehow I'll make you love me, Hawke. I'll steal your heart," she warned, her fingers caressing his cheek, his chin, his neck.

"You cannot steal what is already yours, Shawny," he murmered, pulling her closer into his heated embrace.

Also by Brenna Braxton-Barshon

Southern Oaks

Published by
HarperPaperbacks

Brenna Braxton-Barshon

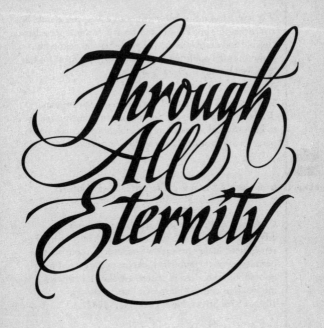

Through All Eternity

HarperPaperbacks
A Division of HarperCollinsPublishers

HarperPaperbacks   *A Division of* HarperCollins*Publishers*
10 East 53rd Street, New York, N.Y. 10022

Copyright © 1992 by Brenna Braxton-Barshon
All rights reserved. No part of this book may be used or reproduced in any manner whatsoever without written permission of the publisher, except in the case of brief quotations embodied in critical articles and reviews. For information address HarperCollins*Publishers,*
10 East 53rd Street, New York, N.Y. 10022.

Cover illustration by Renato Aime

First printing: May 1992

Printed in the United States of America

HarperPaperbacks and colophon are trademarks of HarperCollins*Publishers*

❖ 10 9 8 7 6 5 4 3 2 1

For my treasured daughter, Sheri.
Ours is a bond, my darling, that will transcend my life.
I love you.

And to the man who lives in my heart.
The man who lives in my soul. My beloved husband,
Marty.

Prologue

"I WILL NEVER FORGIVE YOU! NEVER!"

God, how her vow had torn through his heart and nearly destroyed him! That had been two years ago, and now he'd come to take her home. Had come for the angel of hell—and her name was Shawnalese.

Still, he blamed only himself for all that had happened. He had dug her that lethal pit and then he'd jumped into it.

Would she forgive him? He didn't know, and he no longer cared. But he couldn't forget when he had cared. Cared immensely. She had been the world to him.

He leaned against the door as Shawnalese stood motionless at the top of the stairs, her beauty a physical force that struck him and took his breath away. Hundreds of candles flickered in the crystal chandeliers, casting their prism colors across the marble sculptures, across the gilt-framed portraits—across her.

Music floated through the foyer, and beautiful, elegantly gowned ladies, adorned with jewels, drifted by with handsome escorts in satin coats, snug-fitting breeches, and showy laces.

Guests smiled. Laughter tinkled. Gaiety abounded.

Nevertheless, no happy smile curved Shawnalese Grenville's perfect mouth, no laughter slipped past her lips, no gay light glimmered in her green eyes, and she wondered why she'd come. But, with staunch resolu-

1

tion she tried to veil her torment. She lifted her gold-threaded skirts and swept down the staircase.

Without warning, she sensed his presence and stopped midstairs, her hopeful heart and gaze searching carefully for the only man who mattered. Both found him.

"Gayhawke!" The hushed gasp crossed her lips and she battled to recapture her composure.

Exceptionally tall, broad-shouldered and dressed in formal attire, Gayhawke Lawrence Richard Carrington, the sixth duke of Foxridge, looked formidable. Intimidating. His proud bearing was regal, and an aura of power, an air of mystique, surrounded him. Hawke's enigma was not merely from his immense wealth, his distinguished title, or his cavalier disposition, but also from the icy facade which he permitted no one to penetrate. Every man and woman present knew that this arrogantly self-confident nobleman gave quarter to no one. One corner of Hawke's mouth lifted in cold cynicism, and he inclined his head toward Shawnalese in a travesty of a bow.

Frozen to the stair, she nodded aloofly, with an air of defiance that she knew would rankle him. It had been a long time . . . so very long a time. Two years, during which she'd thought of little but revenge. Yet neither time nor her vengeful notions had dulled her remembrance of him, for Hawke's sharply defined features were forever seared into her memory. His softly waving ebony hair framed a treacherously handsome visage, and his strong, square jawline bore the ever-present shadow of a beard. Even Hawke's cleft chin, the only flaw in his otherwise perfect face, appealed to her, and his carved, sculpted mouth, although molded now in harsh censure, was somehow strangely sensuous, beckoning her.

Hawke's fierce, dusky green eyes beneath swooping thick brows glinted at her. But even with all their derision focused on her, she only remembered when those same eyes had sparkled as he teased her playfully or when, in unguarded moments, they darkened to obsidian, reflecting the disillusionment his composure masked.

Shawnalese Grenville knew Gayhawke Carrington for what he was—excitingly dangerous and irresistibly vulnerable—a magnificent, wounded stag.

Everything she hated in a man.

Everything she loved.

Why was he here? Forcing her thoughts from the hopeful, she tilted her chin high and continued down the stairs with all the hauteur she could summon, swept backward in time to the night she had first met him seven years ago. . . .

Chapter 1

NEW ORLEANS, LOUISIANA
SPRING 1781

THE RATTLE OF CARRIAGE WHEELS, THE CLIPPITY-clop of horses' hooves, a Creole's mournful song, the chirrup of crickets—all the myriad sounds of New Orleans at night acompanied Shawnalese as she slipped hurriedly through the dark back streets. She groped her way past the shadowy, unfamiliar areas, her eyes wide and watchful, her ears alert for any sound of danger. Even the moss-hung trees, with their bounty of strange drapings, had taken on eerie, ghostly shapes.

It was a beautiful, warm night, and the full moon cast a mystical light in a cloudless, star-studded sky,

when twelve-year-old Shawnalese arrived safely outside the theater. The fragrance of magnolia blossoms
wafted on the gentle breeze, mingling with that of the
roses and lilacs in the basket she clutched. Anxiously
she faced the theater, bit her lip with uncertainty, and
waited for the beautifully gowned ladies to emerge
with their indulgent escorts.

Shawnalese thought of her mother, ill, urgently in
need of a doctor—and of the many bills they owed. Now
no doctor would attend her mother without the coin in
advance. Shawnalese was desperate, for that morning
her stepfather had been killed in a tavern brawl, and this
was her first attempt to earn money from the streets.

The theater doors swung open and patrons surged
out. With a quickening heart Shawnalese moved
toward one of the couples. "Flowers for your beautiful
lady?" she urged sweetly, but her voice drifted into a
hushed whisper as she offered her prettiest bouquet to
the short, stout man.

"No," he replied curtly without a glance in her
direction, and guided his companion past her.

Turning to a tall man, Shawnalese again extended
her flowers, only to be ignored. Hurriedly she moved
from one couple to another, with no success. She was
in a near panic, for she'd secretly taken her mother's
last coin to purchase these flowers. She grabbed a
balding man's arm and presented her arrangement.
"Flowers for your lovely lady?"

"Take your grubby hand off me," the man snapped
and brushed her aside.

The crowd thinned, and Shawnalese ran to the tall,
powerful figure of one more gentleman. Filled with
determination, she shoved the bouquet at him. "Your
beautiful lady would appreciate these lovely flowers,"
she said in a firm voice. Expecting rejection, she continued on before he could reply. "How dare you insult
your lady by refusing to buy her flowers. One might
think you didn't feel her worthy."

Chuckling in amusement, the gentleman said, "You're an insolent little snip—" Stopping, he stared down into the enormous green eyes that challenged him, stunned by the angelic beauty of the child with the cloud of golden hair and a magnolia tucked behind her ear.

Seizing the opportunity brought about by his confusion, Shawnalese gathered all the flowers into her arms and thrust them toward the handsome man. "I'm sure you'd like to show the lady your regard by purchasing all of these for her."

Amazed by this armful of flowers, the man laughed, and the deep, rich sound filled the night air as he delved into his pocket and tossed a gold coin into her empty basket. "How old are you, child?" he queried in concern. His dark green gaze searched fruitlessly for an adult who accompanied her. "What are you doing out alone at this time of night?"

"I'm old enough to care for myself," she replied, hoping her words belied her fear that he might report her to some unknown Spanish authorities or well-meaningly turn her over to the nuns at the Ursuline convent.

"What's your name?" He hunkered down, intrigued by the feisty street urchin, but more concerned about her welfare.

"I don't . . . I don't give my name to strangers."

"Now don't you try to win me over with your charm." His eyes sparkled mischievously as he reached out to pat her gently on the head before he rose to his considerable height.

"Let's go, Gayhawke," his lovely companion said, only to be ignored.

"I don't have any change, sir," Shawnalese murmured fearfully. She clutched the gold doubloon, felt it grow warm in her trembling hand, and shivered with dread that he might insist she return the coin now that the masses had emptied from the theater and she'd lost all opportunity to resell her flowers.

"You keep it, little magnolia blossom."

"Thank you, sir. Thank you," she mumbled, her voice barely audible as she fought the tears of gratitude that threatened to surface.

"My pleasure."

"Hawke . . . " his companion said.

"May we drop you somewhere?" he asked, again ignoring the woman who stood impatiently beside him. "My coachman"—he motioned toward the waiting carriage—"will be happy to take you home."

"No, thank you, sir," Shawnalese replied, then turned and disappeared into the night, calling back, "Thank you, sir. Thank you."

Hawke stared after the thin child, then with a sigh turned back to his carriage, threw the armload of flowers on the seat, and assisted his companion.

All too soon Shawnalese's illusions crashed when she discovered that men as generous as Gayhawke were almost nonexistent. Gone were her fantasies of moving her mother to a less damp climate, lost in her endless, dire struggle to provide the most meager of staples for the two of them. Gone was her location at the theater when, nearing starvation in the Spanish ruled city, she was forced to settle on the streets in front of New Orleans's cockpits, billiard parlors, gaming halls, and bawdy houses—for there the men were more generous. Gone were her flowers, for men preferred to buy their ladies kerchiefs, carved combs, perfumes, scarves, and trinkets. And gone, out of necessity, was her fear of slipping through the dark streets in the middle of the night, for now she frequented the basements of the bordellos or the waterfront warehouses, where most of the pirates, smugglers, and privateers distributed their ill-gotten booty—when there were no authorities around to harass them. She haggled with the scary pirates, smugglers, and buccaneers, scrambling and conniving to outdo the others there to buy the spoils or duty free contraband from the plunderers of the sea who docked at the New Orleans's wharf.

At the urging of Grizzly, a kind seaman who'd befriended her, she had taken to scabbarding a dagger to her midcalf, a fact kept hidden from her mother by her long, well-mended dress.

"A lass who looks like ye will make good use o' this," Grizzly growled in a raspy voice, and unstrapped the wicked-looking weapon, still in its sheath, from his sash. Her smile of gratitude was the only payment he would accept. He spent the next few hours teaching her how to hold the dagger, how to retrieve it with the speed of lightning, and finally—how to use it if need be.

From then on she practiced with her dagger as Grizzly had instructed her, silently thanking the bearded pirate. Never did she venture outside without it.

Destitution forced Shawnalese to become a child of the streets. A natural cunning helped increase her income. However, as the months lengthened, she reaped the greatest rewards from her awesome beauty, for few men could say no when she held up a trinket, focused her enormous emerald-green eyes on them, and smiled her dazzling smile. Grateful for any advantage, still she found it not enough, for her mother's condition took every coin she earned. There was never enough money, no matter how clever her bartering or how many her sales. Then, all too soon, the cause of her good fortune became the cause of her difficulties. Men began to want to buy her body instead of her wares.

Yet Shawnalese believed she controlled her destiny, for she had learned that survival belonged to the strongest, the cleverest, and the hardest, and she vowed to survive.

The months stretched into eighteen, and came the night she stood at her usual spot in front of the Silver Slipper Gaming Hall and Saloon.

"Hey, princess," a woman's voice called out.

Shawnalese turned to see the lovely Creole madam, Rose, motioning to her from across the street. Hesitantly Shawnalese walked toward the beautifully gowned, jewel-draped woman. Never had she seen the infamous madam up close, and she marveled at the woman's lovely face, her flawless, caramel complexion. "Yes, ma'am?"

"Why's a gorgeous young girl like you workin' the streets selling trinkets?"

"My mother's sick. . . ."

Reaching out with slender fingers, Rose examined Shawnalese's long, luxuriously thick golden hair. "If ya worked for me, you'd be rich, kid. Then ya could get your ma the medicines she needs."

Shawnalese's expression melted into hope. "I—I could become wealthy . . . wealthy working for you?"

"Real rich," Rose assured her, and placed a comforting arm around her shoulders. "What's your name, honey?"

"Shawnalese, ma'am. Shawnalese Grenville. How . . . how could I become wealthy?"

"Just be good to my customers." Rose smiled and gave her a reassuring squeeze. "And keep 'em happy."

"That's all?" she asked suspiciously, eyes wide, envisioning moving her mother to the warm, dry climate that she needed for her recovery.

"That's all, Shawnalese. You come work for me and you'll make more money than you've ever dreamed of. Have beautiful gowns"—she fingered her jewels, which sparkled and flashed in the setting sun—"and jewels. All my girls are named after a flower. That's why I call my place the French Bouquet. There's Violet, Camellia, Lily, Daisy, Jasmine, Poppy, and Iris. Let's see, what should we call you? Maybe Green Orchid, for those gorgeous green eyes. I wonder if there's green orchids? Well, no matter. We'll think of somethin'."

"What . . . what would I have to do to keep your customers happy? I wouldn't . . . I wouldn't have to . . . ?"

"Well, yeah. Of course ya would, princess. But I

keep a guard around all the time, and he looks after my girls real good," Rose answered proudly. "I don't allow no rough stuff."

Paling at her words, Shawnalese blurted, "I can't do that. I won't do that."

"Now don't tell me a girl as lovely as you is still a virgin?" The deep flush of Shawnalese's cheeks was the only answer the madam received, and all she could think of was the enormous sum she would receive for this innocent beauty. Rose had to have this young girl, even if by force. As soon as possible, before some man dragged her into the alley and cost Rose a hefty amount. She'd send out the word for a hundred miles and auction the girl's virginity to the highest bidder. Rose knew she'd make a small fortune with Shawnalese, but much more if the girl came willingly. By the time this child of ethereal beauty had learned all the ways to pleasure a man, Rose could command a huge amount for an evening with her. With that thought the Creole madam said sweetly, "Don't ya worry none about bein' a virgin, honey. I have the perfect man to break ya in—"

"No. I won't do it." Shawnalese shrugged free of the woman's delicately scented arm. "I'll starve first."

"Don't ya care about your ma? Do ya want her to die? I'll move her into a nice place to live and get her the best doctors."

"No. I'll work the streets until I die first. Besides, when I marry, my husband will care for Mama," Shawnalese turned to run back across the street.

Rose's hand flashed out to stop her. "Princess, it's time ya came outta that dream world you're livin' in. No gentleman of wealth or quality is gonna marry a bastard from shanty town, no matter how beautiful she is. Blue blood marries blue blood. The best ya can hope for is some wealthy gentleman to make ya his mistress—until he tires of ya, which'd be about two or three years. Of course, after that you'll go from man to man for a few years, until your youth and beauty start to fade, and then you'll start walkin' the streets, goin' with any man who's got the coin. Or ya can marry some sweet-talkin' boy, and have a passel of kids, and spend the rest of your life in shanty town, old before your time and sick like your ma."

Shawnalese's face mirrored the horror of such a thought.

"There's only one way out of shanty town for you, Shawnalese—at the French Bouquet. Ya don't realize how lucky you are. With that face ya can retire a rich woman by the time you're thirty." The madam sighed and released her grip on Shawnalese's arm.

"I'll marry a man like Gayhawke. You'll see," Shawnalese spat out. Then she raced across the dirt street.

"If ya change your mind, you'll know where to find me," Rose called after her before she turned back to her elegant, iron-gated mansion.

Later, Shawnalese was pacing the street in front of the saloon. Business had been unusually poor. She touched the few brass and copper coins deep inside her pocket and sighed. It was going to be another long night.

Chapter 2

"KERCHIEF FOR THE LOVELY LADIES? PERFUME, OR perhaps an ivory comb to warm a lady's heart?" Instinct told Shawnalese not to approach the two men walking toward her on the shadowy, dark side of the street, but need overcame fear and she hurried toward them.

One man's hand flashed out, catching her unawares,

and his stubby fingers tangled in her long hair. "You've got better'n that to offer, ain't ya, goldie?" He jerked her to him.

While she struggled, the other man, with a few well aimed kicks, demolished her basket of merchandise.

"Turn me loose, you filthy scum!" Shawnalese spat, for her months on the streets had taught her never to show fear.

"Ahh, I've got myself a hellcat, Cal." The man laughed, revealing yellow-stained teeth, and his foul breath spewed hot on her face. "A little spitfire!"

"Get your grubby hands off me!" Shawnalese struggled with all her might, hoping her screams would bring someone to her aid, but the street was deserted.

"I like a girl with spirit," the man snarled before he loosened one hand from her hair to grope at her budding young breasts.

Seizing her opportunity, Shawnalese jerked free, only to stumble into the waiting arms of Cal.

"Let's teach this little lady some manners," Cal grunted. His instructions—to destroy her wares, rough her up a little, and not otherwise harm her—were forgotten as the heat rose in his loins. The other man clamped a hand over her mouth and grabbed her struggling body to help drag her into the alley beside the French Bouquet.

Shawnalese felt them pulling her down with her arms pinned behind her, and she fell, as helpless as a rag doll. She fought the panic that threatened to paralyze her. Her chest felt as though it would burst, her head whirled, and their voices seemed to come from somewhere far off. She bit the hand suffocating her, gasped for air, and cried, "Wait!" Thrashing violently, she pleaded, "Don't hurt me, I'll lie still." Her arms, now in a vise like grip over her head, felt as though they would break.

"No tricks, goldie, or you'll regret it," Cal said, releasing his hold on her wrists when she ceased to struggle.

Cal attempted to cover her lips with a slobbering, wet kiss, the stench of his breath a revulsion. With her heart pounding in her throat, Shawnalese's hand slipped unnoticed down her leg to her calf. With lightning speed she pulled her dagger from its scabbard, plunging it into any flesh within her reach.

"Ya little bitch!" Cal screeched, and jerked up on her arm.

At the snapping sound unbearable pain flashed through Shawnalese.

"Let her go, ya fools! Don't touch her face," a woman's voice called out from the shadows. "Don't touch her face!"

The men ran off into the night and left Shawnalese to kneel alone in the dark back street, nursing her arm. Inhaling deeply, breathless with rage and pain, she muttered, "I know you're responsible for this, Rose." To the tinkle of piano music, she struggled to her feet and stumbled from the reeking byway. Spying a leather pouch dropped on the ground in the struggle, she snatched it up.

Nearby was the destroyed merchandise that represented her only way to earn a living. Shawnalese raised glazed eyes from the mess in front of her to the bordello then turned and slowly made her way through the narrow streets to her mother.

That night the doctor wrenched Shawnalese's dislocated shoulder into position. After he had gone and her mother slept, she removed the pouch she'd found from its hiding place and opened it. Gasping in disbelief, she stared at more coin than she could earn in two or three months.

The next few days Shawnalese stayed at home with her mother, and used the time to sew delicate silk and satin undergarments, tatting them with fine lace and embroidering a monogram on each item, all sewn with the tiniest of stitches as her mother had taught her. It was low-paying work she usually did for the wealthy ladies on long rainy days. Then plagued by her insoluble problems, she went in search of Grizzly, one of the few people she trusted enough to call friend.

The huge, onetime mountain man was leaning against a wharf timber, staring out at the Mississippi River. When he saw Shawnalese, his eyes squinted into a sparkle of blue in his smiling face. "I hear tell that ye had trouble by Rose's the other night."

"Nothing my dagger and I couldn't handle," she replied with more confidence than she felt.

"Tell me what happened, lass." Grizzly's gruff voice was surprisingly tender, and his heavily scarred arm swept her up to sit her gently on a large pier rail. After she related what had happened, he snarled, "Filthy, rotten scum!" He reached to his waist for his cutlass. "Me and a few o' me friends will track the scuds down tonight. They willna bother ye again, and then we'll try to put the fear o' God into Rose. But I figure now that she's had a good look at ye, she'll nae be satisfied 'til she has ye working for her. That means ye're going to have to work down at this end o' town, where me an the lads can protect ye. O' course ye know ye won't make the money here 'cause there's no gents comes down here."

Shawnalese knew Grizzly was right, yet she barely scraped together enough for the ever-increasing cough medicine and laudanum her mother now needed. Dare she move from her more lucrative area? Dare she not?

In a few months the coins from the pouch were used up, and Shawnalese was working sixteen hours a day struggling to survive, and failing. One night, she came home weary and worn down, glanced at her sleeping mother, then slipped out of her dress and onto the sofa. No sooner had she pulled the cover up to her shoulders than she realized that in her exhaustion she'd forgotten to remove her dagger. Sitting up, she placed her bare foot upon the worn cushion, unstrapped her sheathed knife, and tucked it under the rag-stuffed pillow.

Partially awake, Catherine Grenville spied the dagger strapped to Shawnalese's leg. The next evening, while Shawnalese worked the streets, Catherine, was unable to concentrate on anything other than her daughter's welfare. She half listened to her neighbor Odette's cheerful chatter.

"I read zee postings at zee Place d'Armes today, and we 'ave some fancy English duke visiting New Orleans," Odette prattled on, unheard, warming a bowl of potato soup for Catherine that Shawnalese had cooked earlier. "'Is Grace ees up visiting Prince Martinique at Willow Heights. Aristos stick with aristos, you know. Zee posting said 'e's 'ere to see about trade for 'is fleet of merchant ships. Maybe," she mocked, "when Carrington gets back from Willow Heights, 'e'll pay us a call. . . "

Catherine gasped. "What did you say?"

Whirling, Odette stared at the ashen-faced woman. "I was just telling you what eet said on zee posting board at zee square."

"Yes! Yes! But what was the duke's name?"

"Carrington."

"Gayhawke Carrington?"

Frightened by Catherine's pallor, Odette ran to her bedside, fearful she was going to have another devastating coughing attack. "Calm yourself, Catherine. I'm just rattling on about nothing."

"Odette, was the duke's name Gayhawke Carrington?"

"Yes. Yes, I'm sure eet was Gayhawke."

"Oh, dear God! Gayhawke's here!"

Odette lowered her small frame to the bedside. "You know zis duke, Carrington?"

Trembling, Catherine murmured, "Odette, it's the answer to my prayers. Oh, merciful Lord, it's too good to be true." Then she sat up in her bed. "Odette, you must get a message to Gayhawke. Surely he's forgiven me. He must have forgiven me. If so, he'll help me"— she gave way to a spasm of coughing that racked her frail frame—" he has to help me. Shawna's welfare depends on it. Gayhawke Carrington, the Duke of Foxridge, is the one, the only, possibility I have to get Shawna away from the streets of New Orleans."

With tears streaming down her emaciated face, Catherine whispered, "It's Lady Destiny who brought you here now, Gayhawke. It's destiny!"

Chapter 3

A TALL, DARKLY HANDSOME MAN, ACCOMPANIED BY a lovely woman, was strolling through the lobby of the Blue Bayou hotel when a liveried porter intercepted him.

"This letter came for you, suh. The lady said it was mighty important."

Hawke took the brief note and read:

Gayhawke,
I am seriously ill. Come immediately. Please
don't disappoint me. There is a child.

Catherine Grenville
45 Canal Court

Hawke gave the bellman a coin. "Have my carriage brought around at once."

"Yes, suh," the bellman said, and hurried off.

Hawke bent toward his companion.

"Take me with you," she said.

"No," he replied in a bored voice. She was merely one more female, one more bed, in a procession of many over the years.

Moments later Hawke, alone and in full evening dress was on his way to Catherine Grenville, his second cousin. He'd heard nothing of her since she'd disappeared more then fourteen years earlier, yet he still remembered Catherine's lovely face and haunting emerald green-eyes, the famous Grenville eyes. Eyes exactly like those of his mother, Victoria.

The last time he'd seen Catherine he'd been a tall, strong, and angry fifteen. On that day, his sister, Heather, had gone into premature labor with her second child. After the doctor arrived, Hawke had ridden hard to summon Baron Siegfried Von Rueden to his wife's side. Upon arriving at Von Rueden's estate, he'd jumped from his stallion and run into the house, and when none of the fidgety servants appeared to know of the baron's whereabouts, he'd raced from room to room. Upstairs, he'd flung open the door to the master's chambers and discovered Siegfried in bed with Catherine. Enraged by the betrayal of his cherished sister, Hawke had dragged Siegfried from the bed and slammed him against the wall.

"If you ever cheat on my sister again, Von Rueden, I'll kill you!" he roared.

Siegfried paled visibly.

"Do you understand me, Siegfried?"

"Y-yes," Siegfried stammered.

Terrified, Catherine scrambled for her clothes.

After winning the inward battle not to harm his brother-in-law on the spot, Hawke relaxed his grip. When he spoke his deep voice was menacing. "Be assured, Siegfried, this is a promise, not a threat—I will kill you!" Then he released the man his sister adored and commanded, "Get dressed. Your wife is bearing your child."

At those words, a cry escaped Catherine's lips and

she bolted from the room. Some months later she went to France to visit distant relatives and never returned. Rumor had it she'd run off with a ne'er-do-well, but Hawke never learned the truth of it.

As his carriage sped through the night, the words in the note—"There is a child"—whirled in his head. Could the child be Siegfried's?

So much had happened in the more than fourteen years since last he'd seen Catherine, yet so little. At twenty-nine he was still unmarried. He owned vast estates, a mansion surrounded by thousands of acres of lush, tree-studded, English land that rolled down to the English Channel; he had a yacht, a stable of Arabian and Andalusian horses, a château in France, a chalet in the Swiss mountains, a fleet of merchant ships, and investments in several countries. He traveled at will and had more alluring women than he wanted, and a cavernous empty feeling inside. Why was he always searching? What more could he want? He had been everywhere, done everything—what was left?

When Baron Siegfried Von Rueden died in a hunting accident seven years after the incident with Catherine Grenville, Hawke moved his sister and her two sons into his mansion at Foxridge, becoming a father figure to the then twelve-year-old Rutger and seven-year-old Leif. There had been many happy times with his sister, and his two nephews, but it was not the same as having his own family, a loving wife and children from his loins. Without heirs he risked his dukedom, yet he'd been unable to force himself to take a wife. Heather was right. It was inevitable, so it might as well be now, and it might as well be to Lady Hollis Townsende. He'd call on Lord Townsende as soon as he returned to England and hammer out the terms of the betrothal contract and be done with it. It would be the merger of two great family names. Besides, Hollis was beautiful, obedient, and passionate in bed. What more could he want? Why had he had to take a sea voyage to clear his head? If he'd made this decision in England, he wouldn't be in New Orleans right now, riding toward a problem that he suspected would complicate his life.

The carriage stopped in front of a hovel in the heart of shanty town. "There's some mistake. This can't be the place," Hawke called out to the coachman, unprepared for the abject poverty of the collection of surrounding shacks.

"This is Canal Court," the coachman replied.

"Wait for me," Hawke said, and swung down from the carriage. With only the moon to light his way, he walked up the narrow dirt alley to the front door. Knocking lightly, he suddenly realized the lateness of the hour and wished he'd waited until morning. After the second knock met with no response, he tried the knob and pushed the door open.

A candle flickered dimly in the clean, sparsely furnished room, and his gaze fell on the slight figure asleep in the only bed. The once beautiful Lady Catherine Grenville lay before him, obviously close to death. He stared at the emaciated form, at her sunken eyes and mouth and the sallow, waxy pallor of her skin. Approaching the bed, he called softly, "Catherine?" He leaned over and touched her arm.

Dulled green eyes opened slowly. "Gayhawke, you came. I knew you'd come. I knew you would. . . ."

His hand on her arm tightened, as though willing some of his strength to pass through to her. "Pardon me, Catherine, I'll be right back," he excused himself to hurry outside.

"Get the best doctor you can find and bring him here as fast as you can. Hurry," Hawke instructed the coachman, and returned to the tiny one-room hovel. He placed his cloak, hat, and gloves on the shabby sofa before he moved to Catherine's bedside.

"Gayhawke, I beg your understanding. I beg your forgiveness," Catherine pleaded in a halting, weak voice. "The day you discovered me with Siegfried is the only time I was ever with him. I—I swear to you . . . on all that is holy."

Catherine had been a young and, Hawke felt sure, innocent girl who'd fallen prey to the almost beauteous looks of his brother-in-law. Siegfried, with his wife heavy with child, had weakly succumbed to Catherine's beauty. Neither Catherine nor Siegfried, Hawke believed, had acted with forethought. It had simply happened. "I understand, Catherine. Forgiveness needs to come from a man far better than I. How do you come to be here?"

"Some weeks after that incident, I realized I was expecting Siegfried's child, and I reluctantly went to Mother. She told Father." Catherine was taken by a racking spell of coughing.

"A doctor will be here shortly, Catherine," Hawke said, at a loss as to how to help her.

"Father had me exiled to some poor, distant relative in France to await the birth of my child. However, once there, I overheard my guardians discussing the placement of my child after it was born. They'd been instructed to take my baby from me." She paused, and tears trickled down her gaunt face.

Hawke dabbed at her tears with his kerchief.

Catherine smiled. "I've never seen this side of you, Gayhawke." She sighed. "In the middle of the night, I packed a valise, took what little coin I had, and slipped away." She paused, out of breath. "I met a mariner named Casey Jacobs and gratefully accepted his offer to marry me and take me to New Orleans. He was a pleasant enough young man, and I think he considered himself fortunate to capture a young lady of quality, even if she were breeding with another man's child." Another paroxysm of coughing seized her.

When the coughing ceased Hawke asked, "Would you like a glass of water?"

"Yes, please."

Hawke poured the water from the pitcher on the floor and lowered himself to her side to help her drink. He helped her sit up and put the glass to her lips. After she'd taken a few sips, he lowered her back to the bed, and she closed her eyes to rest for a short time.

"I discovered later that Casey believed there'd also be a bountiful purse in it for him. At any rate, he seemed only mildly disturbed when I refused to exchange the vows until after my baby was born. I naively wanted my child to have the advantages I felt the name Grenville would certainly bring." Catherine paused to rest, then continued, "Nothing turned out as I expected. Shawnalese was labeled a bastard. Illegitimate. The name Grenville meant nothing in New Orleans."

Gayhawke glanced around the room, meagerly furnished with the barest of necessities. There was not even a table and chairs.

"Casey insisted that I write to my father and claim my dowry. I received a cold letter from Father. He refused. From that day Casey started drinking, and though I hadn't believed it possible, life progressively worsened. A couple of years ago he was killed in a brawl. I was already ill by then. . . ."

Wordlessly, Hawke pondered her story. He was less sure of Catherine's child's parentage now than he had been before he arrived. Although her story rang true, the child might have been fathered by this Casey.

When she had the strength, Catherine told Hawke about Shawnalese's hard life, then mouthed the words both knew were coming. "Promise me . . . promise me you'll take Shawnalese to live with you at Foxridge. She should be near her brothers." Imploring, her eyes stared into his, and she asked, "When I'm gone, she'll be alone—there's no one. No one but you. I wrote Siegfried for help and enclosed his letter in one to the vicar, asking him to give it to Siegfried in private, but the vicar returned Siegfried's letter and explained that

he had died." Catherine's breathing became labored
and she fought for the strength to proceed.

"Rest, Catherine, you're exhausting yourself."

"Gayhawke," Catherine whispered, and he bent
closer to hear her. "There's no one else to look after
Shawnalese, and if she's placed in the convent, she'll
run away. She's fiercely independent and doesn't realize the danger she's in . . . she's so beautiful"—she
gasped for breath—"and you don't know what New
Orleans is like. I'm surprised she hasn't already been
kidnapped and placed in a bordello. . . ."

"Catherine, I give you my word, I'll see to your
daughter's welfare," Hawke promised, and brushed
her lifeless hair from her brow. "Heather and the boys
live with me at Foxridge now."

"That's perfect. Shawnalese could be with her family, her half brothers. Don't allow my daughter to pay
for my sin any more than she already has, Gayhawke.
Take her to Foxridge to be with her brothers. Please.
I'm begging you—" This time a seizure of coughing
overtook her again, a convulsion so violent it seemed
it would shatter her weakened frame.

Hawke deliberated, for what Catherine asked
would be extremely unfair to Heather. His sister's
memories of her husband were pure and loving, and
she believed he'd been faithful to her throughout their
short marriage. But to appear with a bastard child, a
living memorial of her husband's infidelity, and ask
her to share her home with the young girl, to be
reminded daily of Siegfried's indiscretion . . . Could he
ask that of his sister? Hawke thought not, but first he
had to be positive of the girl's parentage.

"Catherine, how can I be sure Shawnalese is . . . "
Fumbling, he searched for the right words, but there
were none. "How do I know that Shawnalese is
Siegfried's child? Forgive me for being blunt, but I
must know for certain," he concluded, relieved to have
finally put into words what had bothered him since

he'd received her brief note. How would he know?

"You'll know when you see her, Hawke. She's beautiful—like her father." Catherine smiled. "But she has the Grenville eyes."

Another coughing spasm interrupted her, and this time Hawke saw the blood that filled the kerchief.

A short time later, Catherine said, "I know I don't have much time left. Would you bring her here so I can talk with you both?"

"Yes, of course I'll get her. Where is she?" Hawke asked, wondering for the first time about the young girl.

"She's working."

"Working? At this time of night? Where is she working at this late hour?"

Tears trickled down Catherine's face. "She should be in front of Frenchy's Billiard Parlor."

At that moment a knock sounded. Hawke opened the door to admit the doctor and stepped outside to wait.

Sometime later the doctor walked out, satchel in hand. After Hawke paid the man, he asked the question to which he already knew the answer. "How serious is it, doctor?"

"The woman's at death's door. She's in the advanced stages of consumption. I'm making her as comfortable as possible. I'm sorry, but there's little else to do."

"How long can she be expected to live?"

"She's alive now only by sheer force of will. She could go in three hours—three days at most."

Walking back into the shanty, Hawke bent over Catherine's bedside. "I'm going for Shawnalese. The doctor will remain until we return."

Heavily sedated with laudanum, Catherine gave a slight smile before she fell asleep.

Shortly thereafter, the coachman stopped near Frenchy's Billiard Parlor. "Wait here," Hawke said, then bounded from the carriage, his cloak fluttering in the breeze. Scanning the row of alehouses, bordellos, dance houses, gin mills, and sailors' boarding houses, he shuddered and started toward Frenchy's.

"You'll know her," Catherine had said. "Her hair is fair, like Siegfried's, and shimmers with spun gold." Ah, Hawke thought. Mother love. Then he saw her. A halo of hair tumbled below her waist in a waterfall of waves—and shimmered with spun gold. She had an ethereal appearance in the shadowy light, and he sensed something vaguely familiar about the small form as he approached her from behind, then dismissed the notion.

Selling a trinket to a man accompanied by his lady, the young girl appeared not to hear his approach. The couple left with their purchase, and Hawke gently placed his hand on her shoulder. Swifter than he could blink, she whirled to face him, crouching with her basket in one hand and a razor-sharp dagger in the other.

Hawke, stunned speechless, recalled when another street urchin with a cloud of golden hair had caught him unawares, two years before, outside the theater. Could this be that same child? He stared at the girl who faced him with all the courage of a young warrior.

The lights from the billiard parlor shone fully across her face. Unconsciously he sucked in his breath, examining every feature of her perfect, upturned face. An angelic face, a delicately sculpted face that could only be the feminine version of his brother-in-law, Baron Siegfried Von Rueden, and no other. Then his gaze was captured by her enormous almond-shaped eyes, a glorious, jeweled, crystalline emerald green. The famous Grenville eyes. His mother's eyes. Abruptly he realized he still stared at the most exquisite child's face he'd ever seen, and he felt foolish. A corner of his mouth quirked up in an unwary smile, and Hawke stepped aside. "I won't harm you, Shawnalese. . . ."

She stepped backward slowly, tightening her grip on the dagger. "How do you know my name?"

She wielded the knife with an expertise that surprised and impressed him, arcing it before her, a dangerously suspicious flash in her eyes. "I've come to take you to your mother."

"Mama! Is she worse?"

"She's not well and asked me to escort you home. We have some affairs to settle. Forgive my manners. I'm Gayhawke Carrington, the duke of Foxridge, your mother's second cousin. I suppose that makes us third cousins, or perhaps second cousins once removed." His smile was warm, genuine.

"Gayhawke . . ." Recognition flooded Shawnalese. At least a thousand times after that night he'd so casually tossed the gold doubloon into her flower basket, she'd dreamed of his face, had whispered his name. How was it possible she had not recognized him instantly? Second cousin to her mother? Why had her mother never mentioned him?

Somewhat embarrassed, Shawnalese lifted her long skirt to slip the dagger into the scabbard strapped to her calf. She smiled, revealing perfect white teeth. She extended a dainty hand, and inclining his head, Gayhawke Carrington clasped it in his.

"I have a carriage waiting, Shawnalese."

She hesitated, all her senses warning her against getting into a carriage with a stranger, even a special stranger. Even Gayhawke, the white knight of her dreams. Long ago she'd learned there were no gentlemen, only men in gentlemen's clothing. "I'll meet you at home."

Fumbling through his pockets, Hawke found the paper he sought in his waistcoat. "Can you read?" he asked, and offered her the note he'd received from Catherine.

"Yes," she said, and took the paper from his outstretched hand. She quickly read Catherine's handwriting by the dim light. "I'll go with you."

Hawke retrieved the shawl Shawnalese had been

wearing when she'd whirled to face him; he placed it around her shoulders, then escorted her to the waiting carriage, opened the door, and proffered his hand to assist her.

"As fast as you can get there," he said to the coachman, noticing how small and vulnerable Shawnalese appeared. He remembered the anguish and heartache he'd suffered when he'd lost his mother and then, three weeks later, when his father had died. Now she would have the same suffering to endure, and his hardened heart went out to her. He'd had his loving sister to help him through his tragedy, but this young girl would have only a stranger. He had an uncontrollable urge to cradle her in his arms, to stroke her head and tell her everything would be all right. But everything would not be all right, for disease had wasted her mother beyond help. When words failed him, he reached for her hand and squeezed it gently, hoping to pass some small measure of comfort to her. "How old are you?"

"Almost fourteen."

"Almost? When is your birthday?"

"July tenth."

Calculating silently, he sighed with relief. She'd been born nine months and three days from the date he'd burst in on Siegfried and Catherine. He remembered well the date he'd caught them in each other's arms, for his second nephew had been born on that day.

That night Hawke gave Catherine his word that he would take Shawnalese to live with him at Foxridge. As the young girl's distant cousin, he felt responsibility for her welfare until she was a woman grown. Of equal importance, he reasoned, Shawnalese was also the half sister of his nephews, Baron Rutger Von Rueden and Leif Von Rueden, and as such deserved the love and companionship of her family. Besides, she had endured enough in her young life, for she had given up her childhood to care for her terminally ill mother, and if there was any way possible, he vowed he would make it up to her. He would see her well-married, at least as well wed as a child without consequence could expect.

Rising from Catherine's bedside, Hawke walked outside, where Shawnalese waited, and summoned her to her mother's bedside.

After a while, Shawnalese joined him, and at her tear-filled eyes Hawke put his arm around her shaking shoulders, pulling her close to comfort her. He stroked her golden tresses and walked with her in silence. When she started to sob, he wrapped his arms around her, and she buried her face in his neck. At that moment he was engulfed by a tenderness he'd never before experienced.

What strange twist of fate had brought Gayhawke to New Orleans at this crucial time? Shawnalese wondered. Was it destiny, as her mother claimed? Never in her life had a man put his arm around her simply to comfort her. Never had a man been so gentle or tender, not even Grizzly, and the years of hungering for a father, the years of emptiness, of longing for what she knew not, surfaced in a confusion and a sense of loss for all that she had never shared with a man.

She could not accept charity from Hawke, could she? It didn't seem right. Besides, her mother had raised her not to accept charity from anyone . . . yet now Catherine had asked Shawnalese to accept the benevolence of Gayhawke Carrington. Why? If he were so generous, why had not her mother appealed to him when it might have saved her life? What had her mother not told her?

The next day Catherine died and Shawnalese was inconsolable. Hawke stayed with her.

"Shawny," he said in a soothing voice. "Your mother's suffering is over now. She has gone to a far better place." He cradled her in his arms like a babe. There was something deeply moving about the way she snuggled against him and looked up with trusting, tear-filled eyes. He stroked her silken head and rocked her, wondering at his intense need to protect her. "I can't bring your mother back, but I'll always look after you and take care of you," he promised.

Destiny had brought Gayhawke to her when she most needed him. Twice.

Chapter 4

LATER THAT MORNING, SHAWNALESE STEPPED outside and wrapped closer the cloak Hawke had bought her. The spring day was chilly and the damp air penetrating. The sky, like her thoughts, was dark and clouded. Hawke assisted her into the coach, gave instructions to the coachman, and swung inside, seating himself beside her. For a time the coach rumbled over the streets and then stopped in front of the general store. The coachman leaped down, went inside, and returned shortly carrying a feed sack.

Again the coach lumbered on, rocking over rutted dirt roads and into a towering forest before coming to a stop. Alighting from the conveyance, Hawke offered a hand to Shawnalese. She stepped down and glanced about in puzzlement at the untamed forest surrounding Lake Pontchartrain, then followed Hawke to where he'd lowered himself to sit on a felled tree at the lake's edge. He dipped a hand into the feed sack and threw the seeds into the air. In seconds mallards, geese, and all manner of birds surrounded them, fluttering for the delicacy.

He smiled and, with an indication of his fingers, offered her to join him. She reached into the bag, grasped a handful of seed and scattered it in a small nearby clearing. Thus they spent the next two hours, seated side by side, feeding the birds. The wind whipped their clothes, their hair; the only sounds the whir or flap of wings and the twitters, chirps, and squawks of eager birds, and for that brief period she almost forgot that her mother was gone.

Then it was time. "We must leave," Hawke said and offered her a hand up.

"I know why you brought me here," Shawnalese said. "Thank you. I appreciate your consideration."

"My pleasure," Hawke replied and led her toward the waiting coach. He wondered why he felt so deeply for this unknown girl, when he'd done so with few others. What was this strange bond he shared with her?

Leaving the cemetery, Shawnalese, numb with grief, walked beside Hawke toward the coach. Loneliness enshrouded her as the gray clouds disappeared behind the tombs, and a moss-draped tree, its branches spreading widely, dominated her blurred vision. Then they were in the coach and she heard Hawke talking. "I'm sorry, what did you say?"

Patting her hand, Hawke repeated, "Tomorrow a seamstress will fit you for enough clothes for the voyage. I'm taking you home to live with my family and me. We'll sail for England in a week."

In that instant Shawnalese made her decision. She would not accept charity. "Your offer is very generous, but I'll not be going to England with you."

"The decision has already been made, Shawny."

"I've been on my own for almost two years. And, I might add, I've done quite well most of the time." Almost choking on the lie, she inhaled deeply and fought to maintain her slowly disintegrating composure. "I don't wish to seem ungrateful for all that you've done for Mama and me, but I've given my situation careful consideration. It would be unfair to you and your family to burden you with the responsibility of my welfare. Besides, I don't feel comfortable accepting your offer to care for me until I come of age. I'm capable of supporting myself, and I believe we'll both be happier if I stay in New Orleans."

Hawke stared at her, surprised not only by her decision, but at the maturity with which she expressed herself. She was not quite fourteen and educated mostly by her mother. "Now is not the time to make an important decision, Shawny. We'll discuss it when you feel better. However, there is something I want to say, and that is that you're wrong, quite wrong, about being a burden. I not only welcome you into my family, I look forward to it." He was taking Shawny to England and Foxridge—if he had to take her in fetters.

Making no further comment, Shawnalese stared sightlessly out the window the rest of the way to the hotel. That night, after she was certain that Hawke slept, she tiptoed from her bed and dressed hurriedly. Unable to resist, she put on the wool cloak Hawke had bought her, then slipped quietly out of the room and down the back stairs. Once in the familiar dark streets of the city, she breathed easier and made her way to the shanty. Although she had walked these same streets many times over the last two years, nothing seemed the same, the loneliness that engulfed her a sourness in the pit of her stomach. She paused outside her house, then forced herself to go inside, where she undressed, crawled into her mother's bed, and cried herself to sleep.

Waking with a start at dawn, Shawnalese dressed quickly, knowing this would be the first place Hawke would look for her. She made the bed and neatly laid out the wool cloak, rubbing her fingertips over the lovely fabric one last time. She wrote a thank-you note and requested that he not look for her, then laid it on top of the cloak. She searched her cleaning basket and took what little money she had hidden there, unsure how long she might have to stay away from the shack before Hawke gave up and returned to England without her. Then she rushed out the door.

When Hawke awakened to find Shawny gone, he raced to the shanty, discovered her note, then started his search at the cemetery. From there he went to the docks, where Catherine had said she bought her goods.

"She'd most likely be with Grizzly," one old woman replied to Hawke's inquiry. "That's where she's at when she's down here."

A few hours later Hawk was about to leave one more waterfront tavern when a man—almost as tall as he was, but much brawnier—approached him, walking with a slight limp.

"Ye lookin' for me?" Grizzly asked.

Although the middle-aged man's voice was gruff and his immense size threatening, there was an air of decency about him. A handsome head of silver-streaked dark hair fell in shining waves to his shoulders, and a well-kept, matching beard graced his face. Vivid blue eyes that had never looked away from any man, friend or foe, confronted Hawke.

"I'm looking for Shawnalese," Hawke said.

"What's the lass to ye?"

"Shawny's mother has died, and the child's run away. If you're the Grizzly who's a friend of hers, I think you might know where I can find her."

"So that's why she hasna been around. I've been checking everywhere for the lass." Grizzly's face softened in relief. "I was afraid one o' them scum got her again."

Frowning at Grizzly's words, Hawke gestured toward a private table in the corner. "Can we talk?"

After Hawke had successfully convinced Grizzly of the reason for his search for Shawnalese, the big man told him all that had happened to her, which

Catherine, thankfully, had never known.

"From the beginning," Grizzly continued, "that wee one treated me with the kindness and respect she'd treat a gentleman like yerself. If ye havena found her by nightfall, ye'll find me here. Me and me friends will find her in no time. She may hate to give up her freedom, but these streets become more dangerous each day for a lass who looks like she does." Downing his ale, he stared into his empty tankard. "I'll help ye any way I can, but I sure will miss her. I looked forward to being in port because o' her."

From the wharf tavern, Hawke went again to the cemetery. The flaming sun peeked above the horizon and cast its red glow. Silhouetted against the sky, surrounded by the above ground tombs, stood Shawny.

Lost in her grief, she did not hear him approach.

"I've come to take you home, Shawny." Kneeling beside her, Hawke comforted softly, "You aren't leaving your mama. She will always be with you, wherever you are, to guide you."

Tenderly he picked her up and carried her to his waiting coach. Her face nestled trustingly in his neck, her tears trickled down his collar, and the mettle, the strength of character, of the girl with the face of an angel touched a chord in his hardened heart.

That evening, as they dined in the small sitting room of his hotel suite, Hawke said, "I can give you a life of luxury and ease, everything money can buy. . . ."

"Why?"

"Why? Because I care for you. I care what happens to you. Because I cared for your mother."

"If you cared about Mama, why did you do nothing until she died?" Her words were bitter and accusing.

"Your mother ran away from England. I never knew where she went, or what had become of her. Had I known, be assured, I would have seen to the welfare of you both."

"Why are you willing to do this? I know you're too young to be my father," she pressed, lifting her eyes to meet his gaze straight on. Her heart pounded in anticipation of his answer.

"You don't know who your father was?"

Flushing red, Shawnalese answered, "No," her voice barely audible. Then she lifted her head proudly. "Do you not know I'm . . . that I'm illegitimate?"

"Yes. Yes, I do. Your mother told me."

"You're a highborn gentleman, only distantly related to me," she said suspiciously. "Why would you be willing to sully your good name and reputation by taking me into your home when most gentlemen would pay generously to have me disappear?"

"I am my own person, Shawny. I do not follow the rules of polite society."

"What are you not telling me, Gayhawke? What did my mama not tell me?"

Hawke found himself unwilling to disclose the whole of the truth. After all, what difference could it make to Shawny if she knew not who had sired her? Her father was deceased. This way Heather would remain ignorant of the truth, for it would devastate his sister to learn that her adored husband had been unfaithful and that a child had resulted from his indiscretion. After that fateful day when their mother had left, when he was a boy of ten, Heather had tried to be both mother and sister to him. Now he decided that he would protect her from discovering that her husband had fathered Shawny. Abruptly Shawny asked what he dreaded to hear.

"Do you know who my father was?"

"I'm sure that if your mother had felt you should know, she would have told you. If she didn't tell you, why do you think she'd tell me?"

"I don't need charity, Gayhawke. I don't want charity. I pay my own way." Her words were uttered with quiet but determined firmness, and her deceptively composed features belied the pride behind her words. "Besides, like you I'm my own person. I don't take direction very well. I'm used to being free." With that, she stood up. "I do wish to thank you again, for seeing to Mama's resting place and her tombstone. But now I want to go home. I wish you a safe voyage." She turned away, then immediately turned back. "You're truly the gentleman I always knew you'd be."

"Always knew I'd be?"

"One night you bought my flowers and gave me a gold doubloon."

"That *was* you!"

"You remember?"

"I remember, magnolia blossom."

Gayhawke Carrington, the duke of Foxridge, had remembered the sobriquet he had used on that night so long ago. Shawnalese felt warm all over. She smiled, then murmured, "I'd better go."

"Shawny!"

She turned back.

"This is really a subject that's not open for consideration," Hawke said softly. "You gave your word to your mother—on her deathbed." He hated to remind her of her promise. Still, even that was better than taking her by force, his only alternative.

Shawnalese blanched at his words. Her vow weighed heavily upon her. Finally, she said, "I'll do what you ask—as long as we have one agreement clearly understood."

"Which is?"

"There will be no marriage arrangements made for me. If ever I marry, it will be to the man of my own choosing, and no one else's."

Hawke considered her condition and all the reasons he should refuse it, but they were outweighed by the difficulties he would face if he denied her. "I agree. And I have something to which I want you to agree. Don't cut your hair."

It was more of a command than a request, and she wondered why. Then she shrugged. "I won't."

"Shawny, I have a present for you."

"A present?"

"Yes. I came upon it when I bought your clothes." He went into his bedroom and returned shortly with a package, which he handed to her.

Carefully she unwrapped the paper, tied with a white ribbon, to find an oval hand mirror and hairbrush of burgundy, hand-painted with tiny flowers and trimmed with etched silver. Her fingertips caressed the set, and she wanted to clasp the treasured gift from Gayhawke to her breast. Instead she handed it to him. "I can't accept this. It must be extremely valuable."

Understanding her pride, he said the words he hoped would allow her to accept what he wanted her to have. "Would you insult me by refusing a gift selected especially for you?"

Her fingers caressed the brush and mirror, for besides the dagger Grizzly had given her, this was the first thing she'd ever owned that belonged only to her. Wide-eyed, she glanced from the cherished gift to him. "I don't know . . ."

"Your mama would approve. I know it as well as I know how proud she'd be that you'll keep your promise to her."

Her questioning green gaze locked with his determined one. Why was he so kind to her? Not only kind, extravagant. Why was he determined to have her live with him, with his family, in England? With no answers, and no small amount of pride, she lifted her chin and said rebelliously, "I fear you will regret this decision."

Hawke knew that she would keep her word, and he smiled with respect and admiration. Pity the man, who, when she was a woman grown, became bewitched by her. Heaven help him, for surely he would need it.

Shawnalese took his smile to be one of smug satisfaction and could not allow even Gayhawke Carrington, the sixth duke of Foxridge, the white knight of her dreams, to best her. So she said defiantly, "But I won't go without Grizzly!"

Chapter 5

AFTER LONG WEEKS ON HAWKE'S MERCHANT ship, the white cliffs of England rose from the sea.

A short time later the maroon-lacquered carriage, with gilded equipage and emblazoned with the ducal crest of Foxridge, climbed the wildflower-covered downs toward the manor. It drove through the large iron gates, supported on each side by a stone wall stretching in each direction as far as the eye could see, and up the wide, winding roadway, lined with white-trunked birch trees.

Ahead reared the towering mansion of Foxridge. "My home," Hawke announced, and all his pride and love for his vast estate was revealed in those two words. He smiled down at Shawnalese. "The main house was struck by lightning several years after my father's death. It took over four years to rebuild it."

Many times Hawke had visited the charred ruins to brood in dark silence, gratified that the main part of the home of his unhappy childhood had been destroyed, wishing his melancholy memories had been destroyed with it. As a man grown he'd worked with an eminent architect to design and build the structure, combining the grandeur of modern architecture with the romantic beauty of the many medieval castles he'd visited while restlessly roaming England and Europe. To Gayhawke Lawrence Richard Carrington, this mansion was a part of him—his creation, a combination of old world styling and contemporary luxury.

In the distance appeared the bastioned exterior of Foxridge. The crenellated towers stood like silent sentinels against the sky, the mansion dreamlike in the red glow of the descending sun.

Unable to take her gaze from the enormous building, Shawnalese half whispered, "It's like a castle."

The coach rumbled to a stop, and a footman opened the door. Hawke leaped from the conveyance. "We are home, Shawny. Your castle," he teased playfully with a low bow and an exaggerated sweep of his arm toward the imposing residence.

Fear streaked through Shawnalese for the thousandth time. What if Hawke's sister did not like her, or objected to the nature of her birth, or simply did not want her living there?

"Before we go inside I want to show you something," Hawke said, and turned her around.

On each side of her, woodland and meadows swept down to the sea. Off in the distance, the chalk peaks of the Isle of Wight and the shimmering English Channel were cast in the orange-red reflections of the setting sun. Shawnalese gasped. "If this were my home, I'd never leave it, not even for a day."

"This is your home now, Shawny." Taking her elbow, he led her toward the stone staircase that rose in two graceful curves to the entrance.

One heavy oaken door swung open. "Welcome home, Your Grace," the mustached major-domo greeted warmly.

"Thank you, Addison. It's wonderful to be home."

"I daresay, Your Grace, the baroness will be quite nettled that she wasn't here to greet you," Addison said. "The family's at a soiree at the earl of Warsex's."

Hawke turned to the line of servants, hurriedly summoned by the ever-efficient Addison. He introduced Shawny. "This is my third cousin, Miss Shawnalese Grenville. She is now a member of our family." Shawnalese was welcomed politely.

"Shawny," Hawke said, "the maid will show you to your chambers and assist you with your bath. Sleep well—you're home now." After she left, Hawke informed Addison, "I had the coachman take a man called Grizzly to one of the apartments over the carriage house. He'll be a coachman. Have Mrs. Kendall reassigned as Shawny's lady's maid."

Appalled, Addison questioned, "Mrs. Kendall, Your Grace?"

"Yes."

"She's kitchen help, Your Grace. She's not qualified to be a lady's maid to a young lady of the gentry."

Hawke wondered why he tolerated Addison's display of disrespect, but his affection for the man who'd been with the Carringtons for as long as he could remember, and his regard for the man's efficiency, overrode all else. "Mrs. Kendall is always cossetting the kitchen help. My kitchen servants don't need it. Shawny does."

For just a moment a grin touched the lips of the reserved Addison. "Yes, Your Grace."

The next morning Shawnalese awoke to strange sounds in her room. A motherly woman bustled about, arranging a breakfast tray and laying out her clothes.

"Good mornin', Miss Shawnalese. I'm Mrs. Kendall. I've got a bita breakfast an' a spota tea for ya, luv. Will ya be needin' anythin' else?"

"No, thank you, Mrs. Kendall," Shawnalese replied, and sat up.

"If ya don't mind my sayin' so, you're as pretty as a bloomin' princess. 'Course ya would be, bein' a Grenville an' all. Enjoy your breakfast," Mrs. Kendall said, then bustled from the room.

Was this how the wealthy lived? Waited on hand and foot and eating alone? This most definitely was not for her. Shawnalese ate, dressed, and picked up her tray, hoping she could find the kitchen in this mansion that was far larger than the entire Ursuline convent in New Orleans.

A short time later Shawnalese stood in the cavernous great hall. The room was magnificent, crowned with a ceiling that soared to a height of three stories supported by a maze of massive beams that crisscrossed the entire chamber in open splendor. On the west wall, Gothic-arched, leaded windows overlooked the sea, and on the east French doors opened on the gardens of the courtyard, with its stone fountain spewing water into the air.

A footman came into the room, greeted her, and added more logs to the hearths at the north and south ends of the room.

"May I get you anything, Miss Grenville?" he asked cordially. "A cup of tea, perhaps?"

"No, thank you," Shawnalese replied, and the man withdrew.

Over one hearth a relief of knights, mounted on mighty destriers, engaged in battle, while above the other was displayed the Carrington coat of arms. Richly woven tapestries, depicting battles or hunting scenes, hung among the shields and weapons that spoke of battles long past, and flaming wall torches cast their glow over all.

Placed against the walls around the entire room were high-backed carved monk's chairs, interspersed by the silent sentinels of the great hall, arms bearing suits of armor. In awe of the old-world magnificence that surrounded her, Shawnalese found it difficult to believe that this would be her new home.

Minutes later, in search of Grizzly, she left the house to find him looking in amazed wonder at the nine vehicles—coaches, carriages, and one phaeton—

housed in the large carriage house.

"Whew!" Grizzly exclaimed. "Can ye believe one man having all o' this? And ye should see me quarters upstairs, lass. Ye've sure found the pot o' gold at the end o' the rainbow."

Glancing up with troubled eyes, Shawnalese asked, "Then why am I so miserable? Why do I have this knot in my stomach? Why do I wish I were in New Orleans?" Sighing, she looked away. "This isn't me, Grizzly. This is the duke of Foxridge, and all like him, but it'll never be me."

"Aye. I feared that."

"What if Gayhawke's sister doesn't like me, doesn't want me to live here? It's possible, you know. Odette's said many times how uppity the gentry is. She said they don't have much use for those not of their class. Not only am I not their class, but I was born on the wrong side of the blanket, too."

"That might be a problem, lass. And then there's yer objecting to ye calling the nobility by all o' them fancy titles, which isna going to make the family o' this fine duke none too happy."

On the voyage to England, Hawke had said to Shawnalese, "Once we're in England, you'll be required to address those you meet properly, as 'my lord', 'my lady', whatever."

"I learned from Mama and Odette about the titled aristocracy of England and Europe," Shawnalese had replied. "I don't agree with the class system, and I'll call no one 'my lord', 'my lady', or 'Your Grace'."

"Then we have a dilemma to resolve, Shawny," Hawke had said, "for there are times it will be necessary. It merely conveys respect for a titled Englishman, a peer of the realm."

"I'll call no one 'my lord', 'my lady', or 'Your Grace'. Not even you." Nor had she done so on the long voyage.

At that moment a rider came into view, and as he galloped closer Shawnalese breathed, "Gayhawke."

Dressed all in black, he sat arrogantly straight on his Andalusian stallion, England's Warrior. Unaware of Shawnalese and Grizzly at the carriage house, he trotted straight to the stables.

"Grizzly, that's the most beautiful horse I've ever seen."

"Aye. Must be worth a fortune."

The silver Andalusian had a flowing black mane, black tail, and four legs black to the knees. Muscles rippled in his broad chest and sleek silver body, and his long black tail was highly arched.

Hawke glanced up, saw them, and gave a half salute. Then, instead of dismounting, he gave his mount a silent command, and the animal snorted and performed a prancing high step.

To Shawnalese, a king could not have looked more regal.

Hawke dismounted, tossed the reins to a groom, and hurried up the circular stairs and inside.

Moments later a footman came for Shawnalese. "His Grace requests your presence to meet the family."

Then she was in the great hall, not remembering how she'd gotten there, and her heart pounded wildly as Hawke led her to his sister, Heather, Baroness Von Rueden. The lovely dark-haired, blue-eyed baroness smiled and extended her arms in a motherly fashion. Wordlessly Shawnalese moved forward and Heather wrapped her in a loving embrace.

"Welcome to our home, Shawnalese. It will be wonderful to have another woman here. You're even more lovely than your mother. I know we'll be great friends. Please call me Heather."

"Thank you, ma'am . . . Heather."

Then she was introduced to Heather's fifteen-year-old son, Leif.

"Welcome to Foxridge, Shawna," Leif greeted warmly.

Shawnalese sighed in relief. But her respite lasted

only until the regal, silver-haired Dowager Baroness Wilhelmina Von Rueden swept into the hall. When the introductions were performed, the woman peered down her nose and declared frigidly, "You may call me Baroness Von Rueden, young voman."

"Yes, Baroness Von Rueden," Shawnalese replied, intimidated into using the hated title.

For a time the family sat and talked, but after a while, perplexed by the dowager baroness's open hostility, Shawnalese excused herself and left the great hall.

She was not yet out of hearing range before Wilhelmina snapped, "Really, Gayhawke, I cannot imagine of vhat you are thinking to take in a bastard child of no consequence and have her live at Foxridge. You don't even know the child's father. He could be a stable hand. You are bringing disgrace down upon the time-honored name of Carrington. And then to appease her ridiculous notion not to properly address us. It vill be bandied about in every drawing room in London."

Ashamed and humiliated, Shawnalese raced outside, her worst fears realized.

Hawke whirled on the dowager baroness, his eyes narrowed in anger. "There is more courage in one small finger of that 'child of no consequence' than you'll find in the entire being of many of the noblewomen you so admire. And furthermore, Baroness"—his emphasis on the title was contemptuous—"as long as you're a guest at Foxridge, you'll treat that child of considerable character with the respect she deserves. Have I made myself clear, Wilhelmina?"

"Yes, Your Grace."

"Good. See that you don't conveniently forget." With that, Hawke stormed out, turning his thoughts to where they had dwelled considerably the last few days—on Shawny's welfare.

Surprisingly, Shawny was already partially educated, off to a good start, anyway, and now his fifteen-year-old nephew's tutor could nurture her intelligence and tutor her. Her head would not be filled with straw as Hawke believed most women's heads to be. His challenge would be to turn her into a woman of substance, for he knew that once she became aware of her rare beauty, and the ultimate power she would have over men, she would attempt to go the way of all beautiful women, filled only with selfish desires and an all-consuming vanity.

Come hell or hailstorm, he would not permit that. He must protect her from herself. This exceptional child would not become what his mother had. No Victoria she. He would see to that. There would be no pampering, no useless dance and piano lessons, no self-indulgent, extravagant gowns and jewels, no instruction in what women considered charm—the affected mannerisms and pretentious prattle about nothing of importance. Shawny would learn to discuss intelligently everything from literature to affairs of state, and he personally would instruct her on his philosophy of life. She deserved her place among the nobility; after all, she was the daughter of an Austrian baron and a Grenville.

Seeking her out, Hawke found her at the stables with Grizzly, watching a mare with her new foal. He leaned on the stable door beside her and said, "I can help you do wonderful things with your life, Shawny. I want to start with your education. You'll find that if you accept nothing but the best in life, you will usually get it. However, you'll have to work from dawn to dusk. You may not be willing to pay the price for what I want to do for you, and that's what I need to find out now."

She glanced up at him. Why was he insistent on doing so much for her? Even so, she could not surrender her freedom. Not even for Gayhawke Carrington. But more than that, the humiliation of Baroness Wilhelmina's stinging words caused her to reply, "I am who I am, Gayhawke. It's doubtful that you'll change my opinions on many subjects but I have no fear of hard work. Nevertheless, if it's your intention to turn me into a mealy-mouthed, wishy-washy woman who'll agree with your every thought, then we should stop now, before we start. As I said before, I don't wish to seem ungrateful, but it was your idea to bring me here, not mine."

Ignoring the curtness of her words, Hawke replied, "Good. I'm happy we understand each other. Be at the stables at daybreak. Your riding lessons will start then. After breakfast you'll be tutored with Leif."

Thus began Shawnalese's development. However, hers was not the normal education of a young lady of the gentry, for the duke of Foxridge was determined to protect her from herself. She was already fluent in English, French, and Spanish, from having lived with an English mother in the Spanish-ruled French city of New Orleans. Latin and Greek were added to her schooling. She was instructed in geography, history, mathematics, the classic works of literature, the teachings of the great philosophers, and the politics of Britain, France, Spain, and Italy. Thaddeus, the tutor, was a hard and unrelenting taskmaster who brooked no nonsense.

At the same time, Hawke began teaching her, against Heather's and the dowager baroness's protestations, to ride astride and swim. After her first grueling month, Hawke presented her with her first reward, a Russian wolfhound puppy.

"He's my very own? Mine to keep?" she asked in disbelief, and at Hawke's nod she hugged the wiggling, gray-streaked, white ball of fur to her breast.

"His pedigree is the finest," Hawke announced. "The czar of Russia's dogs have none better."

"The czar of Russia?"

"The ruler of Russia."

"What should I name him?" she asked.

"Call him Czar."

"Perfect! Czar he is."

That night when Addison awakened Hawke from a sound sleep to report that Baroness Heather had found Miss Shawnalese's bedchamber empty, Hawke bolted from his bed. Certain he knew where she was, he ran with lantern in hand to the stall where they'd bedded her whimpering puppy. There he found her curled up, sound asleep in the straw, her hound snuggled tightly in her arms.

"Shawny!" Hawke bellowed, his relief now turned to anger. "What do you think you're doing here at this time of night?"

Instantly awake, she glanced up at the towering figure of Hawke. "I couldn't leave Czar here all alone on the first night he's away from his mother. He was crying and afraid. I couldn't leave him here alone, Gayhawke." Her eyes were wide. "You didn't leave me alone when I lost my mother."

Hawke's anger melted, and he sighed. "Well, I can't allow you to stay here by yourself. However, I'll not suffer alone. Grizzly is going to sleep right here with us."

Bounding to her feet with Czar clutched firmly in one arm, Shawnalese stood on tiptoe and threw her other arm around Hawke's neck to hug him tightly. "I love you, Gayhawke," she whispered, clinging to him while Czar struggled between them. Hawke's arm surrounded her thin shoulders, holding her gently. "I know I was wrong, and you didn't scold me."

"We shall have a discussion about that tomorrow," Hawke replied in a much gentler tone than he'd intended. "I'll get Grizzly and be back shortly." Then he gave her a conspiratorial wink.

After Hawke left, she uttered, "Someday you'll love me, too, Gayhawke Carrington. Somehow I'm going to make you love me. I'll never give up until I find a way." She snuggled the wriggling ball of white fur closer, the pup heaved a contented sigh, and both were sound asleep when Hawke returned with a surprisingly good-natured but drowsy Grizzly.

Not long after that, Hawke began instructing Shawnalese in the game of chess, and soon fencing, archery, and firearms were added to her agenda. As the months passed, however, Hawke's delusions of being able to maneuver Shawny to his will evaporated. Frustrated, he complained to his best friend, Viscount Chadwick Leighton.

"The only manipulation done has been by Shawny. She's tried my patience to the point of breaking on so many occasions that I choose not to recall them all. I swear, Chad, her obstinacy is deliberate, to punish me for forcing her to keep her promise. Time and again her words, 'I fear you will regret this decision,' rush back, leaving me to feel that I'm outwitted at every turn. Then, to make matters worse, Grizzly continuously sides with her, for in his eyes she's perfect."

"I warned you to leave her to Heather, ol' chap," Chadwick said.

"Thanks for your support, friend."

"Leave the lass alone," Grizzly grumbled the next morning. "Ye're driving her too hard. She's been through enough."

Heeding the wisdom of the older man, Hawke lightened her tasks, and again rewarded her. He insisted she close her eyes and then led her outside.

With Czar romping at her feet, Shawnalese opened her eyes to look upon the most magnificent Arabian stallion she had ever seen. The beautiful animal held his head proudly. His fiery mane was luxuriantly thick, and muscles rippled beneath the high sheen of his liver-chestnut coat as he pawed the ground.

"You can ride him with pride," Hawke said. "His heritage is the finest."

The red glow of the setting sun turned the satin sheen of the Arabian's burnished coat a fiery red. "He looks as though he's afire," Shawnalese said. "May I call him Wildfire?"

"Of course," Hawke replied.

The tethered stallion snorted and pranced nervously at the wolfhound bounding toward him. Slowly Hawke walked toward the high-spirited animal. "Easy, boy, easy," he soothed, and reached out to grab the horse's halter. Wildfire reared, pawing the air, snorting, wild-eyed, and with laid-back ears. Hawke roughly pulled the stallion down.

"No! No! Don't be rough with him," Shawnalese cried out, running to the skittish animal to throw her arms around his neck before Hawke could stop her. "It's all right, Wildfire. It's all right, love, no one's going to hurt you," she crooned, patting the withers, then the muscled shoulder of the stallion, gentling him. "Don't be afraid. I'm with you, my Wildfire, my beautiful boy. It's all right," she coaxed softly, and to Hawke's amazement, the restive stallion calmed, arching his neck and tossing his head, all the while keeping large eyes suspiciously on Hawke and Czar. Shawnalese continued to stroke and croon to the horse until he stood perfectly still, and in that moment there was an instant fusion between child and animal.

Shawnalese for the first time was experiencing life in the embrace of a loving family. Baron Rutger Von Rueden, Siegfried and Heather's oldest son, came home from Oxford on all holidays and during the summers, and Viscount Chadwick Leighton, Hawke's friend, visited at Foxridge more often than not. Before and after her lessons, most of Shawnalese's time was spent with the men and boys. So she remained a hoyden still, unschooled in the acceptable behavior of a young lady of the gentry, for Hawke forbade Heather's interference.

Early on in the first three years of Shawnalese's stay at Foxridge, there was a bonding between man and child that only deepened over time. From the beginning she had been a needy child, craving Hawke's affection, and she sought ever to be near him. When he was not away he spent his time with Shawnalese and his nephews. Each morning, at daybreak, if it were not foggy, Hawke, Shawnalese, Leif, Grizzly, and Rutger—when he was home from Oxford—galloped over the rolling green meadows beside the forest, across the downs, and beside the surf. Shawnalese treasured those times, so far removed from her life in New Orleans.

Shawnalese spent her spare time in the privacy of her chambers, where she sewed, embroidered, knitted, and tatted lace, making gifts for everyone for Christmas and birthdays.

Hawke had become her mentor, her instructor, her confidant, and her best friend. He never criticized her opinions, never laughed at her, only with her, and he treated her as a child, as indifferently as a little sister. It was a relationship Shawnalese determined to change, for by now she hopelessly, helplessly loved, adored, and worshiped Gayhawke Lawrence Richard Carrington with all the frenzied passion of her being. He had become an obsession; he had taken possession of her heart and abducted it from her body. Now that tender heart belonged only to Hawke.

He was her morning sun, her evening stars. Often when he worked in his study, she would slip into the room and sit quietly on a corner chair nearby. Every now and then he would glance up and give her a dazzling smile.

As Shawnalese neared her seventeenth birthday, an awareness rose in her. She no longer wanted to be a boy, and quite often now her fantasies turned to things of a more feminine nature, beautiful clothes in particular. So when Heather asked if there was a special gift she wanted for her birthday, she hesitantly asked if she might have a fashionable gown, for Hawke had insisted that she wear simple, plain gowns when she was not wearing breeches. Unbeknownst to Hawke, Heather had Shawnalese fitted by her own modiste, and she allowed Shawnalese to select the fabric of her choice. That long-awaited package was delivered to Foxridge on the morning of her birthday.

During the past three years, Shawnalese's body had ripened. No longer gaunt, her high-cheeked, delicately

boned face was exquisitely molded; her thick golden
hair hung in lush natural curls above her softly curving hips.

Anxious about Hawke's reaction to her gown,
Shawnalese sat at her dressing table and stared sightlessly into the mirror while Mrs. Kendall arranged her
hair. Lost in reverie, she vividly recalled the many times
since she'd come to Foxridge when she'd adamantly disagreed with him, causing his temper to flare and his
eyes to darken with anger. Tired of these confronta-
tions, she hoped that if he saw her for the woman she
was, it would put a stop to their endless battle of wills,
and then all their time together would be pleasant. But
more than that, she dared to hope that he would come
to love her as passionately as she loved him. She even
dared to hope that someday she would be his wife.

At last Mrs. Kendall stepped back to admire her
handiwork. Shawnalese's hair was coiffed in a high
bouffant, the long thick curls pulled over one shoulder
in the style so fashionable with Marie Antoinette and
the French courts. "You're as pretty as the bloomin'
queen of France, luv. A mite prettier, I reckon. Yes
indeedy."

Shawnalese moved to the cheval mirror to examine
her new gown and inhaled sharply at the daring
design. Unquestionably Hawke could not ignore that
she was now a woman. But he might also be angry.

"When Carrington sees me in this gown, he's not
going to be at all happy."

Chapter 6

"ONE THING'S FOR SURE, LUV," MRS. KENDALL said as she tucked teeny green satin bows into Shawnalese's hair. "His Grace ain't gonna accuse ya o' bein' a child in this fancy gown. High time, too. The way I see it, you've been runnin' around here far too long in them breeches and nun's dresses."

The years had honed Shawnalese's body into softly curved perfection, and the flowing velvety folds of her gown accentuated every curve and revealed an enticing cleavage. The clever modiste had designed a matching cape of sheer illusion, an added touch of decorum that made the sumptuous gown acceptable for day wear. She stepped into green satin slippers and breathed, "Wish me luck, Mrs. Kendall."

"Don't get your hopes up, luv. I know you're smitten with His Grace, but that charmer's had the besta the ladies try to catch his eye, and ya don't see him marryin' anya 'em, do ya?" At Shawnalese's forlorn look, Mrs. Kendall added, "Bloody hell! Don't pay me no mind. Reckon it dudn't hurt none to dream. Time's awastin'. Hustle on now an' have a good go at it."

Shawnalese hurried from her chambers. She'd spent many hours locating a fabric designed especially to capture Gayhawke Carrington's attention, a color several shades darker than her emerald eyes. Heather had warned her not to choose velvet, but it was the only material she'd found in the correct shade of green.

"Velvet's out of season, Shawna. It'll be too warm," Heather had said. But Shawnalese had her heart set, and Heather had acquiesced.

Nevertheless, Heather had been right, for already Shawnalese felt too warm. Hot, actually. Still, she reasoned, it was worth it. She smiled and envisioned the admiring look on Hawke's handsome face when she swept grandly down the stairs.

"Shawna, hurry!" Leif yelled.

Unaccustomed to the small heel of her new slippers, the many petticoats, and the yards of heavy, flowing fabric, Shawnalese carefully began to inch her way down the stone stairs, envisioning herself tripping and tumbling headfirst—her grand entrance. She paused to catch her breath and tottered precariously. Hundreds of times she'd raced down these same wide, spiraled stairs. Why was it so difficult now? So instead of sweeping majestically down the center of the open stairs, she hugged the single pillar and again started down, appearing, she imagined, the awkward child she tried to escape. Uncomfortably warm from frustration, the heavy velvet, and the petticoats, she stopped again and removed the sheer cape. Suddenly she didn't have enough hands; one lifted her cumbersome skirts, the other carried her filmy cape, and there were none left to steady herself on the pillar rail. She balanced herself, then took the next step down and placed a foot on the hem of her gown. She froze. Dropping her cape, she grabbed at the railing with one hand, backed up one stair, and pulled her gown from beneath her foot with the other.

"Shawna, what are you doing?" Leif laughed in amusement.

She flushed and bent to retrieve her cape, and her full breasts looked to her as though they would burst free of the confining velvet. She turned crimson.

At that moment she straightened and caught Hawke's startled expression as he watched her tedious descent, the green illusion cape in her hand, trailing behind her.

Instead of the look of admiration she had envisioned, Hawke's countenance was dark and brooding.

His winged brows furrowed in outrage, and he stared at her as though she were naked.

"What," he bellowed, "are you doing in that?"

Shawnalese lifted her chin belligerently. Not only was the entire family there to witness her humiliation, but Viscount Chadwick and his love, Lady Laurel Bradford, were there as well.

"I asked you a question, Shawny!" Hawke barked, crossing swiftly to her side. His gaze lingered for barely a moment on the rapid rise and fall of her high, full breasts, daringly revealed by the low-cut gown.

Embarrassed and flustered, she put on the sheer cape, then glanced up at Hawke. "I'm wearing a new gown for my birthday," she replied defiantly.

"Doesn't she look beautiful, Gayhawke?" Heather hurried on before her brother could answer. "Happy birthday, Shawna."

The rest of the family rushed to wish her well while Hawke's gaze burned into her the entire time. After she had opened her presents, Leif cried out, "By Jove, it's time to go swimming. We always go swimming on Shawna's birthday."

And they did, for by the time of her birthday it had usually warmed enough to broach the depths of the English Channel.

Shawnalese hurried to change into Leif's thin breeches and shirt, the cast-offs she'd worn from the first time Hawke had taught her to swim when she was fourteen. Now, however, the once baggy clothes hugged her body. Stepping before the cheval glass, she stared at her reflection with eyes widened. Full, rounded breasts strained for release at the fabric of the shirt, and her hips, now softly curving, filled the once loose breeches. With no time now to find something else, Shawnalese slipped on her spring cloak and hurried downstairs.

Within the hour, the men were splashing boisterously in the cool sea while Shawnalese gingerly made her way across the surf-splashed boulders. Modestly she removed her cape and sat down at the edge of the crashing surf. Swimming to the rocky edge, Hawke reached up and his strong hands circled her waist to lift her into the water. Her arms slid around his neck and she gazed at him worshipfully as he lowered her into the cool sea, his face, his lips, inches from hers. She felt a flush rise to her cheeks, and then all too soon he released her to play with the others. Finally Grizzly, Rutger, and Leif crawled onto the beach, exhausted but laughing. Chuckling with them, Shawnalese stood. Her head and shoulders rose out of the water as Hawke and Chadwick also splashed out of the channel.

"The water's marvelous," she called out. "I could swim the whole day. I'll be out shortly."

Turning back, Hawke hollered to the others, "I'll stay with Shawny. We'll be in directly."

"Hawke, I'll race you to the rocks," she taunted, laughing gaily. "Whoever loses has to bathe Czar."

"It's a wager."

But when Hawke reached her side, she playfully threw her arms around his neck, pulling him beneath the water, surfacing seconds later to laugh at him. Retaliating, he dragged her under, and when they surfaced she clung to him, giggling and sputtering. Standing once again, she reached up and brushed the hair from his eyes, unaware of the disturbed look on Chadwick's face as he observed them from the shore.

Instead of racing, they backstroked side by side toward the distant rocks. Once there, Hawke took her hand and they dove under the water and swam a short distance before surfacing together. Shawnalese shivered in the cool sea, and Hawke, powerless to stop himself, pulled her to him, warming her body with his. To be in the arms of the man she adored sent her senses spinning, and her heart raced out of control as she reached out a dainty finger to trace his lips. Hawke released her, and they tread water with gazes locked, both all too aware of the vibrations between them. His hand covered hers then he pressed each finger to his lips, kissing her fingertips one at a time—ever so slowly—and when he whispered her name, in one movement she was in his arms, pressed tightly against him.

Every hope she'd nurtured over the years materialized, and she closed her eyes, her heart aflame with love. His warm lips covered hers, and she melted at his touch, her world careening crazily while he kissed her sweetly, gently, then deeply, passionately, to snatch her breath away. Kissed her as she had yearned for him to, and it seemed to go on for the longest time, for the shortest time. His lips roamed to her eyes, her cheeks, her ear, then her throat, and she moaned, weakened by his passion. Again his lips consumed hers, his mouth demanding. They slowly sank in the water, but she didn't care, she only wanted this moment with Hawke never to end.

An eternity later, Hawke's arm circled her waist to pull her above the sea, and they came up gasping for air. Forever she'd envisioned his kisses, but no vision had prepared her for this, and her eyes were wide with wonder. Again he pulled her to him, crushing her in his embrace, their bodies molded seductively together, and she felt the rapid beating of his heart, felt his hard, muscular chest warm against her breasts, felt his hard thighs against her softness.

"I'd better take you inside," he murmured, his voice husky with emotion.

Shawnalese nodded, unable to speak. Hawke clasped her hand to dive with her one last time. His arm moved around her slender waist, hers entwined his neck and again his mouth claimed hers under the water.

Together they surfaced in a tight embrace and reluctantly swam toward the deserted shore, she not wanting to leave, not daring to stay. Breathing hard, he stood up in the shallows. He turned and walked toward the beach, his shoulders broad, the span of his back tapering into slender hips and when he turned back to her, he filled the boundaries of her vision. His thick-lashed green eyes sparkled from beneath winged brows, beckoning her. He emitted a strong, irresistible animal heat; a proud, magnificent stag whose muscles rippled with his every motion.

Instead of walking to the beach, he moved toward her, and Shawnalese's heart raced uncontrollably. This was her every dream, her every fantasy come true. She clasped her hands to her mouth to stifle her cry. He reached out and grabbed her wrists in one sun-dark-ened hand and gently pulled her out of the water toward him, capturing her chin with his other hand. Gazing into her jeweled green eyes, now glazed with emotion, he released her wrists, then pulled her into his arms, his mouth once again ravenous on hers. He kissed her longer, more intensely, more passionately, than before, and overcome by sweetness and desire, she felt his lips slowly trail burning, moist kisses across her face to her ear. His hand moved down her back and seared her flesh through the thin, wet fabric.

Moaning, she whispered his name, while his kisses sent wild sensations sweeping through her body. She rose on tiptoe, and her fingers entwined in his damp hair; her lips searched for, then found his. Their bod-ies clung together as his mouth devoured hers. Weak with yearning for him, weak with enraptured love for him, she returned kiss for kiss. Her head was whirling while their hearts beat as one, she hopelessly, helpless-ly lost in the rapture of his embrace.

For the first time in her life, Shawnalese experienced what it was to love someone passionately, and she wanted it to last forever.

Trembling, Hawke gently pushed her from him and took several deep breaths. When and how had Shawny become a sweet nectar he craved? Without a word, he offered her his hand. They walked out of the water onto the beach before he spoke. "You're fortunate,

Shawny, that I didn't completely lose my self-control."
He grinned, feigning lightheartedness, unwilling to
examine what had happened between them. "You
would've found out what happens to angels who fly
too close to the ground."

"Perhaps your chivalrous self-control is my misfortune." She gazed up at him with adoration, hoping he
could not tell how shaken she was.

He was awed by the exquisite, innocent beauty of
which she seemed so unaware. He had known many of
the beautiful women of the world—the courtesans of
Paris, the quadroons of New Orleans, the Scandinavians,
the exotic women of Spain, but all paled beside this
woman-child who stood looking up at him with worshipful eyes. Yet at the same time he cursed his weakness. How could he have kissed Shawny as he had? She
was but an innocent child. Woman-child, perhaps, but
child nonetheless. He was her guardian, her protector,
and he'd taken advantage of her childish infatuation. He
groaned inwardly, for if he'd caught another man kissing
her as he had, he would have called the scoundrel out.
Shawny was not a woman with whom to trifle. She
deserved a man who loved her, a man who would marry
her, and he was filled with self-loathing, for he was not
that man. The child had weaved her way into his heart,
but there was no place for the woman.

"We'd better go before someone comes looking for
us," he said, and turned on his heel to lead her up the
flowered downs and through the towering trees
toward the manor.

Smiling, she skipped along behind Hawke, her heart
burning with love, her brilliant green eyes shining with
happiness. Gayhawke Carrington loved her, and when
the time was right he would be hers and hers alone.

Dinner was early, for everyone except Shawnalese
and Leif was going to the Roswells's ball. After dinner
she turned to Hawke. "I have a gown. May I go to the
Roswells?"

"She'd have a marvelous time, Your Grace," Lady Laurel Bradford interjected, and received a grateful glance from Shawnalese.

"It's not a good idea, Gayhawke," Heather inserted. "Shawna hasn't been taught any of the social graces, and she can't dance."

"She'll disgrace herself, Gayhawke," Baroness Wilhelmina snapped. "And you, too."

At Shawny's beseeching look, Hawke seemed to soften.

"Gayhawke," Heather said, "you know she's never attended a soiree, not even our own, let alone a ball such as this."

"I've watched from the gallery above," Shawnalese admitted eagerly.

Those words gave Hawke pause. Had he been remiss in not allowing her some social contact outside the family? "Would you be content to sit in a corner and watch?"

"Oh, yes."

"Then you may go," Hawke agreed. "However, you'll have to go with the ladies. I've committed to take Lady Melville."

Shawnalese's heart plummeted in disappointment. How could he escort another woman when he loved her?

In her excitement, she took so long to get ready that the family had to wait in the great hall for her.

"Addison," Heather called impatiently, "will you please send someone to check why Shawna isn't here?"

"Don't bother, Addison," Hawke said. "I'll get her." Moments later he rapped on her chamber door. Mrs. Kendall opened the door and he stepped back to permit her to leave. "Are you ready, Shawny? Heather and Wilhelmina are anxiously waiting." Unbidden, his eyes were drawn to the dark shadow of her full, deep cleavage, obscured by the filmy green.

As she approached him, her gaze never left his, and

there, with the gallery candles flickering across them in the dimly lit room, she tried to deny the emotions tumbling though her. Reaching up, she brushed a lock of hair from his brow, their faces inches apart. Slowly Hawke lowered his head to hers and brushed her lips gently, tenderly. Pulling her into his arms, he enveloped her and she felt his warm, moist lips on her face, her throat . . . and again his lips found hers as he kissed her softly, lingeringly, sweetly. She loved his kisses; they melted her to his will. Wth all the idolization in her woman-child's heart, she slipped her arms around his neck to pull him closer. He smelled of soap mingled with the scent of masculinity, and she quivered. How could she act a mature woman when she could not stop trembling in his arms? Then he kissed her deeper, and her senses began to whirl as she submitted to the hunger of his passion. A thousand new sensations splintered through her, leaving her limp and weak.

"I didn't mean for that to happen," he said, visibly affected. "I didn't . . ."

"I did," Shawnalese said breathlessly, then wrapped her arms around his waist and rested her head on his heaving chest.

His arms encircled her tenderly. "Shawny, this cannot continue. You're a child, and my ward."

Heart-smitten, she leaned back in his arms. "Is that the way you kiss a child, Carrington? If it is, then I can hardly wait until I'm a woman grown."

Chuckling, the passion of a moment ago now dissipated, he bent to kiss the tip of her nose.

She rose on tiptoe to brush his lips with hers. "I love you, Gayhawke Carrington," she cried out.

"We'd better go, Shawny, before you tempt me beyond all reason, before I forget I'm your guardian." He stepped back to allow her to precede him through the open door. "You'll change your mind about me after you're grown."

"Nothing and no one will ever change my mind about you," she promised with dreamy awe, sweeping through the door. "Never."

Ignoring Hawke's instructions, Shawnalese twirled awkwardly from one man's arms to another at the soiree. At last, exhausted, she pleaded with her latest partner to sit out the next dance.

While Shawnalese sipped champagne, Chadwick danced his only dance with Lady Laurel Bradford. Forbidden by her father to see Chadwick because of an old family feud, Laurel had been meeting him clandestinely at Foxridge for the past several months. Now Shawnalese dreamed that someday Hawke would gaze at her with the same besotted look Chadwick bestowed on his adored Laurel. Every touch, every glance, every spoken word between them, betokened a regard she'd never before seen.

At that moment Hawke came into view as he danced with Lady Valda Melville, and Shawnalese felt an instant's squeezing hurt. How could Hawke kiss her as he had that morning, as he had that evening, and now hold another woman in his arms? She'd seen Hawke and Valda arrive hours earlier, but she'd not seen Hawke since, for he'd disappeared into the card room until now, while Lady Melville had danced all evening with one man or another. From the pout on Valda Melville's face, it was obvious the woman was incensed by Hawke's negligence.

Suddenly, with an air of indifference, Hawke escorted the viscountess from the dance floor and handed her to another gentleman before moving to Heather's side. Moments later he stood beside Shawnalese.

"Shawny"—Hawke's finger gently tilted her chin up, forcing her to meet his gaze—"what, besides dancing, have you been doing that you shouldn't?"

"Nothing. Oh, Hawke, I'm having a marvelous time."

"Yes, I see the young men have danced attendance on you. However, we must leave."

"Leave? Now?"

"Yes."

"Without Heather and Baroness Von Rueden?"

"Yes."

"Have I done something wrong?"

Her query was sincere, her face innocent, her concern touching, and Hawke's heart went out to her. "Would you like to dance before we leave?"

"Oh, Hawke, I want to dance the whole night." She sighed and jumped to her feet, unable to hide her excitement at dancing with Hawke, unable to disguise her admiration, unable to mask her infatuation.

Reaching up, she brushed a wayward lock of hair from his brow, and Hawke quickly clasped her hand, then glanced around to see if anyone had noticed her affectionate impropriety. Understanding filtered through as to why Heather had insisted that he take Shawny home immediately. To his regret, he realized she was woefully ignorant of propriety. However, she was the only female he'd ever known who was completely without guile, and in that regard she was perfect. Exactly as he'd hoped she would remain. He pulled her into his arms and deftly guided her onto the dance floor.

Hawke's strong arm steadied her body, but not her pounding heart, and then he whirled her around the floor, his handsome face smiling down into hers. She shivered from his nearness, his touch, the power vested in it, and a tiny flame of renewed hope nourished in her breast. She felt her breasts press into his chest, felt her stomach sway against the firmness of his flanks, felt her thigh captured between his, and their bodies moved as one to the music. Breathless, she floated in the arms of Gayhawke Carrington, the white knight of her dreams, the passionate love of her heart.

An amused look stole into his eyes as she gazed up at him with open adoration, and his lips curled into a crooked smile that lifted one corner of his sensuous mouth.

Humiliated that earlier she'd made a fool of herself by pouring her heart out with her declaration of love, she inquired, "Do you find me amusing, Gayhawke?"

He twirled her through the open doors onto the terrace. "I find you tempting, Shawny."

She leaned back and was met with hard thighs molding her even closer as his hand, at the small of her back, held her firmly, unyieldingly. Time stood still as, with gazes locked, their bodies melded together and moved in slow motion to the music floating outside.

Hawke lowered his head to hers, then his lips brushed her temple, his cheek rested against hers, and he crushed her to him, battling for some measure of control.

She closed her eyes and surrendered to the ecstasy of the moment in his arms, the music drifting softly into her rapture.

Presently Hawke set her from him to lead her back into the ballroom. They'd been gone only a few minutes, not long enough to cause any raised brows but long enough to rouse him unexpectedly. What was wrong with him? Steering Shawny across the crowded room, he bade the Roswells good night, ordered his coach, and excused himself to arrange with Viscount Chadwick to escort Lady Melville home. Stopping briefly to apologize to a furious Valda Melville, he returned to where Shawny stood waiting for him. With her hand on his arm, they left the mansion to step into the night air. Unconsciously his arm moved possessively around her waist. With worshipful eyes, she looked up at him and smiled. A footman stood at the coach, his hand on the opened door, but instead of entering the coach, Hawke maneuvered her into the shadows of the manicured grounds.

Chapter 7

"Shawny, I've allowed matters to get out of hand between us today. I'd had every good intention of avoiding you this evening, but . . ." Pausing, Hawke studied her hand where it rested in his, his face somber. "I think you know I can't allow this to continue. I'm your guardian and you're seventeen, still a young girl little more than a child. I care too much for you to permit this to progress."

"But—"

"No, Shawny, allow me to finish. I want you to understand why we can't be together again, not like today, not like this evening. You're too young, too inexperienced, to know your feelings. There's no place in my life for you, other than as it has been between us, as special friends—chums, if you will."

"Chums?"

Hawke caught the pain reflected in her eyes before she turned her head away. "Shawny, look at me." When she turned her face up to his, he continued, "The most difficult deed I've done in my life is to walk away from you now, from what we've shared today . . . from the feelings you arouse in me. If you weren't special to me, I not only wouldn't do it, I couldn't do it." His voice was anguished, and he pulled her into his arms. Lowering his head, he caressed her cheek with his.

Shawnalese leaned back in his arms and peered up at him, her eyes as bright as a kitten's in the moonlight. "Hawke, don't you know that we were destined for each other? Haven't you known that from the first time we saw each other?" With reverent regard she searched his face, his eyes, for an answer. "Why do you deny me?"

Hawke sighed. He had only himself to blame for this situation, for he was well aware of Shawny's childlike veneration. He'd made the first mistake that morning with his witless, uncontrolled behavior at the beach. He'd acted with all the restraint of an adolescent, then he'd foolishly and irresponsibly, if not knowingly, compounded it when he went to her chambers this evening. Now he must rectify two serious blunders.

"If we're destined for each other, Shawny," he replied, carefully treading his way among responsibility, conscience, and concern for her tender feelings, "then nothing can defy destiny." He answered her gently, ever so gently, rubbing his knuckles back and forth across her soft Dresden cheek. "Time is the test of true destiny."

At his gentleness, her love for him burst free, and bending her head, she captured his hand between her cheek and shoulder. "I love you, Hawke." The words slipped from her lips of their own accord, and she glanced up at him with trusting, admiring eyes before she turned her head to press soft lips to his hand.

Hawke groaned. The three words she'd uttered to him so often throughout the years now shattered his composure. How could he tell her he no longer wanted her childish adoration, did not want her starry-eyed declarations of love? For three years he had thrived on her child's love, but now she was a woman nearly grown and there was no room in his life for a woman's love, especially so when there was no such figment of the imagination. "Love" between a man and woman was naught but lust. There was no fire that burned in the heart, only in the loins.

"I'll do anything for you, Hawke. I'll love you forever."

"You don't know what you're saying," Hawke managed to reply, at the limit of his self-control. Shawny not only offered freely everything he ached to accept, but she gave him no respite. And he knew that at this exact moment, if they were in private, he would not, he could not, turn away. He wanted her—no, not her, her delectable little body—more than he'd ever wanted anything or anyone. But he did not want her looking up at him with mooning calf eyes when he yearned to tumble her to the ground and make love to her until darkness turned to dawn. Only the fact that they were mere feet away from several footmen and coachmen kept him from it. However, he mused wryly, doing so would resolve two rapidly increasing problems at one time—his craving and her foolish, obsessive adulation.

With a mind that no longer thought clearly, for the desire shooting through his loins blocked out all rational thinking, he somehow forced himself to say the honorable words: "What you feel for me is simply infatuation. You've no experience with men. You'll feel differently in a year or two after you have some experience. You don't realize what you're saying now, what you're offering." Then, as though someone else had taken possession of his senses, his honor, and his voice, he added, "But I warn you, Shawny, I'm a man. Guardian or no, you can only place so much temptation in my path, and the next time I may be too weak to resist. If that happens, I'll take you to the stars, but I won't marry you. Consider yourself warned."

At that pronouncement, she stiffened and a flash of bitter misery tore through her heart. "How could you suggest such a thing to me"—she beat on his chest with her fists—"after all we've been to each other these years?"

As though he didn't know her, for all logical thought had fled, he looked into the hurt in her eyes and replied coldly, "That was then. This is now." He grabbed her wrists and pulled her roughly against his chest and flanks. She was in his arms, and he smothered her face with kisses as he whispered her name over and over.

There in the darkness, his mouth was ravenous on hers, and a fire flashed through her body. On the brink of an abyss, she wrenched her mouth from his, fighting for air. Again his lips covered hers, hot, eager, kissing her hungrily, and she melted at his touch. Her anger fully gone now, she responded. Her lips devoured his, and her hand cupped his head to pull him closer, their passion leaving her weak.

This had been an even bigger mistake than he'd known it would be, Hawke realized, and released and her as quickly as he had embraced her.

"I'm your destiny, Hawke," she said with all the fervor of her being, and pressed her golden head to his heaving chest, her heart filled to overflowing with love. Silently he encircled her in his arms, and she heard the rapid drum of his heart. "You will love me, I promise you," she said softly, standing on tiptoe to press her lips to his cheek, his chin, his throat. "Somehow, I'll make you love me."

A low moan escaped him as he fought for self-control. "Damn, Shawny," he gasped. Having won the battle within himself, he removed her arms from around his neck. "Do you think I'm made of stone? I can't handle any more."

Moments later, as Hawke assisted her into the coach, she wondered, would he forever be a shattered dream?

"Gayhawke, we're going to talk. Now!" Heather insisted the next morning, her blue eyes flashing, her mouth set in firm resolve. "You've evaded me on this subject for the last three years, but no longer. I daresay you've ruined Shawnalese, and now her reputation is destroyed, fodder for the gossips. The child is disgraced."

At that, Rutger's gaze lifted from the book he'd been reading.

"Really, Heather"—Hawke yawned, placing an

elbow on the stone mantel of the cold hearth—"aren't you being a little dramatic, simply because Shawny can't dance?"

"Can't dance?" Heather scoffed. "When the poor girl wasn't treading on a gentleman's feet, she tripped over them. If only that were the problem."

"Something else is wrong?" Hawke quizzed with raised brow.

"Yes, Gayhawke," Heather replied. "Everything else is wrong."

"You have my attention, Heather," Hawke stated. "Out with it."

"While she talked to the duke of Kensingham, Shawna criticized Louis the sixteenth for bankrupting France by financing the American war for independence and indulging Marie Antoinette's extravagant excesses and court life. Then she wagered with His Grace that France would be in revolution before the decade is out. She not only talked politics, but she actually wagered one pound with the duke of Kensingham."

"Great Caesar's ghost! I'm appalled. It's scandalous," Baroness Wilhelmina huffed, her kerchief clasped in shock to her nose.

"Shawny's right, you know," Hawke agreed.

"Gayhawke!" Heather expostulated.

"Sorry." Hawke grinned and shifted his stance. "Is there more?"

"Much more. I shall never again be able to face the Roswells. Chadwick said that Shawna told Lord Nelson that titles of nobility are balderdash."

Hawke stifled a peal of laughter. Rutger did not.

Casting her eldest son a scathing look, Heather continued, "And I was standing beside Viscount Graham when he angered her and she cursed at him, then insulted him."

"She did?" Hawke and Rutger questioned simultaneously.

"She certainly did," Heather acknowledged, twisting

her kerchief. "To be explicit, she said, 'God's night-gown, you're a pompous toad!' Everyone in that room is wondering where I've been these years that Shawna's been growing up wild, with no direction other than from men and boys. I'll never again present my face outside this manor."

"I tried to tell you, Gayhawke," Wilhelmina snapped. "That child has been growing up like an orphaned heathen. It's shocking. The prattle vill be unbearable. Her name, and yours, vill be bandied from here to London."

Hawke made no comment, and the only indication that Wilhelmina tread in dangerous waters was the darkening of his green eyes, the tightening of his jaw.

"Speaking of which," Heather began again, "Shawna and I visited with Lady Langdon, Lady Kenyon, and the marchioness of Westbridge. To my relief, Shawna sat and quietly listened to Lady Langdon comment on the beauty of the day. At that point Shawna eagerly agreed, then proceeded to remark about the wonderful time she had today swimming with you, Chadwick, Rutger, Leif, and Grizzly."

"Gracious creator of day!" Wilhelmina exclaimed, and sniffed from her vinaigrette of smelling salts. "The girl is ruined. London vill be atwitter."

"That is rather awkward, Hawke," Rutger agreed.

"Gayhawke, if I could have sunk through the floor, I would have," Heather fumed. "Can you imagine what those women are saying right this minute? And to whom? Shawna swimming with five men—and no chaperone. Lady Langdon had to use her hartshorn bottle to keep from fainting on the spot. The whole room was soon abuzz."

Frowning now, Hawke stroked his chin, deep in thought.

"There's more, Gayhawke," Heather persisted.

"You vouldn't listen, Gayhawke," Wilhelmina interrupted. "Heather and I tried—"

"Quiet, Wilhelmina!" Hawke ordered, then turned back to his sister. "Tell me all of it, Heather."

"She argued politics with the earl of Somerfield, spouting Rousseau's philosophies of liberty and equality. While you contentedly played cards with the men, Shawna expounded virtues of equality to a nobleman! And not merely any nobleman, Gayhawke, but the earl of Somerfield, brother-in-law of His Grace, the duke of Berkchester."

"Yes, Heather," Hawke responded patiently, "I'm aware that he's brother-in-law to the duke. Go on."

"Then," Heather continued, "Shawna bumped the arm of Viscount Graham, probably intentionally, and splashed his drink on him. . . ."

"Graham's a mincing fop," Rutger volunteered. "Well known for his liberties with the ladies. I should have liked to hear his stammering when he discovered his garish satin suit and showy laces stained."

"Piffle! The pompous toad deserved it," Wilhelmina interjected, only to receive a withering stare from Heather.

"Everyone here seems to be making light of a grave predicament," Heather protested, twisting her kerchief in her hands. "Of course, Shawna had a marvelous time. She doesn't realize that she was the scandalous talk of the ball, that her name will be bandied about in every fashionable drawing room, by every gossip monger, every crude and coarse man. She doesn't know that she laughed too loud, and talked too much, and on every subject forbidden to genteel young ladies— every subject, Gayhawke. How could she realize? You've never permitted me to teach her anything."

No one replied, and silence pervaded the room.

"Shawna behaved," Heather continued, "as though she's spent the last three years locked up with a scholar, or in the forest and stables with a group of bachelors—which she has. I'd not be surprised to learn that she also discussed the merits of cross-breeding

Andalusian and Arabian horses. After all, that's what she's been taught. Thank God she didn't challenge anyone to a duel. I'm sure she can outshoot and outfence half of the men there." Heather drew in her breath, battling to regain some measure of composure, and went on, "Gayhawke, you've taken a precious child who's borne the tragedies of life, and through your arrogant insistence to direct her development, you've brought her low. I daresay you've not only ruined Shawna's reputation, you've destroyed her life, and any chance that she may have had for a good marriage." With that, Heather burst into tears.

Moments passed before Hawke broke the silence. "Heather, we are having a masquerade. In two weeks. No longer. I will approve the invitation list."

"No one will come."

"Who would dare slight the duke of Foxridge? A man of my consequence could break many of those noblemen you shed tears over, and well they know it. In addition, I'm owed a legion of favors by many others. And has it slipped your mind, Heather, that even though he's ill, I still have the ear of George the Third? You know the king highly regards my sympathetic heart when he's expounding on the latest escapades of his sons. All of England knows it, too. Arrange the masquerade, dear sister. Be sure that I see the guest list as soon as possible. I want the cream of England here. Have Addison prepare it today." Then he turned to his nephew. "Rutger, you have two weeks to teach Shawny to dance." With that, Hawke turned on his heel and stormed out of the hall, Heather's words echoing after him.

"Gayhawke, you can't do this to Shawnalese!"

On the surface everything was the same, yet nothing was the same.

Together as much as ever—riding across the countryside, swimming in the cool channel, dining with the family—Hawke and Shawnalese were never alone. Yet the air between them remained charged. Their brief interlude was relived when their gazes met, when they touched accidentally, in the tone of their voices. When she glanced up, more often then not she found Hawke's gaze boring into her. Tension mounted.

Two days had passed, during which Rutger instructed Shawnalese in dance. Heather had no time to spare, as she was involved from morning to night with elaborate preparations for the coming masquerade ball, so Wilhelmina attempted to teach Shawnalese the socially acceptable behavior of young ladies.

On the third day, Shawnalese burst into Hawke's study. "I'll not spend another second learning that idiotic drivel Baroness Von Rueden is trying to pound into me," she stormed with hands on hips. "I told you when first I came here, Hawke, that I wouldn't—"

Hawke leaned back in his chair. "Please be seated, Shawny."

"I don't want to sit! And I'll not—"

"Sit!" Hawke bellowed. "Now!"

Shawnalese lowered herself onto a chair.

"That's better. You were saying?"

"I realize now that at the Roswells I behaved in a manner that may have embarrassed you and Heather. For that I am sorry, and I apologize, even though it's ludicrous and absurd that a woman is expected to behave as though her brain never developed past the age of five, that she can barely tell her fingers from her toes and needs someone to tell her if it's daylight or dark."

"It's what is socially acceptable, Shawny," Hawke explained patiently. "I've long felt that it's the insecurity of men that's made it so."

"I'm sure you're right. Nevertheless, I won't be the mewling, simpering female the dowager baroness wants me to play. I won't hide behind a fan and flutter my eyelashes, I won't pretend to be enthralled by a consummate bore, and I most definitely will not feign gratitude simply because a nobleman bestows the *honor* to speak to me." Calm now, she smiled. "And if I'm treated with condescension, as though I'm in a state of perpetual childhood, or if I'm told one more time that something is 'beyond my understanding,' or if another so-called gentleman makes an improper comment to me, as Viscount Graham did, I most likely will spill his drink on him also." With that, she rose and walked casually to the sideboard. Removing the stopper from a decanter of port, she picked up the wine and a goblet and walked toward Hawke. "Would you care for a drink?"

"This time of morning? What's gotten into you, Shawny? You know I seldom drink, but never in the morning."

The words were barely out of Hawke's mouth when Shawnalese raised the decanter and poured the red wine over his head.

"What the . . . ?" Hawke sputtered, and jumped to his feet as the port dribbled down his hair, his face, and onto his white shirt.

Shawnalese smiled smugly and moved out of reach. "I didn't have a bottle of port handy when you insulted me the other night, and inasmuch as I don't want to call you out, this seems to resolve the problem of how to satisfy my honor."

"Dammit, Shawny!" Hawke bit his tongue to hold back a string of oaths.

Setting down the empty decanter and goblet, Shawnalese turned and left with a swirl of her skirts. Pausing at the door, she called back over her shoulder, "Since I'll never be what you want, what the dowager baroness wants to make of me, I'll inform her that she may discontinue my lessons. I'm sure you've decided it's best that I not attend your masquerade. I'm not going to stick straw in both my ears and pretend it's growing from within."

"I should have known better than to take a feisty hellion like you under my protection," Hawke bellowed, the port still dripping from his head.

At that moment, Chadwick appeared.

"Beautiful morning, isn't it, Chad?" Shawnalese said happily, and slipped through the door so he could enter Hawke's study. The last she heard was Chadwick quizzing Hawke.

"God's teeth! What happened to you?"

Hawke went to change his clothes, wondering how he was to motivate the independent, willful young woman from further disgracing herself. And then, suddenly, he knew. Shawny deeply loved Heather, and would make her best effort to clear the blemish to Heather's good standing, for Shawny now understood that his sister was held responsible for Shawny's scandalous behavior at the Roswells. Even so, she would not spend another minute under the tutelage of Wilhelmina, nor did he want her to. He would call in his markers to a few influential men. The right word in a wife's ear would restore anyone. And he would make certain the husbands used the right word. Shawny would not be misjudged because he'd erred.

The evening of the masquerade arrived, and Shawnalese was seated at her dressing table, fussing anxiously with the intricately fashioned, towering confection that was her coiffure. Hawke had given her explicit instructions on the style. "You'll be Marie Antoinette," he'd said, and he'd had her fitted for a gown. It still had not arrived, but she'd already decided that if it were buttoned up to her chin, she would not leave her room.

While Mrs. Kendall powdered her hair a snowy white, Shawnalese silently reviewed Hawke's instructions.

"You are to dance with no one but Rutger, Leif, Chadwick, or me. Except to dance, you're forbidden to leave my side, not even for a moment. Finally, you're

not to engage in conversation with anyone about anything other than to greet each guest and comment graciously on his or her costume, smiling all the while."

Mrs. Kendall applied rice powder to her face, to emu-
late the translucent complexion of the French queen,
envied by women everywhere. Next followed a touch of
lip rouge and then a black patch at the corner of her lips.
Worried about the many things that might go awry,
Shawnalese closed her eyes and silently murmured an
entreaty that she not commit a faux pas to further humiliate Heather. When she opened her eyes, she inhaled
deeply, holding her breath, for the image that stared
back at her was that of a stranger. A knock on the door
startled her from her examination. "Yes?"

"Your gown's arrived Miss Shawnalese," Addison
called out.

Mrs. Kendall took from him a bulky, sheet-wrapped
parcel and carefully laid it on bed. She went back for
other packages.

"His Grace asked me to give Miss Shawnalese this,"
Addison said, and gave the maid a handful of straw.
"He said she'd know what to do with it."

Taking the straw, Shawnalese smiled at Hawke's
humor. There was not another man in the entire world
as wonderful. Shawnalese ran to unwrap the sheet.

"Ohh!" she gasped, staring at the most beautiful ball
gown she'd ever seen—white silk, shot through with
gold thread and covered with thousands of brilliants.
Draped panniers revealed an underskirt embroidered
with gold thread, to be worn over a wide oval hoop. In
a trance, Shawnalese dressed and was putting on the
elaborate plumed and brillianted half mask just as a
loud knock sounded at her door.

Mrs. Kendall hurried to open the door to the duke.
Most of the guests had arrived, and as arranged,
Hawke was there to escort Shawnalese downstairs.
Resplendent in a gold-embroidered white tunic partial-
ly covered by a hand-tooled leather breastplate, he

wore sandals laced to his bare knees and a red velvet toga. His awesome presence filled her open door. She felt hypnotized, for he grew more handsome each time she saw him. Smiling with admiration, she remarked, "A more perfect Julius Caesar, emperor of Rome, could not be found." His return smile dazzled her.

"You are impressed?"

"I'm impressed, mighty Caesar." Then, anxiously she twirled for his examination, self-consciously holding her fan in front of the shockingly low-cut décolletage. "Is this how you wanted me to look?"

His gaze lingered on what she attempted to hide from his view. "Marie Antoinette would surely die from envy."

"You are pleased?"

"There's not a nobleman who'll not wish that you were his."

Smiling with relief, Shawnalese looked at him adoringly then reached up to brush back an unruly lock from his brow. His hand covered hers, and her cheeks flushed as she recalled his embraces. Her gaze fastened on the full, sensuous mouth that tormented her, and she longed for him to take her in his arms, to kiss her passionately, knowing he would not. The emotions vibrating between them were tangible. Slowly, his hand on hers slid down and dropped away.

Offering his arm, Hawke tried to ignore what had passed between them. "Are you ready to face the lions?" he questioned huskily. At her silence, he smiled encouragingly. "You'll be fine, Shawny." Then he added the lie: "I'm not in the least concerned."

At that encouragement, she took his arm and floated with newfound confidence down the candlelit gallery.

At the top of the broad, winding stairs, they paused.

Terrified by all the things she could do wrong, Shawnalese gazed up at Hawke and smiled. "I forgot the straw for my ears."

A smile touched his lips. "No matter. No one will

notice."

With determination, Shawnalese studied the crowd-ed great hall, filled with elegantly costumed couples. Then, by prearrangement, the strolling minstrels gath-ered at the bottom of the long winding staircase, and to her horror, all eyes turned toward them. Hawke gave her hand an encouraging squeeze.

Chapter 8

E VEN THOUGH ENCUMBERED BY A MARIE Antoinette gala ball gown, with its yards of billowing, panniered skirts and petticoats, Shawnalese swept regally down the wide staircase, her hand on Hawke's wrist.

Escorting her among the gathered masked visitors, Hawke introduced her to each guest, and she felt as though she were under a quizzing glass, aware of the gazes that slid her way. After strolling with her through the many rooms opened to the guests, Hawke was satisfied that no nobleman had been overlooked and announced that the ballroom was now open. Together he and Shawnalese led the procession, and once inside, Hawke took her in his arms to lead the opening waltz.

Enchanted, she soared in his arms and her heart took wings as he whirled her around the ballroom. Almost every fantasy she'd ever imagined, nearly every wish she'd aspired to, was materializing on this night. Dare she also hope that Hawke returned just a small measure of the infinite love that she reserved only for him?

All too soon she danced with Rutger, costumed, with Grizzly's help, as a pirate, complete with black eye patch, one dangling gold earring, and a plumed hat. Once again she thanked Rutger for the hours he'd spent, and the endless patience he'd displayed, in teaching her to dance as though her feet never touched the ground.

Three years of fencing lessons had given Shawnalese the agility of a cat, and she had learned quickly. Heather had instructed her how a lady, wearing a cumbersome gown, could descend a flight of stairs with grace and aplomb, but it was Rutger who had forced her to practice hour after weary hour. Without doubt, his tireless efforts had surely saved her from humiliation when she was able to glide down the stairs with Gayhawke.

From a distance, Hawke watched Shawny as she danced with the forbidding pirate, and a frown furrowed his brow. She was exquisite. How could he keep her unaffected?

"A magnificent creature, isn't she?" a medieval warlord, the earl of Wellhampton, commented as he walked up beside Hawke.

"Yes. Yes, she is," Hawke agreed, his dusky green eyes following her.

"It would be easier to catch the moonlight than to hold such a woman," Wellhampton said, emitting a deep sigh.

The evening flew by. Shawnalese stood quietly beside Hawke as he conversed with the costumed noblemen, and more often than not she bit her lip to keep from interjecting. When she danced with Rutger, Leif, or Chadwick, Hawke heedfully turned his attention to the female guests.

Fascinated by the magnificently costumed guests, Shawnalese concluded that almost every person of wealth in England was in attendance. Nearly every type of disguise was represented, from the regal costume of King Henry VIII to a court jester, the grandeur of Queen Cleopatra to the simplicity of a gypsy girl.

But the sight that warmed her heart was Chadwick as a knight in armor, a costume designed to conceal his identity from Lord Bradford. Indeed, the ruse worked quite well, for Laurel, costumed as a medieval queen, spent most of the evening dancing in the arms of a clumsy knight, beneath the nose of her ever-vigilant father.

Tired now, the weight of her extravagant gown burdensome, Shawnalese had barely finished her dance with a red Satan Leif when she felt the power of a smothering gaze pinning her to the spot. Out of the crowd Julius Caesar came to stand beside her. Smiling up at him, she tried to breathe normally, and her heart fluttered crazily when Hawke stretched out his fingers and brushed them against her chin.

All evening he had watched her—lusted after her, if he were truthful. What made him seek the bittersweet torture of being with her, when he couldn't be with her in the way he needed? He knew he should not, must not, utter his next words, but he was powerless to stop himself. "You're tired, Shawny," he said. "Would you like to take some air, away from prying eyes, so you can relax?"

"I'd be most appreciative, powerful Caesar."

She slipped her arm through his and followed his lead as he moved toward the French doors that overlooked the courtyard gardens. Hawke sucked in his breath, his gaze fixed on the softly rounded flesh above her decolletage, then, as she preceded him, on the nakedness of her back, the delicate curve of her spine, the soft creamy flesh inches from his hand. She was a tantalizing temptress sent to bedevil him.

She walked beside Hawke through the moonlit fantasy of the lushly foliaged gardens. It was an enchantment of which she'd dreamed many times. Stone pathways wound through the lantern-lit plantings, and stone Renaissance benches, scattered throughout the courtyard, beckoned the visitor to rest and drink in the beauty. Sea nymphs spewed water into the air, and an abundance of trees spread their leafy bowers over all. Did she really walk this midnight Garden of Eden with Gayhawke?

"You've done extremely well, Shawny. You should be pleased." Hawke laughed, and his laughter was deep, warm, and rich. "And you certainly dance better than the last time. I'm amazed that you've also mastered the quadrille."

"Rutger's endless patience deserves the credit. Other than that, I've done little except keep my mouth closed." She removed her half mask. "I fear, left to my own devices, that I would have disgraced you more than the last time."

Hawke chuckled. His arm slipped around her waist to pull her soft body close to the hardness of his, and she smiled up at him as though he were a treasured prize. She nestled her head into the hollow of his shoulder as they walked slowly through the garden wonderland. The warm, gentle breeze filled her nostrils with the fragrance of honeysuckle, and the crickets sang only for her—for her joy, for her misery . . . of unrequited love.

Neither spoke, not wanting to break the spell of the night, not daring to say what was best left unsaid. Stopping at the end of the courtyard, they shared the beauty before them that spoke of another world, another age. A statue of stone, an armored knight astride a rearing horse, protected the splendor below, and the soothing rush of water cascaded across boulders into a winding, stream-fed pond.

At the rear of the gardens, Hawke took Shawnalese's hand to lead her across one of the lantern-lit stone bridges that arched across the curving pond to a domed woodland temple.

The temptation was too much, and Hawke reached out to fondle the soft texture of Shawny's powdered hair, the silken strands curling around his fingers.

Shuddering, she raised her face, lips parted, and her eyes widened with longing—for what, she knew not.

"Green-eyed goddess, why do you torment me?" In one movement he pulled her to him, and she was in his arms, pressed tightly against him. Slowly his head lowered, and his warm, moist lips eagerly claimed hers.

Her arms slipped around his neck, and her hand inched into the curling thickness of his hair as she responded. Her soft lips parted hungrily, demanding more. She shivered, and her senses reeled as his fingers trailed down her bare back and burned into her flesh. He nipped at her neck, under her ear, then moved to the pulsating spot at her throat, sending a million new sensations splintering through her. Weakened knees gave way beneath her, and his strong arm tightened as he expertly bent her into his arms, his lips devouring hers in the dim moonlight, their bodies clinging desperately.

Hawke released her, his entire being kindled in passion's fire. Her full breasts burned into his chest as he fought for control, her inexperience heightening his desire almost beyond constraint. He craved her, craved her beyond all reason and logic, craved her . . . now.

All will, all resolve, gone, Shawnalese proclaimed softly, "I love you, Hawke. You're my everything." On tiptoe, she planted tiny butterfly kisses at the hollow of his throat.

Whispering her name, he again crushed her in his arms, pulled her tightly against him, his lips hot, eager. "Say that to me when you're a woman grown, Shawny," he murmured huskily before his lips claimed hers again.

With a hopeful heart, she wondered once more if he were beginning to love her. "Will you say that to me when I'm a woman grown, Hawke?" she asked breath-lessly when he released her. His lips brushing her neck was her only answer. "Somehow I'll make you love me, Hawke—I'll steal your heart," she warned, caressing his cheek, brushing the unruly curl back from his brow.

"You cannot steal what is already yours, Shawny"— he kissed the curve of her neck—"but there is no place for me in your life."

Crushed, still she clung to him. The fragrant breeze ruffled her hair, and fair strands blew about her flushed face as she battled the anguish that tore through her aching heart.

In control now, Hawke released her and said, "I must return to my guests." With that, his lips brushed her brow, her temple, her lids, and trailed down her cheek.

Shawnalese turned her face to be kissed, sweetly, then demandingly. Elated by his kisses, she wondered if from his desire she could coax love. Might one day, if they shared passion, he come to love her as she did him? Ever hopeful, she whispered, "Don't leave me." The pain of parting was already a deep ache inside her. She was innocent, but somehow she knew the fire that blazed between them was exceptional. "Don't leave me, Hawke."

"You don't know"—his voice broke—"you don't know what you're saying, Shawny. I have to leave— while I still can. We've been out here far too long. Your reputation . . . You go in through the doors to the great hall, and I'll enter through the ballroom. No one will be the wiser," he instructed, releasing her. His hand caressed her cheek one last time, unable to resist.

Her lips brushed his hand, and then she turned to go.

In the gardens, a pair of masked eyes that had secret-ly observed Shawnalese from the moment she and Hawke ventured into the courtyard now watched her solitary departure. Charcoal clouds slipped across the full moon, and every planting became an obscure shadow as the black-cloaked assailant stalked her stealthily.

A strong hand shot out of the darkness to grasp her shoulder and spin her around. Terrified, she faced the menacing black-masked figure unflinchingly, but where her eyes were cold as ice, his were glazed with desire. She shoved his hand away in disgust.

He grabbed her, jerking her to him drunkenly, and one hand clasped her mouth while the other groped at her breast. "Gayhawke Carrington's little plaything will share, won't she?" he sneered.

Reeking of whiskey, the wet mouth slammed over hers as she fought futilely against his overpowering size. Her hand flew to her calf for the dagger that was not there.

He dragged her into the shadowy shrubs: his one hand grasped her breast while the other pawed at her skirts. Off balance, she crumpled to the ground beneath his heavy weight.

Terror streaked through her. She was hurled backward in time to the dank alley beside Rose's French Bouquet. She smelled the rotting garbage, the raw sewage, heard the tinkling pianoforte, the laughter, felt the sweaty hand move up her leg, heard the lewd remarks, felt the alleyway beneath her. Only the coolness she now felt was not the hard dirt, but the soft grass. Unable to breathe, she bit her assailant's lip and twisted away from his ravenous mouth. He again smothered her screams, and she grabbed his groping fingers, struggling frantically to free herself.

Abruptly the black-cloaked figure was jerked from her body, hurled against a tree, and Hawke's large hand clamped the man's throat in a death grip. "I'll kill you, you bloody blackguard!" Then he stripped away the black mask.

Lord Ellsworth's red face darkened as he floundered for air, his hands fearfully clasping Hawke's iron grip around his throat.

Shawnalese scrambled to her feet and stumbled to Hawke's side. "Stop, Hawke! You're killing him!"

"He deserves to die." Hawke's words were venomous, vindictive, icy cold.

"Gayhawke," she pleaded, grabbing at the hand that choked the life out of the older man. "You can't do this. Oh, please, Gayhawke. Please!"

Reluctantly Hawke released his hold, and the nobleman collapsed to the ground, gasping for breath. "If you were a younger man, Ellsworth, I'd call you out," Hawke snarled, his face sinister. "I still should, for you rightfully should die!"

"Please, Your Grace," the man implored, panting. "I was in my cups . . . my wife—"

"Your good wife doesn't deserve the scandal of your death upon a field of honor, nor do your children warrant being reared fatherless." Hawke towered over the cowering baron. "How do I know that I can trust you to keep silent? I'll not have this woman's reputation tarnished."

"You have my word, Your Grace. Trust me."

At that, Hawke's eyes narrowed. "I'll trust you, Ellsworth. One word and you're a dead man. And on that, you can trust me." Pivoting, Hawke picked up Shawny's fan and mask, then clasped his arm about her and led her toward the northern rear entrance of the manor. He brushed her lips softly, briefly, with his, then murmured, "You go upstairs. I'll send Mrs. Kendall to assist you. Heather will be up to check on you shortly."

She lifted grateful eyes to his cherished face and whispered, "Thank you, Hawke."

"My pleasure." He could see the adoration sparkling in her eyes, feel the hero worship, as though he, in shining armor, had charged up on his white destrier to rescue her. He both loved and hated her childish infatuation. Overwhelmed with the feelings of protectiveness he'd always harbored for her, he pulled her into his arms and embraced her tenderly for the longest time. Earlier he'd lustfully held the woman in his arms; now, comfortingly, he held the child. After a time he reluctantly released her so she could climb the back stairs to her chambers.

Her hand grasped his. "Aren't you going to kiss me good night?"

"If I kiss you now, Shawny, it would be the beginning of a beautiful night, not the end of an unfortunate one," he said huskily.

She turned and started up the stairs. Hawke turned to leave and saw a knight in armor with a medieval queen, observers to all, walk from the location of the woodland temple. Cursing, he altered his direction, only to have Chadwick call out to him.

Leaving Laurel where she stood, Chadwick lumbered awkwardly to Hawke's side and removed his helmet. "You play a dangerous game, Hawke," he snapped disapprovingly.

"I don't play games where Shawny's concerned," Hawke retorted.

"Then you're asking for trouble," Chadwick warned. "Unless you intend to marry her."

"Don't be absurd! It was a moment of weakness, nothing more. Don't worry about me, Chad."

"God's teeth, you aren't the one I'm worried about, Hawke! I'm concerned about that naive young lady whom you've reared as a boy, and her obvious adoration of you. Has Shawna ever been kissed before now? Ever?"

"You needn't worry about Shawny, Chad," Hawke replied, anxious to end this conversation. "You should know I'd never do anything to hurt her."

"I know you wouldn't intentionally, but I've seen you hurt many women you hadn't intended to, and I won't see her harmed," Chadwick threatened. "Not even by you, my friend."

The following day Chadwick poked his head in Hawke's study. "Laurel's not here yet, so I decided I'd bother you a while, ol' chap."

"Come in," Hawke responded solemnly. "Close the door. I need to talk to you."

"A problem?" Chadwick closed the door and lowered himself onto a chair.

"Ahh, Chad, my friend. An immense problem."

"Why," Chadwick wondered aloud, "do I have the feeling this involves Shawna?"

At the look of disapproval on Chadwick's face, Hawke sighed. "I haven't shared Valda's bed since before Shawny's birthday." At Chadwick's look of disbelief, Hawke continued, "I can't remember, except on board ship, ever being without a woman for this long. Valda invites me in and I see Shawny's green eyes, those damnable, haunting green eyes, and I make my excuses and come home. Shawny walks by, so that I catch her fragrance, and I want to possess her, or she brushes against me, or puts her hand on my arm, or says my name in that breathy voice of hers, and I crave her so much I can't stand it. What is happening to me, Chad? This is Shawny I'm lusting after. Shawny! The child who goes out of her way to disagree with me—"

"And who goes even further to support you, when need be. Who idolizes and worships you," Chadwick reminded him.

"Exactly. She's little more than an enamored child, yet I'm lusting after her, have been since her birthday two weeks ago, and all I did was kiss her. I don't need to tell you what my dreams are like," Hawke said, rising from behind his desk to sit on the companion chair beside Chadwick.

"You could marry her."

"I thought I made myself clear on that point." Hawke scowled. "I believed I had this under control, until last night. Now I have to accept it's going to be an ever-worsening problem. I can't leave Foxridge, I don't want to send Shawny away. But I'm not going to have a love affair with my ward."

"I'm relieved to hear that. I was getting concerned.

Shawnalese is special to me," Chadwick admitted, hating that he felt it necessary to say this to the man he loved as a brother.

"Special to you! What do you think she is to me?" Hawke flung back. "Just what do you mean, special to you? Do you have some plans for her of which I'm not aware?"

"God's teeth, Hawke! Let's end this right now. You don't realize what you're saying. You're obsessed with her—just listen to yourself."

Caught off guard by his friend's words, Hawke was momentarily speechless. "You're right, Chad. You're right. I'm sorry. I don't know what's gotten into me. Let's forget the whole matter, all right?" he asked, visibly upset over the first heated words he'd ever had with his best friend. "Well, old man, what do you suggest? I won't continue lusting after a woman-child. Neither will I bed Shawny. Nor will I spend another hellish two weeks without a woman."

"Try three months."

"Three months? You?"

Chadwick sighed. "That's how long I've been seeing Laurel exclusively. I don't know what I'm going to do if her father refuses my offer again. Speaking of Laurel, why hasn't she arrived? She's never late."

"Three months! Why haven't you been to see your mistress?"

"I don't want to be with anyone but Laurel. I love her, Hawke. Haven't you figured that out?"

Hawke stared at Chadwick in shock, visualizing the same devastating fate befalling himself. At last he declared firmly, "Shawny has to leave!"

Chapter 9

THE NEXT TWO DAYS HAWKE AVOIDED ALL PRIvate contact with Shawny, even finding an excuse for not riding with her which had been a ritual every day he was home, from the time she'd first sat a horse. Broodingly, he wondered how to tell her he was sending her away. Unsure of where to send her, he had sought out Heather and a decision had been made. Right after that, a distraught Chadwick burst into Hawke's study.

"God's teeth! She's gone, Hawke!" he roared, wildeyed. "Lord Bradford's sent Laurel away, and I can't find where."

"How do you know?" Hawke asked, concerned for his friend.

"I haven't heard a word from her since the day she didn't come here, the day after the masque. I couldn't bear it any longer, so I hurried over to call on Lord Bradford today."

"You went to the earl's manor?"

"I had to, Hawke. I love her!"

"Obviously you haven't been shot, so what happened?"

"Lord Bradford learned that I was the knight in armor Laurel spent most of the evening with. Upon questioning, Laurel told him everything and then said that she'd marry no one but me. The earl, as he stated to me, 'sent her on an extended trip, for an undetermined length of time, until she clears her head and comes to her senses.' Then Lord Bradford puffed out his chest and said, 'No daughter of mine will marry a bloody Leighton.' After that he ordered me out of his house. Wouldn't listen to anything I had to say."

"How can I help?" Hawke moved to pour his friend a brandy.

Taking the snifter, Chadwick said, "Provide me with the names and addresses of every friend, every relative of Bradford's who might conceal her." With that, he downed the strong drink in one swallow.

"I'll prepare it immediately." Hawke sat down at his desk and removed a journal and parchment from the drawer.

"I'll search the length and breadth of England," Chadwick declared. "I'll search the Continent. But I will find Laurel and she'll be my wife."

Later that afternoon Hawke wrote a letter to his friend in France, the comte DuBellay, asking him and the comtesse to take Shawny for the next year or so and see to her finishing. It was merely a courtesy to ask, for Hawke knew the comte would deny him nothing. As though it burned his fingers, he handed the missive to Addison and instructed, "Have this sent by special messenger. I want it to arrive in Paris as soon as possible."

"Yes, Your Grace," Addison replied, and withdrew.

Hawke wandered into the great hall and paced, trying to think how he should tell Shawny. What explanation could he give? He certainly would not reveal the actual reason, that he cared too much, far more than he wanted to, that he could no longer trust himself with her and feared she might become his mistress. They could speak someplace private, so he could try to make her understand that he was doing what was best for her. That she would outgrow her childish infatuation for him and someday thank him.

Where to talk to her? A storm brewed, so they could not ride. And he was not about to tell her in his study. She would most likely pour another bottle of port over him. Smiling at the memory, he admitted begrudgingly that he'd deserved it. Finally he decided on the library. Shawny had a great reverence for books, so most likely she would not throw his leather-bound editions at him. With that, he decided to find her at once, and put the dreaded task behind him.

Turning to summon Addison to send for her, Hawke happened to glance out the window to see Shawny running toward the woodland temple. Ignoring his qualms, he walked out the French doors in that direction.

In the temple, Shawnalese whirled to face Hawke.

He smiled. "I saw you come here and I wanted to talk to you," he said, glancing around the domed circular structure.

"Victoria greatly admired a canvas of an Ionic temple. The painting was not for sale, and my father indulged her every whim, so he intended to build a temple, a replica of the one in the painting. But after the architect drew the plans, Victoria decided she'd rather have windows all around and have the structure set among a forest of trees. She loved the woods and called this her woodland temple. Marie Antoinette has her temple of love, but Victoria had her woodland temple." He grew silent, introspective. After a time he said, "I haven't been here in years. As a boy, I used to come here often. It was my refuge from my father."

"From your father?"

A jagged flash of lightning cracked, followed by a loud clap of thunder. Then an onslaught of rain pounded the roof with a fury.

Hawke crossed to Shawny's side. "My father was struck down in the prime of his life. Confined to a wheelchair, he became cruel and abusive."

"I'm sorry. I didn't know. You've never talked to me about your childhood. So I assumed you've always been an adult," Shawnalese teased, smiling.

"There's also one or two other things I've never told you, young lady."

"I appreciate that, Hawke. I fear I wouldn't be the

eager listener while you elaborated about this lovely woman or that one."

"I suspected as much. Besides, it would be rather boring."

Her laughter tinkled. "Not from all I've heard. Lengthy perhaps but I'm sure not boring. Your reputation is well established, Carrington."

A crack of lightning lit the angry sky, signaling the deafening boom of another roll of thunder. "The storm is getting fierce. Why don't you close the French doors. I'll show you how to enjoy it in here. While you do that, I'll make a fire. Then we can watch the storm without getting wet or cold."

Hawke lit the logs and lowered himself to the rug in front of the hearth. "Come here, Shawny," he said softly, sitting with his back to the fire, knees raised and hand outstretched.

She moved to his side and sat beside him on the rug. He ruffled her hair in a gentle, teasing fashion, placed an arm around her, pulled her close, and nestled her head in the hollow of his shoulder. "Isn't this better?" His lips brushed her brow.

A sigh and her arm slipping to encircle his waist was his only answer as several flashes of lightning eerily lit up the wind-whipped forest.

"Hawke, what did you mean when you said this was your refuge from your father?"

"My father was an angry and tyrannical man. I don't remember him any other way, but Heather is eight years older than I, and she said that father was once kind. I really can't imagine it, however, Victoria and the servants have all said the same, so it must be true."

"Why do you call your mother by her given name?"

"I don't talk about her, Shawny, and I don't intend to start now."

"If your father was restricted to a wheelchair, why did you need to run away from him?"

"A young, active boy made him nervous, apparently

because of his illness, or perhaps his age. I could do no right. Everything I did made him angry. When I was younger he would order me to his side so he could reprimand me with his cane. When I grew a little older, I refused to come when he wanted to punish me, so a footman was ordered to bring me to him. Later on, I ran and hid from the footman. But the servant eventually found me and dragged me to my father."

"We're kindred souls, Gayhawke." Her words were hushed, whisper-soft.

"Kindred souls? How so?"

"It was near the same with me and my stepfather, Casey."

"You never told me."

"It seems there's one or two things I've never told you, either."

"So it would seem."

"After Casey was killed, I was never again afraid to go home. Were you?"

"After my father died, I went to live with Heather. Her husband, Siegfried, was kind to me. Very patient and understanding. It was from him that I learned how a father should behave. Someday I'll have to marry. Perhaps I'll be that kind of father. I like to think so."

"You will be."

"And exactly how do you know that?" he asked, a teasing laughter in his eyes.

"That's how you are with Rutger, Leif, and me. I've often marveled at your patience. I'm sure you would be even more so with your own children."

"I don't know, Shawny. There are times I'm filled with so much anger, so much resentment, that—"

"That you can't control it."

His eyes widened in surprise. "Exactly. How . . . ?"

"I told you, Hawke. We're kindred souls. I used to feel the same way. I still do sometimes, but I've learned to overcome it."

"And how, Miss Goddess of Wisdom, have you accomplished such a feat?"

A flash of lightning streaked into the trees, lighting the room, followed by a loud explosion of thunder. The rain poured harder.

"I refuse to allow myself to think about the bad happenings in my life. If I don't think about them, they don't exist. If they don't exist, I have nothing about which to be angry or resentful. Do you agree?"

"I'll have to give that some consideration." He paused. "You know, I've seen you come out here other times when it storms. Most women I know are terrified of storms."

"I used to be when I was a child. In New Orleans it stormed quite often. Some nights, when I first started selling my merchandise on the streets, I was terrified."

"You worked in the rain?"

"On rainy nights I stood in front of the cockfights, or one of the gaming halls or billiard parlors, and some of the men threw a coin, sometimes two, in my basket and didn't even stop. Many rainy nights I made more money than any other night, for it was all profit. After a while I started to wish it would storm, and I was no longer afraid." She paused, hanging her head, then said softly, "I hated those nights."

"Why is that?"

"Mama always said I should never accept charity. And that's what I was doing. But I couldn't afford to turn down the coin. There was never enough money. At least I had an excuse then." She paused, then added, "I'm doing the same now by living here. Only now I've no excuse."

"Your mother was wrong, Shawny. She meant well, but she was wrong. People who give always receive more than they give away. Those men in New Orleans who were kind to you received the benefit of being more worthy. I'm one of the most wealthy men in England. I've received considerable for the little I've spent on you.

Rutger and Leif adore you, Heather loves you like a daughter, and I receive immense pleasure from having you here—that is, when you're not disagreeing with me." Hawke ruffled her hair affectionately.

"You forgot to mention Baroness Wilhelmina."

"Even our proper Wilhelmina is coming around. I think the problem there is that you don't exactly fit into her neat little mold."

"Because I'm illegitimate?"

His arm at her waist moved around her shoulder, he gave her a squeeze. "Shawny, I measure a person not by his accident of birth, but by his worth. I find you very worthy."

"You've never told me that."

"I didn't realize I needed to." He smiled down at her.

Hawke smiled like no other man she'd ever known—a smile that curved one corner of his mouth upward, then moved to sparkle in his eyes before reaching out to make her feel that no one existed save her.

"To answer your question about Wilhelmina . . . no, I don't believe that's the problem. A little, perhaps. For some reason she does seem to keep her standards unreasonably high, which is why she always manages to find one or more flaws in almost everyone. No, I think you'll agree that you're not exactly the typical upper-class young woman, not quite like other young women with whom she's acquainted."

"I think you'll be the first to agree that I'm not like other women you know, either."

"Ah, you're right there. Not even close." For a short time, only the sound of the storm broke the silence of his contentment. Why did he feel peace and serenity only with Shawny? It had been that way since the night he'd found her. Then she shattered the calm by asking:

"Is that why you don't love me?"

Not love her? He had loved Shawny, the child, to a

depth that had concerned him, and now he desired the woman, in a way that concerned him far more. To consider loving Shawny, the woman, and all the obsessive behavior that would accompany that absurd emotion, was mindless insanity. He shuddered at the mere notion of it, for since her birthday he too often found himself seeking her out.

Without answering her question, he held her tightly; his fingers trailed through her long golden hair and spread it fanlike around her shoulders. After a time he pressed his cheek against her head and asked, "Do you remember when I held you like this in New Orleans?"

"I remember it every day of my life," she said. "Do you know that I love you so much, Hawke, that I ache inside?"

"They say that's the way puppy love, first love, is."

She leaned back in his arm, peering up at him from beneath long, thick lashes. "Is that what you think? Is that why you keep running from me? You think my feelings are merely a young girl's infatuation?"

Wordlessly Hawke stared at her. Lightning flashed across her upturned face, tempting inches from his. She was stunningly lovely. With Shawny, as with no other woman, he felt the need to protect; he wanted to shelter her from the pain of life. It had always been so with her, yet now he also craved her. It had been a mistake to come here. He'd known it before he came, and yet he'd come anyway. Why? So he could seduce his ward, the young girl who was wrapped up in this childish idolization of him? Seduce his Shawny, the light of his life? God forbid!

"You said you wanted to talk to me."

He didn't know when he'd started thinking of her as "his Shawny," but he had. Was it on her birthday? No. It was long before that. And that reality was far more dangerous, far more threatening, than his lust for her, which fired through his loins at this moment. But how could he send her away? How could he not? How could he tell her she had to go? He couldn't. Not here. Not now. "It's not important," he replied at last.

They lay back on the plush Persian rug, their fingers laced. Warm, snug, secure by the roaring fire, they watched the storm that raged around them. Howling winds whispered through the room, and a downpour of rain pelted the roof.

More than anything in the world, Shawnalese wanted to be with Hawke.

Be near Hawke.

Forever.

He needed her to leave.

"Hawke, I could be content with you, like this, the rest of my life."

"You say that because you've never experienced the love between a man and a woman."

"I'm told neither have you. Many poets say making love is sharing the physical with someone you love deeply. You've bedded a woman, but you've never made love, and I pity you. All these years you've wasted your love. A sharing of the passions of the body, but not the soul. A moment of pleasure and nothing more."

Hawke glanced down at her. Unquestionably Shawny needed the genteel guidance of a woman, needed to be taught there were subjects women never discussed with anyone other than their husbands. Yet at the same time he wished it were not so, for he enjoyed being able to discuss every subject in the world with her. Even so, he knew he could not encourage her by commenting, so he sighed and made no other reply.

Believing his sigh to be disagreement, Shawnalese said no more.

All too soon the storm passed, the rain softened to a drizzle, gusting winds gentled to a breeze. The fire crackled, water trickled down the windowpanes, and droplets spattered softly from the roof's edge.

Shawnalese interrupted the tranquillity. "Do you believe in eternity, Gayhawke?"

Why could Shawny pronounce his name in that throaty, breathy voice of hers and it send a chill down his spine? "Eternity? Yes."

"Do you believe love is for all eternity?" When he did not answer, she rolled on her side and looked at him expectantly.

"Marriage vows say 'until death do us part.'"

"No. No. That can't be. If love is not for all eternity, then why is there an eternity?"

He didn't dare look at her. She was too close. Too inviting. Too willing. Too innocent. He should not have come here. To feel all the unexplainable feelings, the mystifying emotions, for which he had no answer. Only fear.

The drizzle became a soft, relaxing sprinkle, and the air wafted gentle and fragrant, filling the room with the fresh scents after a rain.

"I will love you for all eternity, Gayhawke," she vowed softly.

With those words, the woman-child shot a flaming arrow into his frozen heart. Hawke closed his eyes, for Victoria had assured him of much the same. Her "always" had lasted until he was ten, when she'd abandoned him for a greater love. But right now Shawny was here, with him, vowing eternal love, and nothing else mattered.

Time ceased and nothing existed beyond this room. For this span of time, this timeless eternity, there were only two kindred souls and the powerful emotions that vibrated between them.

Later that evening, after dinner, with the family gathered in the great hall, Hawke made his announcement.

"Shawny, I've been discussing the continuation of your education with Heather, and I've decided to send you to France to live with my friends the DuBellays, the comte and comtesse de Chaternay, who will see to your finishing. After that you'll have a season in London, where you should find a suitable gentleman to marry. A female chaperone will accompany you to France, and Grizzly and Thaddeus will remain with you for the duration of your stay there." He announced this as calmly as if he'd suggested that he wanted her to go riding. Only the muscles that twitched in his jawline, the whiteness of his knuckles on the hands that gripped the carved wood of his chair, betrayed his inner turmoil as he avoided Shawny's look of shock. "Naturally, while in Paris you'll be free to see any gentleman you wish, with the DuBellays' approval, of course. You need the experience of being courted."

"I don't wish to go to the DuBellays," Shawnalese insisted. The softness of her voice belied her anguish.

"Shawny, I'm talking about your being presented to Marie Antoinette at court, and having all the lovely gowns you wish. When ready, you'll attend the most fashionable salons, the most exclusive balls, meet the cream of French aristocracy. However, if you prefer to go to London . . ."

"I choose not to leave Foxridge," she retorted with the obstinacy with which he was so familiar.

"Then I shall make arrangements for London," Hawke said patiently, still avoiding her crushed, quizzical stare.

"I refuse to go."

"Perhaps I didn't make it clear—the subject isn't open for discussion."

"I don't wish to leave here, Hawke."

"You're too young to know what you want, or what's best for you."

"You can shackle me to Grizzly and get me there—possibly—but there's no way you can force me to behave as though I were for sale, like one of your trained Arabians. I was above that in New Orleans, and I'm above that now. I won't become a simpering female who hides behind a fan and bats her lashes so that some fop will offer for me. Besides, I don't want a husband. I won't go. I won't!" Pausing, she took a deep breath and her fiery eyes challenged his. "If you wish to be rid of me, Carrington, all you need do is ask—I'll leave. I took care of myself before, and quite well, I might add. I certainly can take care of myself now. You need feel no further responsibility toward me." She leaped from her chair and ran from the room.

Chapter 10

SEVERAL WORDLESS MOMENTS LATER, HEATHER said, "Gayhawke, you must go to her and explain."

Heather's words were met with stony silence from her brother. Rising, she said, "I'll talk to Shawna, Gayhawke. But then an explanation must come from you. That child adores and idolizes you."

Minutes later Shawnalese called out to the knock at her door, "Come in."

"I thought perhaps we could talk," Heather explained as she entered.

"Did Hawke send you?"

"You know better than that, honey. Gayhawke may be the duke of the manor, but I don't do his bidding. You also know that he's man enough to do his own talking—actually, no one speaks for Gayhawke but himself."

"I'm sorry, Heather. I'm unsettled."

"Of course you are, dear." Heather's countenance remained somber. "Shall we be seated?" She walked toward the chairs in the sitting room. Seated, she turned to Shawnalese. "You love him—women cannot deceive each other. It's written all over your face when you look at him. I love him, too—very much. But I also love you. You've become the daughter I never had, and I don't want to see you hurt. You're seventeen and Hawke is thirty-two. He's left a trail of broken hearts of which I've long lost track, and I don't want yours added to the path. Haven't you ever wondered why a titled man as handsome, charming, and wealthy as Gayhawke has never married?"

Shawnalese made no reply. For a long time now she had hoped that Hawke might be waiting for her to come of age.

"Hawke's never been in love, not once—not even close. He finds fault with every woman he courts and yet, since you came to Foxridge, he's deliberately seen only women he'd never consider marrying, as if you've filled the love he's sought in his life, and the women he sees only fill his physical needs. He has no desire to marry now." She spoke as though thinking out loud. "It's strange. I had believed, had hoped, the reason Gayhawke rebuilt Foxridge after the fire was for a wife, but . . ."

Sighing, Heather said, "I used to believe Gayhawke was looking for the perfect woman—or what he thought was the perfect woman. But I've come to learn through our discussions over the years that he won't allow himself to love. I believe he fears being hurt, the way Mother hurt him."

"Victoria?"

"Yes. Has Gayhawke told you about Mother?"

"Only that he doesn't talk about her."

"Some say that Mother was the most beautiful woman ever to grace the English court. She was petite, like you, had curling ebony hair, like Gayhawke's, and the Grenville eyes. Exactly like yours. Mother came to Father an unwilling bride at the age of sixteen, for my

father was fifty-two. Father had been married for many
years to a woman who died giving birth to one more
stillborn child. A widower with no heir, Father
arranged the marriage to the beautiful, much-sought-
after Victoria Grenville, and theirs was a merger of two
great families—the Carringtons and the Grenvilles. I
was born in the first year of their marriage, but
Gayhawke didn't come along for eight more years.
Three years after Gayhawke's birth, when Father was
sixty-four, Father suffered a seizure of apoplexy that
left him incapacitated and in a wheelchair. He had
always been a strong and active man, and suddenly he
was partially paralyzed. Struck down when he and
Mother were the court favorites. Even though he had
an heir to carry on the name, the dukedom, the estates,
Father became bitter, and his temper raged."

With that, Heather paused, the painful memories
assaulting her. Inhaling deeply, she continued, "Father
had never been a tender, loving man, as Gayhawke is,
but now he turned his bitterness on his three-year-old
son, who was active and into everything. He ranted
and raged at Gayhawke for the smallest offense and
even rapped him with his cane or fists if the poor boy
were close enough. Mother, always loving and affectionate, cosseted Gayhawke, and tried to protect him
from Father's rages. I imagine knowing that
Gayhawke was her last child is another reason she
showered him with love and continually fussed over
him. Thinking back, I believe that further angered
Father, for he often accused Mother of coming to
Gayhawke's defense even when Gayhawke was in the
wrong. The more abusive Father became, the more
protective Mother was, and it became an unbroken
cycle. Anyway, by the time Gayhawke was ten, he idol-
ized Mother, worshiped her. Then she ran off with
Julien St. Jeanneret, the comte de Beaulieux, without a
word of good-bye. Only a brief note to Father, begging
his forgiveness. Gayhawke was devastated, incon-

solable. Three weeks later, Father died. We've never heard a word from Mother in all these years. We don't know where she is, or even if she's still alive." Heather paused to blink back her tears. "Mother doesn't even know she has two grandsons."

"You never wrote her?"

"Oh, yes," Heather replied, "I wrote her several times, in care of the comte de Beaulieux, in France, but I never received a reply. I understand he also was married at the time they ran away together. Possibly, if she's his mistress, Mother never received my letters. Certainly Madame St. Jeanneret wouldn't see to it that Mother received them." She sighed. "Anyway, Gayhawke's never forgiven Mother. Will not refer to her other than as Victoria, if he speaks of her at all."

Shawnalese asked the question that burned inside her mind. "Why is Hawke sending me away?"

Heather paled. What should she tell this innocent child who'd slipped into her heart? Naught but the truth as she saw it. "I believe Gayhawke has realized that he did you an injustice by not permitting you to be raised as a young lady of the gentry should be. You should be having your season in London right now, as are other young ladies your age, but I'm sure you realize that's not possible. You're not ready."

"I don't want to marry anyone, but . . . Hawke's told me many times that if you will accept nothing but the best in life, you will usually get it. Hawke's the best there is."

"What you want must be realistic, Shawna. I believe Gayhawke for you is unrealistic—a fantasy."

"Because I'm a bastard of no consequence?"

"No, Shawna," Heather replied gently, cringing at the expression Baroness Wilhelmina had once used. "You may have been born on the other side of the blanket, but that isn't important. Don't ever allow yourself to believe otherwise. Still, you can't force someone to love you."

"You don't think Hawke could love me?" Shawnalese stared at Hawke's sister expectantly.

"No, I don't, dear. Not as you mean, not as a man loves a woman, a wife. Gayhawke loves you dearly—but as a man loves family, a sister. You're precious to me, Shawna, and Gayhawke has crushed so many hearts—I couldn't bear to have yours added to that roster. Considering that you believe you're in love with him, I feel it might be best if you went to the DuBellays for a while. It might help you to realize that the love you have for Gayhawke is really gratitude, respect, the kind of love one has for family—for we are family, even though we're third cousins. They have a daughter, Genevieve, your age. That's why I encouraged Hawke to send you there. You've never had the companionship of a female your own age. Since you came here, you've had little other than men and boys for friends. Gayhawke's given me his word that we'll come to Paris often until you return."

Heather rose and wrapped Shawnalese in loving arms, comforting her. "You're so young, dear. Gayhawke's told me he promised you that you could marry a man of your own choosing. I know you'll find that special one who'll love you in the same way." Knowing Shawnalese fought back tears, Heather forced herself to say the words she felt were best, aware at the same time how much they would hurt. "Shawna, if Gayhawke loved you as a man loves a woman, would he send you away and have you presented to find a suitable husband?"

An unbearable pain ripped through Shawnalese's body. Lifting her chin, she whispered, "I'll go to the DuBellays."

Hawke, Rutger, Leif, and Wilhelmina sat in the great hall exchanging stories about the masquerade, a time normally relaxing and enjoyable for Hawke. Tonight it was not, for Shawny was usually there, excitedly asking questions and laughing at the incidents that happen at all parties. Her absence made him edgy, and he fought an inner battle to go to her, to explain that he'd been thinking of her, not himself, in sending her away; to tell her how hard it had been for him to make that decision, for he realized how empty his life would be with her gone; to tell her how accustomed he'd become to her sparkling personality, her quick wit, her dazzling smile, even her fierce, stubborn independence.

Hours later, as he walked the courtyard gardens, her accusing words still echoed in his mind. He should have explained to Shawny in private rather than surprise her in front of the family. She deserved better than that.

It was the middle of the night, and still a light flickered in her bedchamber. Turning, he strode into the manor and took the stairs two at a time, hurrying to her chamber door.

"Yes?" Shawnalese answered his knock.

Hawke opened the door. A lone candle flickered across her tester bed, made and unslept in.

"I'm here, Gayhawke." Her voice came softly from her sitting room.

"Shawny, please step into the gallery. I'd like to talk to you."

"Heather or the dowager baroness will hear us, Hawke. Cannot we talk in here?"

He groaned. He dared not enter her room. He wouldn't come out before dawn. "We'll talk in the gallery," he ordered. She didn't reply. He'd come to apologize, to explain, to gentle her, yet he felt as vulnerable as a boy. For that he blamed her, then he blamed himself. "Are you coming or do I drag you out?"

She no longer loved him. Actually she hated him, although she had no reason other than that he did not love her. She wished he'd never come to New Orleans, that he were still an elusive dream rather than an impossible one. And she would not be a foolish dolt.

His tall, powerful figure in the light of the flickering gallery candles threw a gigantic shadow on her wall.

She lay down the waistcoat she had made him for Christmas—and was now embroidering with silver thread—and rose from her chair.

As Shawny walked toward him, the diffused lights cast shadows through her shimmering hair, and he sucked in his breath before he stepped aside. She stopped in the gallery, turned, and lifted her gaze to his.

"How could you possibly think I want to be rid of you?" Hawke demanded angrily. "How could you think that?"

"How could I think you wish to be rid of me after you inform me that you're sending me away for years, or more probably forever? After you express your hope that I'd find a suitable gentleman to marry? Is that what you're asking me?" she queried sweetly.

Hawke sighed in frustration. "I've expended a great deal of time and effort on a few other things, too," he reminded her.

She flushed at his words and retorted, "I'm trying to remember."

"You're a child, playing childish games," Hawke said, and grabbed her by the arms, wanting to shake her, yet strangely, at the same time, wanting to comfort her.

"You seem to be telling me that a lot lately."

"Perhaps it's because you seem to be behaving that way a lot lately." He knew he was letting her aggravate him to the point of fury again, even though he'd determined before he came to her bedchamber that he would not allow this to happen.

"Is that what you came here to tell me?"

"You know damn well it isn't!"

"One evenings interlude doesn't make a love affair, Hawke, so don't be concerned about having to push me onto the DuBellays. I'll not throw myself at you again. I only go where I'm wanted."

He battled to keep from shaking her. "You little fool! You've no idea what it cost me to walk away from what you offered. I wouldn't have done it for any other, and I venture to say few other men would have walked away."

She bit back the tears that threatened to surface. Never would she allow Gayhawke Carrington to see her cry. "I want us to be good together, Gayhawke."

"We are good together, Shawny. That's my problem of late. We're too good together. To put it plainly, I'm having a difficult time remaining a gentleman with you. We cannot continue the way we are now—"

"Why?"

"Damn, Shawny! You know why as well as I do."

"No, I don't. I only know that I hurt from loving you, that when you hold me and kiss me, my heart has wings. I only want to be with you, do things with you, do things for you. When you're gone my world is empty—I'm empty. Is that wrong?"

"No, that isn't wrong, but what is wrong are the feelings I'm having for you. Has Heather never talked to you about men?"

"About men?"

Hawke sighed. "One of these times I won't be able to stop with only kisses, and I care too much for you to let that happen. You mean too much to me."

"Why are you telling me this?" she asked breathlessly, turning away from him.

"I have a weakness for you that I've never had for another woman, and it's costing me dearly."

"But," she whispered, head bent, unable to look at him, "I want you to hold me, to kiss me."

"I know you do, and that's what makes it so difficult. Kisses aren't enough for me. I don't want to talk to you like this, but, after the night of the masque, I must."

"Would you force yourself on me, Hawke?"

"No, I wouldn't force myself on you—I wouldn't have to."

Hurt by his insult, she whirled to face him. "Why do you say that?"

"Would you have stopped me in the garden, at the masque?"

"Yes! Emphatically, yes!" she insisted, and pulled her hand from his.

"I say you wouldn't have. You've driven me—you've driven us—to the brink of oblivion twice now. I don't intend to tempt fate a third time."

"If that's what you think, then you don't know me, Hawke."

"How can you be so sure, Shawny? How can you be so positive? I know in the garden that you wanted me as much—almost as much—as I wanted you. Do you deny that?" Seeing her quivering lips, he yearned to take her in his arms, ached to sweep her up and carry her through that door, to lose himself in her arms. How could he want to ravish her and save her from himself at the same time? She faced him bravely, calmly, and he could but admire her.

"No, I don't deny it, Hawke. I admit that I want to be with you, that sometimes it's unbearable. Is that what you want to hear? Do you think that makes me like all your other women? Well, if you do, you're wrong—extremely wrong, because I won't give in to my craving. There's nothing you could do to make me give in, because I'll have your heart or nothing at all." She paused, took a deep breath, and vowed she would not again make a spectacle of herself. "I won't have an affair with you, I won't be your mistress, and I certainly won't be a one-night escapade. That's not for me. The day I permit a man to make love to me is when that man loves me as much as I love him—and that's not the way it is with you." She sighed. "You desire me, you lust after me, you care for me, I'm special to you, but none of those have anything to do with love."

Never had any woman spoken so brazenly to him, and for this to come from an innocent woman-child . . . But he had always encouraged her forthrightness. There was no guile in her, no pretensions or affectations. It was one of the many things he admired about her. Heather was right: Shawny also needed genteel guidance. He pulled her into his arms and stroked her soft, fragrant hair, overwhelmed with feelings he refused to examine. "Hush, Shawny," he whispered, and pressed his lips to her soft neck.

Feeling the tension between them dissolve, she sighed. She hated the discord that had arisen since her birthday. Now she sought only to heal the rift that had driven them apart. Leaning back in his arms, her heart full, she studied his dangerously handsome face. "You're beautiful," she murmured, delicately tracing the bone structure of his face with her fingertips.

"Men aren't beautiful."

"I mean beautiful as a magnificent stag is beautiful."

Closing his eyes, he luxuriated in her tender touch, her sweet scent, her soft, breathy voice. He could not move.

"Why can't we be like this, instead of avoiding each other?" she asked, and slipped her arms around his muscled back, drawing him down to her slowly, tenderly. "Don't send me away, Hawke," she pleaded. "I'm your destiny. Please don't send me away."

He did not want her childish adoration that was no longer harmless. He did not want the complication of a besotted woman-child in his life. He did not want a too-willing ward from whom he could barely keep his hands. She was too dangerous now, for neither could he be near her with out touching her, nor could he stay away.

She was too available.

He was too weak.

"Would you have me hold you like a child until you're a woman grown?"

"It would be better than being separated."

Hawke groaned. "You ask the impossible."

"Aren't you content now?" She ran her fingers up and down his back, silence her only answer. "If you're not, then why do you stay?"

"Because I haven't the strength to leave."

Suddenly he had a premonition that never again would he hold her soft, willing body close to his, never again would he feel her heartbeat flutter against his chest, never again would her arms enfold him, her hands caress him.

"You said I'm the weakness in you, Hawke. I'll build a snare to capture you, and I'll win you. I'll possess your heart and your soul—or I'll have nothing. I'm your destiny, and I'll be the love who enslaves you."

Hawke stiffened. No woman would ever enslave him as Victoria had his father, had him. As Antoinette had Louis XVI. If ever one breathed who was a threat to that happenstance, it was Shawny. Abruptly he released her. He had loved the child, had loved the young girl, but he would not love the woman. Her vow would not be prophetic.

"You're going to France, Shawny. There is no room in your life for me, because there is no room in mine for you." Those words, cool and aloof, were hurtful in themselves, but then, out of fear, out of love, out of fear of love, he added the cut that would turn her away. "I'm making a rendezvous with you now, for when you're old enough, mature enough, and experienced enough to know the difference between desire and a young girl's infatuation. If you say to me then what you did tonight, I once more give you fair warning—I won't walk away from you again. Understood?"

Her hand slapping his face was Hawke's only answer. He knew he deserved it. And then, with that honorable thought, he crushed her to him and his hungry mouth expertly, skillfully, ravished hers until she ardently returned kiss for kiss. Then he set her aside and walked away.

Numb and without hope, Shawnalese watched the man she loved drift forever out of reach. She was a "bastard child of no consequence" and Hawke a powerful duke. The nobility married for wealth, for power, or for the prestige of a title or family name, then looked outside marriage for love and physical fulfillment. She'd never had a chance.

There in the gallery where Hawke left her, she vowed to wrap her heart in ice and distance herself from him emotionally, for she never again wanted to feel the soul-tearing pain of losing a loved one. If that meant giving up her childish fantasies, then so be it. But at the same time she deeply regretted that pride and foolishness had allowed her to believe her love was so strong it would overcome all. Before her birthday they had been the best of friends. Now she didn't even have that, and she blamed herself for teasing and tempting him when she should have known better, for she'd lost the platonic love she and Hawke shared, and it was a bitter loss.

The days before she left passed in sweet torment and ended in anguish when she discovered that much of Hawke's time away had been spent with Lady Valda Melville. Shawnalese's feelings for Hawke swayed back and forth from love to hate. Her childish delusions were merely that.

Then Shawnalese, Grizzly, her chaperone, Thaddeus, Czar, and Wildfire left for France and the comte and comtesse de Chaternay. Hawke watched his yacht sail out of sight, her last words—"I will never forgive you! Never!"—echoing in his ears.

Chapter 11

DURING THE NEXT TWO YEARS, SHAWNALESE WAS taught everything a young lady of the aristocracy need-ed to know. However, to Comtesse DuBellay's horror, and that of the DuBellays' vain and pretentious daugh-

ter, Genevieve, Shawnalese willfully refused to behave
as a young lady should. There were no demure pretenses, no affected mannerisms, no shy coquetry, no
affectations of being unlearned. And the shocking
behavior that nearly caused her disgrace in England
made her the favorite of Paris, for Parisians adored
novelty. They forgave anything but boredom, and
Shawnalese was anything but boring. Polite society
was enchanted.

Yet with all her popularity as the toast of the salons,
with the elegant wardrobe and full social calendar,
Shawnalese was not happy. Actually she was unhappy,
except for the times when she was with Grizzly, Czar,
or Wildfire. Surely, she thought, there must be more
than the superficial, hedonistic life pursued by most of
the French nobility? To her thinking, concentration
solely on where, when, and how soon one could
obtain one's next pleasure was not an admirable
endeavor. She hated her shallow existence. She
yearned for Hawke. Her only measure of comfort was
the gifts she sewed or made for him with loving and
meticulous care. Yet at times she found her thoughts
turning to retribution against Hawke, revenge because
he'd scorned her and heartlessly sent her out of his
life.

Grizzly was her constant companion. In his letter to
the DuBellays, Hawke had introduced Grizzly and
requested that he also be their guest and always escort
her. With the unrest in the streets, an unescorted lady
was not safe riding alone through Paris.

Often Shawnalese visited the Faubourg Saint-
Antoine. This street of craft shops ran alongside a high
wall that reared up ominously on one side—the hated
Bastille, where men were imprisoned without trial,
some never to be seen again. Its shadow loomed over
the most crowded and impoverished quarter of Paris.

Ragged figures shuffled aimlessly along the streets
and dark, fetid alleyways. Men, women, and children

with gaunt faces and eyes dulled by hopelessness, people sunk in the wretchedness of hunger and despair, did not even glance at the handsome carriage. It was simply evidence of one more uncaring aristocrat in the cavalcade that drove through the squalor of Paris, on the way to or from the races or the shops.

Stopping one morning in front of the bootmaker's, Shawnalese was about to accept Grizzly's proffered hand when she glanced up and saw a gentleman exit the shop, only to have a bedraggled woman collide with him and clumsily lift his purse. The man's hand shot out to close around her rail-thin arm.

"You shall pay the price for that," the man snarled. "You filthy rabble aren't filching my purse and getting away with it." He looked around for a gendarme.

"Please, monsieur," the woman begged.

"Monsieur," Shawnalese interrupted, taking Grizzly's hand and stepping out of the carriage, "I believe there's been some mistake." She smiled dazzlingly. "She sought only to do you a kindness. I saw your purse fall myself. Perhaps with your package you were unaware." Grizzly stood quietly at her side, his presence imposing.

The man released the trembling woman. "Be on your way," he grumbled. "And next time watch when your betters are around."

"One moment, madame, please." Shawnalese touched the woman's arm before turning back to the nobleman. "Certainly, monsieur, such consideration cannot go unrewarded?"

Mumbling, the man delved into his pocket and held a coin between his thumb and forefinger.

Gingerly, the woman reached out and took the coin. "Thank you, monsieur."

Ignoring her, the man tipped his hat to Shawnalese and hurried to his waiting carriage.

"Thank you, mademoiselle," the woman murmured gratefully, and turned to leave.

"Madame"—Shawnalese smiled warmly—"have you

no livelihood?" At the look of fear on the woman's face, Shawnalese reassured her, "I mean you no harm. I saw you take the gentleman's purse and . . . well, perhaps I can help you."

"Oh, mademoiselle, I'll do anything for food for my son. I'm a hard worker, and I give you my word I'll never steal from you. My little boy's had nothing to eat for two days and—"

"I understand," Shawnalese replied. "Where's your son now?"

The woman raised her thin arm, and a dirty, tattered young boy ran from the alley to his mother's side.

Hiding her distress, Shawnalese queried, "Where do you live?"

The woman shrugged.

"You have no home?"

"No, mademoiselle."

"Do you have other family?"

Tears welled in her large dark eyes and trickled down her face. Wiping her cheek with the back of her hand, she sniffled. "I lost my husband and three children to the fever, three months past. Auguste is all I have left."

"If you and Auguste will climb into my carriage, we'll get you something to eat, and then a warm bath and bed."

"God bless you, mademoiselle," she said, and burst into grateful tears. "You'll never regret this, I promise you."

Shawnalese was sure the DuBellays would not take in the homeless pair, at least until they looked presentable. So she sent Nadine and seven-year-old Auguste to Hawke's chateau outside the walls of Paris.

A few days later she and Grizzly returned to check on Nadine and Auguste, and Shawnalese barely recognized the beaming woman.

"Nadine, you look marvelous!" she exclaimed. "I hope you're feeling as well as you look."

"*Oui*, mademoiselle. I'm so very grateful to you."

"And is Auguste well?"

"Oh, *oui*. Auguste is staying with the cook's son. The major-domo has hired me."

Shawnalese was happy for Nadine but increasingly concerned for the plight of people like her. Riding home through the narrow, dirty streets full of disease-ridden tenements of Paris, she stared at the bleak faces of the hungry people, their eyes flat, lifeless, their bodies bent, old beyond their years. What could she do to help them? she wondered. Once an impoverished child herself, she knew her heart belonged to the common man, yet now she lived in the luxury of the privileged few.

Shawnalese returned to the DuBellays disturbed. She was pacing her luxurious room when Genevieve DuBellay burst in.

"I'm going to borrow your periwinkle reticule," Genevieve said, crossing the room to open the armoire and retrieve the bag. Receiving no response, she glanced at Shawnalese. "What's the matter with you?"

"When Grizzly and I were returning, we came by the City Hall and the sentries were throwing soup bones to the guard dogs. The starving people were scrambling to get the bones before the dogs. Many of them were bitten."

"So?"

"That doesn't bother you?"

Genevieve shrugged and picked up the reticule. "If the rabble weren't so lazy, they'd find work, and then they wouldn't be starving."

"There is no work, Genevieve. The recession, the critical financial condition of France, have put even the artisans out of work."

"Let the riffraff starve."

"You aristos are all alike!"

"We aristos? And what are you? Besides, why should we care? My François said most of the peasants

and poor are nothing but bastards who don't even
bother to marry. They just breed."

Whirling at that, Shawnalese glared at the young
woman. "If they don't marry, it's because they can't
afford the coin for a license! So many are unemployed.
Taxes takes fifty percent of the wages of those fortunate enough to have work. Does being poor, or a bastard, make them less than human? Does that make
them riffraff? For if it does, then you're living in the
same house as that riffraff you hold in such contempt."

"What are you rambling about?"

"I am a bastard! I lived the first fourteen years of my
life in that same hopeless, stomach-wrenching poverty."

Blanching, Genevieve gasped, "That's not possible!
You're a Grenville."

Shawnalese lifted her chin high and replied quietly,
"My mother was a Grenville. I don't know who my
father is."

Genevieve squealed, dropped the reticule, and raced
from the room.

Within minutes Shawnalese's revelation was made
known to the comte and comtesse DuBellay, within
hours it was the gossip of the beau monde, and within
days invitations were no longer extended.

During the next month, adding to Shawnalese's distress was Genevieve's open hostility. The young woman
refused to speak to Shawnalese and treated her as if she
were beneath contempt. On the evening Genevieve
referred to Shawnalese as "that common impostor" to
visiting guests, Shawnalese quietly excused herself,
went to her room, and packed.

Grizzly loaded the coach with their trunks and
baggage.

"Please reconsider, Shawnalese," Comte DuBellay
beseeched. "Don't leave my protection, you're not
properly chaperoned. You cannot go."

"I cannot stay, monsieur. Genevieve will not accept
me. The situation has become intolerable for me. I'm

grateful for all you and madame have done for me. But I must go. Please forgive me."

"Where will you go?" the comte asked as Grizzly climbed into the coach.

"I don't know, but I'll send you a message as soon as I decide. Thank you for everything. Please extend my apologies to madame."

After the coach pulled away the comte went directly to his study to write his friend, the duke of Foxridge. He implored Hawke to come to France in all haste.

Chapter 12

Grizzly sat in the coach beside Shawnalese and faced a thoroughly unsettled Thaddeus. "Where to, lass?"

"Oh, Grizzly, I don't know. I don't have much money."

"Dinna worry yerself about that. I have a hefty purse from me savings with the duke all these years. He's a mighty generous man, so I'll nae be havin' ye worry about the coin."

She smiled up at her friend and wriggled her hand through the crook of his arm. "Grizzly, I can't use your savings. I'll sell my gowns first. Why don't we spend the night at Hawke's château, and I'll think of something tomorrow. I'd like to talk to Nadine anyway."

"'Tis done." With that, Grizzly rapped on the coachman's portal to give him directions.

Soon all of Paris was abuzz with Shawnalese

Grenville's escapade. The willful ward of the duke of
Foxridge had moved from the comte DuBellay's mansion to the duke's château unchaperoned, openly flout-
ing propriety.

"Spoiled blood," the noblewomen whispered, while
the gentlemen laughed, indulged in scurrilous banter,
and wagered, "Hot blood."

From then on men swarmed around Shawnalese.
Within the month every rake in Paris had made
advances or, in some cases, lewd suggestions. Before
long word would reach England.

That sent Grizzly scrambling for quill and parchment to have Thaddeus write Hawke of Shawnalese's
plight and request that the duke recall her to England.
However, in his haste, Thaddeus neglected to mention
what had caused such intolerable circumstances.

Shawnalese soon refused to accept any gentlemen
callers. Where she had once been deluged with offers
for her hand in marriage, she was now bombarded
with propositions to become a mistress, both offers
often coming from the same gentlemen. Were it not
for Grizzly's nearby presence, she would have been
sorely pressed in discouraging some of her suitors, so
again she took to wearing her scabbarded dagger. The
gentlemen of Paris were no different from the *gentlemen* of New Orleans.

When Shawnalese had first arrived at Hawke's
château, Philippe, the major-domo, informed her, "Of
course you, Grizzly, and Thaddeus are welcome, mademoiselle. My household expense money barely covers the
unexpected support of Nadine and Auguste, but I can
draw from the emergency funds His Grace keeps at the
bank, so don't be concerned. I'll write to the duke . . ."

"No," Shawnalese objected. "Please don't do that.
I'll provide for us."

Shawnalese sold one of her gowns at a fraction of its
cost and gave the money to Philippe for food and
expenses.

During this time, Shawnalese and Grizzly attended the daily assemblage of the liberals to listen to the dissidents at the Palais Royal. Simultaneously Shawnalese, refusing to be discouraged, started to call on the more reputable of the aristocracy, seeking employment as a governess. Yet time and again she met with cool, but polite, rejection. Then came the day when a Madame Garraud was not so courteous.

"A woman of your reputation instructing my Renée?" the comtesse mumbled. "Whatever could you be thinking of?"

The Parisian haut monde was exceedingly liberal concerning married women, and few wedded noblewomen bothered to conceal the fact when they had a lover. It was an accepted way of life. In sharp contrast, the most rigid standards of moral conduct were expected of unmarried women, their behavior to be above reproach. In a city besieged with unemployment and hunger, how was Shawnalese, with her tarnished reputation, to earn a living? For the first time since leaving New Orleans, she felt all the old fears and anxieties.

Heather had visited Shawnalese numerous times, and written to her regularly, but she had neither seen nor heard from Hawke. Yet she knew he'd been in Paris several times, probably each time Heather had. Hawke had banished her from his life, and she did not know why. What unforgivable transgression had she committed? Loving him too much?

While Shawnalese struggled with her predicament in Paris, Hawke was just arriving by carriage at Foxridge, following a month's absence. He was happy, happier than he'd been in two years. Happier than he'd been since Shawny had left. He'd come directly from London, where he'd concluded his business affairs and done a lot of thinking.

He'd faced his confused feelings for the first time, and after several days of wrestling with himself, he concluded what he'd suspected for years, what he'd refused to admit. He loved Shawny. Loved her not with the platonic love he'd borne the child and young girl, but with the love of a man for a woman—passionately, completely, without reservation. He could not imagine his future without her by his side.

He had wasted two years. Originally he'd decided it would be preferable to live without Shawny than to marry a woman who held such power over him. He'd hoped the passage of time would resolve his dilemma. Instead his feelings for her had grown to the point of obsession.

There had never been anyone but Shawny.

Never would there be.

But Hawke realized the two years she'd been away had not been sacrificed for naught. She'd had that time to experience life, to be courted, to discover her true feelings for him. A man of the world, he knew that if he caged her, she would be his for as long as she remained caged. But if he set her free and still she returned, she would be his forever.

He had set her free.

Now it was time for her to return.

Time for her to become his wife so he could spend the rest of his life spoiling her, pampering her, doing all for her that he'd always wanted to do. Perhaps Shawny's vow of eternal love would be more worthy than Victoria's worthless vows of love.

He'd been ten and suspicious; late one night he'd sneaked into the woodland temple to catch her in a passionate embrace with her lover. That night Victoria had abandoned him to run off with the dashing comte. For two weeks his father had ranted and raved but after that the elderly man had broken and sobbed helplessly, endlessly, for his wife, begging for her to return to him. When she had not returned after three weeks, his father, a shell of the former man, died.

At that moment Gayhawke had hated his once strong, tyrannical father for being so weak as to love a woman that much. For that weakness he would never forgive his father. Yet at the same time Hawke had hoped, had even prayed, that his beloved mother would return. And for that weakness, he would never forgive himself. Never again, he'd sworn, would he need a woman's love as he had needed his mother's. Never would he allow a woman to get close. Yet he had. A child with a cloud of golden hair, Grenville eyes, an angelic face, and a courageous heart had crept into his heart. He could no more refuse to love the woman than he could refuse to love the child.

But no Victoria she, for every new letter he received from the DuBellays expounded on Shawny's progress, other than her feisty, independent nature, which, according to the comte, was ever unmanageable. It mattered not. He didn't want her any other way. Besides, once Shawny became his duchess, he would gentle her free-spirited ways.

Smiling at the notion, he bounded from the coach and up the steps to the open door of Foxridge. "Addison, have my valet get me packed. I'm sailing for France with the morning tide. I'm bringing Shawny home." Hawke laughed with sheer joy, unable to contain himself.

Addison, unable to suppress a pleased grin, stood holding the open door through which the duke had just entered. "How long will you be staying, Your Grace?"

"As short a time as possible. Have Baroness Von Rueden's clothes packed also."

"Very good, Your Grace."

Hawke went to his study to read the mail that had arrived in his absence. He read Thaddeus's brief letter, and a scowl formed on his face. Unconsciously he clenched his fists. "Dear God!" He vaulted from his chair and poured himself a brandy. Why was Thaddeus imploring him to return her to England and safety? He returned to his desk and went through his stack of mail. Near the bottom of the stack was the missive from Comte DuBellay. With an ominous foreboding, he slit the seal. After reading the comte's letter informing him that Shawny had left his friend's protection unchaperoned, he hurtled from his chair and roared, "Addison!" Furiously riffling through the rest of his mail, he saw the letter from Philippe. He ripped it open and began to read, his eyes narrowed.

Addison appeared. "Yes, Your Grace?"

"Get my sister. Get her now!"

At the commotion, Heather hurried into Hawke's study as Addison withdrew. "Gayhawke, do I understand you're going after Shawnalese?"

"Yes!" he thundered, traversing his circular study.

"Oh, I'm so happy," Heather said, seating herself. "I miss her so, and I daresay you haven't been fit company for man nor beast since she left Foxridge."

"Don't be too happy, Heather."

"Gayhawke! What's wrong? What's happened?"

Hawke stopped his pacing long enough to pick up the three letters from his desk and hand them to his sister.

Shortly, Heather folded the third letter and murmured, "How could Shawna have behaved this way? She'll never live down the disgrace. Especially here in England. Even so, I'll never believe she's been a party to improper conduct. Not Shawnalese."

"I pray you're right, but if memory serves me correct, you wouldn't believe it of Victoria, either."

"Oh, Gayhawke," Heather moaned.

"We sail for France with the tide. Be ready." With that, Hawke stalked from the room.

Money was running low for Shawnalese. She had searched daily for employment as a governess, to no avail. Today she returned to the château, tired and discouraged. Tomorrow she would seek work as a shopgirl. Certainly, she reasoned, an educated and cultured young woman would have no trouble obtaining that type of work.

Shortly after she returned, she received an unexpected guest.

"I am Madame Brissaud, mademoiselle, and I'm calling as a personal courier of the duchesse de Vordeaux to invite you to the ball the duc and duchesse are having this evening. I apologize for the lateness, but the duchesse had been perusing the invitation list one last time and noticed that you, inadvertently, had not been invited." With that, Madame Brissaud handed Shawnalese an invitation.

"Please give the duchesse my regrets," Shawnalese said.

Visibly upset by Shawnalese's rejection, Madame Brissaud became insistent. "*Non,* mademoiselle. You mustn't refuse. I'm personally responsible for the oversight and will be held accountable by the duchesse."

"In that case, madame, I shall accept. I certainly cannot allow you to be faulted."

That evening, en route to the ball, Shawnalese was sure something was wrong, that the excuse for her invitation was a contrivance. But why? Still, she didn't really care why. After leaving the DuBellays, she'd done little else but search for work and attend depressing, almost hopeless, meetings of the liberals at the Palais Royal. Several times she and Grizzly had stayed there until late into evening, simply to have something to do. At times it was an entertaining place to be, and the only cost was for the food they ate.

"It will be wonderful to dance again, Grizzly. To allow the plight of France and my own predicament to slip away for one evening, even if I have to dance with every rake and knave in Paris." At that vision, she laughed. "If one, only one, of those blue-blooded noblemen makes an improper suggestion, I'll call him out! I've endured enough from the French aristocracy."

Throwing back his head, Grizzly let out a peal of

laughter. "Aye, lass. And I'll wager that ye'd draw his blood, too."

"Wouldn't that set Paris on her tail?"

"Aye. 'Twould indeed."

A short time later, Shawnalese stood motionless at the top of the stairs, wondering why she'd come. Hundreds of candles flickered in the crystal chandeliers, casting their rainbow across the marble sculptures and gilt-framed portraits in the entrance hall.

Music floated through the foyer, and beautiful, elegantly gowned ladies, wearing dazzling jewels, drifted by with handsome escorts in satin coats, snug-fitting breeches, and showy laces.

She forced a smile to her lips, lifted her gold-threaded skirts, and swept down the staircase.

Without warning she sensed his presence and stopped midstairs. Her heart fluttering, her gaze hopeful, she carefully searched for the only man who mattered. He leaned against a pillar, trapping her with his thickly-lashed green eyes.

"Gayhawke!" The hushed gasp crossed her lips, and she battled to recapture her composure, realizing instantly why she'd been invited.

Gayhawke Lawrence Richard Carrington, the sixth duke of Foxridge, looked formidable. Intimidating. His proud bearing was regal, and an aura of power, an air of mystique, surrounded him. One corner of Hawke's mouth lifted in cold cynicism, and he inclined his head toward her in a travesty of a bow.

Frozen to the stair, she nodded aloofly, with an air of defiance that she knew would rankle him. It had been a long time . . . so very long a time. Two years, during which she'd thought of little but revenge. Yet neither time nor her vengeful notions had dulled her remembrance of him, for Hawke's sharply defined features were forever seared into her memory.

Hawke's fierce eyes glinted at her. But even with all their derision focused on her, she remembered only when those same mocking eyes had sparkled and shimmered as he teased her or when, in unguarded moments, they darkened with the pain of disillusionment. She knew Gayhawke Carrington for what he was—excitingly dangerous and irresistibly vulnerable—a magnificent, wounded stag.

Everything she hated in a man.

Everything she loved.

Why was he here? Forcing her thoughts from the hopeful, she tilted her chin high and continued down the stairs with all the hauteur she could summon, her heart pounding in her ears. Her last words to him when she'd been an enamored seventeen echoed through her mind. "I will never forgive you! Never!" But she knew she would forgive him anything.

She catapulted backward in time to the night she had met him, to that fateful night in New Orleans when he'd given her, a desperate child of the streets, a gold doubloon. And from the next time she'd seen him, he had never stopped giving to her. He'd given of his money, generously so, but infinitely more important, he'd given of his time, for her edification. How, these past two years, could she have harbored ideas of revenge against a man who'd shown her nothing but affection, gentleness, compassion, and consideration, until she had, with childish abandon, with naive foolishness, thrown herself at him, and he had sent her away. Revenge? the lofty naysayer of her mind protested. Simply because Hawke was unable to love her? What kind of woman had she become?

Hawke stared at the face he'd dreamed of for two long years. Stared in fascination, in resentment, aware of the emotions simply seeing her had aroused in him. It angered him, for he wanted to feel nothing.

A man paused beside Hawke. "Isn't she a ravishing woman," the man remarked.

"Not bad," Hawke replied dryly.

"Yours for the taking, so I'm told. If my comtesse

weren't here, I'd have a go at—"

Hawke's hand shot out and clenched the comte's cravat, stopping him midsentence. "Apologize for that remark!"

"I-I'm very sorry. I must be mistaken. My apologies, monsieur," the man mumbled, and Hawke released him. Straightening his cravat, the comte hurried off.

The comte's words had struck Hawke harder than a physical blow.

Shawnalese felt Hawke's burning glare touching her everywhere, as if she'd been stripped naked. He had not moved from where he stood, and she felt her heart hammer, felt her knees weaken to the point of giving way at the sight of him, felt all the old feelings of love rush back. Her arms ached to hold him. But then the memory of the mindless, idiotic child she'd been flowed back as though it were yesterday, and humiliation stung her cheeks. How could she have thrown herself at the much-sought-after duke? How could she have been so naive, hoping he would return her love? What a senseless, calf-eyed, mooning little fool she'd been.

With all the grace and sophistication she could muster, Shawnalese glided across the marble floor and proffered her gloved hand. "Gayhawke," she coolly, formally, said in her breathy voice.

"Shawny," Hawke replied huskily, lifting her gloved hand to press his lips there, his gaze never leaving hers. "It's good to see you."

"Is it?" she queried softly. A tremor rushed through her body at his touch, his nearness. The memory of his embraces, his kisses, flooded her senses, and unconsciously she reached up to brush the stubborn curl from his brow. Hawke flinched at her intimate touch as though she'd burned him, and, flushing a deep red, she lifted her chin high.

Curling wisps of golden hair framed her face, and Hawke caught his breath as she lifted thick, sweeping lashes to glance wide-eyed at him with the mesmerizing Grenville eyes, eyes that could draw a man's soul into their crystalline, jeweled depths. Every delicate bone in her face was molded perfection. She was ethereal, the most exquisite woman he'd ever seen. She was everything he knew she would be, everything he'd feared she would become. He offered his arm. "May I have the pleasure?" His query was stilted, formal, as though they met for the first time, as though they'd never shared a deep affection, a special camaraderie, a kindred spirit.

Chapter 13

WITH A DISTANT SMILE, SHAWNALESE PLACED HER hand on Hawke's wrist and wordlessly followed his lead to the ballroom. Why was he treating her with such formal indifference? Who was this dark stranger? Then she melted into his arms and whirled around the ballroom, reliving the last time she had danced in his embrace. The night of the masquerade. Briefly, with cool hauteur, they circled the floor, and then she was being held by the comte de la Trepernay while they twirled through a waltz.

For Shawnalese the evening dragged interminably. She was everywhere but where she wanted to be as hour after hour Hawke ignored her and, seemingly oblivious of her presence, danced with one beautiful woman after another. Humiliated and desperate to capture his attention, she pondered her tarnished reputation, her slandered character, the scandal she'd brought down upon herself. With all of that in mind, she still threw caution to the wind to show Hawke how little she, also, cared. As though forced by a will stronger than her own, she did what she'd never done and before this moment would have refused to do. She encouraged the flirtations of every man with whom she danced. The ballroom soon buzzed at her behavior.

Three dances later, inattentive to the man with whom she danced, she was painfully aware of Hawke with still one more lovely woman in his arms.

"The comtesse de Beaulieux was admiring your lovely gown."

"I'm sorry, you were saying?"

"The comtesse de Beaulieux commented on your gown."

Shawnalese paled. "The comtesse de Beaulieux?"

"*Oui.* Madame St. Jeanneret."

Dear God! Was it Hawke's mother? Composing herself, she asked, "Where is the comtesse?"

"We'll pass her in a moment. She's the woman in the green gown."

As they whirled past the silver-haired woman, Shawnalese stared into a pair of deep blue eyes. She was relieved at first that it was not the green-eyed Victoria Carrington. "Is the comte de Beaulieux present?"

"Of course."

"Would you please introduce me? I have long wanted to meet him."

Minutes later her escort made the introductions and then excused himself. Shawnalese looked up at the still handsome face of the man she assumed to be Victoria's former lover. "You must know from my name why I need to speak privately with you, monsieur."

"Yes, of course," Julien St. Jeanneret replied. "We can use the duc's library." With that, he escorted her there and closed the door. Immediately he asked, "How is Victoria?"

"Pardon me?"

"You are related to the duchess of **Foxridge**, are you not?"

"Distantly. I wanted to talk to you to inquire about her."

"I don't understand."

"You are the Julien St. Jeanneret whom Victoria . . . whom Victoria left with years ago?"

Discomfited, Julien replied, "I am."

"Do you know her whereabouts?"

"Her whereabouts? She's not at Foxridge?"

"No. She's been neither seen nor heard of since she left with you."

"Dear God! I haven't seen her in nearly twenty-five years. Not since the night after we left."

"That can't be. I don't understand."

"We were very much in love. Her young son . . . well, I'm sure you know the story. . . ."

"Yes."

"A short time after her son discovered us, we ran away together. With our affair in the open, there was no longer a reason to remain apart. We desperately loved each other." His eyes clouded in remembrance, his face shrouded in unmasked pain. "It was storming, one of England's cloudbursts, and we traveled all night and all the next day by coach. But when we stopped the following evening, Victoria had changed her mind. She'd cried all the while we were traveling. Said she couldn't leave her son. The boy was so young. Besides, her husband was an invalid, and she feared for the shock to his fragile health. Although she didn't love her husband, she still had a strong affection for the duke. When she left me, we agreed never to see or contact each other again. There was no point. I sent her back in the same coach."

As they returned to the ballroom, Shawnalese floundered in indecision. Should she tell Hawke? Certainly the comte had told the truth. But where could Hawke's mother be? And why? And then, with con-

demning eyes turned toward her, she realized how
long she'd been gone and her folly in insisting on
speaking to St. Jeanneret right then. Impulsively she'd
closeted herself with a man in a room without a chaperone present. Now, as though to further complicate
matters, a visibly distressed Julien St. Jeanneret was
leaving with his angry wife in tow.

Shawny had achieved that for which she hoped—
Gayhawke Carrington's attention. The entire evening,
Hawke had observed her surreptitiously. She was the
statue of beauty, the personification of elegance and
grace. She eclipsed every woman he'd ever seen. But
precisely when he was having second thoughts regarding the scurrilous rumors about her, she'd started to
act the accomplished coquette. And Hawke knew that
in Paris there was no such thing as an "innocent" flir-
tation. Then, as though to further shock him, as
though to corroborate the vicious rumors, she'd disappeared with a man for a lengthy time, unchaperoned.
He would not have believed it if he were not seeing it.

Shawnalese was dancing with the duc de Crenobla.

"I'd heard that you're an extremely stimulating woman.
The rumors underestimate you, mademoiselle," the duc
said before he twirled her through the opened French
doors onto the balcony that led to the terrace below.

Shawnalese protested, "Please take me inside. I
shan't dance with you here."

The young duc's laugh was jeering. "You can drop
the pretenses, Shawnalese. There's no one here to see
us." His head lowered, and his wet lips seared her
cheek as she averted her face. His clasp tightened.

"Turn me loose!"

"Is this not"—his hands grasped her buttocks and
pulled her tightly against him—"what you've been
wanting?"

Bending one knee, Shawnalese raised her ankle
behind her and slipped her dagger from its scabbard.
Before the duc de Crenobla realized what had hap-

pened, the razor-sharp blade touched his jugular. "Inside, monsieur."

Starting to shake his head, the duc felt the trickle of blood move down his throat.

"Slowly," Shawnalese murmured, "if you wish to see tomorrow."

Ever so carefully, Claude-Xavier Ledoux, the duc de Crenobla, shuffled backward the few feet into the brightly lighted ballroom, Shawnalese facing him with her dagger at his throat.

Gasps of astonishment were followed by a woman's scream and shocked murmurs. The music stopped. Shawnalese removed the knife and loudly, clearly, challenged the duc, "You have abused my person and my honor, monsieur, and I demand an apology or satisfaction on a field of honor."

"You can't be serious!" The duc guffawed, his wig askew.

"I am quite serious," Shawnalese retorted for all to hear. "An apology, or I shall call you out."

A hushed undertone moved through the room.

"Have this woman arrested!" the duc ordered. His face flamed and his eyes bulged as he nervously straightened his wig.

Out of nowhere, Hawke appeared at her elbow. "If you sought my attention, Shawnalese, you have it," he snarled.

Shawnalese? He hadn't called her Shawnalese since the day they met, not even when she'd tried his patience almost to breaking. "You flatter yourself, Carrington."

"I want her thrown in the Bastille!" the duc screamed. "Now!"

Two liveried footmen reached for Shawnalese.

"Touch her and you die!" Hawke thundered, his face livid.

The frightened footmen stepped back, and the throng of people moved closer.

"Apologize to the duc, Shawnalese," Hawke ordered, his expression threatening.

She gasped. "I will not! The duc owes me an apology or satisfaction. The choice is his."

Stammering, the duc wiped the trickle of blood from his neck and looked at his bloodstained handkerchief. "This woman's insane! She accosted me. I want her in the Bastille!"

"Monsieur!" Shawnalese shot back. "Shall I tell your peers why I *accosted* you?" At the duc's confused silence, she again ordered softly, "Now apologize, or meet me on the field of honor."

"She lies," the duc de Crenobla said. "Her reputation precedes her. Her behavior speaks for itself."

Instantly Hawke stepped forward, facing the duc. "You have maligned this lady, and therefore you have maligned me. That I will not tolerate." Then his voice boomed sinisterly. "I demand you apologize to Miss Grenville and to me, here and now—or pay the consequences."

The duc turned white, and beads of sweat broke out on his brow. The murmurs of the stunned aristocracy turned into frenzied ramblings.

"No, Gayhawke," Shawnalese implored, and tugged at his arm. "It's all right. I'll leave."

Hawke shrugged her off, and his threatening glare bored into the pompous younger man. "It's your choice, monsieur."

"Please, Hawke," Shawnalese begged, only to be ignored.

Now the duc sweated profusely. "Monsieur . . ."

"You do not want to face me on a field of honor," Hawke said. "Trust me on that." By his mere presence Hawke could dominate a room, but now, in a towering rage, he received the undivided attention of everyone there.

Trembling, the duc mopped his brow with his bloodstained kerchief. "I won't apologize," he said. "She's nothing but a courtesan!"

"You're a liar! Beneath contempt," Hawke said with deadly calm.

Astonished gasps melted into excited whispers, for in calling the duc a liar, Hawke had hurled the ultimate insult, tantamount to a slap in the face.

"No man calls me a liar," Claude-Xavier sputtered, his face ashen. "I will have satisfaction. Unlike your England, monsieur, the choice of weapons and time is mine. Pistols, the day after tomorrow, at daybreak. My second will call on you at midday."

"It will be my pleasure," Hawke retorted. Seizing Shawnalese's elbow, he strode from the room while she ran to keep up with his long strides.

"If," Hawke said to her, "you aspired to go down in infamy, if you endeavored to humiliate me, you have succeeded. Admirably so. All in the space of one evening."

Once outside, he assisted her into the comte de Chaternay's coach. He seated himself beside her, his brow furrowed darkly and his green eyes smoldered as he snapped, "I understand you're occupying my château?"

"Yes."

"Without a proper chaperone?"

The coach lurched forward. "Yes."

"When Heather and I arrived in Paris, we went directly to the DuBellays. Of course when I learned from the comte that you resided at my château, I took the precaution of remaining there until . . ." He could not say it, and that fact further angered him. "Heather's quite fond of you," he barked. "I hate for her to see how low you've fallen."

"How low I've fallen?" Who was this stranger she still loved?

"Let's dispense with pretenses, Shawnalese. All of Paris is condemning your behavior."

"I see," Shawnalese said, and lifted her gaze to his, finding his eyes hard and cynical, boring into hers with a contempt that took her breath away. It was an undeclared war—she battling to remain detached and composed, he determined to overpower her through intimidation. Something primitive and savage emanated from him, something dark and frightening. Leashed power and controlled rage vibrated beneath the surface, and he was both terrifying and exciting at the same time. She shivered as his cold eyes raked her face from beneath half-closed lids.

"Have you nothing to say for yourself? Some excuse, however flimsy?"

She pulled the hood of her pelisse over her elegant coiffure, then shoved her hands deep inside her muff, but even there she could not warm herself against the pain of his icy words. She turned to stare out the small side window and replied softly, "I assume full responsibility for my status. It's all my doing."

Shawnalese's words sent a sourness to his stomach. He had accepted the truth of her downfall, had seen the proof of it for himself, but it tormented him to hear her admit it.

Betrayed. Forsaken.

Damn you, Shawnalese! Damn you! Damn you! He wanted to kill her for what she appeared to be. Wanted to strangle her with his bare hands. He prayed it wasn't so, that it was nothing but a nightmare, but as the duc had said, "Her behavior speaks for itself." How could she? Why did she?

"You said you'd never forgive me for sending you to Paris. Well, I say to you, I'll never forgive you for what you've done, what you've become. Nor will I ever forget."

She turned to look up at him from all the sparkling beauty of the Grenville eyes, and inwardly he cursed her again. Then he cursed himself that, when the child in New Orleans had looked up at him with those same damnable, mesmerizing eyes, he hadn't turned and run in the opposite direction.

"What I've become?"

"Don't use your innocent affectations on me,

Shawnalese. Save that for one of your—ah, what are they called in polite society—admirers?"

"You're despicable!"

"And what are you?" If only he hadn't sent her to Paris. . . . But he had, and now had she become everything he detested in a woman? "Who is the other man with whom you disgraced yourself tonight?"

"Which man?"

"Yes, which man! The man with whom you disappeared into your host's library for over half an hour. That man—or have you conveniently forgotten?"

Even now, in her anger, she could not reveal St. Jeanneret's identity or what he had told her. It was a disclosure that would be extremely painful for Hawke, and she needed first to discuss it with Heather. But what should she tell Hawke now?

"Answer me, Shawnalese. I demand an answer."

"Demand? I don't reply to demands, Hawke. Besides, you're going to believe the worst regardless of what I say."

"After your behavior tonight, how could I believe otherwise?" When that was met with silence, he asked, "What did you do to bring on this incident with the duc?"

Shawnalese felt rather than saw Hawke glare at her. "Does it matter?"

"Answer me. What did you do to cause the trouble?"

"I am presumed guilty? Convicted without a trial? Has it not occurred to you that the duc might be at fault? That he tried to take liberties with me?"

"If the duc behaved improperly, you received that for which you begged. Your conduct was outrageous. Shameful. When there's trouble over a woman, she can usually prevent it—if she wants to." Her face drained of all color and he coolly prodded, "Answer me if you will, Shawnalese. Does it soothe your considerable vanity to have two men duel over your honor?"

Her soft intake of breath was his only answer.

"Does it make you feel more desirable to know that two days hence I'll have killed the duc de Crenobla? It will be the same as murder, for the duc is no match for me."

Turning fiery eyes on him, she snapped, "That's your doing, Hawke. I didn't ask you to interfere."

"Come now," Hawke scoffed, "don't insult my intelligence or yours by pretending that you believed the duc would duel with you."

"Of course I didn't. I'm not a fool. I sought only to humiliate him, as he had me. If you hadn't intervened, I would have achieved that. As you'd say, admirably so."

"If I hadn't intervened you'd be in the Bastille as we speak."

"Then why did you intervene? In prison I'd be out of your way."

"I've been asking myself that same question," he said sardonically.

At that, she turned toward him. Her eyes implored understanding. If only she'd known her ill-conceived actions would end in disgrace, in disaster. "I'm so terribly sorry, Hawke. I didn't think the matter would go this far."

"Great God, Shawnalese! What did you think the duc de Crenobla would do when a woman of your reputation publicly placed a dagger at his throat? Certainly, after that humiliation, you didn't expect an apology? A French noblewoman wouldn't get that from him. There're few men higher in all of France."

"I won't be responsible for your killing the duc."

"You already are."

After a hesitation, she forced the detestable overture from her lips. "I'll apologize to him."

Hawke realized what her offer had cost her in pride, and his voice warmed—slightly. "I think you know the issue has gone too far for that."

"You could return to England."

"I, skulk off in the middle of the night? Surely you jest. I'll face death before dishonor."

"What can I do? I didn't think—"

"You're exactly right—you didn't think. You're highly educated, yet you haven't the common sense of a peasant girl. In all probability, all you could think of was your all-consuming vanity."

"I've admitted I made a mistake. I have apologized. I've offered to apologize to the duc. What would you have me do now? Bare my back and allow you to give me twenty lashes?" Her voice seethed with barely controlled anger. "Or perhaps, Carrington, you would prefer that I grovel? Well, my exalted and noble duke, I no longer grovel. That girl died two years ago, when you banished her to France."

"Yes, I realize that now. That girl is dead." He wanted to hurt her as badly as she had hurt him. "I don't know you, Shawnalese. Nor would I want to if given the choice."

His harsh words destroyed her. For the first time in her life, she wished she were dead. What had happened that the love he had once borne for her turned to hatred?

But then reason overcame emotion. How dare he withdraw his love from her! Love did not have qualifications, restrictions, constraints. There was nothing that Hawke could do that would destroy her love for him. However, at this moment she most definitely did not like him, and if he could say to her what he just had, then certainly she could tell him exactly how she felt. "I don't know this Gayhawke Carrington, either. A fact for which I'm exceedingly grateful."

Battling between rage and desire, Hawke glanced out the window, attempting to gather a measure of control. He saw they neared his château and his next obstacle. "Is there a gentleman I need to throw out of my house?"

Shawnalese stiffened in astonishment, too stunned to reply. He believed the gossip! How, after all their years together, could he think so little of her? The carriage stopped, and she gathered her skirts, flung open the door, jumped from the coach, and raced inside, the blood draining from her heart as surely as if he had plunged a knife into it.

Hawke bellowed at the coachman, "What are you waiting for? Get me the hell out of here!" He needed desperately to escape his sordid thoughts, his black heart.

The next morning Hawke and Heather moved into his chateau. The first matter he addressed was put before Philippe in the privacy of his study. "I want to know everything that's happened since Shawnalese moved in here. Everything!"

"Y-yes, Your Grace. About a month ago, mademoiselle arrived with Grizzly and Thaddeus and said they had moved out of the comte de Chaternay's residence and would need to stay here for a few days until other arrangements could be made. I told her the household money would not stretch to support them and the animals plus Nadine and Auguste as well—"

"Nadine and Auguste?"

"Yes, Your Grace. I wrote you about the half-starved woman and her son. She's a very hard worker, Your Grace, and the boy runs errands. They—"

"Yes, yes. Go on."

"Well, Mademoiselle Shawnalese, Grizzly, and Thaddeus have been here ever since. I wrote to you, Your Grace. Did not—"

"Yes. Yes, I did. Who's been supporting them?"

"I don't know, Your Grace. Two days after she moved in, Mademoiselle Shawnalese gave me more than enough money for the three of them, and has been ever since."

Dear God! Was Shawnalese accepting money from a man? She must be. Where else had she gotten the money to provide for the support of three people for more than a month? "Tell me about the men."

"I don't know if you want to hear it, Your Grace."

"Tell me everything, Philippe. Leave nothing out."

"Well, almost from the day mademoiselle moved in, there have been any number of gentlmen calling. All hours of the day and evening. Most arriving unannounced, without sending a card ahead. Most improper. And men you wouldn't approve of, Your Grace."

"How so?"

"Men of ill repute, men of no consequence, some downright scoundrels. There've been no invitations. That is, until yesterday, when mademoiselle was most improperly invited to a fete by the duchesse de Vordeaux."

"That was my doing. Whom has Shawnalese been seeing?"

"I don't know."

"You don't know. How can you not know?"

"She leaves early in the morning and doesn't return until evening most of the time. She's home most evenings, although there were a few times she was out quite late. She does her studying with Thaddeus during the evenings. Grizzly always leaves and returns with her, Your Grace. Certainly he would know."

"Yes, of course." But Hawke knew it would be a waste of time to ask Grizzly. He was completely loyal to Shawnalese. Besides, Grizzly thought she could do no wrong.

"I know mademoiselle cannot be indulging in the exploits the scandal mongers say."

"Which is?"

"I don't like to repeat gossip, Your Grace. It's most unreliable. A maid got it from someone else's footman, who got it from someone else's coachman, and so on. Besides, I don't believe mademoiselle is that kind of woman, Your Grace. A bit headstrong, perhaps, but certainly not what's rumored."

"Yes. Well, thank you, Philippe. That will be all."

The major-domo withdrew.

Meanwhile, in her bedroom, away from the ears of servants, Shawnalese revealed to Heather all that had happened since last she saw her. Unsure whether or not to mention Hawke and Heather's mother, she explained the incident at the duc and duchesse de Vordeaux's ball that led to the forthcoming duel. Instead of condemnation she received understanding, instead of criticism she received compassion, and then she was wrapped tenderly in Heather's arms and comforted. Together they agonized over Hawke's predicament.

Later that afternoon Shawnalese spoke to Grizzly. She told him everything that had happened at the ball. "I don't know what to do. I can't allow Hawke to fight that duel. I must find some other way to settle this issue. I'll call on the duc. I will apologize. I will beg. I will plead. I will give myself to him if I have to, but somehow I will stop this duel."

"Nay, lass! Ye're talkin' crazy. Ye canna consider such a thing."

Determined, Shawnalese rushed to her room to change, and at that, Grizzly did what he had to do. He sought out Hawke. "Shawna's leaving to go to the duc. Said she'd do anything he wanted if he'd call off the duel. Ye've got to stop her."

Chapter 14

Enraged, Hawke locked Shawnalese in her room, the vision of her in the arms of the duc de Crenobla a revulsion to him. Was there no limit to what she'd do to ease her conscience, to save her reputation?

The next morning, in the cold, misty gray of dawn,

low-hanging clouds enshrouded the trees in gloom and drizzled fine droplets of rain in the clearing. Every sound, an ominous foreboding of pending disaster, pierced the stillness to echo through the murky air. Coachmen, hunched inside their canvas ponchos, sat on their high perches, silent observers to the ritualistic proceedings that preceded a duel of honor.

The Duc de Crenobla, Claude-Xavier Ledoux, drew his second aside. "After the arrangements were made yesterday, I learned that the duke of Foxridge is expert with all firearms. I shouldn't have challenged the man. He's quite capable of killing me. I need your help."

"Of course, Claude-Xavier, but how can I be of assistance?" his second asked.

"Immediately after you've said 'Ready', I want you to silently count to ten before you say 'Fire'. I'll do the same. I'll shoot simultaneously with your calling 'Fire!' That will give me the clear and distinct advantage to shoot early without anyone realizing it. Or at least without their being able to challenge me on it."

"Brilliant!" Claude-Xavier's second exclaimed.

Hawke stood in solitude, his composure a facade. For an angry moment he wished Shawnalese were here to observe the devastation her perfidy would cause; then, not knowing why, he was relieved that he'd locked her in her room and she wouldn't have to look upon the face of death.

Hawke's opponent saw none of the turmoil, only the confident stance of a deadly adversary. Shortly the seconds arrived with the dueling pistols.

It was time.

The gray cloud cover refused to lift, the drizzling rain continued to fall, and visibility remained obscured. The ambulance wagon, equipped with two beds, drew closer to the clearing.

As though on cue, two surgeons, holding black bags, walked toward the dueling field. At a silent signal from the king's brother, a groom brought his powerful black stallion and he mounted. Amidst the grave atmosphere, the principals, seconds, and witnesses walked to the dismal, sodden clearing.

At that moment a coach careened down the rain-rutted road, tottering precariously, its high wheels sending mud and rain splattering in every direction. The thunder of hooves and the churn of wheels reverberated through the eerie silence as the carriage jolted to a halt.

Hawke saw the emblazoned door of his coach fly open and Shawnalese hurriedly descended. "Gentlemen," he said, "I apologize for this interruption. I shall return immediately." With that, he stormed toward Shawnalese and clasped her shoulders just as Grizzly reached her side.

"The lass persuaded the upstairs maid to unlock the door," Grizzly explained. "I couldna stop her from coming, so I came with her."

"Shawnalese," Hawke said in a low voice, "don't further disgrace me in front of my peers."

His eyes, which had sparkled with warm affection when she was a girl, now were icy with indifference, and she withered inside.

At her slump of submission, Hawke ordered Grizzly, "Return her to the coach." Without another glance at Shawnalese, he spun on his heel and returned to the waiting men.

From the distance Shawnalese watched in stomach-wrenching horror as Hawke and Claude-Xavier, their wet, white shirts clinging to their bodies, turned back to back, their pistols pointed earthward.

The rain fell harder. The woods enclosing the clearing were oppressive, the gnarled tree trunks silent witnesses.

Claude-Xavier's second began, "One . . . two . . . three"—his voice cut loudly through the gray-veiled mist—"eight . . . nine . . . ten."

The two duelists stopped, backs to each other.

"Turn!" barked Ledoux's second. "Ready!" He counted to ten. "Fire!"

Simultaneously with the word fire, Claude-Xavier's pistol exploded with a blast of flame and a deadly roar.

The death-bound ball shot into Hawke.

"Nooo!" Shawnalese's scream reverberated through the chilly forest, and she crumpled to her knees, both hands pressed to her face.

Scores of birds exploded into the gray clouds, and the frightened coach horses reared in their trappings, then whinnied and pranced skittishly in place.

The moment hung endlessly in the misty silence of the gray dawn. Then the surgeon raced to Hawke's side.

"Stand back!" Hawke ordered, straightening from the reeling shock. His shoulder was shattered. His once snowy shirt was drenched with crimson, and blood trickled from his fingers, down the gun he still gripped, to drip upon the dampness of the grass. His face flushed livid with fury. There had been subterfuge on this field of honor, and he would have his due. In excruciating pain, Hawke raised his arm with pistol clasped, supporting his wounded limb with his left hand and with lethal precision took slow and careful aim at the head of the trembling Claude-Xavier.

Hawke's voice boomed, piercing the eerie silence. "My honorable"—his words, icy, scornful, deadly, were uttered with black contempt—"duc de Crenobla, you have two choices. You may die by my hand, or you may apologize to Miss Grenville and me. Which shall it be?"

"No!" bellowed the king's brother, sent to oversee the duel, pressing his nervous stallion forward. "The code of honor demands that an apology cannot be extended or accepted until you've fired. You must fire, Monsieur Carrington."

Ignoring the orders, Hawke, with his voice ringing across the clearing, challenged, "What is it to be, Ledoux?" Hawke felt blood trickle down his chest and his vision blurred momentarily, but by sheer force of will, for he would not falter now, he held his supported arm steady.

Staring down the bore of Hawke's pistol, the white-faced Claude-Xavier envisioned the deadly ball that would slay him, and he turned toward Shawnalese, Hawke's pistol aimed at his head all the while.

"Mademoiselle Grenville, please accept my sincere regret for my behavior. I fear I had imbibed too much, and if I offended your person, or your honor, I am truly sorry. I meant nothing that I said. It was merely strong drink talking." Abruptly Claude-Xavier's knees buckled. Trembling severely, he straightened before he turned back to Hawke. "Please, Monsieur Carrington, accept my genuine apology for this unfortunate matter, and for anything I may have said, or done, to offend you. I was wrong, and I regret both my words and my actions."

Hawke knew that within the hour word of Claude-Xavier's apology would race through Paris. He lifted his pistol skyward and fired. Then he staggered, and the surgeon, DuBellay, and Shawnalese raced to his side.

Sometime later, after the musket ball had been removed from his shoulder, Hawke leaned back against the velvet squabs of his coach, having refused to lie in the ambulance wagon. His shoulder throbbed with pain, and he shivered, not only from the chill of the miserable day and his wet clothes, but more from the catastrophe that had nearly occurred this day. Shawnalese sat opposite him, morosely looking out the small side window, and he cursed her treacherous beauty. He had fought two men because of her. How many more would he fight? "Your reputation is firmly established after this duel, Shawnalese," he announced coldly. The bitter edge of irony rang in his voice. "Is your considerable egotism salved now that men have dueled because of you? Is your arrogance assuaged, your narcissism fulfilled? Was it worth it?" At her silence, he said in a coolly impersonal tone, "Have your baggage packed when we get to the château. As soon as the physician attends me, we leave for England."

Shawnalese turned to face him and stiffened under his indifferent, withering glare. "I'll not be returning with you. Nevertheless, I'll pack and leave today. Then you can stay at the château until you've healed."

"We leave for England at daybreak."

"Perhaps you didn't hear me. I'll not be going with you."

"Perhaps you didn't hear me. We will leave for England at daybreak." With that, dusky green eyes challenged jeweled emerald ones. "That is, unless you prefer that I have you shut up in the convent at Montmartre."

Four days later Shawnalese's heart soared as the rocking coach started the climb from Hawke's yacht, the *Phantom Dream,* up the winding road to Foxridge, the only place she'd ever thought of as home. Her joyless mood of the days past disappeared at the familiar sights so dear to her heart.

After stepping down from the carriage, Hawke assisted Heather, then turned to offer his left hand to Shawnalese. She extended a slender, well-turned ankle, and her silk-lined hood fell back, displaying a wealth of long, fair tresses shimmering with spun gold.

Shawnalese raced up the stairs and inside, and there stood Rutger, Leif, the ever-efficient Addison, and a long line of welcoming servants. "Rutger," she squealed, "you're more handsome than ever! How is it possible? You must have thousands of broken hearts by now." The man who'd inherited his father's classic good looks embraced her, and affectionately she turned to Leif. "Dear Leif, do you still have more charm than the law should allow? I can't believe you're so tall. I don't think I'll try to push you from the swing in the hayloft again." She laughed and hugged the man who'd been a boy when she'd kissed him good-bye more than two years earlier.

Turning to Heather, she said, "Oh, I'm so happy to be

home." Her face was radiant and with head back, she twirled in happiness, her long hair swirling through the air, a shimmering golden veil that, when she stopped, undulated in waves down her back to below her hips.

In that moment Hawke knew he should have put her in the convent.

"I say, Miss Shawnalese, it's dreadfully good to have you home," Addison said, smiling broadly.

"Thank you, Addison. It's marvelous to be here. You know the comte de Chaternay's major-domo wasn't half as competent as you."

The capable Addison flushed red, the first time Shawnalese had ever seen him discomposed. Then she was welcomed by Mrs. Kendall and the rest of the staff.

Later Mrs. Kendall helped Shawnalese unpack. "Lordy, it's mighty good to have ya home again, luv. I sure missed ya."

"Oh, Mrs. Kendall, I've missed you, too. Terribly. There wasn't a woman in France I could talk to when I got myself in trouble. What has happened while I've been gone?"

"His Grace's been seein' a bloomin' widow for many months now. The Viscountess Paige Seymour. It's more'n he's ever spent with any lady. An' I hear tell the uppity viscountess has bandied it all over London that His Grace's gonna offer for her real soon now. Maybe after Christmas, which is the first anniversary of her husband's death. Ya might say she mourns mighty short and mighty gay."

Frozen in dread, Shawnalese held her breath, unable to expel it. Gayhawke to marry? She wanted to die. That would explain why she hadn't seen him all the time she was gone. He probably didn't want to be bothered with her continuously throwing herself at him. Ashen-faced and trembling, she placed her gloves in the wrong drawer. After a time she composed herself enough to ask casually, "Does he love the viscountess?"

Chapter 15

SHAWNALESE WAITED AN ETERNITY FOR MRS. Kendall to answer.

"Ain't my place to say if he loves her. She just might end up the duchess of Foxridge." Then Mrs. Kendall looked at Shawnalese's forlorn face. "'Course I know you'd never repeat my words. His Grace's had Her Ladyship here a few times. But he's mighty cold with women. The way I see it, he's no different with this one than all the others. Never did understand why he's that way. Anyway, Lady Heather's been pushin' him to marry for more years than I can remember. He needs an heir. Who knows, maybe he figures it's time."

"Is the viscountess beautiful?"

"Aye, she's a mighty fancy piece. Brazen, too. But I can't take a likin' to her."

"Why is that?"

"Don't rightly know. Maybe it's 'cause her eyes don't smile when her lips do. She seems a right pleasant sort, but there's somethin' 'bout her. . . . Besides, she's not near good enough for His Grace."

Shawnalese smiled, knowing Mrs. Kendall's strong affection for Hawke. "I'm sure you don't think any woman is good enough for Gayhawke Carrington."

"I reckon. Seems like that's where you an' me are alike, luv. Right?"

Dropping her gaze, Shawnalese replied softly, "Yes.

I cannot think of a woman who's deserving of Hawke. He needs someone who understands him, and he's a difficult man to understand."

"Aye. That he is."

"What else has happened? What about poor Chadwick?"

"Ah, poor Viscount Chadwick searched for more'n a year for his Lady Laurel. Can ya imagine a man lovin' a woman that much? Mark my words, he'll find her yet. But maybe not. It's been nigh unto two years now. Prattle says he never heard or received a worda her from the day her father sent her away. He's not the fun-lovin' man he once was. No indeedy. I say he still mourns his Lady Laurel, an' all o' the servants agree."

"Poor Chadwick."

"Aye. Poor Lord Leighton. Baron Rutger's a man grown now. Oh Lordy, he's a handsome one, he is. Yes indeedy. That blond hair and them blue eyes that fair jump out at ya. He sets my poor heart to flutterin' every time I see him. As good-lookin' as his daddy, Baron Siegfried. All the maids are smitten. Reckon I'd be too if I was twenty years younger. The baron's restorin' his mansion, gettin' it ready to move into. Hear tell he'll be assumin' the duties of his title and inheritance now." Mrs. Kendall closed one empty trunk and opened the next one.

"What about Baroness Wilhelmina?"

"The dowager baroness? Word is she'll be movin' with Lord Rutger. Ya know how that woman idolizes her grandsons. She's not about to let 'em get too far from her. What with Lord Leif leavin' for Oxford after Christmas, she'll be hoverin' over Lord Rutger like a mother hen."

"I know you'll miss the dowager baroness if she leaves."

"Hmmph. Not likely. I don't reckon Lady Heather will miss her much, either. Lady Heather is bein' courted by Lord Edmund Spencer, the earl of Fallbrook. I say it's high time. Baron Siegfried's been gone nigh unto twelve years now. But the prattle is that the dowager baroness thinks Lady Heather oughta live out her life a widow. The way I see it, Her Ladyship's mourned long enough."

Thinking about Hawke's family, Shawnalese sought out Grizzly in private the next day. "There's a matter that's been on my mind for several days. I learned something about Hawke's mother at the duchesse de Vordeaux's ball. I spoke with Julien St. Jeanneret, the man with whom Victoria Carrington ran away." She told Grizzly everything she'd learned, ending with, "What with that horrible scene at the ball, then the duel, and Hawke barely speaking to me, I don't know what to do. I dare not mention it to Hawke, but I was wondering if I should say something to Heather, or Chadwick, or possibly even Rutger."

"Nay, lass. Ye know how Hawke feels about his mother. Ye canna go telling anybody. It'll be back to him within the hour, and there'll be hell to pay. Ye're in a kettle o' hot water now, ye dinna want to be heating up the fire. Besides, that was near twenty-five years ago. The woman is either dead or she doesna want to be found. It'd just be opening old wounds with nae good to come o' it."

Shawnalese sighed. "You're right, Grizzly. I'll just forget about it."

During the following weeks, while Hawke recuperated from his gunshot wound, Shawnalese spent most of her time with Rutger, Leif, or Grizzly. She rode Wildfire and romped with Czar. Yet Hawke, dark and brooding, was ever near. His smoldering green gaze raked her, more often than not, from beneath gathered, swooping ebony brows, his sensual lips twisted with mockery and derision.

Never were they alone, not even in the great hall, for he avoided direct contact with her. Their estrangement remained between them, a tangible entity. Gone, as though he had never existed, was the compassionate Hawke who'd given her a gold doubloon, the loving Hawke who'd comforted her when her mother died, the patient and affectionate Hawke who'd seen personally to her development. In his place stood a caustic, scathing man she didn't recognize. Yet he acted that way only with her, and it cut deeply, for he was still caring and affectionate with Heather and his nephews, and she thirsted for the same. Would he never forgive her?

Shawnalese spent more and more time with Rutger. During the years after Siegfried Von Rueden's death, Heather and Hawke's nephews had moved into Foxridge. Now Rutger was renovating the Von Rueden mansion. Each day Shawnalese rode with him to check the progress, and a closeness they had not previously shared developed.

Hawke noticed this evolving affection with deep concern. He couldn't tell either of them they were half brother and sister, not after all these years of subterfuge. Something, he mused as Shawnalese and Rutger again rode off together, must be done immediately, for Ravencroft would not be ready for another three months, and Rutger would be living at Foxridge until then. The developing situation could not wait three months.

Later that afternoon, after Rutger and Shawnalese returned, Hawke's shoulder was throbbing painfully, and he was in a foul mood. Ignoring Shawnalese, he said to Rutger, "I'd like to speak to you in my study."

Crossing the room to his desk, he motioned for his nephew to be seated, but Hawke felt the need to stand. Glancing down at the handsome, fair-haired man, he was struck for the first time by the strong resemblance to Shawnalese. Except for the eyes, Rutger, the image of his father, was the masculine version of Shawnalese. How had Heather never suspected? He turned that disquieting notion aside and addressed Rutger. "I am asking you to discontinue seeing Shawnalese."

"Pardon me?"

"I'd like you to stop spending so much time with Shawnalese."

"Why?"

"Because she's my ward and you two live in the same house. It's not a good idea."

"Why?"

"Why?" Hawke repeated, feeling the bumbling fool. "Shawnalese is no longer the child you knew. . . . There are proprieties, you realize. And you two are riding across the countryside unchaperoned, which invites gossip."

"God's breath! You're quite right, Hawke," Rutger agreed, rising. "I fear I wasn't thinking. Old habits, you know. I'll have Grizzly accompany us from now on. I wager the old boy will love that." Rutger started to leave the room, then turned back. "Sorry, Hawke. It wasn't intentional. I'm devilish lucky Mother or Grandmama didn't draw my blood on that one. Or Shawnalese." He sauntered out, whistling.

At that moment Hawke determined that his best chance for halting the budding relationship lay with Shawnalese, for Rutger was already beguiled. Every sign was there, for he had seen many a witless man with the same besotted look on his face. He would talk to Shawnalese when the first opportunity for privacy presented itself.

The following morning, the house was filled with the aromas of cookies, pies, and tarts, in preparation for Christmas four days away. Although Hawke was unable to hunt, Chadwick, Leif, and Grizzly would be returning with deer, elk, grouse, and pheasant, enough to feed the family and servants, plus Hawke's tenants and their families, for the twelve days of Christmas. It had been a tradition with him from the time he became the sixth duke of Foxridge to furnish his tenants with the feasting for the holiday.

Rutger had been left behind to select the Christmas tree and Yule logs. "Shawna, come with me to choose a tree," he urged, her cloak over his arm. At her hesitation, he assured her, "We shall be well escorted, for there are two men going with us to do the cutting.

Relieved to be away from Hawke's brooding presence, she agreed. Rutger assisted her onto the high seat of the horse-drawn wagon, covered her with a lap robe, and snapped the reins. She sat next to him, her thoughts on Hawke while Rutger chatted and drove the team toward the section of pines, evergreen oaks, and cypresses from the Isle of Wight. Two men silently rode the rear of the wagon, their legs dangling.

"Rutger," Shawnalese started hesitantly, the wagon bouncing her roughly, "is Viscountess Paige Seymour beautiful?"

"Paige? Yes, she's devilishly beautiful—quite spoiled and vain, but rather charming," he answered, guiding the team of horses into the woods.

"Is Hawke in love with her?"

"God's breath! Hawke in love—don't be ridiculous. I daresay Hawke will never love one woman. Chadwick says Hawke searches for the perfect woman, knowing full well there's no such person. But he thoroughly enjoys the search." Rutger laughed and wrapped his arm around Shawnalese, pulling her closer before he released her. "As for myself, I've found my perfect woman."

"You don't think Hawke will marry Lady Seymour?"

"I didn't say that. He might. Mother's been pressuring him for years to marry. He needs heirs. His estates have belonged to a Carrington for almost two hundred years. If he waits, he's only prolonging the inevitable." Turning toward her, he smiled. "Actually, you and I are fortunate Mother's been chafing at Hawke all these years."

"Why is that?"

"Back in 1781 Mother had been badgering Hawke to marry Lady Hollis Townsende, and he promised Mother that he'd decide shortly. Hollis was rather a likable sort, good family and all that. Then the captain of one of Hawke's merchant ships broke his leg right before a trip to America was scheduled. Naturally, Hawke would've had no trouble replacing the man for the trip, but the ship was already outfitted and ready to sail. So he used the excuse and decided to captain the ship to New Orleans. Said the sea air and open space would clear his head, so he could decide about Hollis. That's when he found your mother and you."

Shawnalese turned pale. But for fate, Gayhawke Carrington would never have entered her life the second time. Only the coincidence of a captain's broken leg and a sister's badgering kept her from being in New Orleans right now, living only heaven knew how, instead of at Foxridge with this wonderful family.

"So if not for that, I hazard a guess that Hawke would never have known about you." Smiling, Rutger asked, "Has Hawke or Mother never told you that?"

"No. No, they didn't."

"But for destiny, young lady, you wouldn't be here."

The words echoed in her brain: "But for destiny . . ."

They spent the next few hours selecting the perfect pine tree for the great hall, plus three Yule logs large enough to burn the entire night. They were on their way home when Shawnalese told Rutger, "The viscountess is supposed to be boasting all about London that Hawke's close to a proposal."

"Perhaps so."

She stared straight ahead. Never would she spend one minute at Foxridge if Hawke married.

The jolt of the wagon and two men yelling, followed by a loud thud, jerked Shawnalese from her thoughts. One of the Yule logs had rolled off the wagon. Rutger halted the horses, and while the men struggled with the log, Rutger unexpectedly reached for Shawnalese, pulling her into his arms, his actions hidden from the view of the men by the large Scotch pine tree in the wagon. "Paige's beauty cannot be compared to yours. No one's can," he murmured, and his mouth captured hers in a lingering kiss.

Shawnalese didn't deny his kiss, hoping that he could light the fire in her where all others had failed—all but one. Then empty and lifeless, she pulled away. "You presume too much, Rutger. You're like a brother to me," she rebuked softly, disappointed that Hawke's nephew, with his gentle and considerate ways, could not stir her heart.

Misunderstanding the look of disappointment in her eyes, Rutger sighed, "Please forgive me, Shawna. I didn't mean to take liberties. I couldn't help myself." He paused, then added, "There was a time we may have been like brother and sister, but no more—and your kiss wasn't exactly sisterly."

"Please forget that, Rutger. I didn't mean to mislead you."

"I'm a man, and you're very much a woman. I wish you'd regard us in that manner in the future, and I ask your permission to court you."

"Rutger, I love you dearly. You're precious to me, but not in the way of a suitor." She wrapped her arms around his shoulders to give him an affectionate hug. "Besides, dear Rutger, do you think I'm foolish enough to want all the available women in England after my head because I've taken the most handsome, eligible man out of circulation?" She laughed, hoping to soothe his ego and ease the hurt look on his face.

Hawke had ridden out to meet Chadwick, Leif, and Grizzly returning from the hunt, when off in the distance he caught sight of Rutger kissing Shawnalese, followed by her arms slipping around his nephew in an embrace. It tore through his entrails that Shawnalese might have an interest in Rutger—or any man. Seething with rage, he yearned to thrash Rutger because he dared to touch her, but even more because she obviously wanted Rutger's touch. Of one circumstance he felt certain: Shawnalese had not mourned—either in France or now here—brokenhearted over a lost predestined love. Ahh, how fleeting her "eternal love" for him.

Turning away, he hoped the anguish he felt was nothing more than a bruised ego . . . but he knew otherwise. Furious with Rutger, furious with Shawnalese, but most of all furious with himself for being angry for the wrong reasons, he let out a string of curses and turned Warrior toward the returning hunters. Despite all he had seen at the duc and duchesse de Vordeaux's ball, despite everything Shawnalese had said—and not said—afterward, of late, he'd begun to wonder, to hope, that most of the rumors about her in France were idle gossip. That she had been foolish, headstrong, and impulsive, yes, but wanton, a fallen woman, no. Now, again, her behavior condemned her, and he chastised himself angrily for the pain that shot through him at that discovery. What kind of fool was he? Did he really need to find her in the arms of a lover to be convinced? At that imagining, he knew he must talk privately with her about Rutger as soon as possible.

Late that night, with that notion in mind, Hawke sought her out in her chambers.

Chapter 16

SHAWNALESE OPENED HER DOOR. "HAWKE. Is something wrong?"

"Yes. May I come in?"

She dared not be alone with him, and certainly not here, but at his dark scowl she repeated, "Something's wrong?"

"Yes, Shawnalese. It's not a matter I want to stand in the gallery and discuss."

"What is this about?"

"Afraid to trust yourself?"

Challenged, she stepped backward, and Hawke entered her brightly lit room.

"I saw you and Rutger this afternoon. You're to stay away from him, Shawnalese. Have I made myself clear?"

She flushed at his words, for she'd been unaware

that her embrace with Rutger had been overseen. Feeling defensive and not sure why, she said, "Rutger's too young for me. Besides, he's like a brother."

"Brother? What I saw in the meadows surely wasn't brotherly."

"Rutger caught me off guard, Hawke." She was angry that she'd been overseen, angry that she defended herself, and angry most of all that Hawke was so eager to think the worst of her. Smiling sweetly, she said, "You did say you wanted me to get experience."

"Not with my nephew—not with Rutger. He isn't available to you—in any way other than family. Is that understood, Shawnalese?" Unable to stop himself, he added the insult to hurt her, as she had him. "I'd have thought you'd gotten all the 'experience' you need, in France."

Wounded by his affront, crushed that he'd forbid her relationship with Rutger, she turned her face from him so he wouldn't see the anguish she could not disguise.

At her silence, he said, "You're in England now, not France, and my responsibility. That means you will conduct yourself in a manner befitting your station."

"What station is that?"

"By God, Shawnalese, you'll come to heel if I have to tether you!"

"Come to heel? Like your trained dog? That will be on the same day that you're rolling snowballs in Hades."

"You are not to be alone with any gentleman other than Grizzly. Any time you're with a man, you are to be properly chaperoned."

Leisurely, she scanned the room. "Have you lost my chaperone, Hawke? Should I look beneath the bed to see if somehow she's gotten misplaced? Or perhaps you simply forgot the poor dear and left her standing in the gallery."

Almost beyond restraint, he seized her and gave her a shake. "Do you understand, Shawnalese?"

Jerking free of his grip, she shot back, "You've said what you came here to say. Please leave."

"I do not intend to repeat it, so see that you don't forget. You don't want to know what will happen if you do."

The next morning a new fire burned brightly in Shawnalese's bedchamber. A few guests had already arrived for the holiday festivities and ball. Scurrying from her warm bed, Shawnalese pulled the bell cord, smiling when Mrs. Kendall hurried in. "Oh, Mrs. Kendall, please help me. Lady Paige Seymour will be here today, and I must look my best."

Yet the day lengthened without an appearance by the viscountess, and Shawnalese, quiet and withdrawn, engaged only in pleasantries with the guests, to Baroness Wilhelmina's relief. She moved among the guests in a fog, with Rutger too often at her elbow, Hawke's distant glower warning her. After a time, alone in the crowded room, she was standing next to a suit of armor and staring absently out the window when Hawke approached her.

"You're not discouraging Rutger," he accused quietly.

"What would you have me do, Gayhawke? Slap Rutger for being attentive? Rebuke him for being considerate? Or perhaps you'd prefer I falsely accuse him of some impropriety, and create a scene?" At Hawke's glare and darkening green eyes, she smiled with satisfaction. "I thought not." Then she moved away to join

Heather's suitor, Lord Edmund Spencer, the earl of Fallbrook.

Toward evening, Mrs. Kendall pressed each wave into a pompadour high on Shawnalese's head in the latest Paris fashion and said, "I heard the Viscountess Paige Seymour will be arrivin' for dinner and stayin' the night." She glanced in the mirror at Shawnalese's long, thick, golden twists, caught at her nape by a hammered silver clasp, and pulled them forward to cascade over her shoulder.

Patiently she curled each ringlet that framed Shawnalese's face and wove tiny ruby silk flowers throughout her hair. "Scuttlebutt is there's gonna be a betrothal announcement."

Unaware of what she did, Shawnalese let herself be helped into the ruby, silk brocade gown, stepped into matching slippers, then pulled on her long silk gloves.

Stepping back, Mrs. Kendall sighed. "A bloomin' angel ya are, luv. A bloomin' angel."

Shawnalese's heart thumped at the thought of the evening ahead of her. Was Hawke really going to announce his betrothal to Viscountess Paige Seymour? At that thought her pain was beyond tears. Why did she care? But she did, excruciatingly so.

Moments later Shawnalese stood overlooking the great hall, her gaze coming to rest on Hawke and the stunning raven-haired woman at his side. Unable to turn away from the beautiful profile of the Viscountess Paige Seymour, yet unable to force herself to descend, she stepped back into the shadows of the gallery. The black-haired beauty, with an assurance that proclaimed she was society's pampered darling, engaged in conversation with Hawke while her dark eyes gazed up at him with adoration. Her hand rested possessively on his wrist, and her slender body leaned against his seductively. Did the lovely widow share her bed with Hawke?

As though to answer Shawnalese's silent question,
Paige, unknowingly observed, slowly slid her hand
down Hawke's thigh. At Hawke's responsive, sensual
smile, Shawnalese gave a painful gasp, turned, and
raced back to her room. She longed to ride Wildfire
but could not, for any hole or rock, unseen in the dark
of night, might cause him a broken leg. Instead she
would go to the woodland temple. There, she would
compose herself and somehow summon the heart to
face the woman with whom Hawke was obviously
involved. She hurried down the gallery to the rear
stairs, through the moonlit gardens, and across the
arched bridge to the stone-and-glass-domed temple.
Mrs. Kendall, on her way to the kitchens for dinner,
observed through the window Shawnalese's furtive
departure in puzzlement.

When Shawnalese did not arrive downstairs, Rutger
asked Addison to send someone to check on her. The
major-domo replied, "Mrs. Kendall is in the kitchen,
my lord. I'll have her check immediately."

"Never mind," Rutger replied, "I'll ask Mrs.
Kendall." He went to the kitchens, wondering why the
servant was not with Shawnalese. Minutes later he
was hurrying to the temple.

Shawnalese traversed the large moonlit room in
shadowed darkness, moving absently among the furniture. Intentionally she had not lit a taper.

"Shawna?" Rutger's voice echoed through the
domed room.

"Rutger! You shouldn't be here. How did you know
where to find me?"

"Mrs. Kendall saw you come here. Are you all right?"

"Yes. Yes, of course. I felt the need to be alone
before I faced . . . before I faced the guests."

"The guests, or the viscountess?" When he received no answer, Rutger moved to her side. "You don't still harbor your childish adoration of Gayhawke?"

"Don't be ridiculous, Rutger."

At that moment inside the manor, Heather was asking Hawke, "Have you seen Shawna or Rutger?"

Concerned, Hawke scanned the room. "How long have they been gone?"

"Rutger hasn't been gone long, but I don't believe Shawna has come down this evening."

"Not to worry, my lovely sister, I'll find them." Hawke excused himself, and a scant few minutes later he rushed to the dark woodland temple, his rage barely controlled, his thoughts black. Certainly, he reasoned, Shawnalese knew that he would be occupied with his guests and had planned this liaison with Rutger. His mares in season had more restraint than she.

He flung the open door with a thunderous crash.

Dear God! She knew it wasn't an avenging angel who stood framed in the doorway with eyes blazing, but a demon straight from the womb of hell.

"Rutger!"

The bellowed word ricocheted around the room, and Shawnalese waited for the sound of shattering glass.

"Get into the manor! Immediately! Before I forget you're my nephew," Hawke ordered.

Wordlessly Rutger brushed past him, and Hawke slammed the door behind him.

He felt betrayed.

In the face of those feelings, he felt vulnerable—weak. And for that he hated himself, hated her. From the moment he'd seen her at the top of the stairs, when he first arrived in France, he'd craved her with an intensity stronger than ever. And now he knew she was available. Indeed, had she not already been with half the nobility in Paris?

Now it was his turn.

Hawke's gaze searched the dimness, coming to rest on her shadowy form. "Shawnalese." The contemptuously sneered word cracked like a whip. "Have you anything to say for yourself?"

"I can explain, but you wouldn't believe."

"You're right about that. But then, if I believed you, I'd have to be a bigger fool than I've already been, wouldn't I? Besides, your actions have spoken volumes."

"Wait one bloody minute, Carrington."

"I haven't got a minute—for you. There's the door. Use it." He crossed the room to where she stood, bathed in moonlight, and she took his breath away. His anger and everything else in the world faded to nothingness. There were only Shawnalese and he.

Alone.

She moved to pass him and his hand flashed out, staying her. She was everything he detested in a woman, and he craved her voluptuous little body with an obsession that bordered on insanity.

"Release me, please," she said calmly, and felt his obsidian gaze boring into her. "I should make an appearance before the guests begin to wonder."

"I wonder why you weren't thinking of that minutes before I arrived?" His grip tightened.

"Shall I retrieve my dagger?"

Never had he ravished a woman, and Shawnalese would not provoke him into it now. No, he wanted her eager and willing, and no other way. Years ago he had learned that charm was simply a matter of telling a woman everything she wanted to hear, even though both knew it to be a lie. It was, he had discovered, the game all women sought, and he was always ready to play it. However, with Shawnalese it vexed him to do so.

"Shawnalese," he said huskily, "you know I'm not going to allow any other man to have you. You're mine."

"Yours?"

"I've been waiting, sweet love"—he murmured the sobriquet with deliberate but feigned reverence—"since you became seventeen." He questioned how much of what he said was truth, not lie.

"Waiting while you banished me to another country and hoped I'd marry? Waiting while you treated me with nothing but derision and scorn? Waiting while you found so many times and ways to insult me, as you insult my intelligence now!"

Releasing her, he took two steps backward. "I haven't seen this gown."

"You've seen very few of the gowns you lavished on me."

"Turn around, for I'd like to see this one."

She twirled, a flush rising to her cheeks. "Isn't it beautiful? It's quite extravagant."

He wanted to strangle her for playing her kittenish game of innocence, but he knew it was an amusement many experienced women enjoyed. He marveled at her beauty as beams of moonlight cast silvery streaks across her golden tresses, across her perfect face, across her alluring figure. She was a fair-haired temptress with flawless Dresden skin and delicately sculptured cheekbones. His craving, now a painful ache in his loins, begged—no, demanded—satiation. Shawnalese blushed as his regard dropped to her full, firm breasts, straining for release, with each deep breath, from the snug-fitting fabric. Her full, soft lips, now parted, tempted him to taste fully the sweetness of her youth, the taste that had engulfed him so completely before. He wanted to crush her to him, make passionate love to her, his desire for her more than for any woman he'd ever known. Her ethereal beauty, her youth, her look of experienced innocence, of innocent experience, overwhelmed him, and he battled for self-control. She was in his blood as no other had ever been, and none but she could satiate his hunger.

She puzzled at the glazed look in his thickly lashed green eyes. "Does this mean you like my gown?"

"I like your gown."

"Oh."

Still he stared down at her face and could not force his gaze away. So exquisite was she, he knew surely that hers was a face molded by the Creator, just as he knew surely hers was a soul tainted by Satan.

Held in a void of frozen time, Shawnalese felt herself grow weak with the emanation of power radiating from him, but more than that made her tremble with excitement . . . it was his aura of danger. Challenging danger. Irresistible danger. . . .

Stepping forward, he forced his gaze from the flawless beguilement of her face to pull her into his arms and devour her with passionate kisses. His lips moved to her ear. "You're an angel from hell, sent here to torment me," he said huskily, and claimed her eager lips again, slowly moving her backward toward the sofa, his mouth never leaving hers as he lowered her there.

Breathless, eyes closed, she heard her heart pound in her ears, and when his lips lifted from hers, she sensed him still bending over her. He murmured her name, and she felt his lips searching, then again finding, her soft, willing lips. He nipped, nibbled, then devoured them to send shivers of pleasure splintering through her. Clasped in his arms, she pressed tightly against him, and his mouth, hot, moist, eager, moved slowly down her throat to send wild sensations crashing through her. Her body betrayed her, and, breath short, she whispered his name while he trailed kisses across her heaving breasts. Once more his mouth covered hers, full of passion and desire, and when his hand found her throbbing breast, she moaned with yearning as a flame burned deep inside—for what, she knew not.

For barely a moment her senses returned. "No, Hawke, no!" she cried out, and pushed him away, then felt his trembling hand move from the softness of her breast. How could she have allowed things to progress this far? "Stop! Please stop."

Chest heaving, Hawke rose momentarily, then bent to brush her eyelids lightly with gentle kisses that tickled her cheek before he moved to claim her lips again.

"No. Please . . ."

This time when he forced himself away, she smiled at him and, reaching up, brushed the curl from his brow, the only gesture that could hold him from his intent. With perfect recollection, his thoughts flashed back to the last time he'd been in the woodland temple with her. It was a cherished yet painful memory, and he had relived it often in the past two years. The day they had shared a storm and confidences. The day she had vowed to love him for all eternity.

For one infinitesimal span of time, he held Shawny in his arms.

And it sent shock waves to the stratosphere of his heart.

Slowly she slid her hand down his face and caressed his cheek with the back of her fingers as he bent over her. Again she controlled her emotions and whispered, "I must go."

Then she was gone, as though she'd never been

there, leaving him to curse the darkness, to curse her, to curse her hollow vow.

Racing to her room, Shawnalese looked down at her gown in horror. Where Hawke's body had pressed intimately into hers, the brocade was a mass of wrinkles, and a quick glance in the mirror confirmed it would also take some doing to repair her mussed hair. Unconcerned, she could think only of the temple. What had Hawke called her? "Sweet love." Twirling, she was hugging herself with giddy happiness when a knock sounded at her door. "Come in," she called out.

A maidservant entered, carrying a tray. "'Er Ladyship asked me to fetch you a spot o' tea and to check if you're feelin' up to snuff, miss."

"I'm feeling much better now." She was unable to keep the happy lilt out of her voice. "However, I fear I've mussed my gown. Will you please have it repaired?"

"Yes, miss. An' dinner's in a 'alf 'our," she said, and set the tray on the tea table.

Chapter 17

SHAWNALESE FLOATED DOWN THE CURVING staircase, feeling Hawke's heated gaze and the viscountess's frigid eyes fastened on her.

Wreaths of evergreen embellished with red bows and holly-trimmed garlands decorated the great hall. The Christmas tree reigned majestically in the center of the room, and fires blazed in each of the three hearths. The heady fragrance of evergreen drifted in the air, and the perfume of spice-scented candles floated in and out.

Hawke crossed the room toward Shawnalese, the viscountess clinging to him. The arrogance of her posture, the manner in which she held her head, even the grace of her walk, bespoke an attitude of privilege as her due, bred into her and assumed from the minute she'd been born.

Hawke formally introduced the two women. "Paige, may I present my ward, Miss Shawnalese Grenville. Shawnalese, Lady Paige Seymour."

"His Grace told me what an adorable child you are," the tall, slender woman said as she appraised Shawnalese from head to toe. "It was so considerate of the duke to assume your welfare—and in such generous style." She eyed Shawnalese's elegant gown with a haughty air as though she were already the duchess of Foxridge, then added, "But then, Gayhawke's always generous to a fault."

Seething inwardly in humiliation, Shawnalese barely managed to reply graciously, "I have looked forward to meeting you. Actually, I feel as though I already know you."

Hawke relaxed, admiring Shawnalese's poise, aware she must be fuming at Paige's cutting remarks. Apparently the comtesse de Chaternay had achieved more with his willful ward than he'd realized.

But the scathing look in Paige's eyes brought Shawnalese's pride to the fore. "My condolences at the tragic loss of your husband," she added. "You must be heartbroken."

Paige glared at Shawnalese then whirled to face Hawke. "Your Grace"—she pouted prettily and grasped Hawke's arm—"you've not taken me to greet the dowager baroness."

Shawnalese didn't know what she'd expected of Hawke when she arrived in the great hall, but certainly it was not his casual attitude toward her, his attentiveness to the viscountess, his disregard of the woman's acerbic words. Less than half an hour ago he'd held her in his arms, passionately kissed her, called her "sweet love."

"Dinner is served," Addison announced.

Instantly Rutger stood at Shawnalese's side to accompany her to the dining hall, apologizing quietly for having compromised her.

Disturbed, Shawnalese picked at her food, painfully aware of Paige Seymour. Wealth, arrogance, elegance, breeding—all were there in her feminine perfection. The viscountess, a woman well aware of her beauty, flaunted it with an expertise Shawnalese could admire. Not a woman in Paris was more expert, and Shawnalese wanted to die.

After dinner the guests moved to the festively decorated ballroom. A betrothal announcement now? Shawnalese wondered, and then she was being whirled around the room by Chadwick.

To the casual observer, the ball was a triumph for Shawnalese, for in the course of the evening she was pursued with equal fervor by Chadwick, Rutger, and every available man who could get near. Neither Hawke nor Paige missed the continuous commotion that surrounded her.

Yet to Shawnalese the ball was a dismal failure, and her heart ached as Hawke danced with the lovely widow. His arm was tight about her, and her lace gown swirled through the air as, with his head bent toward her upturned face, they twirled about the candlelit ballroom. Throughout the evening Hawke had not danced with Shawnalese, and it seemed that he was totally unaware of her presence.

Shawnalese felt hurt and rejected, and when Hawke presented her the only opportunity for a few private words with him, she said with all the sarcasm at her disposal, "Thank you, Hawke, for coming to my defense when your viscountess lambasted me earlier."

"What would you have me do? Challenge her to a duel? Allow me another month to recuperate from the last one."

Hours later, Shawnalese sighed with relief when Paige and the last of the guests left or retired to their chambers, for there had been no betrothal announcement. Nor would there be, for the remainder of the overnight guests would leave early in the morning to return to their homes for the holidays. Yet somehow it seemed a hollow success.

The next morning Shawnalese reached for her crimson velvet riding habit. Always when she rode Wildfire across the meadows and downs, jumping the hedgerows with the wind whipping her hair, her thoughts cleared and her problems melted away. After donning her black riding boots and hat adorned with a long black scarf, she snatched up her riding crop and strode determinedly through the doorway.

Deep in contemplation, Hawke stood at his study window as she hurried toward the stable, alone.

Soon Shawnalese was galloping across the meadows on Wildfire, her scarf trailing behind. She felt the power of her stallion beneath her as he sailed over the ditches, and his strength flowed into her magically. Moving into the open, she sprinted across the countryside. At the sound of pounding hooves she glanced over her shoulder, surprised to see Hawke on Warrior, bearing down on her. Slowing Wildfire, she cast Hawke a challenging smile, then urged her mount faster, and they raced across the meadows as they used to. It was exhilarating.

As they galloped across the rolling fields, Hawke reached out, grabbed Wildfire's reins, and brought the panting stallion to a halt at the edge of the forest. He leaped from Warrior, clasped her waist, and jerked her from the saddle. Automatically her arms circled his neck, her inviting lips inches from his as he lowered her roughly to the ground.

"You couldn't get me killed in a duel," he said, grimacing in pain as he rubbed his throbbing shoulder. "Are you trying to do it now?"

"I wasn't . . ." She would neither apologize nor explain something that was not her fault. "What are you doing galloping on Warrior, when your wound isn't fully healed?" she asked sweetly, then tossed his onetime remark back at him. "You haven't the common sense of a peasant boy."

"Don't you ever again defy my orders and leave the manor without an escort."

She jerked free of his punishing grip, drew her leg back, and kicked him hard with her booted foot. Her face flushed, her eyes flashed fire, and she stood with hands on hips in open defiance. In the struggle her hat had fallen off; her hair now tumbled down in a waterfall, and the wind whipped it about her face.

Heaven help me! She's magnificent! Hawke thought. His desire was intense, and by all that was holy, he would have her. It crossed his mind that he was her guardian, her protector; then he rationalized that there was no longer anything to protect. After he'd caught her at the woodland temple he had no doubt she was no longer an innocent young girl. He'd dueled because of her, and he was more deserving than the other men who'd received her favors. Still, he knew she would give him nothing by demand, and although it vexed him to use charm, so be it. Whatever it took.

Raging hunger replaced anger, and with a last twinge of conscience, and some half-formed notion that he merely sought to give them the pleasure they both desired, he gently rubbed his knuckles beneath her chin. "You're breathtaking when you're angry, Shawnalese."

His deep voice was husky, and she shivered, his nearness leaving her weak. Struggling mightily, she fought her weakness. "You may save your charm, Carrington, for all your admiring women." She smiled loftily, and her pride overcame all else. "I no longer find it irresistible. You forget, I've been exposed to a great many fascinating men these last years—at your encouragement, I might add—and I'm no longer the enamored girl you sent away."

His gaze fastened on her heaving bosom, and she felt as though he could see through her riding habit, through her chemise. Her breasts burned beneath his intimate regard, and she couldn't stop her rapid breathing, nor did she want to. For some reason his desire-glazed eyes were excitingly heady. In breeches that hugged his long, muscular legs like a second skin, an open-necked shirt with full, bloused sleeves, leather jerkin, and shining Hessians, he looked every inch the virile nobleman, yet, strangely, he also looked every inch the rogue. She knew she had to leave. She turned when he moved,

Hawke's left hand flashed out and twirled her around to face him. His gaze captured hers, and time hung suspended. They stood motionless. Her soft lips beckoned him, drew him closer, closer . . . Bending her back on his arm, he kissed her and his mouth crushed hers ravenously. He pulled her still closer, and the pressure of high-pointed breasts seared into his chest as she struggled weakly, driving him one step closer to the edge. When at last her mouth yielded to his, she returned his kisses passionately. The breeze whipped her long silken hair caressingly against his face, his neck.

Breathless, Shawnalese fought to maintain control. His lips left her mouth and moved to her ear in a trail of burning kisses, and she heard him whisper before his lips again claimed hers in a kiss turned tender, sweet, loving.

"Oh, Hawke," she cried. "Hawke . . ." With all the fortitude she could muster, she leaned back in his arms and tenderly cupped his face between her soft hands. Rising on tiptoe, with all the love in her heart filled to overflowing, she brushed his lips with hers, gently, sweetly. Her heart soared. He had forgiven her! Forgiven her thoughtless actions in France, forgiven the duel, and forgiven the incidents with Rutger. She knew she should twist from his grasp. She was too vulnerable now . . . he was too overpowering.

"You tempt me beyond all reason, Shawnalese," Hawke whispered, pressing her back toward the beckoning forest even though she struggled weakly. "I've waited a long time to hold you like this," he murmured, and urged her farther back to pin her against the hollowed out trunk of a lifeless tree. "Too long." His mouth ravished hers while the fragrance of her hair teased his senses, while her lips tormented his, while her lush little body tortured him. His fingers moved to work at the buttons of her riding habit.

Wrenching free, she redid the button at her neck, breathless, her mouth kiss swollen.

Breathing hard, Hawke rubbed his throbbing shoulder, relieved to feel something other than the ache that tore through his loins. "Are you this way with all men?"

"And if I were?"

"I see you've gone the way of all women of your kind," he said, annoyed at the indifference of her last words, unwilling to admit they cut into his heart. Even now she still held that power over him, and he cursed her silently.

He hadn't forgiven her, Shawnalese realized. The absurdity of it nauseated her, for he still believed her a wanton woman. He had treated her with all the respect he would show a common harlot. At that painful thought, her pride again surfaced. Never would the confident, arrogant Gayhawke Carrington know that she'd once more played the foolish enamored child. Boldly, defiantly, she lied. "That was quite enjoyable, Gayhawke, now that I'm no longer infatuated with you. A light amusement without any involvement."

Stunned, Hawke said, "You don't even bother with the pretenses of being a lady. Were you taught nothing in France, other than the obvious?"

"Other than the obvious!" The words rankled her, and she yearned to cut his icy heart from his chest. She would show him "obvious." Boldly she reached out and her fingertips tiptoed from his throat to the slash in his chin, then moved to trace his chiseled lips. "You were once my best friend, and I could always say what I thought, what I felt, with you. Would you have me do otherwise now? Would you have me play the sugary, brainless woman that other women must play—a charade?"

Wordlessly Hawke pulled her to him and his mouth lowered to claim hers. He couldn't think to answer her question, he could only feel. And what he felt was the white heat she fueled.

Avoiding his hungry lips, she tugged free. "Really, Gayhawke," she said in a mocking tone, and then cast his earlier words back at him: "You tempt me beyond all reason." What angered her most was that it was the truth. With a toss of her head, she picked up her hat and clambered onto Wildfire to race blindly to the manor, her thoughts raging.

More than two years earlier, when he'd sent her away, it had almost destroyed her; but later—when, from the distance of time, she'd looked back and recognized the temptation she'd placed in his path—she'd realized that he had acted with honor and with her best interest in mind. Now, he acted only out of lust.

How could the caring, compassionate Hawke she'd once known be this cold, callous man? Had he always been this way and her love blinded her? Apparently so. Why did she still care?

While Shawnalese rode toward the manor, Hawke was swearing. Before today, a woman had never cursed him, had never kicked him, and had never scorned him. Yet in one hour's time, Shawnalese had singlehandedly set the record for all three. Plus he'd allowed her to ride away without discussing Rutger with her. It couldn't wait. He would call her into his study today. There he was going to ravish her. And then he was going to kill her. With his bare hands.

After dinner, he approached her in the great hall. "I'd like to talk to you. In my study." With that, he moved in that direction.

"Yes. What is it, Hawke?"

Turning back, he saw that she remained seated. "In my study, Shawnalese."

"There's nothing that can't be said here."

"In my study, Shawnalese! Now!"

Chapter 18

Hawke STORMED INTO HIS STUDY AND Shawnalese reluctantly followed. "Close the door."

"No."

"What's the matter with you?" he challenged angrily, moving to close the door. "You're behaving as though I'm going to ravish you."

"The possibility crossed my mind."

"Don't flatter yourself. Besides, I wouldn't have to. Or have you so soon forgotten the woodland temple, or that this morning I spent some time in the forest with you, engaging in a little 'amusement without any involvement'?"

The minute she'd foolishly said them, she had known those words would return to haunt her, but she had not expected it to be so soon. However, Hawke had no right to fling them back at her. So thinking, with all the calm she could assemble, she announced, "I'm writing a letter to a friend in France. I don't want to make a mistake in spelling your name. Are there one or two d's in blackguard?" With that, she struck his face with a resounding slap. Instead of marching from the room, she stepped back with fire in her eyes to admire her handiwork—the red imprint of her hand on his face.

Only the obsidian-green eyes and the darkened visage betrayed Hawke's fury, for his words were icy calm. "Did you enjoy that?"

"Immensely! So much so I think I'll do it again." She pulled back and swung hard, but her wrist was caught in a vice grip right before her hand smashed against his face.

"Witch!"

Dear Lord, how had their relationship degenerated to this? Nevertheless, she had taken enough from him, and a will stronger than her own urged her to deliberately enrage him, to push him to the limits of his endurance by attacking what he held dearly, his damnable title, and she heard herself say, "Witch? Oh, come now, Hawke, certainly you can do me better than that. With your high regard for titles, I would think you could generously endow me with one of my own. Perhaps"—she jerked her wrist from his tightening clasp and placed her fingers to her temple, in the mockery of thinking—"Queen of Witches. But no, that would hardly do, would it? Then you'd have to bow to my wishes—literally. Rather a ridiculous thought, don't you agree?"

An image of the *Phantom Dream*, slipping sleekly through the waves with sails unfurled, flashed into Hawke's mind and he dearly wished he were there rather than here with her. He also wished he'd neither heard of New Orleans nor been there.

When Hawke didn't reply, Shawnalese taunted, "Please be sure when you're practicing, that it's a courtly throne room bow." Then she marched from the room.

Christmas Eve was normally a joyous day for Hawke, spent with loved ones, family, and close friends, a relaxing day for one and all. But on this Christmas Eve day, Hawke's reflections were dark, his mood brooding, forbidding. He'd thought of little other than Shawnalese meeting Rutger in the woodland temple. Indeed, at the ball he had not been able to carry on an intelligent conversation with his guests or Paige, for when he was not visualizing Shawnalese lying in his arms, he was agonizing over her liaison with Rutger. The notion of what she'd become tore through him. Somehow he had to exorcise her from his mind, from his heart.

With a vengeance, Hawke searched his dressing room, his armoires, his wardrobes, gathering every once cherished gift that Shawny had made for him over the years wanting never to see them again—the shirts with tiny, invisible stitches and lavish monograms, the waistcoat embroidered with silver thread, the kerchiefs of finest linen, and the white cravat, edged with delicately tatted lace. Yet after he'd summoned a footman and instructed him to discard the articles, he called the servant back, snatched the items from the hands of the bewildered man, and angrily tossed them to the rear of his wardrobe.

It had cut him to the heart to find Shawnalese in the woodland temple with Rutger, and for a moment he had wanted to kill his own nephew. That truth disturbed him as much as Shawnalese's apparent wantonness—almost. Then his heart filled with contempt . . . contempt for Shawnalese, but even more, contempt for himself, for he still craved her with a passion that bordered on fixation. He could not continue like this. Somehow he must get her out of his system, must also keep her away from Rutger. But sending her away would solve nothing. Rutger might follow her and he'd already sent her away once, to France, and it hadn't worked: now he desired her more than before. Forbidden fruit, he surmised with a shake of the head. With that thought came the solution. He would eat of the fruit until he was sickened from it. He would make her his mistress!

But she was his ward. Even so, he argued that he would be taking nothing from her that she had not freely shared with God only knew how many men in France. Finding her with Rutger had as good as confirmed every rumor that he'd heard in France. Besides, after he had his fill, he would offer a generous dowry and give her a long overdue season in London. Some poor fool would take one look at her angel face and marry her; then she would become her unsuspecting husband's misfortune. Why that troubled him, he didn't know. But it did, greatly.

Also, it occurred to him that even a substantial dowry would not absolve him from the irreparable damage he would do to her already tarnished reputation. At present the rumors were mere speculation. But if Shawnalese became his mistress, everyone would know the truth. After that, only the most desperate—the lowliest of fortune seekers—would offer for her. However, making her his mistress would solve three problems—Rutger, Shawnalese's hot blood, and, of course, his own ever-present lust. He decided that the day after Christmas he would move her out of Foxridge, out of Rutger's life, and into his bed.

Pleased with himself, Hawke felt better than he had since he'd received the damnable letters from France. He'd give Shawnalese some costly bauble and set her up in her own place, the accepted way a gentleman made a woman his mistress. Eager to have the matter done, he decided to give her a piece from Victoria's valuable collection which she had left behind in her haste. Quite appropriate, too. It was only fitting that one of Victoria's prized jewels be worn by another uncaring, narcissistic wanton temptress.

With that thought, Hawke hurried to his study and removed from the secret panel the half of Victoria's jewels that Heather had insisted should belong to his wife. That evening he left his chambers in the south wing with a necklace and earrings in his pocket. Cautiously he made his way to Shawnalese's chambers in the north wing, alert for Heather or Wilhelmina. He opened Shawnalese's door, stepped inside her sitting room, and locked the door behind him.

"Hawke!" Shawnalese gasped in surprise, walking in from her dressing room.

His gaze caressed her in appreciation. Bathed in firelight, she was breathtaking, bringing to mind the many times he'd come upon her unexpectedly, in the great hall or the library, silhouetted by the glow of an evening fire, and like an awestruck boy he'd stood observing her from a distance. "I'd like to give you a present."

She knew she should order him from her room, knew she could not trust herself alone with him, could not trust him. She also knew that after yesterday she should not even speak to him. So with all of those reasons in mind, she said, "A present? For me?"

He reached into his pocket and handed her a small, ribbon-wrapped package.

"You want me to open this now?"

"Yes, I want you to open it now."

With fingers that trembled, she untied the ribbon and unwrapped the paper to find an engraved silver box. Slowly she lifted the lid and gasped at the dazzling necklace and earrings, glowing blood red in the candlelight.

"They belonged to Victoria," Hawke said softly, and lifted the opulent ruby-and-diamond necklace from its velvet-lined case before he guided her to the cheval mirror. Turning her away from him, he fastened it around her neck while she fumbled nervously with the earrings. Studying her image in the mirror, he moved his hands from her neck, hesitated on her soft bare shoulders, then slid down her arms to circle her waist. How long had he waited for this moment? More than two years. Since her seventeenth birthday.

Shawnalese leaned back against his rock-hard chest. He loves me, her heart sang. How long had she dreamed of this moment? Why had Lady Destiny taken so long to make her claim? Her fingers touched the necklace she would forever treasure. Treasure, not merely for its beauty and obvious value, but for something infinitely more precious, the love it represented.

Moved beyond words, she murmured, "My gift for you is under the tree with the others, but"—his hands, which were gently caressing her ears, her nape, her shoulders, suddenly stilled—"it's nothing compared to this. You know it would be if I had the coin. If I could, Gayhawke, I would give you a crown, with precious jewels, more beautiful than any king's . . ."

At her words, Hawke stiffened. "Your gift for me?" His thoughts flashed back to the presents she made each year for the entire family, even Wilhelmina, working laboriously year round on them. Gifts created with love in each stitch. Gifts that money could not buy. Gifts that he had tried to throw away earlier that day. For an interminable moment he both loved and hated her.

Absently his hands moved from her waist to her arms. Uncertainty pricked at the edges of his mind as he wondered if it were possible that she did not know the significance of accepting an expensive gift from a gentleman? How could a woman of her experience not know? Yet for some unexplained reason, he couldn't say the words aloud. He could not say, "From this moment forward you are my mistress."

For the longest time, Hawke held her like that, and his caresses sent shivers down her spine, arousing a need in her. His lips brushed the nape of her neck, and her heart thumped erratically.

Hawke turned her to face him and saw the glaze of her eyes, the open passion on her face. He wondered how many other men had seen that same look. How many had indulged it? At that thought, he hated her, and his hatred mixed with love until nothing was left but passion.

"We belong together, Shawnalese." Hawke murmured the lovely, lying words and questioned silently why it bothered him to deceive her. So when she relaxed in his arms, he smiled with a victory that was bittersweet before he lowered his head to nibble at her ear. Unquestionably Shawnalese had the infamous hot blood of the Grenvilles flowing in her veins, and he intended to stoke the fires. Lifting his head, he captured her face between the palms of his large hands and gazed into her jeweled eyes, his lips inches from hers.

"What if I said I've fallen in love with you?" He couldn't whisper the lie in a declaration. He pulled her to him and devoured her sweet, welcoming lips before sweeping her up in strong arms, to carry her to the bed. Gently he laid her there, lowering himself beside her.

His lips enticed, intoxicated, and whispered promises she had only fantasized while his hand expertly caressed and aroused, spiraling her into the whirlpool of another world she'd never dreamed existed, leaving her tormented body inflamed and craving more. Only for one brief moment did she realize what was happening and stayed his hand.

"Don't stop me, Shawnalese, unless you can say you don't ache for me as much as I do for you."

Taking a deep breath, she smiled and looked up at him with adoring eyes. "Are you asking me to marry you, Hawke?"

"Marry you!" he gasped, springing up. "I'll possess you, Shawnalese, but I won't marry you."

At that, his words of more than two years ago echoed through her head: *I am making a rendezvous with you now . . .*

She wanted to give him her love.

He wanted only her body.

He'd lied to her, beguiled her, and expected her to give herself to him as though she were a common trollop. Scrambling from the bed, she whispered, "Please leave."

He rose to his feet and murmered, "Remember, Shawnalese, stay away from Rutger." He forced a last lie from his lips before he slipped from her room. "I'm a jealous man." Before the door closed behind him, he saw a lone tear trickle down her cheek.

Shortly thereafter, Shawnalese stood in the gallery

overlooking the great hall, watching Hawke greet the
Viscountess Paige Seymour. He bowed to kiss her
hand, then her cheek; his arm circled her waist, and he
steered the stunning woman across the room to one of
two chairs placed near one of the crackling fires. He
lowered his large frame onto one of the chairs as she
boldly flaunted propriety and eased herself down to sit
on the floor at Hawke's feet. She tucked her long legs
beneath her, and her body leaned intimately against
his thigh. Her every gesture openly displayed her
attraction to the man at whose feet she sat.

Of two facts Shawnalese felt certain: Viscountess
Paige Seymour knew how to use her feminine wiles to
her best advantage when she wanted to—and she
wanted to with Hawke—and second, the viscountess
shared her bed with Hawke. At the thought of him
embracing another woman as ardently as he had her,
Shawnalese's face flushed hot. Less than an hour ago
he had held her in his arms, had kissed her passionately, had embraced her and whispered sweet words of
love, yet now he openly displayed his affection for
another woman. What had happened to her dazzling
knight in armor? With an ache in her heart, she realized that her white knight had been but an illusion, an
alluring, fanciful dream. Even so, there was a measure
of security in knowing that never again would she be
blinded by his brilliant light.

"There you are, beautiful lady," Rutger said from the
foot of the stairs, startling her. "Shall we join the family?" He ascended the stairs and clasped Shawnalese's
elbow. Ignoring her reluctance, he escorted her down
the open staircase and guided her to where Chadwick,
Leif, Heather, Lord Edmund Spencer, and Baroness
Wilhelmina were engaged in conversation.

The Yule logs were lit and crackling fires soon
blazed in the three hearths to bathe the room in a soft
glow. Only a few scented candles burned, their fragrance mingling with that from the Christmas tree and

the abundance of evergreen wreaths and garlands. It was a Christmas Eve much like all others from the time Shawnalese had first come to Foxridge. Yet this year no joy sang in her heart, no happiness sparkled in her spirit, for the lovely viscountess sat at Hawke's feet and Shawnalese could see nothing else.

So when the children from the hamlets and village came, their sweet voices raised to sing hymns and carols, it only reminded her of the Christmases past when she, who with childish need had ever sought Hawke's company, had sat near him in joyous and peaceful serenity. But neither would she allow Hawke or the viscountess to see her pain.

Later that night Shawnalese placed the ruby-and-diamond necklace and earrings in their velvet-lined case, wrapped it in paper, and tied it with the same ribbon. She pulled the bell cord and had a footman place the package on Hawke's bed so it would be the first thing he saw after he left Paige—if he left Paige.

At the stable a few days later, Shawnalese called out, "I'm going riding. Does anyone want to join me?"

"I'll go with you, Shawna," Rutger volunteered.

At Hawke's warning glance, she flushed. "Wonderful!" she cried out. "You must come, too, Chadwick—and I'll have no excuses from you. We'll get Grizzly and Leif, also. I'll be the envy of every woman in England to be escorted by four such handsome men. Would you like to come, Hawke?"

"I have affairs I must attend to," he answered coolly, and noticed Chadwick look up at the obvious lie.

Every day thereafter, Shawnalese rode with the four men. Both Chadwick and Rutger were at her beck and call, enthralled by her beauty and charm. Hawke's dour mood darkened with each passing day as she wrapped his best friend and his nephew around her little finger while she ignored him completely.

During the last days of the festive Christmas celebrations, Rutger became more persistent, his attentions harder to evade. Shawnalese tried to discourage him, but not because Hawke had ordered it. Indeed, in her present frame of mind, that was good cause to encourage him. However, she loved the man like a brother and didn't want to see him hurt. Rutger was dear to her, precious. She needed to consider how best to reject him without losing his friendship. Considering this, she stood waiting while Grizzly and a groom saddled the horses. Czar leaped around her, barking excitedly while she patted his head.

In a dark mood, Hawke came into the stable and addressed the two men without a word to her. "I'd like to speak to Shawnalese. Privately."

Chapter 19

HAWKE'S FINGERS CLOSED CRUELLY ON Shawnalese's arm, and he marched her farther into the stables, farther away from Grizzly and the groom. "I've noticed these past two days that Rutger is always with you."

"As are Leif, Chad, and Grizzly," she retorted, and pulled free of his grip.

"Must you always be surrounded by adoring men?"

"Adoring men? We live in the same house. They're my family."

"Chad doesn't live here, though lately I've begun to wonder."

"Chad is a friend. Your best friend, I might add," she reminded him, absently stroking Czar's head. "Certainly you and Chad aren't still competitive after all these years?"

"Why the sudden interest in Chad?"

Tapping her riding crop against her leg, she said tauntingly, "For some reason, I never noticed until I returned from France that Chadwick is quite handsome. His thick auburn hair, his expressive blue eyes, and he's really quite charming. . . ."

Hawke scowled. "I've noticed how much time you've been spending with him and Rutger, but I assumed your interest was in Rutger."

"I told you before, Rutger is like a brother."

"Yes, I've seen that—twice."

Disconcerted, she bent to hug Czar and scoffed defiantly, "Besides, Rutger is too young for me."

"Too young? He's over six years older than you."

"I prefer a more mature man. Like . . . like Chad."

Grabbing her wrist, Hawke pulled her to her feet. A menacing growl emanated from Czar, who stood with hackles raised and fangs bared. Shawnalese smiled.

"Czar, no! Sit, boy," Hawke commanded, and the big wolfhound obeyed instantly. Turning back to Shawnalese, he warned, "Stay away from Chad, Shawnalese. I've seen him devastated by Laurel. I'll not watch him go through that again. Do you understand?" He released her, but his eyes dared her to defy him.

If Chadwick chose to see her, he was certainly old enough to make that decision for himself. "I have no intention of staying away from Chad. He's a fascinating man, and I enjoy his company. He's considerate and a gentleman, which is more than I can say for you these days."

"I'll speak to Chad and stop this nonsense of yours."

"I'm sure you don't dictate to Chadwick, but suit yourself," Shawnalese said, immensely pleased with herself. Then she asked the question that had plagued her from the time she'd come back to England. "Why did you force me to return to Foxridge? You obviously don't want me here."

Why had he? Because at that time he'd still loved her, still hoped, even when her behavior indicated otherwise, that she was the same girl he'd sent to France. But he certainly wouldn't admit it to her. "Call it noblesse oblige."

She laughed scornfully. "If memory serves me, 'noble' is defined as being high-minded or possessing outstanding character. Which of those two definitions do you feel is more applicable to your behavior toward me of late?" She paused as though considering. "Perhaps we could use both. We'll say the night you tried to seduce me in the woodland temple was 'high-minded,' and the night you brought Victoria's jewels and tried to seduce me in my chambers was 'possessing outstanding character.'"

He glared at her, battling the urge to strangle her. "Be assured, I know what noble means. It's what keeps me from throwing you on your back right here and now, to sample that which apparently made you the much sought after favorite in France." His mouth smiled; his eyes did not. Then he snatched her riding crop from her hand, tossed it across the stables, turned, and stalked off.

He found Paige and Heather in the morning room.

"Oh, Gayhawke," Heather cried out, "did Rutger tell you the marvelous news?"

"What marvelous news, my lovely sister?"

"He's going to ask Shawna to marry him. I believe that's what he's doing as we speak."

Hawke stood speechless. At her brother's concerned frown, his forbidding silence, Heather ventured, "Gayhawke, Rutger is in love with Shawna. Surely you've noticed. He's hoping to marry her."

"Yes, well, Rutger is too young to marry." Hawke felt both Heather's and Paige's eyes boring into him. He waited for the maidservant to pour tea and leave.

Then he asked, "When did all this happen, and how do you know about it?"

"I was suspicious, what with the way Rutger trails behind Shawna like a little calf. So we had a mother-son talk this morning."

"How does Shawnalese feel about Rutger?" he demanded, afraid to believe Shawnalese's recent confession.

"She's been spending a lot of time with him and Chadwick lately, but I don't think she has the slightest idea how deep Rutger's feelings are. Still, he's confident that when the right time comes she'll marry him. You know how all the young girls fall in love with Rutger, as with . . ." At Paige's raised brow, Heather didn't finish her statement. "I suppose Rutger's used to having any woman he wants and thinks that includes Shawna. He has considerable to recommend him, and I know Shawna cares for him, although perhaps not as deeply as he does her. I can't imagine her refusing him."

Neither could Hawke. God, why had he not considered this possibility when he'd decided to keep the truth of Shawnalese's birth from Heather? He had to stop this. He couldn't allow it to continue. He had to tell his nephew that Shawnalese was his half sister—as soon as possible, for if Rutger proposed and Shawnalese accepted, there would be no way to keep her from learning that Siegfried Von Rueden was her father. If that happened, Heather would also learn about Siegfried, the husband she still adored, even in death. At all costs, Hawke must prevent that.

He hurried to the stables meeting the trio just returning from their ride.

"Go into the manor, Shawnalese. I'd like to talk to Rutger," Hawke directed.

Shawnalese, certain Hawke intended to warn his nephew again, lifted her chin with stubborn pride and remained where she stood.

A groom arrived with Warrior, and Hawke swung

into the saddle. "Let's take a ride, Rutger," he said. He headed the stallion toward the English Channel.

The channel was turbulent, sending waves crashing onto the shore, and the chilling wind whipped the green surf to foam. Gulls dove for the fish hurled up by the tossing water, and their squalls filled the air.

Dismounting, Hawke stared across the roiling channel as the cloud-obscured sun cast its rays across the shimmering water. Rather than soothing him, the beauty of the scene before him served only to heighten his distaste for what he had to do.

Rutger dismounted and joined Hawke, knowing from his somber visage, the muscle twitching in his clenched jaw, that this was more than another lecture about Shawnalese.

Hawke kicked at the sand, and the wind whipped his cloak about him. He turned to his nephew. "What I have to say is difficult for me, Rutger, and I'm depending upon your honor as a gentleman to keep this matter private. I especially don't want your mother or Shawnalese to know what I'm about to tell you. Do I have your word?"

Perplexed, Rutger pledged, "You have my word."

"I've noticed the growing interest you've developed in Shawnalese, an interest that is more than platonic. There's no easy way to tell you, so I'm just going to say it. You must give up your attachment, Rutger, because Shawnalese is closely related to you—by blood."

A look of astonishment swept over Rutger's face, melting into pain. "You're a liar!" he exploded. "You're a bloody liar!"

"I think you know I wouldn't lie to you, and I certainly wouldn't contrive such a tale."

"How are we related?"

"She's your sister, your half sister."

"God's breath!" Rutger gasped, his blue eyes wide with shock. "Father and . . . !"

"Yes. Your father and Catherine," Hawke acknowledged. "A one-time incident that ruined many lives."

"I don't believe you!"

"Look in the mirror, Rutger. Then tell me you don't believe me."

Stunned with realization, Rutger suddenly knew Hawke spoke the truth. "You rotten blackguard, why couldn't you have told her—told me? Why did you have to wait until now?" Abruptly he drew back and smashed his fist full force into Hawke's jaw, sending him reeling.

Taken unaware, Hawke stumbled backward and caught himself before he fell. "I'm going to let you get away with that one, Rutger, but don't try a second time," he warned, and pulled himself up to his full height. "Besides, fighting won't change what is. When the time is right, I'll tell you everything, but not now. At any rate, you may accept my word, for I swear to you this is the truth." He rubbed his sore jaw. "And don't breathe a word of this to Shawnalese or your mother. Don't take your anger out on innocent people."

Whirling, Rutger mounted and urged his horse into a gallop along the beach. He crossed the downs, the meadow, and rode past Shawnalese, still at the stables. Without a word he sped up the driveway toward the gates. Minutes later Hawke trotted Warrior back to the stable, filled with an ominous foreboding of what was yet to come.

"Hawke, what's wrong with Rutger? He . . . Hawke, what's happened to you?" Shawnalese questioned excitedly at the sight of his jaw, already turning black and blue.

"I took a fall," Hawke said and slid from Warrior to hand the reins to the waiting groom.

"What's wrong with Rutger? He galloped past me without a word." She was sure that Hawke had forbidden his nephew to see her again, and her eyes widened knowingly. They had fought. "Rutger left Foxridge. Did you send him away?"

Whirling at her accusation, Hawke snarled, "He's my nephew. Of course I didn't send him away." His eyes narrowed with icy contempt. "How many other men am I going to fight because of you?"

She gasped, her hand flew to her mouth, and she turned and raced back to the house.

The remaining holidays passed in a blur of misery for Shawnalese. The Viscountess Seymour was ever-present, and Rutger didn't return to Foxridge but stayed at Ravencroft amidst the renovation, without servants except for the caretaker. Shawnalese and Hawke tolerated each other with a cool aloofness that left her ever more unhappy. At times she didn't know what she'd do without the comfort of Grizzly and Chadwick. The only explanation offered for Rutger's absence was that Hawke and Rutger had disagreed, and Rutger had left of his own free will and was welcome back.

Troubled, Heather confided to Baroness Wilhelmina that she felt sure Gayhawke had refused Rutger's suit. That news was greeted with mixed feelings by the dowager baroness, for through the years she had come to care, even have a certain respect, for the young woman she affectionately referred to as the "feisty moppet." Nevertheless, she wanted her grandson to wed a highborn woman.

Early in January Hawke received a missive from France, and after summoning Chadwick the two spent the afternoon behind the doors of his study. When they emerged, Hawke made an announcement. "The news from France is not good. We all know last year's grain crop was devastating and that the bumper grape harvest depressed the price. But now, what with a severe winter and even higher taxes, the situation has deteriorated rapidly. The economic depression is deepening, and peasants in several of the provinces have rioted. In Grenoble hungry commoners pelted the king's troops with rocks and bottles, and the French soldiers fired upon them."

"Oh, no, Gayhawke," Heather cried out.

"I'm afraid so. Only a few were killed or injured, but revolution is in the wind. We sail for France on the *Phantom Dream* with the morning tide. Chadwick and I both have sizable investments in France, and we cannot delay. We need to assess conditions personally and make decisions regarding our interests there." Turning to Addison, he said, "Shawnalese and Lady Heather will accompany us. Have their maids pack their belongings for an extended stay. Notify Grizzly and Thaddeus that they will also be going."

When Hawke had first brought Shawnalese to England, he had confided her parentage to Chadwick. Now, in private, he told his friend, "I'm using our trip as an excuse to get both Shawnalese and Heather away from Foxridge, for I fear that Rutger, burning with indignation, disappointment in his father, and the pain of having to relinquish Shawnalese, will tell one or the other the truth. With both Heather and Shawnalese in France for a few months, the likelihood of that will be considerably less. Time heals all wounds, and Rutger will come to realize that this is a secret he must keep."

In Paris, every day over the following three months that Hawke and Chadwick were not at the château, Shawnalese and Grizzly went to the Palais Royal to hear the dissidents speak. Shawnalese's sympathies were strongly with the plight of the commoner. Guilt nagged at the edges of her conscience—guilt for still living in the world of wealth, privilege, and excess when her heart lay with the downtrodden, the impoverished, and those who no longer had hope. For fourteen years she had lived in that same unrelenting poverty, had felt the painful pangs of hunger, had experienced the knot of fear, never knowing where her next coin would come from or when. Now she had

one foot planted in each world and was straddling
them both, not sure which foot to move or how.

Shawnalese spread a quilt under the towering firs
overlooking the château. She lay there as the warm,
pine-scented breeze of spring caressed her, causing her
to reflect how different her life was now from that of
the gaunt and gray men, women, and children living in
the shadow of the Bastille, their shoulders stooped
with desperation, their eyes dulled with hopelessness.

At that moment Hawke walked out of the château.
Seeing Shawnalese, he envisioned her naked, entwined
in his arms, her golden cloud of hair spread around
them; soft, fragrant, rousing his senses to madness. A
deep longing began in his chest and spread to his
loins, building with intensity as he watched her. He
had to have her, had thought of little else since his
blunder with Victoria's necklace. For near four
months now she'd driven him to the edge of madness.
After they'd arrived in France, she'd behaved like a
polite stranger. He guessed she was involved with a
man, more than likely the same rake as before she'd
left France, for she left the château almost every day.

He knew that Heather had periodically offered to
accompany her on her outings, but Shawnalese had
made one weak excuse after another to discourage her.
Now even Heather was concerned, for Shawnalese
refused to disclose where or how she spent so much
time away from the château. She was nearing twenty,
long past marriageable age, and she never left without
Grizzly, so neither Heather nor Hawke felt they could
demand that she not leave the château.

Several times Hawke had considered having
Shawnalese followed, then decided against it.
Although he was interested in knowing the identity of
the man in question, he really didn't want to know if
there was more than one. For some reason he was not
prepared to accept that.

A few days ago he'd decided he had to sacrifice his

pride and change his behavior toward her. He'd waited for the right opportunity—and that was today. Chadwick had personal business affairs to handle, and Heather would be spending a good part of the day with the duchesse de Vordeaux. He'd given Grizzly a list of errands that would take up his day after he drove Heather to the duchesse's, and now all three of Shawnalese's guard dogs were gone.

As she lay staring up through the swaying fir branches at the cloud formations, Shawnalese felt Hawke's presence and glanced up to see him studying her from beneath hooded lids. He towered over her, his shirt open at the throat to reveal his furred muscular chest. His booted feet were spaced wide apart, and his breeches molded blatantly to his sinewy thighs. Blushing, she swiftly lifted her gaze from the prominence there but met with amused green eyes. Why did he torment her so?

Chapter 20

"MAY I JOIN YOU?"

"I was hoping you would," Shawnalese said mockingly.

Smiling, Hawke dropped onto the quilt beside her. He felt strangely disturbed as she reached up to brush a curl from his brow.

"I'm sorry, I didn't mean to do that. Old habits die hard."

"I hoped you did." He grinned rakishly.

Take care, Shawna, a voice warned her. There's only
one reason Carrington is being charming. He lay
beside her, safely in view of the manor.

"How do you like the château compared to
Foxridge?" Hawke asked.

Breathing deeply of the strong pine fragrance, she
listened to the gentle breeze whistling through the
giant firs and the peaceful chirp of the birds. "Nothing
could ever compare with Foxridge, not even this. The
château is beautiful, but I can't picture you anywhere
but at Foxridge." He lay so near—yet so untouchably
far. "You belong to Foxridge—your castle."

With the deliberate intent of seduction, he corrected
her huskily. "Our castle, Shawnalese."

She knew his intentions, yet still her heart fluttered
crazily.

"I missed you those years you lived in France," he
said softly in all truthfulness, and stared up through
the sun-filtered trees, afraid to look at her for fear he'd
betray his contempt, for fear he'd betray the love he'd
once held for her.

She shuddered at the words which she would have
given anything to hear when first he'd come to France to
take her home. Now all she could think of was the cold,
callous manner in which he'd taken her love and tram-
pled it beneath his feet. He had crushed her heart like the
rogue he was rumored to be, that she knew him to be.
Rumors, to her regret, she had foolishly refused to
believe.

"I'm never free of you, Shawnalese," Hawke admitted before he uttered the lie. "My arms are empty without you, my world is empty." His hand brushed hers.

She was astonished at his nerve. Was this a game he
enjoyed playing only with her—hot one minute, cold
the next, passionate and loving, then cool and indifferent—a game calculated to keep her between agony and
ecstasy?

Propped upon his elbow, Hawke gazed down at her.

"I could easily forget I have ever known any woman but you." He picked up golden strands of her hair and tickled it across her cheek.

His ploy was obvious to Shawnalese. How could he be so heartless with her, as though they'd never shared the years of love? Well, two could play his game. Gayhawke Carrington was going to have some of his own back. No man would ever warm her heart again, not even Hawke. She still loved him, but unlike before, she no longer liked him. Actually, she disliked him. Never again would she throw away her pride for Hawke. She smiled and murmured softly. "How easily?"

"You're not helping me resist temptation, sweet love." He grinned, the desire to reach out and ravish her almost irresistible.

Sweet love indeed! "Is that what you want me to do, Hawke? Help you resist temptation?" She was furious that he thought her still naive enough to believe his lies, his seduction. How many women did it take to fulfill his insatiable lust? she wondered bitterly. No matter. All he would get from her, she vowed, would be the ice dripping from her heart to extinguish the fire in his loins.

Grinning down at her, pleased with her response, Hawke remembered they sat in full view of anyone who walked out of the château. "What I want you to do is be mine, Shawnalese."

"But, Hawke," she answered, wide-eyed, "I have always been that."

Frustrated, he became more bold. "I'll give you your own apartments, all the beautiful gowns you want. Jewels."

"I share Foxridge and your French château. Why would I want my own apartments? You already give me all the beautiful gowns I could want, and I'd certainly think you'd remember that I really don't have a desire for jewels."

Shawnalese Grenville doing that at which she was

expert. Aggravating him. Tormenting him. Frustrating
him. Infuriating him. At the look of smug satisfaction
on her face, he realized she was taunting him. He
couldn't help but smile. No other woman had ever
bested him at his own game. Let her enjoy her small
victory. It would be a brief one.

Deciding to switch to a safer subject, Shawnalese
ran her fingers up Hawke's arm, pleased with the
response the teasing gesture received. "What is happening with the government?" she asked, knowing as
much as if not more than he. Hawke would probably
have fits if he knew that she and Grizzly had daily discourse with Camille Desmoulins, the leader of the revolutionary movement. If he knew she spent many
hours with him and his group at the outdoor cafes or
in Dominique's print shop at the Palais Royal; if he
also knew she'd written several pamphlets for him and
speeches for the other liberals . . . Hawke's words
interrupted her thoughts.

"The Estates-General, summoned by the king, will
be meeting in Versailles shortly. The people are waiting anxiously, hoping this will be the salvation of
France, the answer to all their problems. However, I
believe it'll be the beginning of all-out revolution."

"Why?"

"The Estates-General are supposedly the governing
body of France. Yet they haven't met for more than a
hundred and fifty years. The king's authority is absolute." Hawke lay down beside her, and his shoulder
rested next to hers, barely touching. "Although the
clergy and the nobility—the first two estates—hold
most of the wealth of France, they are less than two
percent of the population. Still, that two percent has
two-thirds of the vote."

"Why did Louis call for a meeting of the Estates-
General if the outcome is a foregone conclusion?"

"The king is desperate. He needs more tax money,
and he feared, rightfully so, that if he arbitrarily again

raised the taxes of the commoners there would be a revolution. This way when the Estates-General votes to raise taxes, it won't be the king's doing. The commoners will have had a voice through the Third Estate. Louis hopes that will quell any uprising, but I don't agree," Hawke said. "There are educated men, businessmen, and brilliant lawyers from the bourgeoisie who have been chosen as delegates to the Third Estate. If there are no changes, the common man will not walk away this time. If there aren't drastic reforms, the Third Estate will rebel, and all of France will rebel with them."

Hawke had not said anything she didn't already know, but she could not comment, for she would not tell him that she'd deeply embroiled herself in the political intrigue in France. Desperately she wanted to discuss the current political issues with him. They fascinated her, stirred her blood, yet she couldn't, for she feared he'd try to prevent her from returning to the Palais Royal. Of late, matters there had become heated, unpredictable, and fights often broke out. Then a thought occurred to her. "Would you take me to see the opening of the Estates-General at Versailles?"

"I suppose I could. You've comported yourself reasonably for the last three months—or at least I haven't had to duel anyone else," he teased, his dusky green eyes twinkling.

"Ever unforgiving. Are you so judgmental because you're Gayhawke Carrington or because you're a nobleman?" She laughed playfully and ran a finger down his rib cage.

Seizing her hand, he clasped it tightly in his, their fingers intertwining. "There is nothing more I could ever want out of life than what I have right now."

He whispered the lie as though he'd read her mind. Words of love, written on the wind. To how many other women had he uttered those exact words, she wondered. Surely they were too numerous to count;

surely Hawke made every woman feel she was the only one; surely he kissed each woman with demanding mastery and then, with passion spent, forgot her name.

"Nor I," she whispered, almost choking on the barely audible words, so poignantly true. A slight tremor of Hawke's arm was his only response. Closing her eyes, she again lay down beside him and commanded her thudding heart to be still.

To Hawke, it was a marvelous day, and they enjoyed the old camaraderie they'd once shared, a relationship he'd never experienced with another woman. But he'd had to fight the bewitching glimpses of Shawny that kept stealing in. How had he allowed the child to so capture his heart that she still had this hold on him two and a half years later? He knew he'd finally broken down her reserve and only Heather's untimely return had interrupted their incinerating kiss. One more hour and the hot-blooded Shawnalese would have been beneath him, whimpering in ecstasy. He was sure of it.

As for Shawnalese, she felt both victorious and bitterly angry. All day she'd fenced with Hawke in a duel of wits, and she'd parried each thrust expertly, skillfully riposted each lunge. For that she was pleased with herself. So when off in the distance she'd seen the familiar coach approaching, she'd permitted Hawke to capture her lips in a savagely passionate kiss of searing intensity. With Grizzly and Heather arriving in minutes, she knew she was safe from herself. The earth-shattering kiss had been all too brief—and not brief enough—for the ecstasy of it still spiraled through her stomach, still sang in her heart, still whirled in her head. When their lips parted, moments before they could be observed, she'd said haughtily, "Is it your good fortune or misfortune that you've been rescued from me, Carrington?" For that, she was also pleased with herself.

What angered her was that Hawke pompously

believed he'd seduced her, that she'd submitted to his charm. What angered her even more was that he was almost right.

Early on the following day Shawnalese and Grizzly went to Dominique's print shop. The Estates-General were meeting in one week, and she was needed. Besides, she'd written another pamphlet for him. "Mademoiselle, monsieur," Dominique exclaimed, "have you heard the tragic news?"

Monsiuer Reveillon, the great wallpaper manufacturer, proclaimed that the commoners' wages were quite high enough and refused to pay more than the starvation wages he now pays. It was the final insult, and more than five thousand men attacked and sacked his factory and then his house, torching them both.

"How terrible," Shawnalese cried. "Was anyone injured?"

"*Oui!* After that the mob stopped aristocrats on their way from the races, forced the women from their carriages, and made them shout, 'Long live the Third Estate!' The French guard had been called out to stop the rioting and opened fire. Several hundred Frenchmen were killed or wounded."

Later that afternoon Shawnalese stood at the chateau's stone well, lost in thought, when a familiar form emerged from the forest, leading England's Warrior. A groom hurried to Hawke's side, talked to him briefly, then led the stallion away. Hawke sauntered toward her, and she could but admire his powerful build, his animal grace.

"Warrior picked up a stone about three miles back. I removed it, but he seemed a little tender-footed, so I walked him home. Would you like some company?"

"How could a woman refuse such a romantic invitation?"

Smiling, he cranked up the wooden bucket and accepted her offer of a ladle of water. "Fair lady, I have stood observing you from afar for quite some

time now and deign to discover from a much closer
position if such beauty could be of this earth. Is that
better?"

"You're quite charming, Carrington—when you
wish to be."

He groaned and lowered his head toward hers, then
pulled back as he remembered they stood openly within sight of the château. He held out his hand to her.

She shot him a challenging smile, accepted his hand,
and prayed earnestly that he wasn't silently offering up
some bewitching enchantment. Wordlessly they
walked toward the forest, not touching, innocent to
any who might happen to glance their way. A safe distance into the pines, Hawke stopped and turned to
her. In one movement he pulled her into his arms.

She was being kissed as she longed to be, by the
only man she'd ever wanted to kiss. His mouth was
ravenous on hers, hot, eager, passionate, sending wondrous sensations sweeping through her entire being.
Her heart caved in, her body betrayed her, all her
plans vanished, and all notions of vengeance or victory
fled. There was naught but Hawke and her as she
returned kiss for kiss, deeply, demandingly, while his
hungry lips devoured hers. She gave a small moan,
and he planted blistering kisses everywhere—her
cheeks, her throat, and then trailed slowly down to her
heaving breasts. Fire shot through her veins to melt
what little resistance that remained and as she whispered his name, her fingers entwined in the curling
thickness of his hair. Then he kissed her longer and
deeper, his arms crushed her against his granite chest
and flanks, their bodies molded together, and the searing heat that pierced her halfway between her waist
and thighs rose to the crest of her breasts. Wondrous
waves of pleasure engulfed her. Breathing hard, he
moved his lips slowly from her mouth to her ear, and
whispered her name, hotly, tantalizingly, then planted
burning, nibbling kisses there. Shawnalese sucked in

her breath, held it, then released it in one long rush as her body trembled uncontrollably. She was encircled in his arms, and his drugging kisses, his skillful caresses, captured reality and sent it soaring out of reach.

It was quite simple really.

He wanted her.

He would have her.

Here.

Now.

"This is where you belong," he murmured into her ear.

Breathless, she protested weakly, but his fiery, sensuous mouth stilled her protests to work their magic on her once more. She clung to him, felt the passion between them building in intensity, felt his lips trail evocatively down the hollow of her throat with scorching, heart-pounding kisses that moved slowly to the swell of her throbbing breast, felt the delightful sensations sweep through her body. Then she also felt his fingers work at her buttons and submitted helplessly to the gentle touch of his mouth as he expertly began to explore, searchingly, the fullness of her cleavage and smothered her breasts with tiny, tantalizing kisses.

Fully aroused, Hawke encircled her tiny waist with his arm and pulled her soft supple body tightly against the hardness of him, feeling, with no small amount of satisfaction, her surrender completely to his will. Gently he eased them to the bed of pine needles, still locked in each other's embrace, their mouths clinging.

All reality gone, Shawnalese felt his hand slip up her thigh. Drifting helplessly, she inhaled deeply and her nostrils filled with the fragrance of pine needles.

The perfume of pine! Christmas. Deceit! All flashed back in vivid detail. Once again Hawke's deceptive words, his treacherous false kisses, his mesmerizing embraces—all expertly used to entrap—had lured her in. Grasping his exploring hand with hers, she pushed at his chest with the other, to no avail. He was not even aware of her efforts. Releasing his wrist, she instantly held her dagger and cried out, "Turn me loose, you rutting Casanova, or you'll feel my blade!"

Glancing down, he saw the dagger in her hand. Snatching it from her, he threw it as far as he could, then, breath short, he sat up. Riffling his fingers through his hair, he battled to control his unbridled passion.

Shawnalese sat up, more angry at herself than with him.

She'd known exactly what he would do.

Then she'd helped him do it.

"Lecher! Vile rake!" she exploded, accepting none of the responsibility herself.

Gradually Hawke won the battle over his rampaging desires; now he struggled with his urge to strangle her. She gave him no respite. He glared down at her and growled, "What is it that you want, Shawnalese?" At her silence, he added, "I thought I knew, but apparently I was wrong."

She flushed at his meaning. Humiliated, she murmured, "I don't remember hearing a proposal from the almighty duke."

"You can't be serious?" Then his eyes narrowed in deliberation. "I ought to marry you. You'd then get everything you deserve. I would see to that."

Chapter 21

HAWKE KNEW HE'D DO ANYTHING TO HAVE HER, anything except marry her, for she'd make his life a living hell—exactly as she did now. With that thought, he tried to redeem himself from his scurrilous remarks, for he'd definitely never possess her with that tack. He brushed his fingertips over her softly flushed cheeks.

Recognizing the glazed look that had never left his dusky green eyes, she seized the opportunity to regain some advantage in this heartbreaking game of love that Hawke played so casually, so expertly. "Is this a proposal, Duke of Foxridge?" Her eyes twinkled mischievously.

At the teasing in her voice, the taunt in her eyes, he laughed. "No, this isn't a proposal, you brazen vixen. Besides, do you think I'd propose to merely any wench who happened to be walking in the woods?"

"Point well made." She tossed a pine cone at him, and then another and another.

He chuckled as she continued to flay him with pine cones, then his strong arm shot out to wrap around her waist, press her back and pin her to the ground, tickling her.

"No, Hawke. Please. No." She giggled. "Please."

Just as quickly he released her. "I'll honor your pleas for mercy since you now know who is master here."

"You, master? You'll never see that day!"

"Time decides all things."

"Shall we place a wager on it?"

Smiling, he bent over her where she lay on the forest floor, and brushed the pine needles from her hair. But when she stuffed a pine cone inside his shirt, he playfully rolled her among the needles until she was covered with the prickly leaves. Abruptly he snatched his hand away, and his smile turned to a frown. For a brief time it was as it had been before she'd gone to Paris, when they'd been the best of friends, the best of opponents, with nothing in between. Unable to resist, he pressed his lips to hers in a brief, bruising kiss that suddenly turned tender and caressing.

"It seems that's the only way to shut you up." Then he kissed her once more. When he stopped, her eyes were closed and her face turned up, to be kissed again.

"Shawnalese," Hawke barked and her eyes flew open. "You can only tempt me so far without my resistance caving in and you've almost exceeded that already today. We'd better leave, or we won't be leaving for the next three days. The choice is yours." With that he removed the pine cone from inside his shirt, handed it to her, and wondered why he turned away from all he'd done everything within his power to obtain. What was wrong with him suddenly?

Shawnalese scrambled to her feet and left to find her dagger.

Angry with himself that he'd allowed her to escape, frustrated with the ache of desire that still tore through his loins, Hawke warned her while she searched for her knife, "There won't be another incident like today, Shawnalese. The next time you'll get exactly what we both want, I promise you. You don't toy with me. Eventually you'll submit."

She glanced up from where she hunted. "Submit? How do you spell it, Hawke?"

"How do you spell submit?"

"Yes. It's a word with which I'm unfamiliar." Her eyes held a teasing mirth at besting him.

"You spell it, p-l-e-a-s-e G-a-y-h-a-w-k-e." He grinned and sprang to his feet.

"Hah! You and all the king's men couldn't force those words from me."

"There will be no force."

She found and scabbarded her dagger. He sat with one knee propped up, his arm casually resting there, and chuckled. She'd noticed a slight softening in his attitude toward her. Perhaps it was a new beginning, she thought. Possibly with time he'd forgive her the duel he'd fought over her and would realize the rumors about her weren't true, would even come to forgive the incidents with Rutger.

"You were far away, Shawnalese. Is something bothering you?"

It was the first concern he'd shown for her since he'd sent her away, except, of course, for the times he played his games of love, hoping to get her into his bed. "It's nothing, I was simply thinking."

"What troubles you?"

"There was a time I could talk to you, Hawke, tell you how I feel, tell you anything, but now it seems that we're always at odds."

There was a touch of consideration in his question that encouraged her, and she moved to sit beside him. "I have this longing to make a contribution to the world, however small. What or how, I don't know. I only know that I'm not happy with the shallow life I lead. It seems there should be some way that I can help others." She shrugged helplessly. "Possibly it was a mistake for you to educate me, for since I first came to Paris I find myself restless and yearning—for what, I know naught. We're surrounded by misery, poverty, despair. The kind I lived with in New Orleans. I consider all that could be done to help these unfortunate people, people who now live without hope. Yet, what can I do? I must have asked myself that a thousand times." She sighed. "Perhaps I simply yearn to find my destiny."

Hawke stared down at her in stunned surprise, his sense of loss excruciating. Every word out of her mouth had been Shawny, and he hated the icy beauty before him who'd destroyed the child of his heart, for it was a bitter loss.

At the look of wrath on Hawke's face, Shawnalese knew she'd made a mistake in sharing her feelings. She queried softly, "Aren't you going into Paris?"

"Why? Are you anxious to meet whomever it is that you meet everyday after I leave?"

Surprised that Hawke knew of her comings and goings, Shawnalese felt hurt that he hadn't cared enough to find out where she went, or with whom. Then she felt angry that again he assumed the worst of her. "One would think the irresistible duke could persuade me to relinquish whomever it is that I meet every day. Perhaps you're losing your touch, Carrington."

"What would it take?"

"Why don't you simply ask me to?" Triumph gleamed in her eyes.

Suspicious, Hawke turned to look at her. "You've been sporting with me, haven't you?"

"That was extremely unfair of me considering how high and honorably you've been behaving. Wasn't it?"

Laughing, he replied, "It's against the rules."

"Oh, I see. Exactly which book of privileges are those rules in? The privileges of nobility, or the privileges of men?" Smiling, she reached up and brushed the wayward curl from his brow. It was time for a truce. "I would imagine women fuss over your hair," she said sincerely, fingering the attractive ebony waves. "Few men can boast of such a handsome head of hair."

"Sweet love"—Hawke's words were biting, sarcastic—"you've learned my secret. Will you betray me like Delilah?"

"Could I enslave you if I sheared these beautiful locks,

Samson?" Shawnalese tried to calm the wildly beating heart that betrayed her each time she touched him.

"Your beauty enslaves me," Hawke murmured, envisioning her in his bed.

"Is that all that's important to you? What if I were plain—would you turn away from me?"

"If you were plain you'd still be the most desirable woman I've ever known," he answered truthfully.

"That seems to be all that's important to you, Hawke—your desires, your passions of the body and not the heart. I could be anybody, any body, and it would make no difference. I'm not a person to you. You don't care that I have feelings, that I have a heart, a soul."

"Have you?"

Ignoring his remark, she ranted on, bristling with indignation, "I'm merely another woman, any woman—there only for the purpose of fulfilling *your desire*—you hope."

Smoldering dusky green eyes bored into hers, his burning kiss stilled her protests, and when he leaned his body closer, hers surrendered without a fight. Tenderly he enfolded her in his arms, holding her lovingly.

With deliberate intent, with planned malice, both to teach her a lesson, he began a tender assault on her body. Feeling her responding, Hawke smiled inwardly with satisfaction. He would teach her who called the tune. "Sweet love," he breathed into her ear, the only sounds the song of the birds, the drum of his heart.

His lips on hers kissed her softly, sweetly, lingeringly, and time ceased while she languished in his embrace. She trembled in his arms, her anger now gone, and then he released her as suddenly as he had kissed her and shoved her away.

"Other than fulfilling *your desire*, my passionate hell-cat, what else am I to you that you would fault me? Your destiny?" With that, Hawke laughed sardonically, sprang to his feet, and strode toward the château.

She cursed him every step of the way. How could she have behaved so?

"What was that all about?" Chadwick inquired, walking up behind Hawke.

"Damn willful, independent woman! She's enough to goad a man to drink!"

"I see nothing's changed between you two. I saw your little dalliance just now. Do you intend to marry Shawnalese?"

"Marry Shawnalese? If I wouldn't marry Shawny, I certainly wouldn't marry Shawnalese!"

"You don't know that any of the rumors are true, Hawke," Chadwick admonished. "You've not one shred of evidence. Not even a name. Think about it."

"You think I need to catch her in the arms of one of her lovers to know the truth? Five minutes more with Rutger in the woodland temple, and I might have done that exact thing. Or have you forgotten?"

"Well friend, I don't believe those things of Shawna," Chadwick retorted. "And if you weren't so blinded by what your mother did, neither would you."

"Leave Victoria out of this."

"I'm most happy to leave your mother out of it. Can you? She affects everything that you do. You won't trust a woman even when you're staring at her. Don't trifle with Shawna, Hawke."

"Trifle?"

"I know you well, ol' chap. You're like a hound on the scent of a fox."

"What's your interest in this? We've never had a problem over a woman before."

"Shawnalese is not simply another woman, and I give you fair warning, Hawke. If she shows the slightest interest in becoming your mistress, I'll involve myself as her protector. You may own her—for now—but I value her, so heed my warning well, friend. I won't stand idly by and let you hurt Shawna. I'm also informing you now, as of today, that I'm going after her. I'll not see her thrown to the wolves. Before I'll allow her to become your mistress, she'll be wed to me."

"The hell she will!" Hawke roared, his face livid.

Stunned by Hawke's reaction, Chadwick stared at him in shocked silence before he spoke. "Do you mean you'd rather see her become a fallen woman, and your mistress, than married to me?" he asked incredulously, his eyes narrowing. "Do you care that little for her? Or is it that you want her that much?"

Hawke grimaced, for Chadwick had named it—except that it was both: he cared that little for her, and he wanted her that much. "Shawnalese is already a 'fallen woman,' as you generously express it. She's my ward and I won't give my permission for her to wed you, so don't get involved in this, Chad."

"Are you refusing to give me permission to court her?"

"No." Hawke's expression clouded in fury, and bridled anger edged into his voice. "But only because it's my agreement with her that she may see anyone she chooses."

"I didn't realize that included rakes who want only to get her into their bed. Rakes such as yourself."

"It's Shawnalese's decision if she wants to become my mistress. She's hardly the naive child she once was. I'm not going to ravish her. I won't have to—she'll come willingly. And I'm warning you, Chad. Stay out of this. Besides, I don't want to see you hurt again. Remember Laurel?" Chadwick didn't deserve to be burdened with Shawnalese's well-used little body. Besides, he reserved that particular taste of heaven and hell for himself, at least until the hell was burned out of his loins.

"What's really going on here, Hawke? Are your concerns for me? Or am I interfering with your plans for

Shawna?" Chadwick accused, aware of Shawnalese's one-time infatuation, knowing his friend's success with women.

"I'll never give you permission to marry Shawnalese, Chad."

"Well, I don't need your permission—and I do intend to marry Shawna. I made the mistake once of waiting for approval, I won't make it again, even if we have to elope to Gretna Green. So don't be concerned for me. I'm quite capable of protecting myself, if need be. And you've greatly misjudged Shawna. Your distrust of women won't let you see otherwise."

The two friends stood glaring at each other wordlessly, when Shawnalese came into the room.

"Would anyone like to go riding?" she asked, breaking the heavy silence, oblivious of the encounter that had just taken place.

"That's an excellent idea," Chadwick piped up. "Let's go. I'd like to talk to you."

Riding sidesaddle on Wildfire, Shawnalese raced across the fields, Chadwick pacing her on one side, Grizzly on the other. After a time Chadwick reached out and grabbed her reins, slowing them to a canter. "I informed Hawke today that I wished to pay court to you."

Shawnalese's knuckles whitened as she gripped her reins. "What did he say?"

"He has no objection if—"

"Of course he doesn't. Why should he?" Shawnalese interrupted bitterly. "I've cared for you dearly all these years, Chadwick, like family. I . . . it will take a little time for me to adjust to thinking of you in any other way."

"I think you'll find me a man of considerable patience where you're concerned, Shawna."

"I don't know your intentions, and please don't misunderstand my reasons for saying this, but it's because I do care that I must tell you that I'm not certain I wish to marry. Also, I've given my situation considerable thought lately, and I'm not comfortable with continuing to accept Hawke's largesse. After we return to England, I intend to seek employment. I feel Gayhawke and I will be much happier apart." With that, she kneed Wildfire and galloped briskly toward the stables.

Chapter 22

"I'M A WEALTHY MAN, YOU KNOW," CHADWICK teased as he lifted Shawnalese from Wildfire. "One day I'll be the earl of Greystone." He presented his arm, and they started toward the château.

"You know I have no use for titles, and wealth isn't important to me, Chad. Naturally I have no desire to be poor, but . . ." Pausing, Shawnalese continued, "I want you to know that I've been going to the Palais Royal to listen to the speeches of the liberals. I not only agree with them, Chad, I cheer them. I'm a strong advocate of liberty and equality. Hardly wife material for a nobleman, am I?"

"Have you ever mentioned this to Hawke?"

"No," she answered softly. "Hawke's interest in me seems to have changed considerably from the time I first left England to live in Paris. His regard now seems to be . . . of a different nature. Chad, I ask for your word not to tell him about the Palais Royal."

"Is that wise?"

"It is my wish. Have I your word?"

"You have my word." Chadwick hesitated, then asked, "Then you're not involved with a man?"

"Involved with a man? No." She glanced up at him. "Is that what Hawke thinks? Yes, I suppose it is. Well, you might say I'm 'involved' with several men." Chadwick made no comment, so Shawnalese continued, "Camille Desmoulins and the other liberals. I help write pamphlets and speeches for them. I help Dominique in his print shop."

"God's teeth, Shawnalese! You don't know what you're doing."

"I fear I shall never become the lady so many have tried to make of me. Now, I've done naught but talk of myself. You've never told me what happened with Laurel, you know."

"Laurel?" Chadwick's enunciation of her name conveyed a wealth of pain, a wealth of love. "I searched for her for more than a year. Every city, town, and hamlet in England and France. I even went to Spain, where she had a distant relative. Sent her scores of letters, yet I didn't receive a single one from her. If she wanted to, certainly she could have found some manner to get word to me." He sighed. "It's been almost three years. She's probably married and has a child or two by now."

"I'm so sorry, Chadwick. I never knew the whole of it," Shawnalese said, stopping outside the château. "Did her father refuse your suit?"

"Yes. An old family feud that went back many years. It had nothing to do with Laurel or me, but we paid the price for it." His voice broke, and he scuffed the dirt with the toe of his boot. "Laurel is the only woman I ever loved. I thought I could never love again—until now."

True to his word, Hawke took Shawnalese and Heather to Versailles to watch the Estates-General open with a glittering parade. A few days later Shawnalese heard the latest news at the Palais Royal.

"My fellow countrymen," the speaker cried out, "there is hope at last, for today our delegates have demanded the right to vote by population. They also demanded freedom of religion, of the press, of speech, of assembly, the right to be taxed only through representation, and equality before the law."

Rousing cheers echoed through the crowd.

A few minutes later Shawnalese and Grizzly entered Dominique's print shop, and she picked up the latest pamphlet to read that the cost of the four-pound loaf had gone still higher, and that hunger deepened. Peasants in the provinces, the pamphlet said, now survived on husks and boiled grass, and in Paris the impoverished could only afford bread made from soured or pest-infested grain. Disease ran rampant.

New Orleans flashed into Shawnalese's troubled thoughts, and for a moment the painful gnaw of hunger tore at her stomach. "Dominique," she said, "I've written another pamphlet. Do you want me to start setting it to type?"

"*Oui*, mademoiselle. *Oui*," Dominique replied. "Have you heard about the miracle?"

"Miracle? No. What's happened?"

Dominique wiped his ink-stained hands on his apron. "In answer to a prayer, someone has reopened a small cafe in the Faubourg Saint-Antoine, a nobleman, 'tis rumored, and is feeding the famished each a cup of vegetable soup and a large chunk of cornbread."

"Oh, Dominique, that is the answer to a prayer!"

"Do ye know this to be true?" Grizzly asked.

"*Oui*," Dominique said, leaning his bulk against a table cluttered with assorted pamphlets. "I went this morning to investigate for the newsletter, and the unemployed, homeless, and starving wind through the alleys and streets in a never-ending thread. Those too

weak to stand in the line are served in the streets or
alleys where they slump."

"Ye dinna know who the saint is?"

"Non," Dominique replied. "The man's hired locals
to unload the wagons, cook, dole out the food, and
wash the cups. Mademoiselle, monsieur, the wagons
never stop rolling, and the cafe never closes."

Shawnalese and Grizzly continued to go to the
Palais Royal almost daily, as embroiled in the politics
of "reform or revolution" as ever. Sundays were quiet
and peaceful, a welcome respite from the plight of
France. On one Sunday, Shawnalese, finished with her
evening meal, said, "If you'll excuse me, I'll change
clothes. Chad has offered to take me for a carriage
ride." She caught the withering look Hawke flashed
Chadwick.

"Take Nadine and Grizzly with you," Hawke
ordered.

"But of course," Shawnalese replied coolly. "You've
no need to mention it."

Sometime later, the brilliance of the full moon
reflected on the horses and carriage, hoofbeats reverberated in the air, their rhythmic resonance mingling
with the soft winds that blew a light perfume throughout the countryside. All were the sights, sounds, and
fragrances of peace, contentment, and happiness—but
Shawnalese was neither at peace, content, nor happy
as she rode beside Chadwick.

"Stop the carriage, Grizzly," Chadwick said, and
turned to Shawnalese. "Shall we walk awhile?"

They strolled along a country lane while the conveyance waited. Chadwick talked, and Shawnalese's
thoughts, as usual on Hawke, abruptly snapped to
what he was saying.

". . . and knowing what we might be facing with the
French government, you shouldn't go to the Palais
Royal again." Her surprised expression turned to one
of anger.

"I suppose Hawke put you up to this?"

"Hawke put me up to nothing. Does your whole world still revolve around Hawke, that you can have no other thought in your head?" Chadwick exploded, now fully provoked. "Or is it that you still hope his world will revolve around you?"

Wincing at his words, at what must be obvious to everyone, Shawnalese placed her hand over his. "I'm sorry, Chad, I didn't mean to insult you. I'd never intentionally hurt you, for you mean too much to me." She suddenly found herself in his arms, and his warm lips claimed hers in a kiss that left her altogether unmoved.

"I apologize, Shawna, for being curt. I was merely thinking of your safety and your reputation. The situation in France is rapidly deteriorating, on the edge of revolution." He lifted her hand to his lips, held it there, then again pulled her into his arms. "Shawna, I have discovered I'm falling in love with you. Love not as friends as we once were, but as a man loves a woman."

Catching her breath, Shawnalese pushed him away. Never had she allowed a man other than Hawke to take such liberties. "You move too fast. Since I left Foxridge, I've been taught the charades that are supposed to be acted out between men and women. I cannot play those games with you, Chad. You're too close to me. I'm too fond of you."

"We don't need charades between us. If I ask you to marry me, will that convince you I'm not playing a game?" Chadwick ignored her shocked gasp and his mouth lowered to close over hers, but she evaded his kiss.

When he released her, she hesitated a moment, then asked, "Chad, are you aware that I'm . . . Do you realize that I was born illegitimate? I don't know who my father is."

"Of course I'm aware. What possible difference can

that make? I haven't misrepresented myself as the Prince of Wales," Chadwick teased, "that you might think you need evidence of royal blood, have I?"

"No." She sighed and felt a warm glow flowing through her. "Please give me a little time, Chad. I need to consider this."

"A little time, and no more. One month, perhaps two. We know each other too well to have need of a lengthy courtship. We'll be back in England by then."

She felt Grizzly's eyes, from where he sat on the coachman's seat, bore into her, and she turned away, for he knew well how she felt about Hawke.

The following morning Shawnalese, with her Christmas sewing and a quilt, started toward the side door when she heard a carriage arrive and saw Hawke appear from nowhere to accept a large basket of flowers from the coachman. Hawke frowned and walked toward the château with the basket. Puzzled, Shawnalese moved back into the room. Without a word, he marched in and handed her the basket.

"How sweet," she said, taking the bouquet to set it on the table. Pleased with the scowl that formed on his handsome face, she opened the card to read:

> *The most lovely flower wilts by comparison to the beautiful lady who has stolen my heart.*
> *Chadwick*

Slipping the note among her sewing, she commented as though to herself, "At least one gentleman in this château knows how to treat a lady." She turned to leave, and Hawke grasped her shoulders with a biting grip, pulled her roughly into his arms, and kissed her hard. For a moment his kiss galvanized her, then she coldly pushed him from her. "Perhaps you should take lessons from your friend."

"You expect me to court you?" Hawke spat. "Surely

you jest!" Still, his thoughts flashed back to the night of the masquerade and the earl of Wellhampton's words: "It would be easier to catch the moonlight than to hold such a woman." Without question, she now was fully aware of her power over men.

At that moment Heather entered the room and saw the floral arrangement. "How lovely. Who are they from?"

Hesitantly Shawnalese answered, "Chad."

Obviously surprised, Heather smiled. "That's wonderful, Shawna. But you be careful," she warned, sipping her morning tea. "Except for Laurel, Chadwick has a scoundrel's reputation with women."

"A reputation like Hawke's?"

"Not quite that bad," Heather replied, chuckling at her brother's grimace.

The following day at the Palais Royal the air rang with condemnation. "The king has turned on the people and barred the Third Estate from their chambers. But our representatives won't be defeated. They have gathered on the indoor tennis court and taken an oath never to separate until the new constitution giving the commoner a voice in government is established. Long live the Third Estate!"

"Long live the Third Estate!" the crowd shouted. "Long live the Third Estate!"

Two days later Shawnalese learned that the king had intervened with a royal speech: "If you three estates cannot agree, I the king will myself achieve the happiness of my people." The implication—nothing would change.

Protest reverberated through the air at the Palais Royal. "We've been betrayed by our king!" the liberals cried out. "No more king!"

"No more king!" the crowds chanted. "No more king!"

Shawnalese stood frozen as the deathly seeds of revolution thundered through the air of the Palais Royal, through the air of Paris, through the air of France.

Three days later she paced the château's gardens, anxious for Hawke and Chadwick to leave so she could hurry to the Palais Royal.

Through his study window, Hawke saw her and grinned with satisfaction.

For days now he had tried to banish her from his thinking, but regardless of how intensely he concentrated on his business affairs, regardless of with whom he engaged in political discourse, regardless of how deeply he slept, Shawnalese's jeweled green eyes, shimmering golden hair, and voluptuous little body crept into his thoughts and sped to his loins, driving him half-mad with desire. Nowhere could he escape her insidious invasion of his mind and body.

She passed by his window again, and his grin broadened into a triumphant smile. During those same days, he had contemplated the words that would stir her heart, and now there she was walking outside his window. It was the perfect opportunity. Without the slightest twinge of conscience, he walked out of his study, snatched from the vase the bouquet of flowers Chadwick had sent her, and sauntered outside. If she wanted to be romanced before she'd warm his bed, then so be it.

Shawnalese saw him with flowers in hand crossing the manicured grounds toward her. Certainly he wouldn't try anything so obvious, would he? She sighed, for she was in no mood for his game playing today. She should be at the Palais Royal right now. She had written two more pamphlets and another speech to be printed, but Gayhawke Carrington wanted to play more silly games. More dangerous games.

As he approached she recognized the flowers Chadwick had sent her. How *dare* he? Hawke could not even buy his own flowers in his pursuit of her. How dare he! By the time he reached her side she was furious. Not simply furious, enraged.

He winked and gave her his most begiling smile.

Her longing to sneer almost overwhelmed her, and she ached to wipe the arrogant, self-assured expression from his handsome face. Only strength of will kept her from doubling her fist and walloping him. With all the calm reserve she could assemble, she smiled her own sweet smile of welcome and with a concerned look inquired, "Do you have something in your eye?"

Without the least hint of embarrassment at her question, Hawke returned her smile, offered her Chadwick's bouquet, and in a most seductive voice said, "I had to check if what I saw outside my window was genuine or merely a celestial figment of my imagination."

In a delectable, gentle tone that belied the rage broiling within, she said, "If you're here, as usual, to attempt to seduce me, I suggest that you take my flowers and your speech and leave."

So he took her flowers and his speech, and he left.

The next morning Shawnalese bearded Hawke in his study. "I've decided to accept your apology," she said.

"My apology?"

"For your technique yesterday morning—my flowers, your speech."

He grinned and leaned back in his chair. "I didn't apologize."

"Well, I knew you wanted to. Only your stubborn pride kept you from it. So I'll accept the apology you would like to make."

"If it's an apology you want, if you'll walk with me in the forest, unchaperoned, I will apologize."

"You are a shameless, despicable, depraved rake."

"I knew it!" Hawke shouted, jumping to his feet. "I knew you still loved me."

Her eyes opened wide and her lips formed a perfect circle.

He chuckled in triumph. She giggled. He laughed.
She laughed with him.

A short time later, Hawke walked outside when a
courier delivered still another large, crystal vase
arrangement of flowers for Shawnalese. Without the
slightest twinge of conscience, he read the note;

> *I'm counting the days.*
> *Chadwick*

Hawke stared off into the forest of swaying pines.
He wondered if he'd made a strategical error with
Shawnalese, been too confident, too sure that the
young girl's love for him still beat in her breast. Why
did she resist him when she probably had denied few
others? For the second time in as many days, the earl
of Wellhampton's words—"It would be easier to catch
the moonlight than to hold such a woman"—rushed to
haunt him. But he did not want to keep her, he argued
silently, he only wanted to linger with her for a while.
For the first time in his life, Hawke was unsure of himself about a woman.

And now he felt the hounds baying at his heels.

A distant rumble interrupted his ruminations.
Thunder? He looked in the distance toward the sound
and dust-clouds hovered over the road. Instantly he
knew: regiments of troops. The king's army.

Family and servants rushed from the château to a
nearby hilltop to view the endless procession of armed
soldiers—many fierce-looking and foreign—marching
to drum cadence, with cannons trailing.

Shawnalese stood frozen, her heart pounding wildly
as the formidable army advanced. The air reverberated
with the tramp of soldiers, the beat of drums, the
thunder of horses' hooves, and the rumble of rolling
cannons and artillery wagons. The dust hung ominously in the air as King Louis XVI prepared to put down
resistance and resume the absolute monarchy with an

unprecedented buildup of troops. Thirty regiments of French, Swiss, and German soldiers now surrounded Paris and Versailles.

Cannons were aimed at the Hall of Assembly in Versailles where the deputies of the Third Estate worked with conviction on a new constitution for France—on the indoor tennis court, vowing they would leave only by force. "The king has turned on his own people," the dissidents at the Palais Royal exhorted loudly. "The king knows French soldiers will not again fire on Frenchmen, so now he orders in Swiss and German troops. I say let us die at the hands of foreign soldiers, but let us die free!" A week later Hawke and Chadwick left for Fontainebleau.

"We'll return within the week," Hawke said. "This trip will complete our affairs in France, and then we'll return to Foxridge immediately. The king has matters well in hand, and with troops camped right down the road there's no fear for your safety. Actually you'll be safer here than with us, because of all the riots in the provinces. Heather and Shawnalese, you're to stay at the château until we return. Don't take any chances by going into Paris." He turned and looked directly at Shawnalese. "Do you understand, Shawnalese?"

"I understand, Hawke."

Glancing at her suspiciously, he said, "I want your word that you won't go into Paris until we return."

Aware of what he suspected, from what Chadwick had told her, she replied, "You have my word that I won't see any of my suitors while you're gone."

A scowling Hawke left with Chadwick shortly thereafter.

"Heather, Grizzly and I are going to the Palais Royal," Shawnalese said.

"You can't do that" Heather protested, "you promised Hawke. Besides, there's too much unrest in Paris."

"I promised Hawke I wouldn't see any beaux, and

you have my word that I won't. I've promised some friends that I'd meet them at the Palais Royal today, so I must go. Grizzly will be with me, and you can see the king's soldiers have things well in hand."

Heather sighed and relented, so when Shawnalese and Grizzly left each day thereafter, she told Heather where she went.

Four days later Shawnalese and Grizzly rode to the Palais Royal amid thousands of angry men and women gathering there. She rushed to the print shop. "Dominique, what is happening?"

"Oh, mademoiselle, 'tis terrible," Dominique exclaimed. "At the urging of Marie Antoinette, the king has dismissed Jacques Necker, the director general of finance. With Necker goes France's hope for salvation. 'Tis the final straw!"

The next day all of Paris was in a roar; a sea of people, fifteen thousand or more, gathered at the Palais Royal, Shawnalese and Grizzly among them. Panic, terror, and suspicion kindled into a frenzy, and passions rose to fever pitch. Camille Desmoulins leaped onto a table in the gardens and gave one more of his fiery speeches. Noticing Shawnalese, he gave her a hand up onto the table, then jumped down and disappeared into the crowd. All eyes turned toward her, for it was unheard of for a woman to speak publicly. Yet there she stood in the middle of a table in the Palais Royal, surrounded by nearly fifteen thousand revolutionaries.

Chapter 23

STANDING ON A TABLE IN THE CENTER OF THE Palais Royal, Shawnalese scanned the thousands of expectant faces lifted toward her. Camille Desmoulins had roused the crowd to a feverish intensity, and instinctively she knew he expected her to keep them riled until he returned. She reached up, took the pins from her hair, and shook her golden mane into disarray. Cheers went up from the predominantly male audience. Then she took the red and blue ribbon clutched in her hand, the cockade of old Paris and not that of the monarchy, and pinned it in her hair. A roar echoed through the air, followed by shouts of approval from the women. Her small fist shot into the air, and she cried out, "Parisians, stand up and be counted! You are victims! This is your chance to change history—not suffer it. Rest not until France is free!"

The crowd exploded. "Free France!" they chanted. "Free France! Free France!"

Camille Desmoulins sprang onto the table, eyes inflamed, in each hand a pistol. The militia of the king would not take him alive. Grizzly swept Shawnalese from the table.

"Friends!" Camille shouted. "Shall we die like hunted hares? Like sheep hounded into their pinfold, bleating for mercy, where is no mercy, but only a whetted knife? The hour is come, the supreme hour of Frenchman and man, when oppressors are to try conclusions with oppressed. And the word is—swift death or deliverance forever. To arms!"

"To arms!" echoed the crowd as one great voice, and they poured onto the streets of Paris, shouting, "To arms!"

French soldiers stood at the ready, and the command, "Fire!" was given. But not a trigger was pulled. Only the angry rattle of musket butts hitting the ground resounded. Never again would Frenchman fire upon Frenchman.

French soldiers deserted en masse. All troops withdrew to outside Paris, for even the foreign soldiers refused to fire upon civilians or their deserting members. On that warm and cloudy Sunday the mob of commoners took over Paris and the cry "To arms!" echoed throughout the city.

The strong arms and willing hearts of the smithies made steel-pointed pikes while the work-roughened hands and stout hearts of the women made cockades of red and blue, the colors of Paris.

Late that night the mob burned the custom offices at the gates of the high, eighteen-mile-long wall that surrounded Paris. Now deserters from the French guard of the crown defended the entrances to Paris—on behalf of the commoner.

July 14 dawned cool and cloudy. Against Heather's protestations, Shawnalese insisted on going to the Palais Royal. "History is being made, Heather. I won't miss it. I'm well known by everyone there, so I'll be safe. Besides, Grizzly's with me. And you'll be safe here, for the king's army stands between you and Paris. We'll leave the carriage for you and go on horseback."

As Shawnalese and Grizzly entered Paris they encountered a huge sea of people, armed with swords, pikes, cudgels, and other arms, moving toward the Invalides, the arms depot, tramping to the beat of drums. The masses charged the Invalides and seized the loaded cannons and empty muskets, for the defending French troops refused to fire on the Parisians.

Yet powder and shot was needed for the muskets,

and that was stored in the hated Bastille. An unarmed delegation of bourgeoisie, with a flag of truce, raced ahead to demand the peaceful surrender of the arms, powder, and shot stored in the high-walled fortress-prison that loomed on the edge of the Faubourg Saint-Antoine.

Though it had fallen into disuse years earlier, the Bastille represented centuries of oppression to the people of France—a potent symbol, the manifestation of the king's power to imprison, without charges or trial, anyone at will, for an indefinite duration.

The cry went up, "To the Bastille!" and the mob of thousands turned toward the detested Bastille.

A man recognized Shawnalese and shouted, "She's the lady from the Palais Royal!"

"Let her lead the way!" another man yelled.

"Take down her hair!" a woman screamed.

Large hands reached out to pull the pins from Shawnalese's chignon, and her long golden hair tumbled down; small hands pinned red-and-blue cockades to her wildly tossed hair, then more—until her head was covered. Two burly men hefted her to their shoulders.

"Free France!" the passionate roar rang out. "Free France! Free France!"

To the beat of drummed kegs, men, with the cockades of old Paris pinned to their hats or chest, and women, with cockades in their hair, flooded through the narrow, squalid streets of the Faubourg Saint-Antoine to besiege the Bastille, gathering more people as they marched. Two cannons rumbled behind.

Shawnalese rode on the shoulders of two men who led the throng of fire-eyed thousands. Along the way a torch was thrust into her hand, and with her head covered with red-and-blue cockades, she became the symbol of a free France—the vainqueuse de la Bastille—and the first person the soldiers guarding the Bastille saw.

Grizzly reached up and pulled Shawnalese from the

open target she presented on the shoulders of the two men.

"Oh, Grizzly," she cried out, trying to be heard above the din, "surely there will be blood shed here today. There must be some other way."

"Aye. But the king and the nobility refuse to consider any other way, lass. Ye know that."

As though to answer her fears, overhead from the fortress, one great gun, its mouth soaring skyward, boomed a warning. The governor of the Bastille had refused to surrender.

Suddenly, those inside the Bastille poured a fiery hail of shot into the people, and Grizzly went down in blood.

"No!" Shawnalese screamed, dropping her torch, collapsing to her knees over the lifeless body of her beloved friend.

As muskets from the Bastille positioned for a fresh assault, a strong arm swept the woman with streaming golden hair to safety, shielding her body with his. The wild mob came to life and, ravenous for revenge, charged the Bastille.

Another volley of fire roared into the crowd, and the man who stood in the spot where Shawnalese had knelt moments before dropped. She twisted in the arms of the captor who'd saved her life and looked into the enraged face of Gayhawke Carrington.

In the midst of blood, fire, and carnage, Hawke had come for her, and she clung desperately to him.

All around her pandemonium exploded, and Hawke, with Shawnalese in his arms, spread his booted feet wide to stand protectively over Grizzly's body. A sea of humanity, roaring men and screaming women, burst past them, and Shawnalese threw her arms around Hawke's neck and sobbed against his cheek. "Oh, Hawke, they've shot Grizzly! They've shot my Grizzly."

The acrid smell of gunpowder permeated the cloud

of smoke, and moments later Chadwick stood at their side.

"Get Shawnalese out of here," Hawke bellowed above the thunderous din as the bolting throng pushed and shoved them. "I'll get Grizzly."

As Hawke heaved Grizzly over his shoulder, men climbed the first drawbridge of the Bastille and the clang of axes against chain rang through the air. Other men assembled the cannon from the Invalides.

Chadwick lunged forward away from the Bastille, shoving and pushing against the thousands who surged forward, who dragged and pulled them back. Shawnalese clutched at Chadwick's coattail, followed by Hawke shouldering Grizzly.

The loud crash of the Bastille's drawbridge slamming down resounded, followed by an outburst of tumultuous cheers, even though the portcullis still barred the way. Musket fire from the Bastille filled the air, trailed by the wails and cries of the wounded and dying.

The Invalides cannon, leveled at the Bastille, roared behind them, followed by the deadly sound of soldiers marching toward them. From the garrisons outside the city, two detachments of the French Royal Guard, in full uniform and armament, advanced in double time.

"Faster, Chadwick," Hawke yelled, for his friend parted the barrier of onrushing people to clear a path for Shawnalese and Hawke with his heavy burden. Commotion and chaos reigned as they struggled onward amid the turmoil and hysteria.

They plunged forward past the marching soldiers, and Chadwick moved into the doorway of a smithy shop, followed by Shawnalese, then Hawke. The howling Parisians swept past them, and Hawke lowered Grizzly to the cobbles to search for his wound.

"Shawnalese," Hawke shouted above the fracas, "tear off a strip of your petticoat. I need something to stanch the flow of blood." With her dagger, she slashed her rid-

ing habit, and he rolled the cloth and pressed it to the
wound. Then he checked for and found an exit wound,
did the same there, then jerked Grizzly's belt from his
breeches and tightly bound the bandaged wound.

Wave after wave of the pike-armed, and uncontrolled, masses raced past them. Men shouted, drums
beat, wounded cried, muskets fired, women screamed,
soldiers marched, and cannons boomed. These and a
hundred other sounds engulfed them, and the shrieks
and cries rose to a piercing crescendo.

Hawke glanced at a distraught Shawnalese, who
knelt beside him to wipe Grizzly's lifeless face. "He's
alive," Hawke murmured into her ear, more gently
than he'd intended.

Then a shout rang out, "Aristos! Aristos!"

Hundreds of eyes turned toward them, sheltered in
the doorway, surrounded by a Paris gone rabid.

"Kill 'em!" a voice thundered

"Kill 'em!" another echoed.

The crowd crushed in around them in a nightmare
of screams and threats.

"No! No!" a deep voice cried out. "It's the man what
feeds us. It's the nobleman what brings the free food
to the cafe!"

"*Oui.* 'Tis. 'Tis him!" another man yelled.

"An' that's the lady from the Palais Royal," still
another bellowed above the uproar.

Volleys of gunfire exploded through the air, followed by the boom of the Invalides cannon and another round of musket fire. Smoke mingled with the
pungent smell of gunpowder.

"Monsieur!" A ragged, gaunt woman tugged timidly
at Hawke's sleeve. "They don't need my help," she
called out over the noise. "I'd consider it an honor to
take ya to the gates o' Paris."

"Me too!" a voice howled above the clamor.

"And I," another woman screeched over still more
gunfire.

"And me!"

"Our horses are at Nicolas the blacksmith's," Shawnalese yelled back.

"We can't get to 'em, mademoiselle," one bony woman shrieked. Then, as the thought occurred to her, she shouted, "I could send my lad to fetch 'em and meet us at the gates."

"Our horses are at Henri's livery," Chadwick called loudly.

"My two boys will get 'em for you, monsieur," another woman hollered to Chadwick.

Quickly Chadwick gave instructions, pressed the necessary coin plus several more into the outstretched palms, and five young boys raced off in different directions.

An honor guard of sixteen bedraggled women surrounded Shawnalese, Hawke with Grizzly, and Chadwick, and escorted them safely through the bedlam, through the streets of a frantic, turbulent Paris, where madness ruled the hour, to the gates of the walls at the outskirts of the city.

On their way, criers raced by, with bells clanging, to spread the word that the French Royal Guard, to the roll of drums, had lined up in front of the old fortress and with a blaze of flame had fired upon the Bastille. Hence the people of France in military uniform, armed with swords and rifles, and the people of France in rags, armed with pikes and cudgels, side by side stormed the Bastille.

And the cry went out, *let neither French man nor woman lay down until the torch of freedom burns over all of France!*

Revolution and France was afire!

Sometime later Hawke carried Grizzly into the kitchen at his château. With Paris in open revolution, a doctor was unavailable.

"What can I do to help?" Shawnalese asked, physically sick at the sight of Grizzly drenched in blood, fearful that he might be mortally wounded.

"Wash down the table with alcohol so I can lay Grizzly down," Hawke ordered, then cried out his instructions in rapid succession. "Heather, bring the laudanum, drawing salve, and another bottle of alcohol. Philippe, kindle the fire and get pails of water heated, then bring linen for bandages. Chadwick, get the poker and put it into the fire, we'll need to cauterize this wound. Nadine, get needle and thread. Somebody find me a knife."

Everybody scattered while Shawnalese hurriedly scrubbed the sturdy trestle-table top with alcohol. Then Hawke laid down the groaning man. "He's lost considerable blood. We have to stanch the flow if he's to live. Help me cut away his clothes, Shawnalese. Time is of the essence."

Taking her dagger, Shawnalese cut away the blood soaked shirt while Hawke worked on the breeches. Philippe hurried in to throw a sheet over Grizzly's lower body, then began to cut strips from the sheets into bandages.

Chadwick ran into the room, shoved the poker into the flames, and moved to Hawke's side. "What now?"

"Get some cognac and force as much down him as you can, then help me roll him onto his side."

Chadwick poured a large drink of cognac down Grizzly's protesting throat. The semiconscious man coughed, then another drink was forced into him before they rolled him to his side.

"The ball went clean through," Hawke announced. "He's bleeding from the front and back. Get a good grip on him, Chad. Shawnalese, pour alcohol into his back wound."

"We haven't any more alcohol."

"Then use cognac. Philippe, hand me the poker."

Shawnalese, feeling faint, closed her eyes as the red-hot poker cauterized his back and the smell of burning flesh assailed her nostrils. Hawke returned the poker to the fire, then retrieved it, and they quickly did the same with the entrance wound.

"You'll need to sew both wounds, Shawnalese," Hawke ordered. "He's already lost too much blood to risk the loss of more. Can you do it?" His gaze captured hers.

She blanched at his words, then glanced at the ashen face of her beloved friend. "I can do it," she murmured, and with trembling hand took the needle and thread from a softly weeping Nadine.

"I've always admired your stitches," Hawke said, and smiled.

Shawnalese's heart stirred at his gentle humor, at the glimpse of the Hawke she'd once known and his attempt to soothe her.

"What were you doing in Paris after you'd given me your word that you wouldn't go?" Hawke asked.

Her fingers moved with a swiftness and dexterity she didn't know she possessed. With the back wound quickly closed, she performed the same ministrations on the front, then looked up for the first time, relieved to see that Grizzly lay unconscious.

"Hawke, I didn't promise you I wouldn't go into Paris," she finally replied as she took a last stitch. "I promised I wouldn't see any suitors, which I didn't." She covered both wounds with a drawing salve to help prevent infection, and Grizzly was quickly bandaged.

"So because you chose to play verbal subterfuge with me," Hawke began, "even though you knew my intent, your friend may die."

His words tore through her—because they were true. "Aye. It's something"—her voice broke—"something I may live with the rest of my life." Hearing Nadine's sobs, Shawnalese glanced up. Clearly, the woman loved Grizzly, too. Shawnalese gave her a squeeze. "A bear couldn't kill him, most assuredly a musket ball won't."

"Philippe, put him to bed until we leave," Hawke directed, his anger with Shawnalese evident in the tone of his voice.

"Until we leave?" Shawnalese asked.

"France is in revolution," Hawke replied. "No aristocrat is safe. What do you think would have happened to us if that man and those women hadn't intervened? You and Heather can't be protected from an enraged mob. As we speak, criers ride throughout France to spread the word. This is the beginning, I would imagine, of a long and bloody revolution. I'm taking you home to England, and we leave today." He turned to Chadwick. "I believe in these circumstances it is safest for us to travel at night. We'll only have to be concerned about brigands, not mobs and rioters. Do you agree, Chad?"

"Unquestionably."

"But, Grizzly . . ." Shawnalese protested.

"We'll make him as comfortable as possible. I won't risk Heather's safety, or yours. Chad and I will outride." Hawke turned to his major-domo. "Philippe, inform any servants who want to leave with us to be ready in two hours. After you've put Grizzly to bed, give him laudanum, then summon every manservant here. There is much to do if we're to have any chance of leaving France alive."

Two hours later the coach, hitched with six horses instead of the usual four, was ready for their departure. Normally the journey from Paris to the coast would take three days, but they intended to travel in all haste.

Muskets, pistols, powder, and shot filled one of two boxes beneath the seats of the coach. The other box contained medicines, bandages, breads, cheeses, water, the remaining laudanum, and the single remaining bottle of cognac. Blankets lay over all. Every eventuality had been considered. Warrior and Chadwick's mount each carried two scabbarded muskets. Harcourt, the groom, tethered Wildfire and four spare horses behind the coach, for under these circumstances not a horse would be had in all of France. To keep the weight to a minimum, only two trunks, which contained the barest necessities, were tied on top.

There was none but Hawke and Chadwick to protect the coach, for what Frenchman could be hired to safeguard them from revolutionary Frenchmen? Added to that was the problem of who would drive the coach. Other than Nadine and her son, Auguste, none of the servants chose to leave France.

"I have no experience, Your Grace, but I would be honored to drive your coach," Thaddeus volunteered.

"I'll go with him, Your Grace," Harcourt offered. "Between the two o' us, we'll get ya to the coast."

"I appreciate that, gentlemen, and you'll be well paid for your services."

While Hawke and Chadwick were otherwise occupied, Shawnalese scabbarded Wildfire with two muskets, untethered him, and mounted. She shoved a pistol, primed and loaded, into the waistband of her riding habit as Thaddeus and Harcourt climbed to the coachman's seat. Czar, with his great tail wagging and his eyes bright and excited, stood between them. Two footmen carried Grizzly into the coach, then assisted Heather and Nadine. Auguste scrambled in behind them. Under the dark of evening, the time had come.

Hawke and Chadwick, with swords hanging from their sides and a brace of pistols in their waistbands, bounded from the château and mounted.

Hawke handed Thaddeus and Harcourt each a flintlock and a pistol. "I'm asking you not to shoot at anyone unless it's necessary for your protection. We want only to leave France peacefully. However, after what I've seen this day, I'd be remiss in not giving you something with which to defend yourself. There is no talking to a rioting mob, and we have no idea what we're going to encounter." Then he turned a dark glare on Shawnalese. "Get off that horse and into the coach."

"Gayhawke—"

"No."

"Carrington—"

"No!" Hawke bellowed. "Get in the coach. Now!"

"I can shoot almost as well as you, and better than Chad," she protested.

"God's teeth, Shawna," Chadwick lashed out, affronted.

"We aren't going to shoot anyone," Hawke stated. "We're only armed in the event that we're attacked. Now get in the coach where you'll be safe."

"If I ride Wildfire, Grizzly can lie down on one seat."

The slight tremble of her lower lip was the only indication of her concern for her beloved friend, but Hawke didn't miss it. With more patience than he intended, he said, "You can lay Grizzly's head on your lap."

She did not tell him Grizzly's head rested on Nadine's lap. Instead she argued, "My weight will slow the coach."

Hawke started to dismount. "Your slight weight will make no difference, and you know it."

"No," Shawnalese tossed back, nudged Wildfire, and started down the drive.

Hawk saw the flash of defiance in her eyes and smiled in spite of himself. "Damned independent vixen!" he grumbled, and trotted to the front of the coach. "Let's go."

The reins snapped, the trappings rattled, the coach started with a jerk, and Hawke raced to catch Shawnalese.

They hadn't traveled far when guards from the king's army stopped them. "'Tis not safe to travel, monsieur," the sergeant warned. "The Bastille's fallen. The mob's gone insane and beheaded the governor of the Bastille and some other officials of Paris. Right now they're racin' through the streets with the men's heads on their pikes. Word is they might turn on the aristos next."

Shawnalese, riding between Hawke and Chadwick, gasped. "But we're English."

"Don't make no difference, mademoiselle," the

guard answered. "They wouldn't know you was English 'til the shootin' was over. Rioters would only see the blooded horses, the coach of an aristo, and your fancy travelin' clothes. I'm sorry I can't give ya escort, but we're waitin' orders from the king. Louis, as usual, can't make up his mind."

"Thank you, Sergeant," Hawke said. "We'll just have to travel without escort. We have no choice, for we must return to England while we still can."

The soldier glanced from Chadwick to Hawke. "Ya should put the lady in the coach where she'll be safer, an' go back to where ya came from. 'Tis danger you're headin' into."

Chapter 24

Hawke snatched the reins from an unsuspecting Shawnalese. "You will ride inside."

"Hawke . . ."

"Not a man under my authority ever dared to defy my orders. You will not be the woman who does." He leaned out of his saddle toward her. "The question is not whether you get in the coach, but how you get in. Willingly or by force."

Shawnalese sighed and slipped from her saddle.

"Tie Wildfire's reins back and his stirrups up," Hawke instructed. "When we're in open country and it's safe, you may ride him."

Auguste jumped down to assist her with the stirrups and into the coach.

Hawke jerked the two muskets from their scabbards on Wildfire and handed them inside to her. "Now reach out and rub Wildfire's muzzle." She looked at him questioningly. "Just do it, Shawnalese. If Wildfire knows you're in the coach, he'll follow. Then he can run free."

She smiled and did as instructed.

Minutes later a grim-faced and concerned Hawke and Chadwick led the coach and six, into what they knew naught. Neither doubted the gravity nor precariousness of their situation.

Night gripped the countryside with menacing darkness. Low-hanging, dark-edged gray clouds intermittently obscured the overcast moon to hurl darting shadows behind every tree, behind every shrub. The wind whispered ominously past their ears as the thundering horses and rumbling coach fled the threat of disaster that hung heavy in the air.

Hour after hour Hawke's and Chadwick's alert eyes scanned every dark shape, every shadowy configuration, as they galloped over the hazardous roads, the coach lumbering behind with churning wheels. Then a gunshot echoed, and a shout split the night.

Ahead a fire blazed. A barricade at the bridge!

Reining in Warrior, Hawke held up his hand to signal a stop. Thaddeus hurled an oath and floundered with the reins before he hauled back with a jerk and jammed his foot on the brake, only to slip off, then strike again. The coach came to a jolting, tottering halt and nearly flung Shawnalese and Heather to the floor. Trembling with relief, Thaddeus dropped the reins and lowered his head into his hands.

In the glow of the bonfire, six men and the barrels that blocked the bridge could be seen clearly. Firelight glinted on the steel of their weapons. Dressed in peasant garb, three men carried pikes and scythes while two men's flintlocks and another man's pistol pointed directly at them.

With concentrated thoroughness, Hawke searched the surrounding fields for any crouched figure, any previously unseen threat. Seeing none, he kneed Warrior and trotted forward cautiously. Chadwick rode back to the coach, reined his horse around beside Thaddeus, and sat facing the scene ahead.

Shawnalese, with a racing heart but a firm hand on her flintlock, leaned out the coach window.

"Why is the bridge barricaded?" Hawke asked in English.

"We don't speak English," said one burly Frenchman.

"Why is the bridge barricaded?" Hawke repeated. Although his French was perfect, he spoke the words with as heavy an accent as he could affect. He wanted no mistaken impression that he was a hated French aristocrat.

"You're English?"

"I'm English."

"Do you have any French aristos"—the man spat— "with you?"

"No. I have my family and French servants."

"We want no trouble with the English." With that, one man lowered the butt of his flintlock to the ground, the second slung his rifle across his shoulder, muzzle skyward, and the third man shoved his pistol into his waistband.

Hawke announced, "We merely wish to return to England. If you will remove the barrels, we'll be on our way."

"We'll have to inspect your coach. No French aristo gets over this bridge."

Hawke thought of Grizzly, wounded, unconscious, and in Chadwick's silk nightclothes. They couldn't prove that Grizzly was not a French aristocrat. They could not even explain how he'd been wounded, for these men certainly would not believe the truth. "I'll not have my family inconvenienced in such a manner. There are three women and a young boy."

"Then you'll have to return to Paris, monsieur. No nobleman's coach crosses this bridge without being—"

Hawke whipped out his brace of pistols and pointed them at the man. "My patience is exhausted, monsieur. Remove the barrels and allow us to pass in peace. We mean you no harm."

At that, Shawnalese called Wildfire. The stallion trotted to the coach, and with musket in hand and Heather's protestations ringing in her ears, she threw open the door, untied the stirrups, and scrambled onto Wildfire's back.

Chadwick, his musket aimed, galloped to Hawke's side, followed closely by Shawnalese. The night burst into chaos, and mayhem reigned as a warning gunshot, fired by one of the peasants, shattered the calm of night, followed in quick succession by two more gunshots. The wild-eyed coach horses reared, came down with a thud of flying hooves, panicked, and bolted forward at full gallop while the coach careened crazily behind. Hurling an oath at the runaway team, Thaddeus snatched for the reins that were fast disappearing over his footrest to dangle beneath the pounding hooves of the six horses.

To the peasants, armed riders and a coach and six bore down on them at breakneck speed. Gunfire mingled with the sound of stampeding horses and the rattle of churning wheels as the conveyance crashed through the flimsy barrier and sent empty barrels flying in every direction. The coach rumbled across the bridge and took the curve wildly before disappearing in a cloud of dust.

Another barrage of firing split the air. Chadwick shuddered and slumped forward in the saddle, and Shawnalese cried out as a musket ball pierced her leg.

Hawke galloped to her side, unaware she was wounded. "Get the coach! I'll hold them off here"—he glanced at the slumped form of Chadwick—"and then Chad and I will catch up with you." At her hesitation, he bellowed, "Go! Go! The coach is out of control.

And keep going. Don't come back."

A musket ball whizzed past her. How could she leave him?

"Go, dammit!" Hawke cursed. "Go!"

She bore her weight in one stirrup, leaned low over Wildfire, slapped the reins across his withers, and felt the power beneath her as the stallion sped down the road after the coach. With each long stride, hooves flashed quicksilver, nostrils flared, and eyes blazed in the mighty head that jolted up and down. The horse stretched into a fleeting gallop, and each jarring hoof-beat shot pain up her wounded leg. They flew through the night and never slacked the pace. With mane and tail whipping in his breeze, the animal sailed over a fallen trunk without breaking stride and devoured the road in his perilous race.

By the faint light of the cloud-obscured moon, Shawnalese sighted the precariously swaying coach. Fearing the worst, she tied her reins together lest they be dropped and clung to the stallion's mane. Wildfire sensed the urgency and surged forward. They overtook the horses tied to the rear of the jouncing carriage, then were beside the coach itself, and finally galloped side by side with the lead horse. The pain in her leg tore through her entire body, and she fought back nausea and waves of dizziness as she leaned out of her saddle to grab at the lead horse's bridle. She knew if her strength failed her, if Wildfire failed her, she'd be flung beneath twenty-four powerful hooves pounding the ground, to certain death. She lunged for the bridle and missed, tried a second time and missed again, then straightened in her saddle to speed neck and neck down the dirt road. She waited for the flash of pain in the calf of her leg to subside. Once more she pulled Wildfire closer to the laboring lead horse, stretched out of her saddle, and lunged. This time her hand clasped the leather and she hung on desperately, gasping, sure her arm was being wrenched from her shoul-

der. With her clinging to the bridle, they raced
onward, smoke drifting from the braked wheel.

Shawnalese didn't have the strength to halt the runaway team and with her injured leg couldn't try to
mount the lead horse. Knowing nothing else to do, she
reined Wildfire into the stampeding lead horse, causing the animal to break stride; then, with her hand still
clutching the bridle, she jerked the horse's head with
all her might. The runaway stumbled, then straightened, and she prayed Wildfire had the remaining
stamina to do what she asked as she urged him in
front of the thundering team. Once there, she gradually slowed her galloping horse, and the team behind
slacked as they did, until finally they were halted.

She dared not look inside the coach to see if this had
been a fatal ride for Grizzly, to see who might have
been injured. Hawke needed her. "Thaddeus, have
Harcourt help you turn the coach around and back it
into the lane"—Shawnalese pointed down the road
they had just raced up—"between those trees. Pull the
blinds and cover the windows with blankets before
you light a lamp inside the coach. Not a speck of light
must be seen from outside. Hawke needs me. God
willing, we'll be right back. If we're not here within
one hour, change teams and leave without us. If
Auguste is all right, have him stand guard. We might
have trouble finding you. Understood?"

"Yes."

"Let me have both your pistols. I don't know what I'm
heading back into. Rearm yourselves with the weapons
from beneath the coach seat." Shawnalese took the two
pistols, shoved them into her waistband with the other
one, checked that her two flintlocks remained tightly
sheathed, whirled Wildfire around, and galloped off in
the direction from which she'd just come, riding with her
heart in her throat. Was Hawke dead? Was Chadwick?

As she neared the bridge, she spotted Chadwick's
riderless horse by the side of the road, cropping grass,

Chadwick's motionless body lay on the ground nearby. "Dear God!" she gasped, the burning pain in her leg forgotten in her concern for Chadwick, her concern for Hawke. Ahead on the bridge, Hawke, with his sword glinting in the firelight, fought three men armed with pikes and scythes. One motionless form lay on the ground while another man staggered down the road and still another, the nearest, sat on the roadside reloading his flintlock.

Backing with quick, sure steps across the bridge, Hawke, with his sword in his right hand and Warrior protectively at his left side, skillfully fought three men wielding lengthy iron pikes or swinging razor-sharp scythes. The noise of metal clashing against metal rang through the air as he nimbly parried the deadly aim of a pike, then, dancing on booted feet, riposted the lethal swing of a scythe, his swift sword whipping around the weapon to spin it from the attacker's grasp and send it sailing into the river. He grinned with satisfaction. The odds were even now. Two of them against him. No contest. He dodged the sharp jab of a pike, whipped his flashing blade with a flourish, and lunged into a ruthless attack of rapid thrusts, stalking his prey, knowing that if his skill did not desert him, he would not have to kill.

Hawke's two opponents drew back, then charged him like savage bulls. Dexterously sidestepping the murderous aim of the one pike at his groin, he met the other highly raised pike with all the muscle of his powerful sword arm, parrying it before riposting, before swirling agilely to block the death blow from the other man. The sharp point of his swift rapier found its mark, and one screaming man collapsed heavily to the ground, clutching his side, while on muscular legs Hawke leaped out of reach of the wild, vicious swings of the other pike. He feinted, then lunged and parried yet another strike from the considerably longer pike.

Shawnalese rode hard toward the scuffle, pulling her rifle from its sheath as she galloped toward the man who was loading his flintlock. Assessing the situation, she lowered her flintlock and gave her stallion the silent command to jump. Wildfire soared out of the darkness, knocking the man head over heels. From the hand of the tumbling peasant came a flash and a roar of his rifle before it flew through the air and down the riverbank. She whirled her stallion about and charged. Wildfire skidded to a halt at Hawke's side, and she aimed her pistol at the pike-bearing man. "Throw down your weapon," she demanded, and the man complied. She slipped another loaded pistol from her waistband and handed it to a sweating Hawke.

"You and your cohorts"—Hawke paused to catch his breath—"take your wounded and get out of here before I change my mind." Warrior stood seventeen hands high, but Hawke grabbed his mane and effortlessly catapulted himself onto the saddle. "I'll leave your weapons here and you can come back after them. We aren't French nobility, and from the beginning we meant you no harm." He waited as two men carried off a moaning comrade and a fourth struggled to help his wounded friend to his feet.

"If I find that my friend is dead, and if you or any of your friends come after us, I promise you that I will revenge his death and not one of you will be left standing. You have started this fight. I will be the man who ends it!" He turned to Shawnalese and snapped, "Don't you ever dare defy my orders again. I needed no help from you."

She was stunned by his rebuke, and the agonizing pain that ripped up her wounded leg joined the one that tore through her wounded heart.

"Let's get out of here before some bourgeois patrol happens by," Hawke commanded. "Is the coach under control?"

"Yes."

They whirled their horses west, to Chadwick and his horse. Hawke bounded to the ground and bent over

Chadwick. "He's alive, but barely," Hawke said, more to himself than to her. "Take Chad's horse with you," he instructed as he hefted his unconscious friend onto Warrior and mounted behind him. "There's not enough light here to see a cursed thing. If there's a patrol nearby, they'll be here fast, so I've got to get him to the coach if he's to be saved."

"You'll need to follow me, Hawke. The coach is hidden in the trees." Pain darted up her leg, accompanied by hot flashes and nausea. Shawnalese fought her light-headedness. There was little blood. Why did her leg hurt so terribly?

"Lead the way with wings on your heels. Chad's more dead than alive."

Shawnalese, with reins in hand to lead Chadwick's horse, and Hawke, with Chadwick's motionless body across his stallion, galloped into the night, riding hard and fast. When she neared the area where she'd stopped the coach, she slowed Wildfire to a canter, thankful that the moon had slipped from behind the dusky clouds. For several minutes the winded horses trotted onward, and her concerns grew. Had she passed the concealed coach? At that moment Auguste and Czar jumped from behind a roadside bush to signal her.

Shawnalese and Hawke turned their lathered horses into the lane and trotted to the coach. Thaddeus and Harcourt rushed to meet them.

"How's Grizzly, Thaddeus?" Shawnalese asked in a low voice, and slipped to the ground. Pain shot through the calf of her leg, it gave way beneath her, and she clutched at Wildfire's mane for support. Czar bounded to her side, his wet and eager tongue on her hand welcoming her.

"The stitches held quite well, but I daresay Grizzly was in terrible pain," Thaddeus answered softly. "Nadine changed his bandage, then gave him more laudanum. He's resting comfortably now."

"Thaddeus, get everyone out of the coach quickly

and quietly," Hawke demanded in a hushed tone. "Harcourt, give him a hand. Chadwick is gravely wounded."

"Auguste," Shawnalese said as Thaddeus and Harcourt hurried to obey Hawke, "how are Heather and Nadine? Are they injured?"

"*Non*, mademoiselle. Only bruised and bumped."

"And you?"

"I'm fine," the young boy answered proudly. "Harcourt walked the horses and rubbed them down before he changed teams. We're all ready to go."

"Good. Auguste, will you please find me a large stick to use for a cane?" she whispered, for she had discovered her wounded leg wouldn't bear her weight. "I've hurt my leg a little, but please don't tell anyone."

Auguste scurried off.

Minutes later Shawnalese had readied everything inside the coach while Hawke cut Chadwick's jacket and shirt from his blood-soaked body. At Hawke's deep inhalation, she glanced up. All she could see was Hawke's white shirt covered with blood. "Oh, dear God!" she cried out, her agonized gaze lifting to his eyes. "Oh, God! Oh dear God! Hawke, you're wounded." Her vision blurred, everything swam around her, and she felt as if she were drifting, drifting . . .

Hawke stared at her. She still loved him. After all that had happened since she'd first left England, she still loved him. He shrugged, for unlike before, he no longer cared. He didn't want her love; he wanted only her lush, voluptuous body. Wanted her beneath him, writhing in ecstasy as she had with so many other men. "I'm not wounded, Shawnalese. This is Chad's blood."

Weak with relief, she forced herself from her dazed state and asked, "What can I do to help?"

"The musket ball entered directly above Chad's heart. It's still in there, and it has to come out."

She bent over Chadwick and held the lantern close to examine him for the first time. "It appears the wound is deep," she said softly. "What do you think?" They both bent for a closer examination of the ugly, gaping hole that slowly oozed blood.

Chadwick, now semiconscious, groaned in pain.

"You'll have to do it," Hawke informed a startled Shawnalese. "Chad's conscious, so I'll have to hold him down. One jerk, one wrong move by him, and . . ." His eyes implored her understanding and he willed her his strength to do what must be done.

"Oh, Hawke," she whispered. "How—"

"Shawnalese, Chad's life depends on you—there's no one else. You can do it. I know you well, and I know you can do it—you have to."

"I can do it," she announced.

"Good girl." Hawke reached for the cognac and forced some down Chadwick's protesting throat. Chadwick groaned again, then stammered, "How . . . how are we to . . . to get out of France?"

"Have another drink and don't worry, Chad," Hawke mocked with a lightness that belied his fear for the friend he loved like a brother. "Perhaps I'll pin those damnable red-and-blue cockades all over Shawnalese's head and she can lead us out of France."

A brief smile tipped the corners of Chadwick's lips before Hawke forced another sip of cognac down him and then another.

Shawnalese took the bottle from him and corked it. "I'm going to need the rest for your wound, Chad."

Hawke retrieved a coil of rope from the box beneath the other seat. "Chad, I'm going to tie you down to keep you as still as possible," Hawke said, and started to tie Chadwick's ankles before he could protest. Next came his knees, then, last, his wrists behind his back. After taking the lantern from Shawnalese, Hawke hung it above Chadwick's head, removed the protective globe, and put the blade of his knife into the flame. While he worked, he said, "Shawnalese, at the château I'd asked you what you were doing in Paris."

Without answering, she handed him her crochet hook and tatting needle, and he placed those in the fire, then maneuvered around her to bend over Chadwick.

"I wanted to see what was happening, Hawke. That's why I went into Paris."

With no choice, they worked under extremely adverse conditions. The coach was cramped. With every movement their bodies brushed and bumped. They couldn't stand up, nor could they lay Chadwick straight.

"Cleanse his wound exactly as we did Grizzly's," Hawke instructed, preparing to pin Chadwick's shoulders to the coach seat with all the strength he possessed, knowing his friend was conscious and must be held perfectly still.

"I will, but I have to kneel on the floor," she said, for she couldn't remain bending with only one good leg.

"Whatever's most comfortable."

Now she drew upon her inner strength to do what she had to do. Readying herself mentally, she poured a little cognac into the wound and on a clean piece of cloth. Gently she cleansed the destroyed flesh exposing the bloody muscle under the skin.

"Is that why," Hawke asked, "you've been going to the Palais Royal while Chad and I were in Fontainebleau?"

Heather had told him. "Yes, that's why. I'm ready to begin with Chad's wound now." Hawke's smile urged her on, and she reached for the knife still in the lantern flame, wiped it on the cognac-soaked fabric, and slowly probed for the ball, while Chadwick futilely tried to twist away from her. He cried out, and his brow beaded with sweat. She shook her head at Hawke.

"Cut the skin and probe wider and deeper. We can't leave the ball there."

She fought her faint feeling, wiped the perspiration

from her brow with her sleeve, then made a larger slash over the open wound and tried again, slowly exploring wider and deeper while blood gushed from the wound. She probed more deeply, ever aware of how near to his heart she must be working, intent on her slow, laborious task.

Chadwick's lower body thrashed wildly, and she withdrew her instrument.

"You can do it, Shawnalese. I'll get on the other side of you," Hawke said, and crawled over her to place his weight on Chadwick's waist. "I wish we could squeeze one more person in here."

"I'm going to try this time with my crochet needle," she said more to herself than to Hawke. Using a cloth, she reached for the red hot piece of metal. After it cooled enough to hold, she once again began her slow, tedious search.

Hawke's knees straddled Chadwick's waist as he sat on his friend to keep his lower body from squirming. His one hand gripped Chadwick's right shoulder while his arm surrounded Shawnalese, where she knelt over the injured man, and his other hand pinned the left shoulder. Hawke's chest pressed intimately against her back, his face buried in the fragrance of her soft hair, and he wondered how desire could be flashing through him when his friend lay in jeopardy, so near death.

"I've found it. I've found it," Shawnalese cried. Seconds later Chad had passed out, and using both her knife and the hook, Shawnalese slowly manipulated a flattened, ugly piece of metal from Chadwick's chest. As she did, blood spurted into the air.

"Move! Move!" Hawke commanded, shoving her aside to cauterize the vein wound. "You can sew him closed now. We've done our best."

A short time later Shawnalese shifted from her kneeling position in the coach to sit on the floor and lean back against the seat. Chadwick's wound was stitched closed, covered with the last of the salve, and bandaged. Deathly white, he remained unconscious. How had this day turned into such terror and calamity? How had dreams of glory, dreams of liberty, equality, fraternity, and dreams of a free France become such a nightmare? Suddenly she was so hot, so weak, and the entire one side of her body, not merely her wounded leg, felt numb.

"You did marvelous work, Shawnalese," Hawke complimented, and gave her shoulder a squeeze. "I knew I could depend on you." He smiled and blew out the portable lantern. "You can rest outside now. This mess will be cleaned up in no time and we'll be on our way."

She wanted to say, "Hold me, Hawke. Tell me that you came to the Bastille because you love me and not merely because you're my guardian." But she knew the folly of that wishful thinking, so she smiled wanly and said, "Hawke, I'm afraid I need your help. I don't think I can move." With that, she lifted the skirt of her riding habit to reveal the torn and bloody flesh of a large gunshot wound in the calf of her leg.

Chapter 25

ICY FEAR SHOT THROUGH HAWKE, AND HE BENT TO examine Shawnalese's leg. His worst fear was realized: the musket ball was embedded in her leg, and they were without cognac and had very little laudanum and no salve.

One anguishing hour later her leg had been dressed and Hawke, heavily armed, rode out of the forest on

Warrior, leading two horses. He could still see Shawnalese turn to look up at him with the trusting eyes that haunted him. With only a little laudanum to relieve the pain and no cognac or alcohol to help guard against infection, he had removed the large piece of flattened lead from her calf. Within minutes he'd located the ball, for it lay shallowly embedded beneath the skin. A ricochet, a wicked-looking and painful injury, but little more than a flesh wound.

As he rode through the shadowy moonlit night, he recalled the terror that had volleyed through him when he'd seen Shawnalese's leg. It was a terror that had not torn through him when he'd seen Chadwick's injury, and now he refused to examine why. Turning his thoughts from what he didn't want to know, he reined Warrior onto the lane that led to a darkened farmhouse. All their lives depended on what he did now, for this was his only chance to get those he held most dear out of a France gone mad.

At daybreak a handsomely dressed nobleman astride a blooded silver Andalusian stallion led a spirited, blooded Arabian stallion. A rickety wagon piled high with straw and drawn by two plow horses creaked down the road some distance behind.

Nothing appeared unusual about the wagon, about the peasant man and boy on the driver's seat, or, from a distance, about the three peasant women who rode on top of the straw. No one saw the handsome wolfhound riding in a pocket atop the straw or the two wounded men buried, all but their faces, beneath the straw.

At the same time, a farmer astride one of Hawke's coach horses and accompanied by Harcourt rode toward Paris, where, if the man spoke to no one en route, he would receive a substantial bonus. A broad smile covered the man's wrinkled face, for this was the first good fortune that had come his way in his fifty-some years. A fine coach and nine coach horses—worth what he considered a treasure—had been signed over to him and, except for the horse he rode, were in his barn.

Hawke was equally pleased with the agreement, for the man couldn't reveal the circumstances of his stroke of luck to anyone in time to cause them harm. The farmer would be treated as a guest of the duke of Foxridge but not given his bonus until three days after he arrived at the château. By then Hawke and everyone would be on the *Phantom Dream* sailing for England.

Four days later two coaches pulled up in front of Foxridge and Hawke descended with Shawnalese in his arms. Addison stood in the open doorway.

"Addison, get four footmen out here right away," Hawke ordered, and bounded up the curving stairs to the mansion. "I'm taking Shawnalese to her chambers. Have Chadwick and Grizzly taken to the guest chambers next to hers. Then send two grooms on my fastest horses to find Dr. Fleming. They are not to return without the doctor. No excuses."

Sometime later the doctor joined Hawke, Heather, and Leif in the great hall. "Although the man Grizzly is quite weak from loss of blood, he's in the best condition of the three. No fever, no infection. With bedrest and good nourishment, he should be fine. The young woman's wound is the slightest, but it's badly infected. I'm sorry to say Lord Leighton is in a bad way. I'm sure you don't want to hear the details, but I had to reopen his wound. He'll need round-the-clock care. We must keep his fever from climbing. I'd guess he'll reach his crisis point tonight or tomorrow night. I should be able to tell you more about him tomorrow."

The next day, while Chadwick hovered between life and death, Grizzly gradually improved, but Shawnalese worsened.

On the second day, Dr. Fleming came down to the great hall to report to the family again. "Lord Leighton has not gotton any worse, so I am more optimistic about him," he announced. "However, I daresay the news regarding Miss Grenville is not at all favorable. She's vacillating between unconsciousness and delirium. It's not a good sign."

Hawke took up a bedside vigil. He had a compelling need to be near Shawnalese, as she'd always had to be near him, before he'd sent her to France. He smiled at the treasured memory. If he was at Foxridge, she would find him. If he was busy, or with someone, she'd tarry nearby like a faithful puppy, always keeping him in sight. Now he glanced at her, in a fitful sleep, so small, so innocent looking, her hair a spread of golden threads against the white sheets. It was as though she were once again his Shawny, and the agony of the imagining tore through his vitals.

The following morning the doctor returned to examine her. "Your Grace, she's taken a turn for the worse, and a decision must be made."

Rutger and Leif were her brothers. It was their right to be involved in this matter, Hawke decided. "The family will meet you in the great hall, doctor."

Minutes later Hawke, Rutger, Leif, and Heather assembled in the great hall. A grim-faced Dr. Fleming joined them.

"Miss Grenville's condition has slowly deteriorated," he announced. "Far worse, there's a red streak running up her leg."

"A red streak?" Hawke repeated.

"I daresay her blood's poisoned."

"Dear God!" Hawke groaned, and his searing anguish almost overcame his control.

"Oh, no!" Heather cried out. Rutger and Leif glanced at each other fearfully.

"There are two choices. Amputate her leg or try bleeding her first"—he paused at the gasps in the room—"so I'm asking your permission to bleed her immediately," Dr. Fleming said.

"No! I forbid it!" Hawke blurted out. Panic such as he'd never known shot through his body.

"Then I must amputate. I know it's a dreadful decision, but I know little else to do, Your Grace. None survive poisoning of the blood."

"Never! I won't allow it!" Hawke roared. "I've seen the butchery of surgeons' amputations. I've also seen many a soldier bled. Few survive either. It makes no sense to me to take someone weakened by illness or injury and weaken him further by bleeding him."

"Your Grace, I'm telling you, the blood in that leg is poisoned. If I amputate now, and if she doesn't get blood poisoning again, or gangrene, she will live. Or if I bleed that leg, we might have a chance to save her. If we do neither . . ."

A glazed look of despair spread over Hawke's face. "We must consider this, doctor. I don't know if I could approve an amputation, and I'm opposed to bleeding."

"There is no time to consider, Your Grace," the doctor insisted. "If you make no decision, you will have decided to let her die. And if we wait, it most likely will be too late."

Heather cried out, and knowing he dare not say more in her presence, Hawke turned to Rutger and Leif. "You two discuss this. I'll return in ten minutes. We'll decide then." With that he leaped from his chair and took the stairs to the north wing two at a time. When he entered Shawnalese's chamber, the drapes were drawn, the room dim.

"She's awful sick, Your Grace." Mrs. Kendall sniffled. "An' her alayin' there lookin' like an angel. Somehow it don't seem right, her bein' so kind an' all."

"Has she been awake?"

"No, Your Grace. She's outa her mind with the fever. Keeps talkin' nonsense, then she sleeps awhile. I keep spongin' her an' forcin' water down her throat, but she ain't no better. Seems a mite worse. The doctor wants to bleed her or . . ."

"Yes, I know." Hawke stumbled across the room, shattered. How could he make the decision that might end her life? How could he not make the decision that might save her life? Never had he felt so helpless. He caught his breath as he stared down at her slender form.

Mrs. Kendall had brushed her hair and arranged part of it fanlike on the white pillow, while the rest had been pulled down over each breast to end in curls above her thighs. Narrow white ribbons had been woven among the golden strands. Her arms were bent and her hands rested, one on top of the other, over the counterpane at her tiny waist. Except for the high flush of her face, she looked as though she had already crossed over death's threshold. At the image, a sob escaped his lips, for clearly Mrs. Kendall didn't expect Shawnalese to live.

Mrs. Kendall offered, "Can I get ya a cupo' tea, Your Grace?"

Too choked to reply, he nodded, and she bustled from the room. A gnawing anguish seared inside, filling him with a wretchedness of mind, spirit, and body, such agony that he felt sure he'd certainly die from the pain.

Now he knew what he'd refused to countenance since he'd gone to France after Shawny and found, instead, Shawnalese. He still loved her. Had never stopped loving her. Would never stop loving her. She had entwined herself too deeply around his heart, and they had shared too closely a bond, one he could never relinquish, a slender thread that forever bound him to her.

Forever bound him with her.

Easing himself to the side of her bed, he reached for the basin of cool water and sponged her face, then placed the cool cloth on her brow. She burned with fever, and he picked up one small hand. Her fingers curled around his, her glazed eyes fluttered open, and she smiled wanly.

"Gayhawke?"

Her pronunciation of his name was uttered in the husky, throaty voice that never failed to send shivers down his spine. "I'm here, Shawnalese."

"Shawnalese?" she whispered. "Hawke, I forgive you. Cannot you forgive me?"

God help him! Could he forgive her? Forgive her when she'd destroyed the woman-child he'd loved more than he'd ever loved anyone or anything? No, even now he could not forgive her, for she had destroyed the Shawny who ever lived in his heart. But he could, and he did, love her in spite of what she'd done, what she'd become. Still, if her believing he had forgiven her would help give her the desire to live, then he would utter any lie. "Shawny . . ."

Yet by the time he'd forced the name from his lips, she had drifted back into the netherworld of the critically ill, leaving him alone to decide whether to make the terrible decision—for he knew Rutger and Leif would leave it to him.

A soft tap on the door drew his attention, and he moved to open the door to Nadine.

"Grizzly says eet ees important to talk to you for a minute, Your Grace," Nadine said.

"I can't see him now. Tell him we're doing everything we can."

"Eet ees about Miss Shawna, Your Grace."

"I understand he's concerned, but I must return to the doctor," Hawke said. He closed the door and hurried down the gallery.

"Gayhawke Carrington!" Grizzly bellowed. "I'm the only chance she has to live!"

Hawke rushed to Grizzly's side, then assisted him to his bed.

"Ye let that ignorant doctor amputate or bleed her, and she's good as dead." Grizzly looked at Nadine. "Turn yer back, woman," he ordered, and pulled the nightshirt Nadine had forced on him from his large body. "Take a look at me, Hawke."

Hawke stared at the long, deep scars on Grizzly's shoulders, arms, chest, abdomen, one thigh, and leg. Deep claw gashes, large bite marks. Never had he seen a man so terribly scarred.

"There's more exactly like them on the back o' me. Now dinna ye wonder how a man who's been mauled, mangled, and chewed on, like I was, lived to tell about it? An Indian found me, more dead than alive, and nursed me back to health. And I know exactly how he did it."

Less than five hours later, four litter-bearing men carried an exhausted Grizzly into Foxridge. He had been rushed by carriage to the *Phantom Dream* and sailed to the Isle of Wight. There the four men had borne him by litter into the giant redwoods, where— on an outing several years ago with Hawke, Rutger, Leif, and Shawnalese—he'd seen the exact herb his Indian rescuer had used on his own wounds.

Into the large kitchens of Foxridge, under Grizzly's scrutiny, the leaves of the plant were washed and crushed and mixed with the thickness of tree sap into a balm, exactly as his Indian friend had done. Part were chopped into a small amount of water to boil, and the rest was rushed to Shawnalese's chambers. Minutes later the doctor, under the watchful eye of Grizzly and Hawke, prepared once again to clean the wound.

The pungent odor of the steaming herbal water drifted through her room. Hawke held Shawny, who thrashed in pain as the doctor treated her. She rambled in a restive delirium and cried out when the stinging paste of warm tree sap and herbs was spread on her torn flesh. Over that went herbal leaves and then, on top, cloths steeped in clean, hot water.

Each time the cloths cooled, the same procedure was repeated, but as the hours passed several thin red streaks crept still higher up her leg, almost to her hip. Dr. Fleming changed one more poultice, checked the surrounding swollen flesh, and shook his head in hopelessness.

Hawke wondered if he'd made a fatal mistake in insisting to Rutger and Leif that they try Grizzly's way. Exhausted beyond physical tiredness, he placed his arms on Shawnalese's bedside and rested his head there.

"Your Grace," Mrs. Kendall said gently. "Don't mind my sayin' so, but ya oughta be gettin' some rest. Ya've not closed your eyes for more'n two days. Why, I've been to bed twice since ya have."

"Not now, Mrs. Kendall."

"Then if you gentlemen will step into the gallery, I'll freshen the little luv a bit an' wake the good doctor."

Heather tiptoed from Chadwick's chamber. "Chad's awake. He's still burning with fever, and he's so terribly weak." She tried to smile encouragingly and swiped the hair from her brow before she suddenly realized they all stood in the gallery. Fearfully she cried, "Shawnalese!"

Hawke shook his head and Heather disappeared into Shawnalese's room, to reappear shortly, sobbing.

"Rutger, send for the clergyman," Heather murmured, and collapsed into her brother's arms. "Oh, Gayhawke, she won't wake up, she hasn't moved, hasn't uttered a sound, she's barely breathing." She burst into tears. "The doctor says she's in God's hands now."

Grizzly, with the aid of a footman, struggled to Shawnalese's bedside where Hawke, Heather, Rutger, and Leif were gathered. He bent over her motionless form. Hawke, unable to bear the heart-wrenching scene any longer, slipped out to the gallery.

As he stood there, memories assailed him of Shawny in his arms. The night he'd told her he was sending her to France. How many times since then had he regretted that decision? Every long, empty day, every lengthy night of sleeplessness. Before the child Shawny had come into his life he had known only emptiness. She, with all her defiance, with all her obstinance, and with all her worshipful love, had filled the void. Until he'd sent her away. His shoulders slumped. Now he couldn't imagine life without her. For all that he loved her, for all that he hated her, he didn't want to live without her. He knew that if she left him, a far worse emptiness than the one he'd once walked with would stretch endlessly before him. God, she couldn't die!

He had to return to her, somehow to pass his strength to her. He opened her door and looked at the doctor for a sign of hope, only to have the physician shake his head. "Everyone please leave for a while. She needs her rest," Hawke demanded softly, the tone of his voice causing Heather to hurry from the room, gently pulling a weeping Mrs. Kendall behind her. Rutger, Leif, Grizzly, and the footman filed out, and Hawke closed the door behind them.

He sat down on the edge of her bed and bent to kiss her tenderly. He pressed his cheek to hers, more aware than before of her shallow breathing, her burning fever. His trembling lips moved to whisper unheard words in her ear, until the doctor's hand on his shoulder caused him to sit up.

"She can't hear you, Your Grace."

He glanced up at the bleak-faced doctor. "Isn't it time to change her poultice?"

"It's useless now, Your Grace."

"I say when it's useless. Change the poultice. Then leave me alone with her."

Dr. Fleming did as ordered, then hurried from the room.

A half hour later Heather slowly opened the door. Behind her stood two footmen carrying Chadwick between them.

Hawke, with red-rimmed, hollow eyes and a three day growth of beard, lifted his head from Shawnalese's.

"Gayhawke," Heather said, "Chadwick would like to—"

"Get him out of here!" Hawke bellowed. "She's mine! She always has been. She always will be. Get him out of here! She's mine."

Heather quickly shut the door. "Oh, dear God! Gayhawke's losing his mind. He's losing his mind."

Chapter 26

IT WAS A MARVELOUS LATE JULY DAY, WITH PUFFY clouds chasing through the sky and the fragrance of flowers wafting on the soft breeze. Hawke walked up to Shawnalese where she sat in the gardens taking the sun. He reached down and tucked the lap robe more tightly around her. "You appear to be feeling much better," he said, and hunkered down on a large boulder across from where she sat on a stone bench. Czar lay at her feet, tail thumping. "I'm at your disposal, fair lady. My only intent is to keep you from being bored until you have to return to your bed. However, there's one forbidden subject. I will not argue Rousseau's philosophies of equality with you. I am a duke, and I intend to remain a duke."

Shawnalese smiled. "I wouldn't dream of suggesting you surrender your dukedom, exalted nobleman. Nevertheless, since you've brought up the subject, there's much more to Rousseau than his views of liberty and equality."

"Such as?"

"His laws not only of what we are, but of what we ought to be."

Hawke groaned, but she ignored him. "I've given that considerable thought since I came so near to dying, and I believe more than ever that I was spared from death to do something better with my life."

"Heaven forbid. Don't tell me you're going to lead another revolution?"

"Hawke, I'm serious. Besides, I didn't lead the revolution. I've already explained that to you. That was none of my doing."

"Ah, I understand you're going to devise some other clever way to get me killed. You've used up one of my lives in a duel, another to rescue you at the Bastille. Surely your ingenious little mind can devise seven other resourceful and entertaining, if not dazzling, ways to kill me."

He grinned with the most marvelous, teasing half smile that let the sunshine in to warm her heart. Finally! He had forgiven her.

"Actually, Carrington, you do have to agree that the two times I sought to have you killed were anything but boring. Dramatic, actually."

"There's no denying that. You will have to give it serious contemplation if you're going to top a duel and a revolution. I can hardly wait for the next time."

"I shall promise to use all of my ingenuity to conceive something elaborate—befitting a man of your station, as were the last two—if you will make me a promise in return."

"What is that?"

"You must be a better sport about all of this. I won't play this game with you, Hawke, if you're going to be as ill humored as you were after the duel."

Her words were spoken in jest, but the sadness in her eyes, the soberness of her face, told him she was not amused. Hers was a gentle rebuke that caused him to ponder. Certainly she didn't think he'd changed his treatment of her, altered his feelings, simply because he'd fought a duel she'd provoked? Surely she realized that her surrender to the Grenville hot blood was the cause? Yet he could not ask her for an explanation, could not give one of his own, for at her deathbed, although he hadn't been able to forgive her for what she'd become, he'd learned that he could forget it. He'd decided he didn't want to live without her. Even so, the only way he could live with her was to forget everything that had happened after she went to France. So from that moment, Shawnalese no longer had an unsavory past. There was only today and all their tomorrows—together.

Now Hawke wanted the enmity between them eradicated and their former closeness restored. He'd never shared a relationship with a woman such as he'd had with Shawny, and he wanted it back. With that in mind, he teased, "I'll give your request consideration if you'll agree not to try to get me killed in the meantime."

"I suppose I could restrain myself for a time." She wanted so badly to be friends with him again. Nothing more, for she realized the futility of that. "I don't know how I allowed you to distract me from what I started to say, but you did. Anyway, since I've returned from the abyss of death, I've come to believe I was spared for a higher purpose—my destiny."

"Your destiny? I thought I was your destiny." He tossed the words flippantly so she could not detect her words had cut him.

"You are my destiny, Hawke." She spoke softly. "I've known that since you came to New Orleans the second time. I've never doubted it for a minute since."

Joy flooded through him. He had never felt like this in his life. He'd always been so totally in control of himself, of his feelings. Confused, unable to understand these kinds of emotions, he fought the urge to pull her into his arms and never let her go; but then he set the feeling aside. He might have been foolish enough to fall in love with her, but he wasn't foolish enough to betray himself by revealing it.

"Apparently," she went on, "I'm not *your* destiny. Regardless. As you once told me, time is the test of destiny." Suddenly she was exceedingly tired. She knew she needed to rest, but she didn't want to leave him now. Although it was not what she dreamed of, they communicated now in a way they hadn't since she'd first gone to France. It was a beginning.

"I believe there's more than the destiny of the heart, Hawke. There's also the destiny of the soul, that of which Rousseau speaks—becoming all we ought to be."

"What do you think you ought to be?"

"Something more than the pampered ward of an English nobleman. My life so far has served no purpose."

His gaze captured hers. Would she forever have this mysterious hold on him? Would she always say the words that inspired him? God, he hoped so. But never could he let her know the control she held over him. He said mockingly, "Leading France toward independence is not a high enough plane for you? You want to be Joan of Arc?"

"Carrington, don't taunt me. I'm most serious. I did nothing in France of which I'm proud. If I were Camille Desmoulins, I'd feel I had made a worthy contribution. I respect and admire him greatly."

Stunned by her admission, he wondered if the liberal journalist had been her lover. He forced the unwanted imagining from his mind. That was yesterday, and with Shawnalese there must be no yesterdays. "If you've been contemplating as you say, 'the destiny of your soul,' then you must have reached some conclusion."

"No. No, I haven't. That's why I'm mentioning it to you. I thought perhaps you might have some idea. . . ."

"I'm afraid you're going to have to be patient. My understanding of Lady Destiny is that she seeks you out, not the opposite. If you're destined for great deeds, it will happen." Shawnalese might have lost the purity of her body in France, but not the purity of her mind and soul, and he valued those two far more than the other. "You know, I have often heard you expound the philosophies of Rousseau, but there is one of his persuasions I don't remember you mentioning."

She blushed, for she knew exactly what he was going to say. She'd promised herself, when he first joined her in the gardens, that she would do and say

nothing to annoy him. That she'd disagree with him
about nothing. She would remain poised and imper-
turbable, regardless of how ludicrously he behaved.
There were fences to mend. With that intention, she
clamped her mouth shut, determined to keep it shut.

"Why," Hawke asked, "have I never heard you laud
Rousseau's opinion that 'women must be weak and
passive, man active and strong'? 'Woman was made to
be subservient to man,' he said, 'and woman must
make herself agreeable and obey her master, and such
is the purpose of her existence.' Actually, now that I
think on it, I've noticed that you neither subscribe to
that philosophy nor live by it."

She knew he was deliberately baiting her, that she'd
laid her own trap. Everything was back to normal, and
her heart took wings. Nevertheless, she determined to
maintain their fragile peace, so she bit her tongue and
said nothing.

Most amused, Hawke grinned and watched her
silent struggle. "I didn't hear what you said."

Shawnalese looked up at him grinning in that smug,
superior fashion he always used when he'd bested her.
Yet try though she did, and the Lord knew she tried
mightily, she could not fail to parry his remark. "No
one ever accused Rousseau of being perfect," she sputtered, "which he most assuredly was not." Unable to
help herself, she added, "Such drivel could only come
from the lips of a man bestowing pontifical attributes
upon men."

"Welcome home," Hawke said. His grin broadened
into a smile. In his mind, in his heart, he reached out
and pulled her close to embrace her with all the love
in his being. In actuality, he did not move.

With sparkling eyes and a most joyous feeling, she
returned his smile. "You've never told me, Carrington.
How did you come to be in New Orleans the first
time?"

"I went to Willow Heights in Louisiana to visit a

friend—and to give a child a gold doubloon." He paused at her startled look, then said, "Now, I've kept you from abject boredom for long enough. I can see you're tired." With that he stood, swept her up, and carried her to her room to rest. Czar bounded behind. After her recovery, she had asked for Czar, and her adored wolfhound had slept beside her bed ever since.

July turned into August, and Shawnalese regained her health rapidly. Her speedy recovery, after the herbs started to draw the poisoned blood, had been miraculous. She'd knocked at death's door one day, and three days later she'd taken her first sun in the gardens.

But Chadwick recuperated slowly, and Grizzly had suffered a setback after he'd gone to locate the herbs for Shawnalese. Both men were still confined to their chambers.

When not resting, or visiting Grizzly and Chadwick, Shawnalese spent her time with Hawke, and the halcyon days drifted one into another. Except for unexpected moments when Hawke stared off into the distance, with eyes glazed and expression brooding, it was as though she'd never gone to Paris.

One afternoon she again sat in the gardens, taking the sun and trying to tat a lace reticule for Heather.

"I don't know why you bother bringing your sewing out here. You know I'm not going to let you sew." Hawke chuckled, taking the nearly completed reticule from her to set it in her basket on the ground. Her long golden hair whipped wildly about her face, and he reached out to brush it back, its silky texture caressing his skin. He bent to retrieve the slippers she'd kicked off, tiny shoes so small that he found himself thinking they should have been made of glass. His gaze fastened on her shapely legs, displayed to perfection as she scrambled to her feet.

"I'm feeling marvelous today. Perhaps we could go for a walk. I'm restless. What I really want to do is race Wildfire across the downs."

"Forgive me, fair lady, for not rescuing you from your boredom earlier, but I had a matter to arrange."

"A matter to arrange? Hawke, whatever are you—"

"I thought a picnic might cheer you." He smiled disarmingly and pointed at the two footmen standing nearby, a large wicker basket between them.

"Oh, Hawke, how wonderful—how thoughtful. You know how I love picnics." She laughed with delight, impetuously throwing her arms around his neck to hug him.

Soon they were bouncing on their way in the carriage.

"A private picnic by the sea. And it's such a beautiful day. Does this mean you've forgiven me?" she teased happily as the open carriage, drawn by two matched blacks, took a circuitous, scenic route.

"Yes, it is a beautiful day," he agreed, ignoring her question.

They passed through villages and hamlets of red-brick buildings, and Shawnalese realized she'd acquired the same passionate love for the unique beauty of Foxridge as Hawke had. The nearby forest beckoned with its woods of oak, birch, beech and evergreens, but the downs on each side of the road, covered with nodding wildflowers, whispered enticingly, Come share my fragrance, my beauty.

They topped the ridge where the woodland and the downs swept down to the shimmering sea. The surf crashed against the white cliffs, and off in the distance the craggy white rocks of the Isle of Wight rose majestically, billowing clouds hanging low in the clear blue sky to graze their pointed tops.

Hawke swept her from the carriage and carried her along the cliff edge toward a tree bent by the strong sea winds. The coachman and footman spread the picnic lunch beneath the twisted branches of the gnomed silver birch. With the sea flinging itself against the rocky shore of the island, with a fine mist spraying into the air, and with the breeze whipping them lightly, they enjoyed their picnic.

More than anything, Hawke wanted to throw Shawnalese to the fragrant downs and have his way with her. Instead he said, "Conditions are worse in France."

"You've had some word?"

"The marquis de Montpierre, my friend who witnessed my duel, smuggled a letter out to me. All of France has gone insane. There is rioting in the cities, villages, and provinces. Half crazed mobs have murdered many aristocrats, and even their servants. Then they carry the victims' heads around on pikes to show their power and contempt. Adding to the chaos, brigands loot and pillage. The Third Estate is still working on a constitution, and the bourgeois militia is trying to maintain order, but they can't be everywhere at once. Not an aristocrat is safe. The guards at the gates of Paris won't permit any of the nobility to leave."

Shawnalese sighed. "Even though we can almost see France from here, it seems so far away. It would be so easy to cloister oneself in the sanctuary of Foxridge and ignore the cares of the rest of the world as though they didn't exist. I believe that's the subtle seduction of being wealthy that one must guard against." Absorbed by the natural beauty that surrounded her, she murmured, more to herself than Hawke, "If only I never had to leave here. . ."

"Leave here? Why would you have to leave?"

"My life isn't here, Hawke. I know that now. I had once hoped it was, but that was a childish fantasy." She turned from his achingly handsome face to stare out to sea. "You once said to me that there was no place in your life for me. I've accepted that, and I treasure that we're again friends. But I must say those same words to you, for now there's no longer a place in my life for you. As soon as I'm well enough, it will be time for me to move on." Smiling, she reached up and brushed the curl from his furrowed brow. "This and Foxridge is all wonderful." With a sweep of her arm, she gestured around her. "No, not merely wonderful, magnificent. Still, this isn't me, Hawke. It never has been. I have this restlessness deep inside."

Hawke smiled. By the time he returned from France, she should be fully recovered. Then he'd tell her that he would marry her and spend the rest of his life satiating her Grenville "restlessness." It was a small sacrifice. He'd lost count of the times he'd wished he had reached that decision before he sent her to Paris. Setting that regret aside, he said, "Let's simply enjoy the day and we'll talk when I return from France."

"Return from France!"

"The marquis needs my assistance to get his family out of Paris."

"You can't go to Paris, Hawke. Even with considerable good luck we almost didn't make it safely out of France. You'll never get in and out alive."

"I can't turn my back on the marquis."

"Please, I'm begging you. Don't go."

"I have to. I need to check on the DuBellays, too." At her frightened face, the warmth of her concern flooded through him. "Don't fear. I'll be safe."

"How can you believe that? Because you fed the hungry of Saint-Antoine? That won't get you safely from the coast of France to Paris. That won't get the marquis and his family out of Paris. You won't have an escort of starving women this time. Hawke, you can't do this!"

"Shawnalese, please don't worry. I'll be perfectly all right."

The following morning, Hawke sailed with the tide for France. From the carriage, Shawnalese watched the *Phantom Dream* sail out of sight, and an icy fear coiled around her heart.

The next three weeks, she spent most of her time

with the men at Foxridge—Grizzly, Leif, Chadwick, and sometimes Rutger. There had been no word of Hawke. To distract her, Chadwick invited her to walk in the gardens.

"It seems this will be the only opportunity I'll have to speak to you privately," he complained good-naturedly.

"Perhaps we should sit, Chad. You're still weak, not fully recovered." Shawnalese sat on one of the stone benches overlooking the fountain, and Chadwick lowered himself beside her.

"I've thought of nothing but you since I started recuperating, Shawna." Chadwick lifted her hand to hold it in his. "I want you to be my wife."

She was astonished. She had done nothing to encourage him. Indeed, since his illness she hadn't been alone with him until now.

"I don't want to wait any longer," Chadwick insisted. "Life is too short. We can have our betrothal ball in two or three weeks, Mother will make the arrangements for everything, and we'll be married a month after that."

Chapter 27

"DON'T YOU STILL LOVE LAUREL?"

"Part of me will always love Laurel, just as part of you will always love Hawke. But I know we can live with that, for given enough time, you'll help me forget Laurel and I'll help you forget Hawke."

She stared at the fountain and could think of nothing but Hawke. Where was he now? Was he safe? Why had there been no word?

"Shawna, you've given my life meaning once again—I need you. I want to share my name and my life with you." He paused, and turned her toward him. His deep blue eyes captured hers, and his hands clasped hers gently. "Shawna, I promise you, I can make you happy. I can make you forget the hurt, the pain. I've been through it, I know what you're going through—I'll make you forget Hawke—I promise you."

Filled with compassion and understanding, she looked up at Chadwick's handsome face. If only he could make her forget Hawke—even for a little while.

Chadwick smiled down at her. "I promise there would never be anyone but you. We and our children would have a wonderful life together."

Why had there been no word from Hawke? How could she consider anything about her life without knowing if Hawke was safe? How could she sit calmly in this beautiful garden discussing marriage with a man she loved only as a friend when Hawke might be imprisoned, might be hurt, might even be . . . "Chad, we must find out if Hawke is all right. It's been three weeks. He might need help—"

"God's teeth, Shawnalese! He knows how to take care of himself. He wouldn't have gone without a plan. I just asked you to marry me, or didn't you even hear me?"

"Yes. Yes, of course I heard you. But I'm so worried about Hawke, I can think of little else."

"I see nothing has changed. Not a bloody thing! If you don't give me an answer by tomorrow, I'll assume your answer is yes. You're going to have to say no if you don't want to marry me."

"Chad, please try to understand."

"I do understand. I understand too well. But before you decide to say no, consider carefully. I'm offering you marriage, children, a beautiful home, and my love and fidelity. I know it's meaningless to you, but you'll also be a countess someday. I value you, Shawna, and I can make you forget Hawke."

Chadwick had offered her everything a woman could want. He would be a considerate husband and a good father, and he had a wonderful sense of humor. What more could a child from shanty town wish? Gayhawke Carrington? Why wait until tomorrow? She already knew her answer. She would never marry anyone if not Gayhawke Carrington. Chad could never make her forget Hawke. Not even Hawke could make her forget Hawke. Even so, she cared deeply for Chadwick and didn't want to hurt him.

"There's no reason to wait. I already know my answer, Chad." She knew he wouldn't be crushed by her refusal, for Laurel still lived within his heart. Still, he deserved all of her consideration. She smiled tenderly, then squeezed his hand.

At her smile, Chadwick knew her answer too. He was as good as betrothed. "I'm not concerned that you'll change your mind. You can tell me tomorrow. Don't forget, I'm taking you to the Hardwickes' ball tonight. I've been a convalescent too long. If I spend another day inside this house I'll go daft."

"Of course."

Chadwick stood up, and before she realized what he was about, he bent and, with no regard for propriety, kissed her briefly before he started toward the great hall.

As Chadwick entered the great hall, he almost bumped into Hawke. "Hawke, ol' chap. It's good to have you home. Shawna and I were getting worried about you."

"Yes, I saw you were."

Chadwick grinned triumphantly. "Ah, I daresay you saw us in the gardens."

"I and probably everyone else in the place. What's happening, Chad?"

"Congratulate me, ol' man. I think Shawna is going to marry me."

"Like hell she is!" Hawke roared, his face a mask of rage.

"What is that supposed to mean?"

"It means Shawna is not marrying you," Hawke retorted.

"And why is that?"

"Because I'm her legal guardian, and I say she's not."

At the commotion, servants started to gather, but a wave of Addison's hand sent them scurrying.

"We'll continue this discussion in my study, Chad. Now!" With that, Hawke turned and stormed off, Chadwick close on his heels. When the study door banged shut, Hawke whirled to face his best friend. "When she almost died and I refused to let you see her, I apologized to you for my behavior. That was then. This is now. Know that I am not grief-stricken now, not out of my mind, as then. And for what I am about to say, I will not apologize. I say to you now, as I did then, she is mine—she always has been."

Meanwhile, a distressed Addison bolted into the garden. "Miss Shawnalese!"

Shawnalese was surprised to see Addison—who never hurried, was never unsettled—rushing toward her frantically. "What's wrong, Addison?"

"His Grace and Lord Leighton are in a terrible row. . . ."

"Hawke's home?"

"Yes, and he and Lord Leighton are having heated words. It's never happened before. I'm quite concerned where it might lead. . . . I—I thought perhaps you might be able to prevent. . . ."

Paling, Shawnalese ran into the manor. Addison's words floated after her.

"They're in His Grace's study."

As she approached the closed door, she heard the angry words.

"Are you saying you're going to marry her?" Chadwick questioned at a piercing level. "If you are, I'll step aside."

"I'm saying she belongs to me. You can't have her."

"The hell you say! I *will* marry Shawna. With or without your permission."

"Over my dead body!" The tone of Hawke's voice left no doubt that he intended to back up his words.

Shawnalese opened the door. "Stop!" she cried out. "Stop this minute! Please. I'll not have you two arguing because of me. I won't have it." Both men turned to stare at her. With an aching heart, she commanded herself to composure and spoke calmly. "You can discuss this at a later time. It's time to dress for the Hardwickes' ball."

"I'll be taking you, Shawna," Chadwick stated firmly.

She glanced at Hawke.

"Don't change your plans on my account," Hawke snapped. "I'll not be going."

"I'll meet you in the great hall, Shawna," Chadwick said, and paused to wait for her to leave.

She stepped aside. "I'd like to speak to Hawke for a moment, Chad."

After he left, she closed the door and confronted her guardian. "I wish to make something clear, Hawke. Explicitly clear. I belong to no one but myself. Not to you. Not to anyone. Only myself. And now I would like you to explain a matter to me." Her gaze, reflecting a mixture of anger and hurt, captured his and held. For a moment she said nothing and experienced the feeling that they played the childish game of "who looks away first, loses" in their endless battle of wills. She asked softly, "Why is it that, although you don't want me yourself, you don't want anyone else to have me? What have I done that you have so little regard for me? So much contempt? Or is this simply part of your caste system—I'm of ignoble birth and unworthy to marry a nobleman?"

Unworthy? If not for her wanton ways, there would be no woman more worthy. What woman had a more noble heart than she? What other woman, aristocrat or commoner, had the mettle? What other woman had written pamphlets and speeches, not of scurrilous sedition against the king, but moving, inspiring discourses on the rights of all mankind? She would marry none but he, and after that she would know no other man. Of that he had no doubt. Yet he didn't say what he thought, didn't tell her how he felt, didn't even answer her questions. Instead, his gaze still locked with hers, he said, "You don't want to marry Chad. You don't love him."

"And why do you say that?"

"Because you love me."

She inhaled sharply. Were her feelings still so obvious, even to him? Apparently so. Abrubtly her pride came to the fore. "Love you? Right now I don't even like you. How could you have said such a thing to Chad? If I hadn't come, would you have called him out? Your best friend—your lifelong friend?"

Hawke knew she was right. Because of her, he'd almost come to blows with his best friend. How many more men would he fight because of her? What was this, the third, the fourth, time? Was he so besotted that he'd never again know a reasonable thought or responsible deed regarding her? Setting aside that troubling reflection, he asked, "Do you deny that you love me?"

"I once loved you more than anything—more than sunlight, more than laughing children, more than the air I breathe. I lived only for you. I became all I thought you wanted me to be. I'd have given you my life, but then you sent me away." She paused, stubbornly refusing to look away from the gaze that bored into hers. "You're partly right in thinking I love you. But you see, the Gayhawke Carrington I loved was the man who gently comforted a young girl who'd lost her mother.

That's the Gayhawke I love—will always love. The Gayhawke who stands before me is a stranger I don't know. Which one are you, really? The one I knew and loved before I went to Paris, or the one I met in Paris? And what is this barrier you erect to keep the rest of the world out? And why?"

"Do you want to marry Chad?"

"Is this your method to avoid answering my question?"

"Which question is that? I've avoided quite a few."

"Yes, I know. Let's begin again. Why, when you don't want me, do you not want any one else to have me?"

He moved forward until he felt the heat from her body. She refused to step back. With their gazes still locked, he could but admire her defiance, the regal proud tilt of her head. She was magnificent. His hands clasped her shoulders gently, and his voice turned husky. "What makes you think I don't want you?"

Unable to think, unable to breathe, she forced her gaze to remain fastened on his and saw the slow softening in his eyes, the increased desire.

"You don't want to marry Chad," Hawke murmured, and slid his arms around her back to pull her into his embrace. "He could never satiate your passions."

Her heart slammed against her chest, her pulse fluttered wildly. "And you could, Gayhawke?"

Her throaty voice was almost his undoing as he battled his desire to take her right there, right then. No woman had ever fired his loins, his heart, as she did. Somehow he knew that good, bad, and everything in between, it would always be so. Now he had to learn to accept it. "I could."

"You'd like that, wouldn't you, Carrington?" she challenged, then struggled to free herself while she still had some presence of mind. His iron grip tightened. "Sorry. This isn't my day to become a nobleman's plaything."

Still their gazes remained fused. "I can think of only

one way," he murmured, "to keep both of us from losing this war of wills."

At that, his head lowered to capture her lips with a gentleness that melted her resolve. Barely, just barely, she fought her weakness for the one man she knew she could never have—the one man who still dominated her thoughts, her dreams, her world. She longed to throw her arms around him, to cling submissively. His kiss revealed none of the antagonism of their encounter but was only tender caress, a delicious seduction of her lips, seduction of her heart.

"Every time ya put on a new gown, luv, I think it's the prettiest I've seen," Mrs. Kendall said in admiration of the satin ball gown. She fussed with the huge, off-the-shoulder puffed sleeves that ended at the elbow. "Mark my words, every eye'll be on ya."

Shawnalese tugged at the lace-edged, blushingly low décolletage, then sighed in resignation as it slipped down again. "I don't really want to go, Mrs. Kendall, but I can't think of an acceptable excuse. Oh, well, perhaps I'll enjoy dancing. I haven't danced since Christmas."

At the lack of enthusiasm in Shawnalese's voice, Mrs. Kendall glanced up. "Keep up your spirits, luv. There's nothin' like kickin' up your heels to chase them blues away. No indeedy."

Mrs. Kendall was wrong, for Shawnalese had to force every smile, coerce every word from her lips. Ever lingering at the edges of her mind was Hawke's kiss, his altercation with Chadwick, and the dreaded refusal she must give Chadwick tomorrow. She was whirling around the room in the arms of some unknown man when she saw *him*. He strode into the room with the unmistakable stamp of arrogant nobility on his face, looking more handsome than any one man had a right to be. Soon she was floating in his arms, unable to hide her pleasure in seeing him. The evening suddenly come to life.

"What brings you here, Carrington?" The hand at her back burned through her gown, and her heart fluttered crazily.

"You do."

"I?"

"I knew you wouldn't enjoy the evening if I wasn't here." He grinned down at her, a teasing light in his eyes.

"How generous of you to give of yourself so unselfishly—and so modestly. More than likely you're here to make certain I don't lead Chad astray."

"That too," he agreed, chuckling.

"Or because you two have made a wager as to who will get the last dance."

"Chad told you about that, did he?"

"Yes, and also of the much larger wagers you used to make regarding whom the lady in question went home with. You're naught but naughty boys in gentlemen's clothes."

"I shall have to speak to Chad about his careless prattling." The music stopped, and they walked from the dance floor.

"My dear fellow," Chadwick interrupted, "you've had her long enough. Besides, Lady Seymour wishes to see you. She seems to think you've been avoiding her since you came home from France in July."

Hawke stepped aside. "Perhaps that's because I have been."

Shawnalese stood at Chadwick's side, all too aware of the Viscountess Paige Seymour clinging possessively to Hawke. Forcing herself to look away, Shawnalese smothered a gasp of disbelief, for Lord Bradford had arrived—and beside him walked his daughter, Lady Laurel Bradford.

Chadwick glanced up and stiffened.

Thereafter, Shawnalese felt as though she'd attended a play being acted out before her eyes. Chadwick

attempted to make conversation with her but failed
miserably, staring hypnotized at Laurel Bradford, who
returned his gaze as though in a trance. At the same
time the beautiful Lady Paige Seymour expertly
worked every feminine wile on Hawke. Turning away
from Paige, Shawnalese spoke to Chad loudly enough
for everyone nearby to hear. "You simply must welcome Lady Bradford home. I'll join you shortly."
Then, for his ears only, she added, "It might be the
only opportunity you have. I'll keep Lord Bradford
busy." With that, she moved in the direction of
Laurel's father.

Chadwick joined the group that surrounded Laurel
and soon steered her to a quiet corner of the immense
room.

Laurel had been sent to the United States. She had
written numerous letters to Chadwick the first year
and a half, assuming they'd been posted. But then
when she'd received no letters in reply, she'd assumed
Chadwick had lost interest and ceased writing to him.
Even so, she had not been able to take interest in any
other suitor.

Now a nervous and anxious Laurel tried to put
Chadwick at ease in his distress. Having recovered
from the initial shock of seeing him after so many
years, the heretofore reserved and withdrawn young
woman suddenly became her old vivacious, bubbly self.

Meanwhile, Shawnalese talked comfortably with
Lord Bradford, somehow able to hide her resentment
at his having kept apart for so long two people who
still loved each other.

"For three years now," Lord Bradford said, "my
daughter has refused to be courted. Now I've lost my
beloved wife, I'm growing older, and I wish to have my
only daughter with me, and hopefully grandchildren. I
only hope Lord Leighton hasn't become involved since
my last inquiry." His eyes questioned her.

Shawnalese's heart leapt, for Lord Bradford, aware

that Chadwick would be here, had brought his daughter to the Hardwickes' ball hoping to achieve a reconciliation between Laurel and Chadwick. "Chad isn't involved," Shawnalese assured him, "for no one but your daughter could fill his heart. He loves her still. He's a wonderful man—you couldn't find one who'd be a better husband to Laurel."

Relieved, Lord Bradford sighed. "When I saw Lord Leighton with you, I feared I'd made a grave error. So, now that you know we both have the same purpose in mind, perhaps you wouldn't mind if I no longer keep my back to my daughter. I would enjoy looking at her lovely face."

Shawnalese glanced at Chadwick and Laurel, amazed at the transformation in Chadwick's expression. The two were oblivious of everyone but each other. Chadwick threw back his head, laughed at something Laurel said, and caught Shawnalese's eye. Suddenly, he sobered, as though he'd only now remembered his proposal and thus his commitment to her.

"Excuse me, Lord Bradford, I'd like to welcome your daughter back." Shawnalese floated across the ballroom. "Laurel, I'm so happy to see you. We've missed you terribly." The two women chatted comfortably for a time, then Shawnalese said, "Please excuse me, Laurel, but I need to borrow Chadwick. I'll return him shortly." She smiled, then glanced at Chadwick's now somber countenance.

"Chad, have you seen the Hardwickes' magnificent library yet?" Shawnalese took Chadwick's proffered arm to lead him in that direction. Silently, he followed her down the wide corridor and into the candle lit library.

"Chad, I believe you know I love you," she said softly, and caught his look of despair before he masked it. "Hawke's put a considerable amount of time, money, and effort into trying to make a genteel lady of me, but I'm afraid he'll never succeed"—she laughed softly—

"for I know this certainly isn't the time, or place, but I need to give you my decision on your proposal, and I need to give it to you now." At his slight intake of breath, Shawnalese cupped his face between her hands. "Dear, sweet Chad, I love you, and I know you love me—we love each other as dearly as if we were brother and sister. But I think we both know that isn't the kind of love with which to start a marriage, and—"

"Shawna . . ." Chadwick interrupted, taking her hands in his.

"Please hear me out. Hawke has taught me that if you refuse to accept anything but the best, you will usually get it. You had the best once—that special love—with Laurel. You can't accept less than that now . . . and neither can I," she said, and wrapped her arms around him. "I tried to tell you this earlier, but I fear something I said or did allowed you to misinterpret my answer. So I'm asking you now, to release us both from any misguided commitment." She looked up into his shadowed face, and at his silence, knowing he struggled with honor, she added, "I ask this for both of us, not only you. My heart is bound to Gayhawke, I am bound to Gayhawke. He is all that I am, all that I can ever become. I loved him yesterday, I love him today, I will love only him through all of my tomorrows. My eyes have never seen any but he." She took Chadwick's hands in hers and implored understanding. "You see, Chad, Hawke doesn't merely live in my heart. Hawke lives in my soul."

At that moment, unknown to either of them, a tall figure slipped silently into the library.

Chapter 28

CHADWICK HUGGED SHAWNALESE TO HIM. "OH, Shawna, I love you. I will always love you," he cried out joyously.

"I know. And I'll always love you, exactly as I do now," she promised, tears of happiness overflowing to trickle down her cheeks.

Hawke's voice boomed out of the shadows of the dimly lit room. "I hate to break up this tender love scene, but we are guests of the Hardwickes, or have you forgotten? I'm sure this passionate indiscretion can be replayed at a more opportune time, when you won't be insulting your host."

Shawnalese stiffened. Again she'd been discovered in a compromising situation, one that had to look as incriminating as Hawke assumed it to be. And once more Hawke condemned her out of hand, without an explanation.

"Gayhawke Carrington, you—"

"Hawke, you don't understand," Chadwick interrupted.

"Chad, don't . . . please," Shawnalese implored.

"I understand a hell of a lot more than you think I do," Hawke raged, his face dark with fury, his fists clenched at his side.

"And I understand you're a bloody jackass," Chadwick exploded, trying to maneuver around Shawnalese, who had positioned herself between the two men.

Abruptly Shawnalese turned and, with a deliberate intent to rankle Hawke, stood on tiptoe and twined her arms around Chadwick's neck. "Please, Chad," she whispered for his ears only, "for my sake, go to Laurel—with my blessings. I don't want a scene here, and I won't beseech Hawke to allow me to give an explanation. Go to Laurel. Now. I beg of you."

Wordlessly Chadwick circled his arm around her trembling body and brushed past Hawke. He stopped at the door and turned back. "God help you, Hawke, for you're the biggest fool I've ever known."

Chadwick and Shawnalese started toward the ballroom when the sound of Hawke's fist smashing into the wall echoed in their ears.

Rutger paced the great hall at Foxridge. As long as any of the family remained awake, Addison assigned at least one servant to be in attendance. Tonight Nadine performed that function. She was sitting inconspicuously in a dim corner, waiting to be of service, when Hawke arrived home from the Hardwickes and hurried into the great hall.

Nadine stood up. "Good evening, Your Grace."

"Good evening, Nadine. Where is Shawnalese?"

"I don't know, Your Grace," Nadine replied, and looked to Rutger for an answer.

"Where is Shawnalese, Rutger?" Hawke asked. "Has she gone to bed?"

"She was rather nettled. She changed clothes and went out. Said she needed to be alone. What have you done to her now, Hawke?"

Ignoring Rutger's question, Hawke asked, "You let her go out alone this time of night?"

"Let her? God's breath! You know you can't tell Shawna what to do. Besides, I wager she's with Grizzly."

"Not at this time of night. She's not at the woodland temple?"

"No. She left by the front. Czar's with her."

"What are you doing here, by the way?" Hawke questioned. "Is everything all right?"

"Everything is fine. I brought Shawna home. I'm staying over, but I wanted to wait until she returned before I turned in."

"I'll go get her."

"She's probably riding Wildfire."

"Wildfire! If she's gone riding, Rutger, you'll get the thrashing she deserves."

"What's gnawing at you, Hawke? You've done something else to unsettle her, haven't you?"

Without answering, Hawke spun and left. Shawnalese was not with Grizzly, nor was she in the stables with Wildfire. There was only one other place she could be.

Aggravated that Hawke had discovered her in Chadwick's arms, frustrated that he'd assumed the worst of her, Shawnalese cursed her bad luck. Uncertain what to say to him, what to do, unable to think clearly, she'd left the Hardwickes and raced to the serenity of the sea. She'd had the presence of mind to bring her pistol, Czar, and her dagger, which was strapped to her calf. Certainly the strenuous exercise of a vigorous swim, the cool water of the English Channel, would relieve some of her distress. With no one to see her, she'd stripped down to her chemise, and then impulsively tossed her chemise aside as well. Uninhibited, with the warm breeze caressing her nakedness, she felt considerably better even before placing a toe in the water.

Shortly after that, Hawke walked along the sands looking for Shawnalese, and Czar bounded toward him. He petted the wolfhound on the head and ordered, "Watch, Czar." The big dog sat, alert and watchful, guardian of his master and mistress on the beach, sentinel of their privacy.

The English Channel, bathed in moonlight, shimmering in starlight, rippled gently toward the shore. The hushed whisper of a fragrant breeze kissed the sea, swept the shore, and the rhythmical rush of the tide lapped softly. The moon played hide-and-seek with puffy gray clouds and cast its intermittent beams across the shore, across the water, across the chalk peaks of the Isle of Wight. Then he saw her, cloaked in moonlight, rising like Venus from the sea.

Hawke glanced from her to the pile of clothes on the beach and back to her. If she walked ashore in all her naked beauty, he knew what would happen, and he didn't want that. Why, he didn't know. He knew only that he loved her enough to want to marry her before possessing her. He wanted to give her that much. Tossing off his coat and his waistcoat, he dropped to the sand, hurriedly removed his shoes, and leapt to his feet. Unaware of his presence, Shawnalese walked toward the shore, a temptation no man should have to resist. Otherwise fully clothed, he walked into the water toward her. The moon slipped from behind a cloud, and he sucked in his breath.

Shawnalese waded toward the shore, exhilarated and restored from her swim. She could face Hawke's condemnation now, could look him straight in the eyes and apologize for nothing. There was nothing for which to apologize.

The moon peeked from behind the clouds, endowing its soft light, and she gasped. Hawke, fully clothed, splashed directly toward her.

And there she stood—as naked as the day she was born. She took a step backward, then another, and another, until the water covered all but her shoulders. Hawke followed relentlessly until he stood inches from her. *Don't let him touch me*, she entreated. He said not a word but stood staring down at her. He was shrouded in moonlight, and his wet shirt clung to his broad shoulders, to his massive chest. She could do nothing but stare back. Unable to breathe, she swallowed, then sent up a different prayer. *Please let him touch me, take me in his arms, tell me he understands.* But she knew the duke of Foxridge had not sought her out, had not waded into the sea, fully clothed, to comfort her. Hell knew no fury like Hawke when he was enraged.

"I've come to apologize for my crude behavior earlier this evening."

Gayhawke Lawrence Richard Carrington, exalted peer of the realm, duke of Foxridge, apologize? Impossible! "Pardon me?"

"I'm extremely sorry for my conduct at the Hardwickes. Before he left, Chad explained what happened in the library. . . ." Hawke paused, then continued when she made no response, "That was an admirable deed you did for Chad. I hope . . ."

Shawnalese's hand reached out to caress his cheek, then slid down his muscled chest. The water washed against her back, and the moon disappeared behind a dusky cloud, leaving them shrouded in its diffused light. "We don't need apologies between us, Carrington—not ever—not for anything," she whispered, unable to speak aloud. "I realize what doing so has cost you in pride, and I thank you, but even more, I admire you."

With those murmured words, she shot one more salvo into his heart. He had been an offensive boor, and instead of faulting him, she'd given him accolades for admitting it. He had to get out of the water, had to get away from her, for at this moment not even the water cooled his ardor. With a husky voice, he murmured, "I've said what I came to say. I'll leave so you can get dressed, then I'll take you back to the house. You're not safe here."

She clasped his arm, steadying herself while her other hand dove into the water and came up with her dagger.

He laughed. "I should have known." He stared down at her, the goddess of the sea, the goddess of beauty, the goddess of his heart, and felt his resolve weaken. "You're still not safe here"—his voice broke—"trust me on that."

She scabbarded her dagger, and he turned and started toward the shore. She followed. The water dripped from her full breasts, fell away from her tiny waist, and now surrounded her softly curving hips. She stopped, but Hawke walked straight ahead. His wet shirt hugged his unusually broad shoulders, clung to his bulging biceps, cleaved to every rippling muscle in his tapering back; his trousers adhered to him like a second skin. What must it be like to be loved by such a man? She heard a soft voice and realized too late that it was her own. "Gayhawke . . ."

He hesitated, shuddering.

"Gayhawke," she repeated in a sensuous caress.

He couldn't help himself. He knew it and God knew it. He turned back. Heaven help her, for she'd just sealed her own fate.

"Perhaps I don't want to be 'safe,' Carrington." The moon moved from its hiding place, and Hawke faced her from a distance of a few feet. She knew she should cover herself, or perhaps be embarrassed, but she didn't and she wasn't. There was no shame for what she felt for him, only a love that demanded to be fulfilled. There was nothing but Hawke. All else faded. "Let me love you, Gayhawke."

Frozen where he stood, calf deep in water, he took in her beauty. Simply looking at her inflamed his senses, torched his body. He slowly unbuttoned his shirt and tossed it ashore. His trousers followed. Naked, he walked toward her with deliberate slowness. She was a woman well experienced, and he wanted her to fully enjoy the sight of what would soon take her to the heights of rapture.

Her heart slammed against her chest, her pulse raced wildly, and she held her breath. Her gaze lowered from his face to his furred, muscular chest and fastened there, wanting to drop lower but not daring to. She had never seen a nude man before, had never wanted to—until now. A little at a time, she let out her breath and lowered her gaze.

He grinned arrogantly. Women had always appreciated his attributes, and he could see Shawnalese was no different. For the first time in his life he was grateful for his endowments, for he knew he would erase the memory of every man she'd ever known. And he intended to spend all night doing so. "Think I can cool your hot blood?"

Flushing, she didn't reply. This was a mistake. Again she'd offered him her love. Again he wanted only her body. His apology had changed nothing. She took a step backward, then another. "Stay back," she whispered, for she knew he didn't love her, now knew he would never love her.

Time staggered to a standstill.

He advanced.

She retreated.

She'd whispered, "Stay back." Her body whispered, "Come closer." So he said, "Stay back? You're one of those women who like to play games?" He moved forward. "Play 'catch me if you can.' And you know I can." His arousal ached now, his desire for her irrational. He hadn't yet touched her, and still his response raced out of control. The water reached almost to her breasts when he caught her, crushed her to him, and his kiss drove her head back with a brutal force. His mouth slanted ravenously across hers, with months of hunger for a woman—with years of hunger for her—then opened to devour her lips in a sizzling kiss. She struggled weakly. He ignored it. With urgent need, he seized her buttocks and clasped her to him fiercely, and the hardness of his desire pressed into her abdomen, the strength of his chest mashed her breasts. There was no subtlety, no finesse, no respect, in his actions, only pure, unadulterated lust.

She felt pleasure course through her body, leaving

her limp, unresisting. He lifted her, forced the boldness of his hunger against the softness of her woman-
hood, and began a circling movement. She tingled
deep inside with glorious surges of mysterious, delicious longing. Moaning, she opened her mouth to his
thrusting tongue, encircled his neck with her arms,
and clung breathlessly to him.

Feeling her surrender, Hawke swirled his tongue
into the cavern of her sweet mouth, to twist around
hers, to tantalize hers.

Lost, unable to stop him, unable to stop herself, she
tantalized back, mimicking everything he did.
Groaning, he swept her up in his arms and stumbled
to shore, his mouth never leaving hers. Dropping to
the sand, half in the water, half out, he mounted her,
kneed her thighs apart, and stroked her velvet softness while the cool surf rushed over their hot bodies.
As his mouth moved from hers, a shuddering sigh
escaped her lips. She arched to his hand and sighed,
"My love . . ."

"This," he murmured while he expertly manipulated
the dewy warmth of her to receive him, "is what you
love, Shawnalese, not me." Then he moved to suckle one
rosy tip to taut anticipation, then the other. The next
wave broke over them, and he smiled. She was as hot
for him as he for her. Guiding himself to her tight
sheath, he groaned when again she arched to welcome
him. "I knew you'd be like a mare in season," he uttered.

Tonight he would have her three times. Five times.
Until he dropped, until she begged him, No more.
Desire flooded him as he entered her and thrust to
give her what they both craved; the swells of the sea
pulsated with him, with them. At the delicate barrier,
he froze. It couldn't be! Withdrawing, he pushed forward again, ever so slowly, ever so gently, only to be
stopped once more by the fragile shield. Dear God!
Shawny!

What had he done? Retreating from her body, he

dropped to the sand beside her and pulled her into his arms. Filled with self-loathing, filled with contempt for himself, he could think of nothing other than the way he'd just treated her, of the crude things he'd said.

How many other times had he done as much?

Never had he insisted on a detailed explanation of what had happened in France. He'd simply judged her and found her guilty.

He sat up and stared out to sea, remembering all the times he'd tried to seduce her. His ward. His Shawny.

Now he wanted to tell her how he felt about her. But how—after the way he'd treated her, after all he'd said and done these last ten months—would she ever believe what lived in his heart? If he said what he felt, she would think it one more lie, one more attempt at seduction. Never could he make it up to her, but he knew he'd spend the rest of his life trying. Beginning right now.

In spite of all his ill treatment of her, she had still offered him the most valuable treasure she possessed: her virtue. It was a precious gift he could not accept, for he was not worthy. Even so, the day would come when she would know that he loved her, had always loved her, and for no other reason than that did he want to marry her. After that, with a most grateful heart, he would ask her to marry him, and then he'd accept her gift of purity.

Shawnalese sat up beside him. "Have I done something wrong?"

He enfolded her in his arms and lowered her to her back, enveloping her in an endless embrace. The tide surged over them, then ebbed. "Shawny, I'm so sorry. Sorry for everything. Can you ever forgive—"

Small fingers on his lips stilled his words. He clasped her hand and pressed each fingertip to his lips, one at a time. The moon moved behind a cloud, and they lay on the beach unmoving, his body partly covering hers where he leaned over her. Reverence and con-

tentment reigned supreme until she reached up and
brushed the lock from his brow, murmuring,
"Gayhawke . . ."

Their gazes met and held on the moonlit beach,
locked in the magic of the moment. He dared not
move, dared not hold her tighter, dared not drop his
gaze to her lush little body, for his willpower threatened to collapse.

"I'm cold."

Welcoming the interruption, he rolled to his side
and leapt to his feet, offering her his hand. "You get
dressed. We're going back to the house." If they didn't
leave now, they wouldn't leave before dawn.

She sat up, her eyes at his thigh level. She inhaled
deeply and accepted his hand, and her gaze moved up as
she did. He was a marvelous specimen of masculinity.
Overcome by a torrent of seductive emotions, she was
drawn to him, flung into a whirlpool of tumultuous feelings that sucked her down. She felt herself drowning in
the fathomless depths of his eyes, in the abyss of his
bewitchment. "I don't want to leave," she said softly. The
palm of her hand pressed against his furry chest, and she
stepped closer. "I want to stay here . . . with you."

"No." His one word was husky, choked.

The sea swirled around her ankles. "I'm cold,
Hawke."

He groaned. "I'll get your clothes." Her hand stayed
him.

"I don't want my clothes. I want your arms around
me."

"No, Shawny. Not now."

"You don't want me?"

Seconds ticked by like an eternity. Heaven help him!
Once more he thought of all he wanted to do to atone
for his behavior these many months, for his behavior
tonight. She deserved to be courted, to know she was
valued for herself. Deserved to be bedded the first
time as his wife, not on a deserted beach.

"You don't want me," she said. It was not a question, but a statement, for she knew why. "I'll not ask you to marry me. Just love me."

If he made love to her now—when his heart overflowed with love for her, when mysterious emotions flooded through him, when his body cried out only for her, and when he felt like laughing and crying with relief, with joy, with immeasurable happiness—he would be lost for all time. But he was snared by a trap of his own making. He had loved Shawny too deeply, had desired her too long. All lofty principles, all good intentions, fled, and he clasped her in his arms. God help me . . . God help us both.

"Shawny . . . Shawny . . . Shawny . . ." Her name on his lips was a litany of love. Then, with all the pent-up hunger within him, he sought her softly parted lips, his self-control breaking like a dam to sweep them both along.

Gently he nipped at her mouth, one hand clasping her to him while the other slipped down her back. She quivered at his touch, at the tenderness of his delicious kiss, a slow, drugging kiss that lingered and savored and sang through her veins. His lips whispered across her cheek to her ear, to nibble there while his hand moved up to cup the soft firmness of her breast. Her senses reeled, and the pounding in her heart leapt to her head.

With the fire in his loins threatening his restraint, Hawke willed his body under control, for she was the woman he loved, and he intended to take her slowly, take her gently, with him. He swept her up and carried her higher on the beach, out of the water. Lowering her to the sand, he tickled his tongue into her ear, and she shivered. His hand moved from her breast with a painful teasing, across her taut abdomen to the soft fur at her thighs.

She shuddered in ecstatic anguish. He reclaimed her lips and parted her thighs. Currents of yearning spiraled through her, the moan she heard was her own, and she returned his kisses with wild abandon. His tongue slipped into the honeyed cavern of her mouth, to meet and curl sensuously around hers before he explored, searched, and caressed every part. Transported on a soft, billowy cloud, she languished while his fingers brought her to a dreamy ecstasy, then to higher heights, where she writhed under his touch, swept along in the tide of his passion, of her passion. When his hand moved to her thigh, she moaned a protest.

Lifting his lips from hers, he whispered, "We have all night, Shawny."

His words, as though far off, drifted into her mind, and she knew that if he kept this up all night she wouldn't live to see the dawn. Still, she didn't care. She was caught in the power of his enslaving drug. To be in Hawke's arms was the fulfillment of her every dream. To have him doing all these wondrous things to her was to surpass her every dream. To have him call her Shawny again was to return her heart to her—and it beat only for him.

Chapter 29

A RAPTUROUS TIME LATER, SHAWNALESE, INTIMATE-ly joined with Hawke, floated to some unexplored place beyond the stars, taking him with her. For that instant that knew no time or space, they soared with the wings of an eagle, of one body.

One breath.
One soul.

"You are now my wife, Shawny." Hawke gazed at her in the moonlight and kissed her tenderly. "I never dreamed it possible to know such contentment."

They lay on the beach entwined in each other's arms, wordlessly watching the puffy clouds cross the full moon in the star-filled sky, listening to the rhythmic pulse of the surf, the rhythmic beat of their hearts.

For some time he held her in his loving embrace. He had taken her to the stars, but once there his innocent Shawny had taken his hand and led him far beyond— to soar in an ecstasy into the rapture of paradise, a mystical place he'd never before explored. "Teach me," Shawny had said. Then she had taught him the difference between bedding a woman and making love. After that, what could he possibly teach her? Overcome with emotion, he broke the peaceful silence. "Shawny, Shawny . . . What are you doing to me, love?"

Unwilling to ask what he meant, she smiled up at him.

At the beauty of her nakedness, he murmured, "Already I'm craving you again."

"Is that all I am to you, Hawke—a craving?" She lowered her lashes to hide the hurt.

"Craving? No. Exquisite obsession comes a little closer." Leaping to his feet, he towered over her in all his naked glory.

She swallowed.

"I'll race you to the sea." Smiling playfully, he offered her a hand up.

"For some reason, I think I'm too weak to move from here. I wonder why."

Laughing, he swept her up in strong arms, and while she clung submissively, he carried her into the water. "The cool water will buoy you up . . . and then I'll make you weak all over again."

"You're as ardent as I knew you'd be, Gayhawke Carrington."

"Thank heaven you're right there with me."

"Aye. I fear I am—and it's all your doing."

"It would appear we have a joyous future ahead of us."

Her heart hammered wildly. Could he possibly mean . . . ? She forced the hopeful from her mind, for she would never again live in hope only to wither in despair.

For a time they romped in the water, until she glanced up at his eyes, glazed with desire. His fingers traced each feature of her face. His hand reached beneath the water for her breast to gently caress her there before moving lower, then lower. Her knees weakened.

"Be prepared to spend a lot of time in my arms, for I'll never have enough of you." He smiled, as though to himself, before adding, "Heaven knows I waited long enough." He bent to kiss the hollow of her throat, then, backing toward the shore, he drew her with him.

This time she experienced none of the pain she'd known before, only the wonderful feel of his love swelling inside her body, inside her heart, and she cried out with hunger, her hands caressing his buttocks, urging him on. He withdrew, and she moaned in protest until slowly he started the escalating rhythm that carried them both to new heights. He slid his hands under her derriere, guided her into a rhythm to match his, and she floated in the exquisite torment of unbelievable pleasure, a heated passion that raged through them both.

She murmured his name and he cried out hers, as a peak of fire consumed them both and carried them skyward to soar gloriously through the heavens, to dip and glide in ecstasy, to spin and spiral in rhapsody, held in a space of frozen time in that kingdom of love they shared.

Shawnalese sighed, happy, contented, and refused to think of tomorrow. She took his hand, still clasping hers, and pressed it to her cheek for a time. He was the master of seduction—the seduction of her body, the seduction of her heart, the seduction of her soul.

Hawke couldn't speak, for the joy in his heart drowned his voice. Still, if he couldn't tell her how much he loved her, he could show her. A virile lover, he did.

All night.

As dawn approached, Shawnalese shivered, naked in Hawke's arms, laughing as he playfully covered them with sand and prolonged as long as possible the time when they must leave their enchanted beach.

"You've awakened a sleeping tigress, Carrington. Don't be surprised to find me beating on your chamber door some night," she teased.

Hawke had decided that he'd continue with his original plans: to give Shawny the consideration she deserved. He would leave for London tomorrow and buy her the most extravagant diamond ring he could find, then return and propose formally to her. He did not want her to think his was an impulsive, unplanned, or obligatory proposal. Never again would he treat her ill. That meant a lengthy betrothal. But now that his Shawny had been returned to him, now that he had sampled paradise, he was not going to endure another lengthy abstinence. "You may be beating on my back, love," he replied, "but there will be no doors between us. Hereafter you discreetly sleep in my chambers. There won't be any well-worn paths between our rooms." The words had barely left his lips before he realized his error in uttering them.

She gasped. "I will not!"

He could not retract his words, but neither would he again allow his willpower to flee. As impatient as a boy, he'd started to propose to her several times through the long and magical night but had managed to bite back the words each time. He would not put his wishes before her welfare. Shawny needed to know that she was loved. As a young girl she'd been needy for his love, and now he could see that as a young woman she still was. No doubts must loom between them. He'd pay her proper court; then, after he'd proposed, after she wore his ring, after their wedding date was set, she would see the sense of moving into his chambers. With that goal in mind, he tried to smooth his blunder. "I must leave for London tomorrow, Shawny. We'll discuss this when I return." He smothered her with sweet, loving kisses.

At dawn's faint rays, they slipped into the manor. No torches flamed in the great hall, no candle flickered in its shadowy dimness.

Glancing around, Hawke exhaled with relief, for no servant observed their entrance. He reached into his pocket and pulled out a closed hand. Sand trickled to the floor. They both glanced down at the sand, then back at each other, and smiled. He reached out and took her hand, turned it palm up and placed a spindle seashell there. "A memento of tonight." Then she was in his arms, and he kissed her closed eyes, her cheek, her ear, her throat . . . His hand slipped familiarly inside her blouse to fondle her breast.

Lost, she whimpered softly.

Hearing her moan, Rutger sat up on the sofa, where he'd fallen asleep, and witnessed their intimate embrace.

Hawke kissed her with a fiery passion that she returned with equal fervor. His hand moved from her breast to explore her supple body, then stole under her skirt and up her thigh while she clung to him with a hunger that betrayed their intimacy. When she gave a small sigh, he swept her into his arms to carry her up the winding staircase, Czar trailing behind.

Minutes later Hawke crossed the gallery toward his room in the south wing. Rutger roared, "Carrington, come down here!"

Instantly Hawke knew they had been observed.

Hoping to keep an incensed Rutger from waking the household, he bounded down the stairs.

Nadine, startled awake by the shout, hurried toward the great hall from her post in the dining hall where she'd fallen asleep. Addison would severely rebuke her for dozing while she was in attendance to the family. Drawn up short by the personal conversation, she could not help but overhear.

"By God, you will marry my sister!" Rutger thundered. "You will marry Shawna!"

"Let's talk in my study, Rutger. Your bellowing will wake everyone, if it hasn't already."

Enraged and uncontrolled, Rutger shouted, "You'll marry Shawna, or I'll call you out."

"Call me out? Would your death get her married?"

"I'm aware of your prowess with weapons, Gayhawke. In the event of my death, Leif would stand in my stead. Then you could explain to Shawna why you killed her brothers and also to Mother why you killed her sons."

"You've told Leif that Shawny is his sister?"

"Of course."

Hawke cursed. At this moment he could happily take the lash to Rutger, and he felt the explosive situation degenerating by the second. He grabbed Rutger by the arm. "Outside, Rutger. I'll not have you shout the house down."

Unable to help herself, Nadine raced to the window.

The sun was rising. Rutger's arms flailed the air as he shouted, "The question isn't *if* you are going to marry Shawna, but how soon."

Hawke shook his head. "Shawny deserves to be properly courted first."

Rutger's fists clenched and unclenched. "God's breath! You're talking to me, Hawke. Rutger. You've 'courted' women for as long as I can remember, and you're still not married. I'll tell you what my sister deserves, and that is to be married after being deflowered by a rake like you."

Hawke shook his head in frustration. "I didn't intend for last night to happen."

"Yes, and I don't intend to be the baron of Ravencroft."

Enraged, Hawke grabbed Rutger by the shirtfront. Rutger looked down at Hawke's hand on his chest. "If this is to end in a duel, I'll hurl the insult now."

Instantly Hawke released his nephew, his face grim. Dear God, how had matters deteriorated to this sorry pass? He nodded in agreement. "I will marry Shawny, Rutger. There's a matter I need to see to in London. I'll propose as soon as I return." He groaned aloud, for now Shawny would pay the price for his indiscretion. She deserved to be courted, and now that too was being cruelly snatched away from her. But for consideration of her feelings, he would willingly marry her today. Would prefer it.

"The only matter you will see to on this day, Hawke, is proposing to Shawna. I won't have her spend a week or more thinking you have abandoned her, and I won't have you return with a changed mind, forcing me to go through this again—or, worse yet, hunt you down in London."

Because Rutger was his nephew, Hawke ignored the insult. "Consider it done. As soon as she's up."

"And I want the announcement made to the family today. You'll not wriggle out of this."

"I'll make the announcement after I've talked to Shawny."

An angry Rutger and an angrier Hawke shook hands.

While Hawke and Rutger exchanged heated words, Shawnalese lay in her bed, thinking. For not one moment did she regret her night in Hawke's arms. She loved him with an intensity bordering on obsession. However, against the brightening rays of a new day, their night of love had to be accepted for what it was: a brief interlude, nothing more. She had submitted

pou, no, not submitted, enticed him, for she had
mention her, would never marry her. Even so,
had not even ht, bewitched and besotted, she had
only passion for h. implied that he loved her. He
woman. Her face flame. The night had been one of

By that same light of day, d been but one more
she'd come to a turning point in. o recognized that
have left Foxridge long ago, but no fe. She should
had a choice. If she stayed, she knew she no longer
mistress. At that imagining she shuddered. Still, she
didn't regret what she had done. She would live the
rest of her life on the memories of last night, for never
would she marry any but Gayhawke.

With that vow went the children she yearned to
have, and she fell into a troubled sleep, making plans
for her departure.

Chapter 30

In the afternoon, Hawke joined Heather,
Rutger, and Leif in the great hall. "Shawny's not up yet?"

"No, she's not, Gayhawke," Heather replied. "I wonder why? She left the Hardwickes before I did. I hope
she's not sick."

"She's not sick, Mother," Rutger said, scowling.
"She and Hawke came to an understanding last—"

"Rutger!" Hawke warned. What w— ...ked.
nephew? Shawny had yet to be talssion. He was
"What kind of an understandin—, Rutger was sure
"Later, Heather," Hawke an—rted, "Hawke has an
Rutger stared at Hawke— "Hawke has an
going to renege on their—
of it. With that in mi—
announcement to m— ...licement?" Heather pressed.
"What kind of— tell me what is happening?"
"Will someone at his nephew. He couldn't tell the
Hawke gla—he'd talked to Shawny. What was Rutger
family bef—
thinking—
His —cle's angry silence told Rutger all he needed
to know. "Hawke's marrying Shawna," he announced.

At the gasp from the top of the stairs, Hawke looked
up to see Shawny. He cursed beneath his breath. What
could he say to her? "I told Rutger before I asked you"?
Then Heather would wonder, if indeed he hadn't asked
Shawny to marry him, just what kind of "understanding" they had. And never would he humiliate Shawny
by admitting the truth. The confusion on her face tore
at his heart. He smiled, hoping he could somehow make
her understand, and walked to the stairs to greet her.

"Rutger couldn't wait to tell Heather our good news.
That we're to be married," Hawke said, bending to
press a kiss to her cheek and whisper, "Don't act surprised. I didn't tell them I haven't yet asked you. You
weren't meant to overhear the announcement."

All the ashes of her dreams rekindled and blazed in
her heart. Hawke wanted to marry her. He loved her.

Then Heather, Rutger, and Leif surrounded her with
cries of congratulations. The wedding date was set for
three months hence, December 1, 1789.

"Why so long?" Rutger protested, anxious to have
the deed over and done with.

Heather smiled at her eldest son. "That's the minimum time required to prepare for a wedding of the

willingly—no, not submitted, enticed him, for she had asked Hawke to make love to her—knowing full well he didn't love her, would never marry her. Even so, throughout the night, bewitched and besotted, she had poured out words of her love. But Hawke had neither mentioned the word nor implied that he loved her. He had not even feigned love. The night had been one of only passion for him, and she'd been but one more woman. Her face flamed at the notion.

By that same light of day, she also recognized that she'd come to a turning point in her life. She should have left Foxridge long ago, but now she no longer had a choice. If she stayed, she knew she'd become his mistress. At that imagining she shuddered. Still, she didn't regret what she had done. She would live the rest of her life on the memories of last night, for never would she marry any but Gayhawke.

With that vow went the children she yearned to have, and she fell into a troubled sleep, making plans for her departure.

Chapter 30

IN THE AFTERNOON, HAWKE JOINED HEATHER, Rutger, and Leif in the great hall. "Shawny's not up yet?"

"No, she's not, Gayhawke," Heather replied. "I wonder why? She left the Hardwickes before I did. I hope she's not sick."

"She's not sick, Mother," Rutger said, scowling. "She and Hawke came to an understanding last—"

"Rutger!" Hawke warned. What was wrong with his nephew? Shawny had yet to be talked to.

"What kind of an understanding?" Heather asked.

"Later, Heather," Hawke answered.

Rutger stared at Hawke's dark expression. He was going to renege on their agreement, Rutger was sure of it. With that in mind, he blurted, "Hawke has an announcement to make."

"What kind of announcement?" Heather pressed. "Will someone please tell me what is happening?"

Hawke glared at his nephew. He couldn't tell the family before he'd talked to Shawny. What was Rutger thinking of?

His uncle's angry silence told Rutger all he needed to know. "Hawke's marrying Shawna," he announced.

At the gasp from the top of the stairs, Hawke looked up to see Shawny. He cursed beneath his breath. What could he say to her? "I told Rutger before I asked you"? Then Heather would wonder, if indeed he hadn't asked Shawny to marry him, just what kind of "understanding" they had. And never would he humiliate Shawny by admitting the truth. The confusion on her face tore at his heart. He smiled, hoping he could somehow make her understand, and walked to the stairs to greet her.

"Rutger couldn't wait to tell Heather our good news. That we're to be married," Hawke said, bending to press a kiss to her cheek and whisper, "Don't act surprised. I didn't tell them I haven't yet asked you. You weren't meant to overhear the announcement."

All the ashes of her dreams rekindled and blazed in her heart. Hawke wanted to marry her. He loved her.

Then Heather, Rutger, and Leif surrounded her with cries of congratulations. The wedding date was set for three months hence, December 1, 1789.

"Why so long?" Rutger protested, anxious to have the deed over and done with.

Heather smiled at her eldest son. "That's the minimum time required to prepare for a wedding of the magnitude required for the duke of Foxridge."

A solemn Rutger prayed that Hawke had not gotten Shawna with child. After that thought came another. What about between now and the wedding? If indeed it were not already too late, he wouldn't have his sister's name prattled about in every drawing room. "I insist that Shawna stay at Ravencroft until the wedding. Grandmama is there to act as a proper chaperone."

"He's right, Gayhawke," Heather agreed before Hawke could object. "We don't want to invite idle gossip by having Shawna live at Foxridge now."

Everyone of social prominence was invited to the wedding. Monogrammed invitations, bearing the ducal crest of Foxridge, were sent by courier to every country within a reasonable traveling distance.

"Only a royal wedding could attract more excitement, or more people of consequence," Heather said.

The next three months were a whirl of social activities, among which was Chadwick and Laurel's betrothal ball, Gayhawke's and Shawnalese betrothal ball, Chadwick and Laurel's wedding, and countless receptions, balls, soirees, and other fetes. Shawnalese made numerous trips to London for the design and fittings of a wedding gown and trousseau, plus the myriad arrangements and countless details for a wedding of this import.

During that time, Hawke and Shawnalese were never alone for more than the ten minutes of privacy alloted them by the dowager baroness, the chaperone designated by Rutger. Rutger also instructed Grizzly to accompany Hawke and Shawnalese on their daily rides, giving her cause to wonder at Rutger's overzealous, self-appointed protection. Fortunately, on these outings Grizzly often rode at a discreet distance, giving them privacy of conversation. However, as December 1 neared, passions too long denied blazed with a fury that left them both weak and wanting.

Three days before the wedding, a courier arrived at Ravencroft with a letter for Shawnalese, which the butler presented to her on a silver tray. Reaching for the letter, she recognized immediately the large scrawl, and a shiver snaked down her spine. For a moment her thoughts flashed backward in time to when, after her mother's death, she'd discovered among her mother's things a letter in this same handwriting. It had been from Lord Maynard Grenville, the earl of Stratland, her mother's father. Sometime after her marriage, according to Catherine's diary, she had written to her father, informing him that he had a granddaughter named Shawnalese and pleading for her dowry money. The earl of Stratland's reply had been cold, cruel, and to the point: "I have no daughter named Catherine."

Shawnalese's grandfather's unforgiving response, his indifference to Catherine and her infant's needs, had forced his daughter, a noblewoman gently reared in luxury, to spend her life in abject poverty—indeed had been responsible for her illness and premature death.

Now that same Lord Grenville, according to his missive, wanted to acknowledge his granddaughter—and on the eve of her marriage to one of the most wealthy and powerful dukes in all of England. Why had this man not come forward at any time during the last six years? He had to have known who she was, for everyone in England knew a Shawnalese Grenville had been brought to live at Foxridge.

Shawnalese excused herself to write a reply. May God have mercy on her soul, she prayed, for she had an unforgiving heart. She returned shortly and handed the wax-sealed note to the waiting footman. It read: "I have no grandfather named Maynard Grenville."

The day before her wedding, while she waited for Hawke, Shawnalese walked the grounds of Ravencroft in solitude. She wanted to race Wildfire across the downs and over the hedgerows. But she couldn't, for one or more of the hundreds of guests would see her and soon be riding with her. Her only privacy these days was in her chambers and, for the moment at least, in the copse of trees where she walked.

More than anything in this world she wanted to be the wife of Gayhawke Carrington—but she did not want to be the duchess of Foxridge. Tormented by the thought, she envisioned tomorrow with both a joyous and troubled heart, for with her marriage to Gayhawke, she would become a pampered noblewoman, useless to everyone but herself.

The last three months had been the happiest of her life, with Hawke in constant attendance, the two of them recapturing their former bond and camaraderie. Even so, the continuous round of fetes had left her bored and restless, as they had in Paris—and she knew why. That was not how she wanted to spend her life. Yet as the duchess of Foxridge that would be how she'd be obligated to live. She sighed. Perhaps as the wife of a duke there would be some altruistic endeavor she could adopt. At least she'd be at Hawke's side, eventually surrounded by their children. That would make up for everything else, would it not?

Then she faced the other matter that gave her no peace. Hawke had never said he loved her, not once. His every gesture said it, his every thoughtful deed said it, his consideration and gentleness said it, but still she longed to hear it from his lips. Hear it over and over, be it truth or lie. On her left hand an extravagant marquise diamond flashed a rainbow of colors in the sun, and she remembered when Hawke had given it to her. "A ring befitting the duchess of Foxridge," he'd said. She would have preferred a simple band presented with "All my love." Was the word love forbidden among the nobility? Was the emotion condemned? Touted as unfashionable by the haut ton? No matter, she decided. She would teach Hawke the meaning of love, and someday he would say those most precious of words and mean every one of them.

At that moment she glanced up to see him riding Warrior toward Ravencroft. She raced out of the trees, waved, and called out to him. He galloped to her side and swept her into strong arms to sit her in front of him.

He kissed her exuberantly, passionately, lingeringly, and when his lips lifted from hers, he grinned. "We should have thought of this long ago. No Grizzly, no Wilhelmina." He kissed her again and kneed Warrior toward the sea.

"Hawke," she protested weakly, "the guests. Whatever will they think?"

"I don't care. Do you?"

"No."

At that, he kissed her again, then again.

They arrived at the edge of the white cliffs that overlooked the Isle of Wight, overlooked the beach where they'd made love. Hawke dismounted and lifted her down. "Come here," he urged, patting the ground next to him. It was a cold day, and Shawnalese wrapped her cloak around her and knelt beside him, her heart in her throat as he placed his arm around her and pulled her down beside him. Gently he hugged her to him before he bent to brush his lips against her brow. "It's been over three years since you sat here and argued—excuse me, I mean discussed—philosophy with me. Do you remember?" he inquired, pressing his cheek to her brow.

"I sat next to you like this over three years ago?" she asked with all the feigned astonishment she could muster, for she remembered well everything she'd ever done with him.

"Well, not literally like this. I wasn't holding you, or kissing you"—he gave her only part of the kiss he wanted to—"like that. We were having one of our many disagreements about something or other. You don't remember?" Disappointment sounded in his voice.

"What had we been doing? Riding?"

Something in her voice caused him to look down at

her. "Why, you little vixen—you've been teasing me."
He laughed, and a faint light twinkled in the depths of
his green eyes.

"Would I do something like that? To be exact we . . .
shall I say 'debated' the class system of the nobility."

"Well, I won't debate with you today, Shawny. I
know the folly of that, and I will not jeopardize my
son by so doing."

"Jeopardize your son?"

"Yes. If we start on this subject, I may not have
one."

She smiled. "Ah, Carrington, you ever warm my
heart." His face was inches from hers; her gaze captured his, and she felt him tremble.

"If I don't kiss you soon," he murmered, "I might
devour you."

She laughed at his foolishness and closed her eyes as
his head lowered to hers. Then she was lost. Lost to the
pleasure of his hungry lips slanting across hers in a
heady ravishment of her mouth, lost to the excitement of
his sensuous tongue swirling around hers in a ritual of
mating, lost to the senseless thrill of his hand, which
slipped up her leg in a mind-drugging caress that left her
weak, wilted, and craving more. Consumed by the sensations that splintered through her, she returned kiss with
kiss, tongue with tongue, and when her hand moved
over the boldness of his desire, Hawke shuddered.

Abruptly he released her, his breath ragged and
short. "Much more of this and we won't be back in
time for the ceremony tomorrow." He smiled and
pressed her head to his shoulder.

"I love you, Hawke," she whispered as he held her
tenderly, and he answered her with a kiss. "My heart
aches with love for you." Her arms wrapped around
his waist, and her head pressed to his wildly beating
chest. This time he answered by kissing her deeply,
passionately. His body, lean and hard, pressed into
hers. She broke from his embrace, breath short. She

needed desperately for him to tell her that he was not marrying her out of a noble obligation because he'd taken her innocence. "Tell me you love me, Hawke. I need you to tell me that you love me, too." She threw her head back to look up at him.

The words caught in his throat. Why couldn't he force himself to say the three words that meant so much to her? In reality, he not only loved her, he loved her to distraction. He worshiped her. Then he realized the truth: he clung to the last vestiges of his old fears, to his vague uncertainties. Still, even now he felt vulnerable, afraid that with those words would go all his strength, afraid that one admission would give her the power that could demolish him, a power no woman had ever had. It was too great a weapon to place in the hands of any woman, but in the hands of Shawny it could destroy him.

Pressing warm lips to her brow, he reached into the inside pocket of his jerkin and withdrew a parchment. "Perhaps my wedding present will ease your mind."

Shawnalese took the paper Hawke handed her, broke the wax seal, and read the enclosed note:

> *Shawny,*
> *Whenever I look up and you are there, I will know it is because you want to be.*
> *Gayhawke*

Shawnalese glanced at the enclosed bank draft in her name. The sum £250,000 stared back at her. Her face flushed with disbelief, and she looked up at him in puzzlement. A heaviness settled in her chest, and a knot formed in the pit of her stomach. "I'm not marrying you for your money, Hawke. What have I done to earn your doubt? Is this what you really think of me?"

Ignoring her questions, he said, "That bank draft is in your maiden name. It's yours whether or not you marry me. That's enough for you to live on quite comfortably the rest of your life. If you arrive at Foxridge tomorrow"—he chuckled, as if his words were being said in jest, even though he jested not—"I'll always know you didn't marry me for wealth." Grinning, he pulled her back into his arms and added in a teasing voice, "I already feel quite certain you're not marrying me for a title."

She tucked the bank draft inside the top of her gown. "We'll discuss this after we're married. I won't allow anything to upset me today or tomorrow. And you, my darling, do not get my wedding present to you until after we are wed and I'm living at Foxridge."

"Your wedding present for me?" he asked, as pleased as a boy.

"Yes. It's a gift I'm sure you will treasure"—she reached up and brushed the cleft in his chin with a brief kiss—"and there's a drop of love in every thread."

Pleased, he smiled. "Are there many threads?"

"Too many to count."

"And is there any left?"

"Any love?" At his nod she smiled. "I have an infinite amount of love for you, Carrington. A bottomless well."

By midmorning the haze had cleared and the day was sunny and bright. Neither rain nor fog would mar this, the day of the marriage of the sixth duke of Foxridge. Nearly eleven hundred guests were there, the cream of England, the aristocrats who'd fled France, and several noblemen from Scotland, Austria, Switzerland, and Spain. Dressed in their finest, they filled the rooms.

An army of florists had lavishly decorated Foxridge with greenery and all manner of white flowers, their fragrances wafting through the air. The ceremony would be performed in the ballroom which had been transformed into an indoor garden with a bounty of trees, plants, and a bower of white flowers. Hundreds of white candles would be lit before the ceremony. Gilded cages of white doves, crowned with white satin bows, were placed around the perimeters of the room, and after the ceremony the doves would be freed to fly away.

As Hawke mingled among the guests, strolling violinists filled the manor with the strains of lilting music. He wished Shawny were with him, if only so he could look up and see her. A deep longing, an unexplained emptiness, overcame him, and he attributed his feelings to Shawny's insistence that she would not see him today until she walked down the aisle to him. He smiled, certain the hundreds attending the wedding would behold the most exquisitely beautiful bride they could ever hope to gaze upon.

At Ravencroft Shawnalese, in a daze of joy, stood at the window of her chambers that overlooked the front grounds. The activity from below caught her attention. Four black horses, mounted by liveried outriders—in maroon and gray, the colors of the duke of Foxridge— cantered to place in the circular drive, followed by six maroon-plumed white horses, in maroon Morocco trappings, pulling the gilded baroque coach Hawke had ordered for the occasion. Four coachmen, two front, two rear, rode the gilt-and-glass coach. Behind came four more black horses, mounted by liveried outriders in maroon and gray. The wedding procession, which would depart from Ravencroft and wind through the hamlets and village to Foxridge, was forming.

"Come, luv, let me help ya on with your gown. Ya don't want to keep His Grace awaitin' on this day," Mrs. Kendall said, beaming.

Shawnalese moved from the window, pulled on her silk stockings, slipped lacy garters on her legs, then stepped into dainty, pearl-encrusted satin slippers. Mrs. Kendall and Nadine helped her struggle into the petticoats that would keep the skirt of her lace-and-silk taffeta gown billowing fully from her tiny waist.

"I'm so happy Hawke sent both of you," Shawnalese said, barely able to contain her exuberance. "Rutger's servants are quite capable, but it's wonderful to have the people I care about to help me today, the most marvelous day of my life." She twirled with happiness.

A grim Nadine and a buoyant Mrs. Kendall carefully carried the creamy wedding gown across the room to Shawnalese and struggled to slip it on her.

"Love agrees with ya," Mrs. Kendall chattered as she buttoned the back of the gown. "Doesn't it, Nadine?"

Without answering, Nadine gave Shawnalese's golden hair—arranged as Hawke had requested, cascading down her back in a waterfall of rippling ringlets to her hips—a final touch before her veil was positioned.

Shawnalese stood quietly as the two women attached the veil to her tiara.

Mrs. Kendall stepped back and gasped at the apparition who stared back at her. "No angel ever looked more beautiful, luv. No indeedy."

Nadine bit her lip and turned away, teary-eyed.

"Nadine, what is bothering you?" Shawnalese asked. "You've been upset and unhappy ever since you arrived. Auguste is all right, isn't he?"

"Oui."

"Grizzly isn't upset with you, is he?" At the shake of Nadine's head, Shawnalese probed, "Are you ill?"

"Non."

"Have you been scolded?"

"Non."

"I'm not leaving until you tell me," Shawnalese insisted. "You know I'll help you with whatever is bothering you. It will be all right."

At Shawnalese's gentleness, at her concern, and on this her wedding day, Nadine could bear no more. She burst into tears.

Shawnalese placed a comforting arm around the weeping woman and urged softly, "Please allow me to help, Nadine. Certainly it's not that bad."

"You're gonna muss your gown, luv," Mrs. Kendall scolded gently. "Lordy, Nadine, this is a pretty kettle o'fish."

Sniffling, Nadine glanced at the woman who'd rescued her and her son from the streets of Paris. Auguste was now a healthy and happy boy. She would ever be indebted to the tenderhearted Shawnalese. For three months Nadine had been tormented by what she had seen and heard when she'd unwittingly become a witness to the scene between Hawke and Rutger at Foxridge. She couldn't repay Shawnalese's kindness with deceit about something so important. With that decision, she burst out, "I wanted to tell you before, but you've not been at Foxridge. Zee duke ees marrying you because your brother threatened 'im with a duel."

Chapter 31

"WHAT ARE YOU TALKING ABOUT, NADINE? What are you saying? My brother? I have no brother."

Then the whole story of what Nadine had overheard poured out—that Rutger and Leif were Shawnalese's brothers, that Rutger had threatened to duel Hawke if he didn't marry Shawnalese—and ended with what Nadine had seen outside. "Zee baron's arms waved angrily through zee air, zee duke's face was dark and 'e kept shaking 'is 'ead no, just kept shaking 'is 'ead no. Zhey were shouting, but I couldn't make out zheir words, and zee baron kept clenching and unclenching 'is fists. Zhen zee duke grabbed zee baron by 'is shirt-front—and oh, I was so scared zhey were going to fight, but I could see zee baron keep zalking and zhen zee duke let him go. A little bit later, zhey shook hands and came back inside. But both of zhem looked very angry."

"No! Hawke wouldn't do that to me—I know he wouldn't do that to me," Shawnalese cried out in disbelief, a flash of pain ripping through her. She battled the blackness that threatened to envelop her as her world, her happiness, collapsed around her. "It can't be true . . . it can't be true!"

"Bloody hell, Nadine! Ya daffy woman. Get the baron . . . get Grizzly . . . get someone," Mrs. Kendall bellowed, her own self-control exploding. "Hurry! Go . . . go!"

Minutes later Grizzly paused at Shawnalese's open chamber door. She stood at her window, staring out, looking more of a vision in her elegant gown and veil than even he had imagined possible. Perplexed by her apparent serenity, for Nadine had been hysterical, he entered the room. "Ye ready for me to escort ye down to the coach, lass?" At his question, Shawnalese turned and he saw her white, stricken face. Her lower lip trembled slightly and he knew she battled for control.

"Come in, Grizzly," Shawnalese said softly. "Please close the door. We'll not be going anywhere."

After sending Grizzly, with no explanation, to Shawnalese, Nadine learned that Rutger was in his apartments dressing for the wedding. She raced there and was admitted to the baron's sitting room by his valet. Rutger entered shortly. "Milord, Miss Shawna needs you right away. Eet ees urgent!"

At the servant's obvious distress, Rutger asked, "Is something wrong, Nadine?"

"*Oui,* milord."

"Well, what is it?"

She glanced from Rutger to the valet and back to Rutger. "*Mon Dieu!* I can't say."

Rutger dismissed his valet, and a rap sounded on his door. He opened the door to the dowager baroness. "Come in, Grandmama. You look as lovely as a bride."

"Rutger dahling," Wilhelmina said, "I know flattery gets you everyvhere, but never vith your grandmama." She smiled as he kissed her cheek. "Vell, almost never."

Rutger turned toward Nadine. "Now, what is the problem, Nadine?"

Nadine glanced from the dowager baroness to Rutger. "I can't say, milord."

"Out vith it, young voman," Wilhelmina ordered, her tone insistent. "Tell my grandson vhat is the problem."

Intimidated, Nadine allowed her words to pour out. "Miss Shawna knows zhat you were going to challenge 'is Grace to a duel."

Wilhelmina gasped.

"God's breath!" Rutger cursed.

"She also knows 'oo you are, milord," Nadine added as tears streamed down her cheeks.

"That will be all, Nadine," Rutger said. "I'll go to Shawna."

"Vhat does she mean, who you are, Rutger?"

Wilhelmina's words echoed after Nadine, and she realized she'd made a terrible error.

Meanwhile Grizzly—dressed in formal wear, for he would give away the bride—crossed Shawnalese's room and placed an arm around her. She laid her head on his shoulder. "Are ye getting wedding jitters, lass?"

"Who is my father, Grizzly?"

"Yer father? I dinna know. What's this all about?"

At Shawnalese's silence, Mrs. Kendall stopped her pacing and related what Nadine had said.

A knock sounded at the door. "Shawna," Rutger called out. "May we come in?"

Mrs. Kendall opened the door to Rutger and a white-faced dowager baroness. "That will be all, Mrs. Kendall," Rutger said, and she bobbed a curtsy and left. "Please excuse us, Grizzly."

"I want Grizzly to stay," Shawnalese said softly. "He's my family. . . . Are you?"

"Yes, Shawna," Rutger replied. "I'm your brother. Half brother."

She leaned against the window, composing herself.

"Straighten yourself, Shawna," Wilhelmina demanded. "The Von Rueden blood flows in those veins. The Von Ruedens are strong. In ill vinds, ve vhip, ve svay, ve bend, but ve never break. Our roots are deep."

Shawnalese turned her regard on the dowager baroness, only now realizing their relationship, and stated the obvious: "You're my grandmother."

"No, child. I'm your grandmama," Wilhelmina replied with tears in her eyes. "I once said you were a bastard of no consequence. However, through the years I have learned, of far more importance, you are also a child of enormous character. I should have known—vhen you not only defied every nobleman in England, but also every aristocrat in France—that the Von Rueden blood raced through you. I am exceedingly proud to claim you as my granddaughter. Can you forgive a stubborn and foolish old voman?"

"How long have you known who I am?"

"Five minutes."

A smile tipped Shawnalese's lips. "How could I not forgive you? Gayhawke says stubbornness is one of my more desirable character flaws. Perhaps I inherited it . . . Grandmama." With that, she embraced the grandmother who'd been a stranger to her for the last six years. How could Hawke have kept her family from her? Why had he? Then Rutger too hugged her, and the lost years slipped away.

A few minutes later Shawnalese asked the question to which she did not want the answer. "Rutger, did you threaten to duel Hawke if he didn't marry me?"

A grim-looking Rutger did not reply.

One glance at her granddaughter told the dowager

baroness that if she did not do something quickly, there
would be no wedding. She knew the scandal would be
terrible. All of London, all of England, all of Europe,
would be atwitter. "Shawna dahling, the vedding cara-
van is formed, the guests' coaches and carriages are
lined up. Everyone must be vaiting for you to come
downstairs. Ve shall be monstrous late. Perhaps you
could delay this discussion until after the ceremony."

"There isn't going to be a ceremony, Grandmama,"
Shawnalese announced, and reached up to remove her
veil.

"You don't know vhat you're saying child. One does
not leave the duke of Foxridge vaiting at the altar. Not
even my granddaughter." With that, Wilhelmina
snatched the veil from Shawnalese's hand and started
to replace it.

Shawnalese heaved a sigh. "Rutger, how long have
you known about me?"

"Since shortly after Christmas. That's why I left
Foxridge."

"Rutger dahling, ve'll talk about this after the vedding."

"Does Leif know?" Shawnalese inquired.

"Yes," Rutger replied. "I told him."

"Does Heather know?"

"No."

The dowager baroness sighed in frustration. She
envisioned the great names of Carrington and
Grenville bandied about amidst ridicule, snickers, and
mockery.

"Why did Hawke agree to marry me?" When
Shawnalese received no answer, she whispered, "Only
because you threatened to challenge him if he didn't?"

"Shawna, I hazard a guess that Hawke loves you. . . ."

Shuddering at his comment, she recalled the morning she'd stood at the top of the stairs to the great hall.
Hawke's face had been dark with fury. Then Rutger
had announced, "Hawke's marrying Shawna." Now
she knew beyond a certainty: Hawke had not only had

to be challenged to marry her, he hadn't even been able to force the announcement from his lips. Rutger had had to perform that distasteful deed himself. Naked pain reflected in her eyes, and grief and despair seared her heart. Swallowing the sob that rose in her throat, she suggested softly, "After this, Rutger, I don't believe the truth can be kept from Heather. It would be better if she were told by you rather than guess, or learn through servants' gossip. You might want to have the guests made comfortable. Tell them there is a delay."

After Rutger left, Shawnalese rose in determination. "Grizzly, I never again want to see Gayhawke Carrington. Will you ask Nadine to help me pack?"

"Nadine?"

"How can I think unkindly of a faithful friend who told me what Gayhawke should have, what my brother should have? Nadine's mistake, Grizzly, wasn't in telling me the truth, but rather, in not telling me sooner."

"Where are ye going to go, lass?"

"Away from Hawke. I don't know where. Anywhere. I not only never want to see him again, I don't want to hear his name." With a lightheartedness she did not feel, she added, "I'll see to it that Rutger puts away his gun, then I'll not need to worry about Hawke coming after me."

"I'll be going with ye, lass."

She smiled. "I hoped you would."

After Grizzly left, Wilhelmina asked, "Are you sure this is vhat you vant to do, child? Don't you think Gayhawke deserves to be heard? You're bringing disgrace and humiliation down around him. He'll never outlive the scandal."

"Nadine informed me of what happened and Rutger couldn't deny it. Should I stay and ask Hawke to confirm it? I have my pride, Grandmama. I won't marry a man who has to be challenged before he agrees to marry me. Neither will I marry a man who doesn't love me. I have seen that particular hell on earth—in my mother's marriage." She removed her veil again.

A short time later Grizzly instructed two unsuspecting footmen, "Will ye carry these three trunks out the side door and to the coach waiting near the gate. 'Tis just like a woman to be unable to make up her mind on what clothes she wants in her trousseau."

The footmen laughed and nodded in understanding as Grizzly grumbled. Nadine and Auguste waited inside the driverless coach.

Shawnalese folded the bank draft Hawke had given her inside a note to Chadwick. She sealed it and handed it to Wilhelmina. "Grandmama, I'm asking you to send a messenger in all secrecy to give this to Chad. It's important that Gayhawke not know. Will you do that for me?"

"Of course, my dahling. Now I vant you to do something for me." Wilhelmina removed the enormous diamond brooch from her bosom and pressed it into Shawnalese's hand. "Please do not refuse my gift of love. I know you have no money. This vill take care of you until you're settled. Then I vill come to see you." She smiled tearfully. "I never much liked it, anyway. It's vulgarly large."

"Thank you, Grandmama. Will you explain to Rutger for me?"

"I shall, but I imagine Rutger already suspects there vill be no vedding. You'll let me know vhere you are as soon as you're settled?"

"Of course. But promise me you won't tell Hawke."

"Sveet child, do you really think Gayhawke von't know vhere you are vithin days, if not hours?"

Shawnalese shuddered, for she knew her grandmother was right. "Please tell Heather I'm . . . I'm so very sorry. . . . And ask Rutger . . . please, not to interfere."

"Yes, dahling, I shall tell them."

"Don't tell Hawke about my message to Chad."

"You have my vord, my dahling. Godspeed. I'll see you soon."

Shawnalese put on her cloak and pulled the hood up over her hair. She turned to leave and saw the wedding gown and veil. Then she remembered the ring. She slipped the diamond from her finger and handed it to Wilhelmina. "Please give this to Hawke."

Unable to speak, Wilhelmina nodded her silver head.

Minutes later Shawnalese slipped out the side door. Alone, she stumbled down the drive, her heart near to bursting. Glimpsing the shimmer of the English Channel through the trees, she paused, looking toward the beach where Hawke had made love to her. At last she turned away and was continuing down the drive when a whinny captured her attention. Off in the distance, the gilded coach and maroon-plumed white horses awaited the bride—in vain.

A short time later Grizzly drove the coach past Foxridge, and Shawnalese turned, her heart aching, to look one last time at the mansion that had been her home. Then with staunch resolution, she turned away from her past and faced forward to race with the coach into her future and a freedom she hadn't known in six years—one that now filled her heart with despair, for it was a freedom and future without Gayhawke Carrington.

Within minutes after Shawnalese left Ravencroft, Hawke leaped from Warrior and raced into the mansion. Rutger's brief note had said there would be a lengthy delay and offered no explanation. "Where is Shawny?" he demanded.

"In her room," Rutger replied. "But first, Hawke, I need to talk to you—in my study. You don't want to see Shawna before you've heard what I have to say."

Minutes later Hawke rushed from the study to Shawny's chambers. God, what a mess! And now, added to everything else, his Shawny thought that her brother had had to challenge him before he would marry her. How could she think otherwise?

Hawke burst into Shawnalese's chambers and confronted Wilhelmina. "Where's Shawny?"

"*My granddaughter* has decided she doesn't vish to marry you. Perhaps you know vhy?"

Hawke raced to the dressing room, then back to the sitting room. "Where is she, Wilhelmina?"

"She has left."

"Left? Left the estate?"

"Left you. Had you no concern for her tender heart, Gayhawke?"

"Did she leave me a note?"

"She left you this"—Wilhelmina held out the dazzling diamond ring—"and she left her vedding present to you under the bed."

Taking the ring, Hawke slumped against the door. "Where did she go?"

"Do you care?"

"I care, Wilhelmina."

"I don't know vhere she vent. I vould tell you if I did, for I believe you have finally discovered vhat I have known for years—you love my granddaughter. But I haven't exactly been the kind of grandmama in whom she felt she could confide. Had I known your secret, I vould have been." She sighed. "How could you have kept us apart? Shawna is my only granddaughter. She vas living with her family, her brothers and me, and never knew it. How could you have robbed us of that pleasure?"

Hawke rushed away. After he'd discovered that Grizzly, Nadine, and Auguste were also gone, after he'd learned footmen had carried three trunks to a coach, after he'd learned a coach and four was missing, and after he'd searched the local villages, he returned to Ravencroft. A lone candle flickered dimly in her darkened room. There he sat with his head in his hands. Her presence surrounded him. He closed his eyes, remembering the perfume of her hair, the softness of her lips, the tenderness of her embrace, and her image burned into his memory in the achingly lifeless room.

Slowly he rose from her silk chair and walked to her bedside table. His fingers moved from the hand-carved scented candle Rutger had given her, to the crystal horse from Grizzly, to a hand-painted, porcelain slipper from Heather, to a book from Leif, and lingered on the hand-painted silk and ivory fan he'd given her, feeling her nearness by touching the gifts she treasured.

His chest felt as if it would collapse as he agonized over the suffering she must be enduring now, and again he was the cause of her torment. After this, could there be any forgiveness? Could there be any love left? He wondered how his joy, his happiness, his whole life, could have been snatched away from him so quickly—without warning. She was there—then she was gone.

Where would she go with little or no money? The bank draft! Could she have taken the bank draft? Stark, naked fear glittered in his eyes as the possibility built in his mind. With that kind of money in her possession, she could disappear forever without a trace—he would never find her, or worse yet she could easily be murdered for such a sum. Unwittingly he had given her the means with which to elude him forever. However, he knew he'd find her and bring her back if he had to go to the ends of the earth. And he was leaving now.

Then he remembered the wedding present Wilhelmina had said was under Shawny's bed. Drawn there unwillingly, knowing her gift of love would only add to his torment, he lifted the skirts of the bed and peered beneath at the large, sheet-wrapped bundle, almost as long as the bed. He dragged out the heavy article, tied on each end with silver ribbon, and unwrapped it. He recognized the backing as that of a tapestry, and with a swift jerk he unrolled it. Before him lay the perfect image of England's Warrior—his silver Andalusian stallion, with black mane and tail, and four legs black to the knees—rearing on muscular hind quarters. Warrior's contour, musculature, conformation, even the glint in his eye, was so expertly captured that he almost expected it to come to life. It was handsomely bordered with the Foxridge colors.

He knelt with her tapestry, wrapped in the warmth of a drop of her love in every thread, while he knew she fled cloaked in the icy torment of his duplicity, believing he didn't love her.

A knock sounded at the door.

"Come in," Hawke called out.

"Your Grace, there's a courier downstairs," the footman said, handing Hawke a silver tray with a missive resting on it. "The man says it's most urgent."

Hawke broke the wax seal to read:

> *Gayhawke,*
> *I desperately need your help. My life and those of my family are in peril.*
> *All of France has gone insane! The king and queen are under house arrest and being held in Paris. Nobles are not safe in the streets, some not even in their homes.*
> *Please, I implore you, come in all haste and bring me and my family to the safety of England.*
> > *Your devoted friend,*
> > *Maurice DuBellay*
> > *Comte de Chaternay*

"Where is the courier who delivered this?"

"Downstairs, Your Grace."

"Have him shown into Rutger's study. I'll speak with him there."

Minutes later Hawke closeted himself with the courier. He had to make a choice. He could follow his heart and go after Shawny, with the possibility of the DuBellays' blood on his hands, or he could try to rescue the DuBellays and lose Shawny forever.

"God help me!"

Chapter 32

"WHO ARE YOU TO DuBELLAY?" HAWKE ASKED the messenger.

"A trusted servant, monsieur."

"Are you returning to Paris?"

"Yes, monsieur."

Shawny was with Grizzly and therefore safe. She had the bank draft, thus was financially secure. Also, in all probability she never wanted to see him again. For how many years now, had he caused her little but pain?

He could not abandon a friend whose life, and those of his family, swung in jeopardy in order to pursue the woman he loved. He had managed to get the marquis de Montpierre and his family safely out of France and could do the same for the DuBellays—if he left now. "I'll be ready within the hour. We sail for France."

In London the seaborne chill pierced to the bone. Thousands of chimneys spewed black smoke that merged with the thick fog, and a soot-laden cloud enveloped the city. London loomed as bleak and gloomy as Shawnalese's future.

For two hours Grizzly had searched for reasonable rooms to let, and the report of each unaffordable rent sent them deeper into the sordid area of London.

Shawnalese, Nadine, and Auguste were waiting in the coach while Grizzly inquired at still one more place. A thin layer of soot covered every surface, rotting tene-

315

ments reared up on both sides of the filthy lane, and
wretched, foul alleyways separated one deplorable
building from another. Here even the smell of coal and
tar couldn't overcome the stench from the gutter.

"How do these people survive such suffering?"
Shawnalese asked aloud, expecting no answer from
Nadine.

"What choice 'ave zhey?" Nadine replied.

Shawnalese sighed, glanced out the window for
some sign of Grizzly, and stared into the gaunt, filthy
face of a street urchin. Clinging to the boy's befouled
rags, a little girl looked at Shawnalese with huge,
solemn eyes, her small face red and chapped by the
cold. Frowning, the child pranced and stomped her
shoeless feet, wrapped in dirty rags, in an attempt to
warm them. Behind those two stood another, a small
boy wearing a threadbare coat—much too large and
with strips of lining hanging down—and no shoes or
stockings on his feet. He kept his eyes lowered and
periodically glanced at her furtively.

Shawnalese's heart caught in her throat. "Dear God,
Nadine," she cried out, "somebody must help these
poor children." She opened the coach door, fumbled
in her reticule, and pressed a coin into the grubby
hand of the boy with beseeching green eyes. Before the
urchin raced off, she grasped his angular shoulder.
"What is your name?"

"Timothy, ma'am."

The little girl limped forward and opened a tiny
hand. Shawnalese pressed a coin, into the child's palm.

"'Er name's Margaret," Timothy said.

The third child remained where he stood and cast a
desperate sideways glance at her. She held out a coin
and he snatched it from her hand and ran.

"'E ain't got no name," Timothy volunteered.

"I'll be back, Timothy and Margaret. In two, three
days' time, so watch for me," Shawnalese promised as
threadbare men, women, and children, who grasped

their rags about them, surrounded her.

Grizzly limped from the lodging house, lurched through the huddle, swept Shawnalese up, and placed her in the coach. "Ye all right, lass?"

"Yes," Shawnalese replied, the single word barely audible.

"Dinna worry. We'll get ye a nice clean bed and a good hot bath, and ye'll forget about this misfortune."

She smiled, a serene look on her face. "I don't want to forget, Grizzly. I'm not meant to forget."

"Are ye sure ye're all right, lass? No one hurt ye?"

"No. None of these poor unfortunate souls would harm me."

At that, Grizzly reached into his pocket to retrieve some coins and pressed one into each outstretched hand. With a mumbled word or a nod of thanks, the poor wretches shuffled away. "I have all o' me stash tucked away at Foxridge. Ye should've let me stop to get it."

"You know I couldn't do that, Grizzly."

"Aye, I know."

"Besides, I won't live on your savings."

"Well, I sure wish I had some o' it right now. We're none too flush, ye know. Oh, I think I've some good news."

"Which is?"

He looked at her strangely. For three days, ever since she'd fled Ravencroft, she had not smiled, had barely said a word, yet now she almost seemed herself again. He set his reflections aside, for he'd never been good at comprehending a woman's ways. "I just figured out that we've been getting snookered. The landlady takes one look at me in these gent's clothes, and then she peeks at the handsome coach with a duke's crest, gold ornaments, and four blooded horses, and she most likely assumes I'm one o' the debauched nobility up to no good, and she's going to make me pay—at four, maybe six times her normal rate. We'll head back uptown, I'll stop down the street, and since Nadine is in her servant's clothes, she can go check on two rooms. We're lucky she never had a chance to change into her fancy clothes for the wedding."

"You're brilliant, Grizzly. But first I want you to drive around this area. I want to see all of it."

"Ye dinna want to be doing that, lass. It's a pathetic sight. The worst me eyes have seen. The landlady up there"—he motioned toward the building from which he'd just come—"said this is Spitalfields, the district where all the silk weaving's done. That's why there's so many urchins and sickly here. They work, or did work, in the silk factories."

"The children, too?"

"Start out at five years, sometimes four, she said. There's no laws against wee ones working."

"Dear God!" Shawnalese closed her eyes, and when she opened them they blazed with determination. "I'm home, Grizzly. I'm finally home."

"What are ye talking about?"

"From the time I left New Orleans, I've felt that I didn't belong. I felt I stood on the outside looking in, like a little girl at the window of the candy store. Yet unlike that child, I didn't want what I looked at. Here I'm home. I'll never have children of my own, Gayhawke's children, but the homeless little ones of London can be my children."

Grizzly glanced from Shawnalese to Nadine, who shrugged in puzzlement. "It's all right, lass. These last days have been terrible for ye. We're going to get ye something to eat and then a nice clean room."

Her hand flashed out to clasp his. "Grizzly, I'm not ready for Bedlam. In Paris I sat in the fashionable, intellectual salons and discussed philosophy. Here I can live my philosophy. Here, as Rousseau says, I can become all that I should be. Here, in Spitalfields, helping these doomed children, is my destiny. I know it."

"How are ye going to do that, lass? Ye've little more than some costly gowns and an expensive bauble from the dowager baroness. That wouldn't last long down here. Then what?"

"Grizzly, dear, I haven't determined how I'm going to. I've barely discovered what I'm going to. But I have three days in which to do it. Miracles have been, and will again be, achieved in three days."

"What's in three days?"

"I told two of my children that I'd be back within three days. I have a promise to keep—and I will not come empty-handed."

Spent, Shawnalese lay on her bed, flooded by memories of Hawke. Precious, treasured memories. Assailed by a devastating sense of loss, she wondered if she had made a mistake in fleeing. Would it not have been better to live as Hawke's wife, even though he didn't love her, than to forever live without him?

Filled with anguish, she forced her thoughts to the plight of the children in Spitalfields. So much needed to be done—and with almost no money remaining. She lay awake wondering how to accomplish the impossible, and Hawke's words of many years ago rushed back. He had been speaking to Leif, a younger son with only a small inheritance. "Money attracts money, Leif. Regardless of how impoverished you are, never divulge it. Behave as though you have an endless supply of finances, for the wealthy and the successful deal only with the wealthy and the successful."

The next morning Shawnalese awoke early, though she'd had little sleep. At the knock on the door, she volunteered, "I'll get it, Nadine. It must be Grizzly and Auguste."

"I'm hungry as a bear, and Auguste says he's hungry as two bears," Grizzly said as he entered the clean but tiny chamber. His size seemed to fill the room. "If this place was any smaller, there'd only be one wall."

Auguste giggled, and Shawnalese glanced from

Grizzly's beaming face to Nadine's smile of approval. So much had happened since leaving Paris that Shawnalese hadn't kept abreast of matters. Now she had strong suspicions where Grizzly had gone on his solitary rides while they stayed at Ravencroft.

"Grizzly, I know you men are famished, but I have an extremely important call to make. If I'm to be successful, I must see this . . . this person at his home before he leaves for the day. Would you mind waiting to eat?"

"Nay, lass. We men can wait, right, Auguste?"

"Right," Auguste echoed.

"I knew when ye were all dressed up like a bloomin' duchess that . . ." Grizzly paused, disconcerted. "Sorry, lass. Me mouth 'twas in motion before me head."

"It's all right, Grizzly. We can't walk around pretending it didn't happen." She pressed her fingers to her trembling lips and paused to compose herself. Somehow she had held together on the nightmare of her wedding day and the three days since; she wouldn't break now. "Gayhawke always said time was the true test of destiny, and he certainly was right about that. I'm going to call on the nobility for donations to help those poor foundlings."

She dove into her reticule, withdrew her grandmother's diamond brooch, and pinned it to the lace jabot at her throat. "We're going uptown in style. Grandmama said this brooch is vulgarly large, but I imagine the baron I'm going to call on will view it more as extravagantly expensive."

"Aye. Canna deny that. Who's the baron ye're going to see? And why him?"

She inhaled deeply, then blurted, "Lord Ellsworth, the baron of Ashworth."

Grizzly's mouth flew open. "The baron who attacked ye three years ago at Hawke's masque?"

"The very same."

"No, lass. Ye canna do that. They'll have ye in Newgate for blackmail."

"Grizzly, I have no intention, by word or suggestion, of such a deed. The baron's quite wealthy. I hope that my appearing at his home for a charitable donation will prompt him to be quite generous on behalf of a worthy cause. If guilt or fear, rather than benevolence, motivates his generosity, the end result will be the same. I'm convinced he's the key to my success or failure, that I have the greatest opportunity for success by starting with him."

"Starting with him?"

"Oh, yes. Once I have that first donation, the second should be much easier. What nobleman of pride and means could refuse to contribute after Lord Ellsworth has? As I understand it, the baron of Ashworth isn't recognized for his generosity."

"Ye intend to call on all the nobility for donations?"

"Every last one, for a beginning."

"A beginning?"

"Yes. There are also many wealthy businessmen in London, commoners who'll be impressed when I wave this duke's or that earl's name as contributor. Oh, Grizzly, my head is filled with thousands of ideas on how to raise money for those pitiful little children. But more on that later." She turned to Nadine, who sat in bed with the covers pulled up to her chin. "Grizzly will turn his back while you dress, Nadine. Then we're off to see the baron. What remaining reputation I have will certainly be destroyed. The *ton* will bandy it about how fortunate Gayhawke is that I cried off." She swallowed a sob and turned away.

Frowning, Grizzly said, "Carrington's a bloody fool!"

"That's not true," Shawnalese objected. "You see, Hawke can't help it that . . . that he doesn't love me, any more than I can help it that I do love him. You either love someone or you don't."

An hour later Shawnalese sat in the drawing room of the baron of Ashworth. A footman entered the room and announced, "His Lordship." She breathed a sigh of relief, not sure what she would have done if the baron had refused to see her.

"Please be seated, Miss Grenville," Lord Ellsworth said, and his fingers nervously traced the pocket of his breeches. "My congratulations. I understand you're to be married to the duke of Foxridge."

Masking her surprise, she smiled. Of course, he wouldn't know the truth, for he hadn't been invited to the wedding. And since she'd fled directly to London, perhaps the guests wouldn't return before today, or even tomorrow, to spread the gossip of what she'd done.

Shawnalese knew she should tell him that the betrothal and wedding were off, but hers was such a worthy cause, and it would benefit her for him to believe she was the future duchess of Foxridge. Momentarily, the sound of Hawke threatening the baron on the night of the masquerade echoed in her ears. Undoubtedly, judging from the hole Lord Ellsworth was about to wear through the pocket of his breeches, it still echoed in his ears, too. Smiling sweetly, she said "Thank you," and sat down.

Lord Ellsworth lowered himself onto a wing chair. "To what do I owe this honor?"

A half hour later she had described in vivid detail the homeless children she'd seen in Spitalfields and had told him of all her plans. Absently she fingered her grandmother's brooch and said, "I knew you would want to be the first contributor to this worthy cause, and I realize that you'll be making a donation purely from altruistic motives, but I still insist on placing an article in the *Times* and the *Chronicle* extolling your generosity, so you receive the recognition you deserve from your peers. Of course all donors will have a name plaque on the selected building."

"Ah, yes. That will be fine," Lord Ellsworth said and reached in his drawer to pull out a paper. Dipping quill in a nearby ink pot, he scribbled a note, shook the drying sand on the paper, blew it off, and handed it to her.

"Give this to my banker and he'll issue a draft."

She took the paper and her heart sank to her feet. It was for a paltry 1,000 pounds. She looked up with a beguiling smile. "The duke of Foxridge gave me a bank draft, drawn on the bank of England, only a few days ago . . . for £250,000," she said in all honesty, and returned the baron's paper. "I'm sure you didn't mean to, but I believe you forgot one of the zeros. Gayhawke says that people who give always receive more than they give away. They receive the benefit of being a more worthy person."

Wordlessly he snatched the paper from her hand, tore it up, and wrote another. This time he included another zero. She graciously accepted the document, examined it, folded it carefully, and placed it in her reticule. Instead of rising, she hesitated. "I know how honored your wife would be if you made a like donation in her name . . ."

Chapter 33

SHAWNALESE CLASPED HER RETICULE CONTAINING the two bank drafts from the baron of Ashworth and tried not to run to the coach. But she had a promise to keep to the children of Spitalfields, and her heels would not stay on the ground. She went directly to the bank to obtain the money before the baron could change his mind.

Sometime later, with a wildly beating heart, she sat in the coach outside Hawke's London town house and prayed that he was not in residence. She wasn't yet ready to face his wrath—or see his beloved face. At her insistence, Grizzly stood on the doorstep—she'd seen him refuse the invitation to go inside, probably fearing Hawke's anger—and talked to the butler, explaining that Shawnalese had great need of the duke's coach and four for the next few days, after which it would be returned. She was not willing to risk that Hawke, in his humiliation and rage, wouldn't have her arrested for stealing his property. Certainly his fury over this latest incident would be greater than it had been before and after the duel.

Grizzly returned shortly. "Hawke's not here, lass, and the butler was shocked that the wedding dinna take place. I told him where ye're staying in case he wants the coach."

"In all probability the guests are still at Foxridge, enjoying the lavish entertainments meant to amuse them for the rest of the week. I imagine they're celebrating the cancellation of the marriage of the duke of Foxridge to a commoner of no consequence. Hawke probably celebrates amidst them, with Lady Paige Seymour on his arm." At the image, a bitter jealousy stirred within her breast and a new anguish seared her heart, but she jerked herself from her self-pity. "Grizzly, I'll take advantage of these few days until the *ton* returns to London, and call upon Hawke's detractors, those not invited to the wedding."

In their haste to leave Ravencroft, only Shawnalese and Grizzly had been able to bring their clothes. Nadine and Auguste had only the apparel on their back, for the rest remained at Foxridge. Shawnalese, Grizzly, Nadine, and Auguste went to a secondhand store and purchased clothing. When in Spitalfields they would dress more in keeping with its residents.

But for the next two days, Shawnalese wore her finest, her grandmother's diamond brooch at her throat. The first evening she excitedly reported to Grizzly and

Nadine, "I've collected 28,000 pounds more. Of course, I was unable to persuade anyone to be as generous as Lord Ellsworth, but I didn't expect to. I asked that the donation be made in the nobleman's wife's name, or at least in both names. That way I'll have the advantage of dealing only with the wives in future."

"Good. Ye've lost none o' the touch ye had in New Orleans."

"I'm not so sure, Grizzly. My first visit was unexpected, and the men caught unawares. And in view of the exceedingly generous donation from Lord and Lady Ellsworth, I believe these men chose not to suffer loss of face by declining or making a scant, obligatory contribution. Also, with these six it probably helped for them to know I've lost favor with the duke of Foxridge—for I told all but Lord Ellsworth that the marriage has been postponed indefinitely. However, the next time I call on four of the six noblemen, I will probably be told, 'His Lordship is not in.'" Shawnalese didn't say that the other two had responded favorably more from an ache in the loins rather than a swell of the heart; when next she called and they ascertained beyond doubt that she was not willing to "earn" their largesse, she wouldn't be received a third time. Many of the gentlemen of England, like those of France, like those of New Orleans, were naught but men in gentlemen's clothes.

"What will you do eef zhat 'appens?" Nadine asked.

"What I did with the baron's wife," Shawnalese replied. "After I receive the note from whoever to his banker, I'll have tea with his wife and thank her for her generosity and benevolent heart. Then I'll make an appointment with the woman and take her to meet the children she's so selflessly fostering. After that, what mother of means will be able to say no to future donations?"

"Aye, ye're right about that."

All donations had been placed in a drawing account

in the Bank of England, titled "Childhaven Foundation,"
even though no legal sanction from the government or
license had been acquired. The *Chronicle* and the *Times*
had accepted the articles from Shawnalese and printed
them at no charge. She sent gracious letters of commen-
dation to the donors.

Not enough hours existed in the day as Shawnalese
and Grizzly searched for a building in the area of the
silk-weaving factories. "We must locate here in
Spitalfields, Grizzly. No abandoned, orphaned, or runaway child, hungry, weak, or ill, can walk any great
distance from these fetid alleys."

Finally, out of desperation, she rented an abandoned
warehouse badly in need of repairs. The building had
sat vacant for several years and was obtained at a low
rent. "Now we hire the locals at a fair wage plus
meals, with preference given to older children, homeless, unmarried and unemployed mothers, and the
general unemployed, in that order," Shawnalese told
Grizzly. "Do you agree?"

"Aye. But 'tis a mighty big undertaking, lass."

Grizzly, with Auguste's help, supervised the massive
cleaning up while Shawnalese and Nadine started on the
priority of the day—food, blankets, and coal for fires.

Shawnalese went directly to Covent Garden mar-
kets, then to Butcher Row. She'd lost none of the bar-
gaining ability she'd learned on the streets of New
Orleans and left many a merchant to wonder how he'd
been bested by such a sweet-looking young woman.
The foods were delivered to specified hired women in
the tenements in Spitalfields, for them to cook for the
workers and children, until such time as the warehouse was equipped for that task.

"I've written a plea for donations of blankets, warm
clothes, and coal, coke, or peat," Shawnalese said to
Nadine. "We'll take it to the *Chronicle* and the *Times*.
I'm sure they'll run it at no charge. Then we'll begin
the rounds of the secondhand shops for blankets and

warm clothes. I've collected an enormous sum of money, but with all there is to do, I must be frugal."

They returned at dark with the coach loaded with blankets and warm coverings. However, there had been no time to make arrangements for coal.

Grizzly and two men unloaded the coach just as a wagon filled with coal and metal containers pulled up to the warehouse. "'Tis our first donation," Grizzly cried out as men from the *Chronicle* were already starting to unload the newspaper's contribution. That first night, the homeless waifs and adults, with warm food in their stomachs, bundled in all manner of warm coverings, huddled around the red glare of fires, and slept in the huge filthy warehouse, grateful to be out of the bitter cold, whipping winds, and dampness that descended on London at night. Childhaven was under way.

With so much to do, little time remained during the day to grieve for Hawke. Still, each night when Shawnalese crawled exhausted into bed, her mind, her body, her heart, turned toward him. Lying stiff and miserable, she wished something could banish the emptiness within her and make the pain go away.

All of the *ton* was gossiping about Shawnalese literally leaving the Duke of Foxridge waiting at the altar. "The poor duke," they all said, then concurred there was nothing more shocking that she could do.

They were wrong.

Soon she tapped optimistically at each and every one of their doors for donations—and received none. What nobleman would dare affront the duke of Foxridge by giving her so much as a brass farthing, even if they wanted to?

Two different short Christmas stories about children, written by Shawnalese, ran in a series over seven days in the *Chronicle* and the *Times*, each ending with a plea for warm clothes, blankets, and toys. Donations flooded in.

Next she called on the businessmen, seeking bedding ticks, candles, kettles, and kitchenware. "Like a streetwalker who'll go with any man who has the coin," the *ton* whispered. "Has she no pride? Fortunate Gayhawke," they prattled. "Wouldn't it be a pity if the duke had been burdened with the likes of her as his wife? Perhaps His Grace has learned his lesson and will now choose a suitable wife from his own class."

Anxious widows and mothers with daughters of marriageable age nurtured renewed hopes and made plans so as not to be overlooked by the venerated duke.

Shawnalese anguished through yet one more sleepless night, tormented that she'd run off blindly without confronting Hawke, without allowing him to say one word in his own behalf. Was the Hawke who had taken her innocence the man she'd known and loved before Paris? Or was he the dark and brooding stranger she'd met in Paris, with whom she'd spent months of hell? She realized these were questions to which she would never have answers.

Four days before Christmas, Shawnalese, Grizzly, Nadine, Auguste, and twenty-eight carefully selected "foster mothers" moved into the warehouse. Childhaven would be separated into families of seven—six children and a foster mother.

Soon Christmas Eve day arrived. A tired and dejected Shawnalese returned from a long outing, changed clothes, and slid onto a wooden bench at one of the many tables in the warehouse, across from Grizzly and Nadine. A cup of tea warmed her hands, and she pulled her two sweaters around her to ward off the never ending dampness. "I know I should be ecstatic, for so much has been accomplished in the three weeks we've been in London. But two more refused to give me a contribution, and another six refused even to receive me. I thought certainly on this day I wouldn't be refused."

"Ye canna get discouraged, lass."

"Oh, Grizzly, it's obvious now that I'm being cut

dead by the nobility with whom Hawke associates. And that's the majority. The *haut ton*. The wealthiest, the most powerful, those of ultimate consequence."

"Do you zhink zee duke has ordered eet?"

"No, Nadine," Shawnalese replied. "Hawke may despise me, but he wouldn't allow innocent children to suffer because of his feelings. I imagine it's the *ton's* respect for Hawke and contempt for me that's influenced it."

"Ye know Childhaven isna running short o' funds, for ye've collected 48,000 pounds and spent very little other than for food and wages."

"Yes, I know, Grizzly, but I have such high aspirations for these children. To prepare them to survive in the world they need nourishing food, a reasonable education, and to be taught a trade. I have the expense of the foster mothers, all the other help, rent, heat, clothing, doctors, and maintenance. Forty-eight thousand pounds will not provide all of that for the one hundred and twelve who live here now, until they're grown. Many, for the first time in their lives, have hope. What will I tell them when the funds are gone? How will I turn away those who are yet to come? Suddenly my burden seems so heavy."

"Aye, but ye've the heart to handle it."

"Aye, I'll handle it. But I'm so terribly worried since I'm being ostracized by the nobility."

"Dinna worry, lass. I feel it in me bones that somehow things will work out. Ye've done miracles here already," Grizzly said, glancing around the large warehouse.

"Jamie's right, Shawna—"

"Jamie?"

"Jamie MacPherson. Grizzly," Nadine explained. "Did 'e never zell you 'is given name?"

Shawnalese smiled at Grizzly's sheepish expression, his reddening complexion. "No. No, he didn't."

A young boy of six or so appeared shyly at Shawnalese's elbow. The child who'd been with

Timothy and Margaret and never been given a name, had been christened Lawrence Richard by Shawnalese, after Gayhawke Lawrence Richard Carrington. He had softly waving ebony hair like that Shawnalese had so often run her fingers through during the three months of her betrothal, and she smiled to herself, wondering what the shy, fearful little boy would do if she yielded to her urge to do the same to him. A sensation of intense agony and desolation swept over her. Was she never to be free of Hawke? Everywhere she looked, he was there; everything she saw reminded her of him; every special moment she experienced, she wished she could share with him. She was a helpless prisoner of her thoughts, her feelings, and she didn't know how to escape either.

She wanted never to see Hawke again, wanted never to hear his name, yet at the same time it disturbed her no small amount that he hadn't bothered to try to see her. Unquestionably he knew where to find her, for his London major-domo had been given the address, and she'd written to Rutger, Leif, and Grandmama, and a long letter to Heather, so they also had her address. Apparently he was the Gayhawke of Paris, with the unforgiving heart and no consideration for her pain.

Unable to resist, she reached out, pulled Lawrence Richard into her arms, and ran her fingers through the thick waves of her foster son's hair. Margaret, her foster daughter, limped to her and was quickly lifted to Shawnalese's lap for a hug. Then she placed her arm around the bony shoulders of Margaret's older brother, her other foster son, twelve-year-old Timothy, and smiled into his haunting, dusky green eyes.

Chapter 34

During the next two weeks bricklayers built oversize hearths and constructed brick ovens for the kitchens. As the cooking area neared completion, Shawnalese employed a senior cook, then hired assistants and kitchen help from among the homeless adults. Large larders accommodated the kitchens, and the cooks prepared all meals on the premises now.

New mattress ticks and pillows were delivered, and a mixed match of upholstered sofas and chairs, part donated and part purchased, arrived. Nadine supervised the arrangement of the furniture into a comfortable sitting area, and Childhaven took on the atmosphere of a home.

One day soon after, the door opened, cold air swept in, and Shawnalese looked up to see Heather, Rutger, Leif, and the dowager baroness. She raced to greet them and gave each of them a hug. "Oh, I'm so happy to see all of you." After she told them what she'd been doing, she proudly showed them through the building.

A short time later they relaxed together in the sitting area. Shawnalese held a drowsy Margaret and rocked the child absently. "I'm terribly sorry that my actions have brought scandal down around you." Her eyes shimmered. "As I said in my letters, I didn't intend to hurt any of you . . . I couldn't think, I could only feel. And I felt only pain. I had to leave—and now I'm glad I did."

Heather's and Wilhelmina's eyes widened at her last words.

"You see," Shawnalese explained, "as the duchess of Foxridge I certainly wouldn't be here to help these poor children. That great lady of fate didn't lead Hawke to me in New Orleans so that I might marry him, but so that I could become all that I should be. I've come full circle from the slums of New Orleans."

When the family came again the next day, Shawnalese asked Rutger, "Do you suppose now that Thaddeus has no one to instruct, I might hire him?"

"Certainly not," Wilhelmina interjected. "Thaddeus is employed by me now, to teach my great-grandchildren. He did so vell with my grandchildren that I vould not risk losing him. The agreement is already made." She sighed. "However, dahling, the poor man vill have nothing to do for at least five years. I could loan him to you until one of my grandchildren starts the next generation."

"Oh, Grandmama, thank you. I promise I'll return him as soon as Rutger or Leif has need of him."

"Thaddeus has been teaching me about this Rousseau fellow you set such store by," Wilhelmina admitted proudly. "Frankly, I think some of his philosophies are balderdash. Most especially his opinion that voman vas made to be subservient to man and that voman must make herself agreeable and obey her master as the purpose of her existence. Piffle! Only a man vould conceive or endorse such an idiotic theory."

"Grandmama," Shawnalese said, smiling, "I'm terribly proud of you."

The silver-haired woman beamed. "As I am of you, my dahling."

Shawnalese didn't want to ask, had fought an inner battle not to ever since her family had arrived, but still she said, "How is he?"

"We don't know," Rutger replied.

"You don't know?"

"He's in France." At her swift intake of breath, Rutger added, "After you left, Hawke received an urgent message for help from the DuBellays and left immediately for France."

Heather turned to see Shawnalese's white face, her stricken look. "You still love him," Heather murmured.

"Yes. Part of me will always love him, but it's too late. This is my life now. There's no room for this"—she swung her arm in the direction of the children who played at the tables—"in the life of the duchess of Foxridge, so now there's no room in my life to be the duchess of Foxridge."

The family stayed in London for several days and visited each day for as long as Shawnalese's busy schedule permitted. When they'd arrived they'd brought all the belongings Shawnalese, Grizzly, Nadine, and Auguste had left behind, as Shawnalese had requested in her letter. Before they left, each of her family members gave Childhaven a donation, and Heather announced that she'd finally accepted the earl of Fallbrook's proposal.

The next day, feeling dejected with her family having returned home, feeling tormented as she'd been every moment, waking or asleep, since learning Hawke was in France, she unpacked her treasured mementos and set them by her bed.

Then, with an arm around Timothy's shoulders, she walked to the kitchens. Little Margaret limped up to her, crying. Shawnalese knelt to kiss the lightly skinned elbow. Suddenly Shawnalese's nerve endings tautened and she glanced up.

Hawke!

He stood there cloaked and booted, emanating dangerous raw power—the epitome of man. Slowly, in her faded muslin gown, she rose to her feet, capturing his gaze. Her cheeks flushed warm. She had wanted never to see him again—he had robbed her of the closeness and love of her family, he'd had to be challenged to a duel before he'd agree to marry her, and then he hadn't come to give her the apology she deserved. Yet now, irrationally she felt like crying with joy because he was here.

She stood transfixed as Hawke, with the use of a walking stick, limped slowly toward her. Her heart caught in her throat, and a hot rush flooded through her. How could she feel as though she were dying, when she had died on December 1st?

As he neared her, her small hands clenched and unclenched and she regarded him with an intense suffering in the depths of her eyes. Gone was the child-like worship, and he ached for her pain more than his own. "Shawny," he greeted softly.

An eternity ticked by before she managed to reply, "Gayhawke." His dusky green eyes searched her face as though he gazed at her for the first time and was trying to memorize each feature. In a gentle caress, his fingers trailed over her cheek, over her jaw, and cupped her chin. His look was more potent than his caress, and she turned her head to be free of his touch, free of his engulfing gaze.

"May we talk?"

She hesitated. "If you can be gentlemanly."

"I can."

"Then yes," she replied. "Forgive me, this is my son, Timothy, and my daughter, Margaret. Children, please meet Gayhawke Carrington."

With barely a lift of one brow, Hawke acknowledged, "Timothy, Margaret."

"Mr. Carrington," Timothy replied, and Margaret shyly buried her face in Shawnalese's skirts.

Lawrence ran to her side and clung to her leg. She smiled down at the small boy. "This is my other son, Lawrence."

"Lawrence Richard," the boy piped up proudly. "This is my mum now, and she named me Lawrence Richard."

Hawke had not wept since he was five, when he'd

cried after receiving a particularly harsh whipping from his father. Then his father had thrashed him again, for a Carrington did not cry. He blinked and forced back the forbidden tears before his gaze captured hers. "My coach is outside."

She wanted to cry with joy, with relief, for he was safe. She wanted to flay him with her fists for depriving her of her two brothers and grandmother, for robbing her of a feeling of belonging, but she couldn't do that either, for the distance of time had allowed her to understand why he had done so, had also allowed her to realize that only his concern and consideration for her welfare had prompted him to take her into his home at all. His had been a deed fraught with risk. Hawke could have placed her in a convent or an orphanage, hired caretakers, or simply walked away, but he'd done none of those. She could not say she would have done the same if she'd been in Hawke's place. Still there remained the worst cut of all, that he'd had to be challenged before he would marry her—even after he knew there'd been none but he.

She wanted to hate him for that, but she couldn't. She felt only hurt and humiliation. "Your coach?" she calmly said. "No, I'd prefer to talk here."

"If you like."

Bending, she smiled at the children. "You run along now."

The two youngest scampered off, but Timothy, who had borne the height of misfortune with courage and pride, looked up at her and asked, "Are you all right, Mum?"

"I'm fine, Tim."

She moved toward the tables. "Would you like a cup of tea?"

"No. Thank you."

Shawnalese sat at the table and snuffed the candle. In the dimness her face would not so easily betray her feelings. "How did you injure your leg?"

"I'm sure you wouldn't want to hear it. Nothing noble, I assure you."

"Then I definitely want to hear it."

A smile tipped the corner of his mouth. "I wasn't bested by a saber. I wasn't felled by a musket ball or bayonet. A pike was thrust into my thigh—wielded by a woman, no less." When Shawny didn't laugh, he added, "I was fleeing France with the DuBellays and we were discovered."

"Are they safe?"

"Yes."

"I'm glad."

After a lengthy, strained silence, he said, "Tell me what you're doing here."

Then she told him about Childhaven—most of which he already knew—and her plans.

The beauty of her face and the ripeness of her figure vanished, for all he could see was the sunshine in her soul. She was the personification of goodness, and he loved her to a depth that was frightening.

When Hawke uttered not a word, Shawnalese said, "I have your coach and four here"—she pointed toward the far end of the building—"and they've been well cared for. I'll have them sent to your town house today if you need them." Why was she sitting here talking about everything except what she wanted? Behaving as though they were strangers, making impersonal conversation with the man with whom she'd shared the most intimate of acts? If he had come to apologize or explain, why did he not get it over with and leave?

"Damn the coach and four. I'm here to find out how soon, and where, you wish to be married."

She gasped. "You needn't be concerned about Rutger, Hawke."

"I never was concerned about Rutger."

Her face flushed in anger. "I know that to be an outrageous lie. I wouldn't marry you if you were the last man on this earth. Now if you will excuse me, I have work to do."

"Shawny!"

She leaped up and hurried into the kitchen where the women were preparing supper. Hawke limped toward Grizzly, who talked to him at great length before he proceeded to give Hawke the grand tour, such as it was. Then, in mortification, Shawnalese saw the friend she wanted to strangle show Hawke where she and her three children slept.

"What with her fund-raising," Grizzly said, "and doing all the buying, she's away a lot. She felt she wouldna have the time for more than three wee ones."

Hawke hardly heard a word Grizzly said, for he noticed that on a trunk beside her bed, as they'd been on her bedside table at Ravencroft, sat her treasured mementos. Missing was the silk and ivory fan he'd given her. But then his gaze moved to her painted night table and fixed on the oval hand mirror and hairbrush of burgundy trimmed with etched silver that he'd given her in New Orleans. Resting beside the set lay the spindle seashell.

The mirror and brush were a gift he'd given a child he was already beginning to love, and the shell he'd given a woman he loved beyond imagination—and she could not leave them behind when she'd fled from him.

Minutes later Hawke left and Grizzly approached Shawnalese. "I'm going to hitch the horses and drive Hawke's coach to his town house, lass. He said his coachman would bring me back."

"Did Hawke ask you to do this?"

"Aye. But dinna worry yerself. He said he had need o' it tonight, but that he'd have his coachman here at seven sharp to take ye anywhere ye wanted to go, and that he'd not leave ye without transportation. I told him 'twould be nice if we could use it a couple o' days until we buy a wagon and a couple o' horses."

"And?"

"He said that would be fine."

Hawke was severing all ties. Certainly he didn't need

the coach, for he kept a coach and a carriage at his London town house.

The next morning at seven, Shawnalese, dressed in her muslin gown, put on a warm cloak and left with Grizzly to run errands and to buy a wagon, horses, and trappings. Grizzly opened the door to Hawke's coach and gave her a hand up. Inside sat Hawke. Before she could back out, his hand clasped her arm.

"Sit down, Shawny. Please . . ."

"What do you want? I must see to errands."

"If you'll be seated, I'm sure you'll be more comfortable. I thought perhaps I could see to your errands with you."

"Grizzly, don't leave," Shawnalese called back.

"I believe I can select a suitable wagon and dray horses as well as Grizzly."

Still standing on the coach step, she started to descend.

"I'm sure the children would love to accompany us," Hawke suggested. "It should be enjoyable for Timothy and Lawrence to help select the horses. It was a pleasure I was never allowed to enjoy with my father."

She turned back, not daring to look at him, so she spoke to the button on his coat. "Why are you doing this?"

"If you will please be seated, I promise not to kidnap you or ravish you. Grizzly can get the children, and I'll tell you what this is about."

After thinking about the many reasons she shouldn't do as he asked, she turned to Grizzly. "Will you please get the children? Have Nadine bundle them warmly." She accepted Hawke's hand into the coach, lowered herself onto the gray velvet squabs, and faced the man who could still destroy her life, the man who almost had. Glancing away from his cherished face, she asked the coach handle, "What is your explanation?"

Chapter 35

"YOU ONCE SAID TO ME, SHAWNY, THAT although we couldn't be to each other what you had wished, you hoped we could at least be friends. I now say that to you, and I felt that taking you and the children out today might be something nice for two friends to do."

She didn't believe him for a minute, but she couldn't determine his true motive. Besides, she reasoned, she did need the use of his coach. . . . "Friendship. Nothing more. However, Hawke, you may not want even that, for I am no longer the girl you once knew. I won't crawl, as I once did—"

"Crawl? You? Hah!" He had won the duel—she was going with him—but he knew that Shawny, with her forthrightness, with her guileless ways, emerged the victor, for he was as pleased as a boy.

First they went to Covent Gardens for fresh fruits and vegetables and then to Butcher Row. On the pavement there another market flourished, this a grand one. There wagons, carts, barrows, and boards on trestles held nearly every kind of small merchandise imaginable, from looking glasses to scented soaps to Bibles. The children gaped in awe at the wonders that surrounded them.

After that, Hawke purchased a wagon, an enclosed chaise cart, a coach, four dray horses, and all the equipment needed to pull them. "A donation to Childhaven," he explained. They all shared a lengthy picnic at Hyde Park, where the children marveled at the marble-arched entryway, at the fashionably dressed nobility strolling or riding handsome blooded horses. By the time they left at dusk, all of the *ton* knew that the duke of Foxridge had spent two hours at Hyde with *that* woman and three beggarly children.

Inasmuch as the coach would not be available for a month—unbeknownst to Shawnalese, at Hawke's request—he took it upon himself to escort her on all her errands the first week. Her children always accompanied them, and theirs became exactly what he'd suggested—a friendship. Other than the hand that lingered too long when he assisted her, there was no intimacy of touch, only the gazes locked in expectation, in hope, in longing, before quickly looking away.

Gradually they drifted into the easy familiarity of their onetime relationship—the bantering, the friendly disagreements, and the discussions of politics. Still, neither her breach of promise, the secret he'd guarded, his having to be challenged before he'd marry her, nor even their one night of love was ever mentioned.

During the next three weeks, Hawke took Shawnalese and ten of the children—a different ten each time—to see the wonders of London. It mattered not that all the days were gray and dusky, for in the winter the rays of the sun never penetrated the dense clouds of smoke and soot that spewed from the thousands of chimneys. They ended their days in the open-air amusements of the crowded Vauxhall Gardens with its colonnaded temples and statues, and after eating they watched in childish glee the puppeteers orchestrate a three-act play.

On the evening of the first visit to Vauxhall, the *ton* gossiped in shocked dismay. "How could the duke of Foxridge demean himself in such a manner after she left him waiting at the altar? He needs a sniff of a burnt feather for giddiness."

After three weeks of Hawke being a friend, of his being the perfect gentleman without so much as a chaste kiss, Shawnalese allowed herself to be persuaded to go up the river to Ranelagh, the ultimate of London's pleasure gardens. Beautifully gowned, she went with Hawke, who dressed in formal wear, to supper and a concert in the rotunda built on the model of the Pantheon at Rome.

Afterward, with deliberate intent, Hawke promenaded with his Shawny, first the arched interior of the rotunda, then the magnificent gardens. They strolled along the lantern-lit gravel paths that wound among the cascading waterfalls and great trees, festooned with colored lanterns, in the spacious, lush gardens, bringing back memories of when he'd strolled the gardens of Foxridge with Shawny masqued as Marie Antoinette—a lifetime ago.

Word spread quickly about Childhaven, and new children arrived each day. In the black of a cold, rainy night, Grizzly discovered a baby girl on their doorstep. Happily received, she was named Heather.

Shawnalese said, "I need to start my fund-raising again, Hawke. When will the coach be ready?"

He had no choice. He lied. "I checked on it yesterday. It's going to be another couple of weeks."

"That makes no sense to me. That coach looked ready to pull when you purchased it."

"The man sold it to someone else for a higher price. I've ordered another. No problem. I'll take you on your fund-raising."

"I can't ask you to do that."

"You didn't. I volunteered."

That day the duke of Foxridge forced himself to have tea with three ecstatic noblewomen, while Shawnalese received three exceedingly generous donations from their husbands.

Excited, she exclaimed as the coach stopped in front of Childhaven, "Oh, Hawke, wouldn't it be marvelous if all the aristocracy would open up their hearts? Why,

eventually I'd be able to buy the building and build a
second floor—"

His mouth closing over hers stilled her words. A
magical kiss, a kiss of wondrous tenderness, it curled
around her heart and swept her into another sphere
where naught existed but beauty and love and soaring
ecstasy. There was only the loving embrace of his
hands delicately cupping her face, of his gentle mouth,
which sensitively, lovingly, promised all that his lips
did not say, of his heart pounding wildly against her
fluttering breast to steal her breath away. Shaken to
the core, she pulled away, threw open the door, and
fled, not so much from Hawke as from herself, to the
sanctuary of Childhaven.

Late the following afternoon, Hawke came into
Childhaven without his walking stick and gave her a
smile that set her heart to racing.

"Walk with me. I have something for you."

"All right," she agreed, and they set off toward the
end of the building where the horses were stabled. He
pulled a document from his pocket and handed it to
her. She unfolded the paper and stared at the deed to
the warehouse. Stunned, she glanced up at him. "Why
are you doing this?"

How many times had he cursed the weakness that
caused him to postpone the moment he must reveal
what sang in his heart? But still he couldn't force the
words from his lips. Instead he said, "I should think
that was obvious, Shawny."

He had not said "I love you," which she hadn't
expected. Neither had he said "I'm sorry," which she
had expected. If neither love nor apology, then why
else did he come bearing extravagant gifts? Suddenly
she knew. With a heavy heart, she interpreted his
words, his gesture, to be the same as when he'd
given her his mother's diamond and ruby necklace.
He wanted her for his mistress. She wanted it, too,
and that angered and bothered her far more. In

France she'd told him to take her flowers and his speech and leave, and her pride yearned to tell him to do so now. However, although the deed was in her name, this was really a gift to all the unfortunate children, and she couldn't refuse it out of pride. Yet neither would she pay for it with her body—even though she wanted to.

"I thank you, and every little lost soul in here thanks you." She paused, then added the words that would leave no doubt in his mind. "Inasmuch as this is a donation, with no conditions, I accept gratefully."

"There are no strings, Shawny. It's strictly a contribution."

Had she misjudged his reasons? Allowed her raging hunger for him to cloud her thinking and assume his actions to be a mirror of her own unfulfilled passion? "Thank you, Gayhawke."

"There is something else." He withdrew another document from his pocket. "I just learned that you sent this to Chad. Now, as then, there are no stipulations. It's yours to do with as you please."

She knew what it was before she accepted it. As always, he knew how to tear her heart from her. Wordlessly she accepted the bank draft for £250,000 that he'd given her the day before their intended marriage. Childhaven was now secure.

His gaze captured hers, and he murmured, "I forgive you, Shawny. Can you not forgive me?"

For an interminable time, afraid of her love for him, afraid of her reawakened desire, afraid of disgracing herself, of shaming herself, of making an utter fool of herself one more time, she stood immobilized in wordless pride and watched him turn and walk out of Childhaven and out of her life.

She had no idea how long she'd been standing there when Timothy raced to her side. He'd finally begun to gain a little weight, and his once gaunt face had filled in.

"Are you all right, Mum?"

She hugged her son. "Do you need something, sweetheart?"

"Nadine said there's a gentleman to see you."

Minutes later Shawnalese was sitting in a private corner of the large sitting area with Julien St. Jeanneret, the comte de Beaulieux, Victoria Carrington's self-confessed lover.

"My family and I fled the madness of France," Julien said. "We are temporarily living in London until I find a suitable country estate. But as to the reason of my visit, ever since I learned that Victoria disappeared after we separated, I have been unsettled in my mind. I've had three investigators checking into the matter for almost four months. As you know, it's a twenty-five-year-old trail. After every other avenue had been explored, these men next looked at reported deaths of unknown personages and unmarked graves in the area between Foxridge and where Victoria and I separated." He hesitated. "I'm afraid I have bad news. As I told you, the night Victoria and I left it stormed all night and continued to rain torrents all the next day and evening when my rented coach turned back. The coachman apparently tried to cross one of the flooding creek beds in the dark of night, and the coach and horses were swept into the raging waters. Both Victoria and the coachman drowned. She was unrecognized and her identity never discovered. One of the investigators talked to the widow of the doctor who signed the death certificate. The woman not only remembered Victoria, but also described the gown she wore." He paused to compose himself. "The widow also had this." He handed Shawnalese a small silver locket on a chain. "It isn't a costly piece of jewelry, but it's a highly valued one. Her son had selected and bought it for Victoria with his accumulated allowance. She was wearing it the night we left together. I feel the family should know. Will you please tell them and give them my condolences, and regrets?"

"Certainly," Shawnalese said, fingering the small silver locket.

Julien reached into his pocket and handed her a paper. "This is the name and address of the church-yard where Victoria is buried, and also the name and address of the doctor's widow."

"Monsieur, I am indeed grateful, and on behalf of the Carringtons, I thank you. If I could ask one small favor of you?"

"But of course."

"If you would drop me someplace. I have a valuable gift to deliver."

Shortly thereafter Shawnalese sat beside Hawke in the drawing room of his London town house. She had told him everything she'd learned, had revealed the identity of the man she'd unthinkingly disgraced herself with at the duchesse de Vordeaux's ball in France, had given him the paper with the addresses.

"I realize, Gayhawke, since you have never loved a woman deeply, that what your mother did in running off with Julien St. Jeanneret is difficult for you to understand. But please consider that your mother at the age of sixteen was forced into a marriage she did not want, and to a fifty-two-year old man she neither knew nor loved. Had your father's unfortunate illness not turned him into a bitter man, perhaps your mother would not have fallen in love with St. Jeanneret. When your father was struck down, I feel sure he withdrew his love not only from you, but also from your mother. After seven years of this coldness from your father, I imagine she was quite vulnerable. I suppose it's not important now, but what is important is that your mother could not and did not abandon the son she loved and adored, or her ill husband. She turned back to come home to you and your father."

Hawke sat with his elbows on his knees and his head in his hands.

"I have a gift for you, Hawke. It was a gift of love

from a son to his mother. She was wearing it when she drowned."

Shawnalese handed him the silver necklace, then pulled him into her loving embrace as he had done with her when her mother had died. She soothed not the man, but the boy within, understanding that he had never allowed himself to grieve for his mother. That he did now.

The candle flickered out, and for a long time they sat in the darkness of the drawing room as he opened his heart to her, to tell her about all of his childhood, about his mother. After his grief was spent, she felt the healing in his arms, which tightened around her.

"I had better go now," she whispered into the softness of his hair.

His clasp tightened. "Don't leave, Shawny. I need you."

How could she leave him now? When he grieved. When he needed her. When he was in anguish, and his heartache was her heartache. She wanted to explain, *I cannot stay. If you touch me now, I will crumble. I cannot stand against you when you are suffering, for when you are wounded, I feel the pain. I'm defenseless and I know if I don't leave I will awaken in your bed.* But then if he could find solace in her arms, she would find the same in his. She whispered, "I'm afraid."

"Of me?"

"Of myself."

For a moment they were frozen in place and time, gazes locked and the understanding that blazed in his eyes warmed her heart. She stayed right where she was.

It was sometime later that she became aware of him as a man. She felt his warm breath, felt the slow rise and fall of his chest, felt the arms that held her gently. She nuzzled her head into his shoulder, then twisted in his embrace to trail tender kisses up his neck and across his cheek until his lips found hers in the shadowy drawing room.

She intoxicated him, filled the empty void within him, swelled his heart to bursting. He wanted to love her until they were one, forever joined, and such all-consuming love both exhilarated and terrified him.

With ragged breath, he scooped her up in strong arms, carried her to his room, and placed her on her feet. She trembled and ached with need, then recognized the naked, raw desire in his eyes. Her hands slid from his shoulders to his neck, up the chiseled contours of his face, to entwine in the curling length of his ebony hair. She lifted her face before his mouth, warm and wet, closed upon hers. Hands at her waist, he drew her closer, closer. She arched against him and he groaned before his hips swiveled against her to send surges of pleasure splintering through her.

His tongue slipped into the sweetness of her mouth to thrust in the imagery of lovemaking. She trembled, then wrapped her arms around him, clinging in senseless ecstasy as he undid the fastenings of her gown to let it slip to the floor. Her heart pounded wildly against the hardness of his chest, and she was dimly aware of his hands as they undid the ties of her pantalettes. They fluttered down around her ankles, and she shivered as his fingers skimmed up her stocking, up to the bare flesh above, to the inside of her thigh. Unable to move, she stood immobile as he performed his magic on her quivering body.

Then he pulled at his shirt, jerked at his breeches, and she murmered a protest. Her chemise was rent from her body and fluttered to the floor.

She was naked except for her stockings, and he stepped back to see the lovely perfection of her. He wrenched off one boot, then the other. She kicked off her slippers, stepped free of her drawers, and a primitive sound rumbled from his chest before he swept her up, carried her to his bed, and bent over her, his eyes glazed with raging desire.

"I have gone through five and a half months of hell without a woman, waiting for you, and you are damn well going to know it."

"You haven't been with anyone since me?"

Hurt reflected in his eyes. "Shawny, in my heart you are my wife. Don't ever doubt me, you'll never have reason to," he murmured tenderly, and cupped her face in his hands, his lips brushing her cheek before they found her mouth to kiss her sweetly, lovingly.

His flickering tongue devoured her body, his lips ravished her mouth, and then the power of him entered the moist warmth of her and passionately plundered her being. She catapulted with him to explore the timeless region of that world only they shared, locked in the throes of passion as wave after rapturous wave tore through them, whirling them through a wondrous journey of the miracle of love.

Afterward, Hawke fell into the deep sleep of the emotionally tried and physically assuaged. Shawnalese, however, struggled in the anguish of having her body fulfilled, but not her heart. Even though she knew there could never be a marriage between them, and knew Hawke didn't love her, she had willingly, eagerly, come to his bed. Had seduced him, actually. There was a name for such a woman. Mistress. She shuddered, and the words of Rose, the Creole madam in New Orleans, rushed back unbidden: "The best you can hope for is some wealthy gentleman to make you his mistress—until he tires of you, which'd be about two or three years."

Shawnalese's pride, her self-respect, wouldn't permit her to live the slow death of being Hawke's mistress for the next two or three years. Of what had she been thinking these last weeks when she had allowed one marvelous day with him to seduce her into the next, living only for the joy of being with him, all the while knowing they had no future together?

Slipping from the bed, she dressed hurriedly, tiptoed into the next room, wrote a quick note, placed it on her pillow, and in the middle of the night once again fled Gayhawke Carrington.

Sometime later Hawke stirred with a smile. Never in his life had he been so happy. He reached for Shawny but found only the note on her pillow.

Chapter 36

LIGHT FILLED HAWKE'S BEDROOM, AND THE PIL-low next to him still carried the impression of Shawny's head. With an ominous premonition, he picked up her note to read:

> Dear Hawke,
>   There is no future for us together, and I choose not to see you again.
>   In remembrance of all that we have been to each other, I ask this of you. Please make no attempt to see me, for naught will change. Allow me to have last night as my final memory of you, of us.
>   May God hold you in the palm of his hand.
>   Shawny

This last month, not wanting to break the fragile bond between them, he had waited for the right opportunity to explain why he'd never told her who her father was. He'd intentionally not explained about Rutger's threat to duel him, waiting until he felt he could convince her of the truth. He'd apologized for nothing. It never seemed the right time and they were seldom without the children. Yesterday she had come to him with a precious gift, her comfort and her love.

And exactly as the night on the beach, he had taken all he needed, plus all he wanted, without thought to her needs, her wants. Once more he had been unable to say, "I love you." Again he had allowed his passion to burn out of control without first telling her he wanted to marry her. Now no apology would suffice.

He didn't know what to do. Didn't know what not to do. Caught in the whirlpool of indecision for the first time in his life, he returned to Foxridge. Once there, he spent the day with Heather. He told her about Siegfried and Catherine and explained why he'd never told her the truth, then apologized for all the pain she had ultimately suffered.

"I suspected the truth after you refused Rutger's suit with no logical explanation," she said softly. "At first I believed you loved Shawna and intended to marry her yourself, but when we were in France and you treated her so abominably, I started to have second thoughts. I do understand, Gayhawke, and I thank you for trying to protect me. Siegfried was a good husband and loving father. I've been able to accept his betrayal. Now I'm moving ahead with my life. Edmund Spencer and I are to be married."

At that, Hawke told her about their mother, adding, "I stopped on the way from London and made arrangements to have Mother's body disinterred. She will be buried here at Foxridge, where she should be." After that, unable to discuss his anguish, his regrets about Shawny with Heather, he hurried to Greystone to see Chadwick.

After explaining all that had happened with Shawny after he'd returned from France, Hawke admitted, "I think I've destroyed her love this time, Chad. She certainly must view what happened as my wanting only to make her my mistress."

"God's teeth, Hawke. After all you've put her through, how could you add the final cut? Unless you really don't love her."

"Not love her? I'll love Shawny until the day I die."

"I know that, ol' chap. I felt it was time you said it aloud. The first time's the hardest, you know." Chadwick grinned.

For a moment, Hawke stared at his wise friend. Then he asked, "What do I do now?"

"I can tell you what not to do. With the high and honorable regard in which you've treated Shawna this last year and a half, I suggest you refrain from challenging her to a duel. She'd not only show up, she'd probably have the audacity to shoot you or run you through with her rapier."

"Spare me the lecture. There's nothing you can say that I haven't already said to myself. And how can you jest when my life is a shambles? Dammit, Chad, when Laurel disappeared I didn't make light of the situation."

"I didn't deserve it. You do."

Hawke stood up to leave.

"Sit down. No more teasing. I've something to tell you."

Hawke sat, looking up expectantly.

"I told you that Shawna released me from my marriage proposal so that I could be with Laurel."

"Yes."

"But I never told you exactly what she said about you. I think it might help you decide, perhaps not what to do, but how." At Hawke's quizzical look, he continued, "I remember her words perfectly because they left me with no guilt at doing as she bid. Shawna said, 'I loved him yesterday, I love him today, I will love only him through all of my tomorrows. My eyes have never seen any but he.' Then she said, 'You see, Chad, Hawke doesn't live merely in my heart. Hawke lives in my soul.' That, my friend, is why I called you a bloody jackass and a fool."

Hawke lowered his head into his hands, calling himself all the names Chadwick had not. Yet self-flagellation wouldn't win Shawny back. "I don't know what to do. I've always known what to do with other women. But they aren't willful and independent. They don't defy me and outwit me at every turn. They aren't . . . Shawny."

"I don't know what to advise you, Hawke. It seems the biggest problem now is to get her to listen to anything you have to say. My Laurel's a sweet and gentle soul. Who better to guide a bumbling fool like you? She's as wise as Solomon."

"Laurel? I'm not about to tell your wife—"

"Hawke, you don't need to tell her specifics. Simply tell her you've been an idiot and a dolt—again."

Hawke took Chad's advice, and a short time later Laurel said to him, "Shawna's been gone two and a half months now. I would think she'd be terribly homesick for Czar and Wildfire. She's never really been separated from them before, has she?"

Hawke leaped from his chair. "Thank you, Laurel," he exclaimed, and kissed her on the cheek before he raced out.

"Hawke," she called after him. "That should get you in the door. Still, there are things a woman needs to hear."

He turned back. "I'm not a man of pretty words, Laurel."

"They don't need to be pretty, or lengthy, but they need to come from the heart. But, more important, you talk, you discuss, until daylight turns to dark, if need be. With that comes understanding. Then you compromise."

"Chad is right about you. You are as wise as Solomon," Hawke said, and dashed out.

Shawnalese stood discussing the construction of a second story and stables with a building engineer, the third such man with whom she'd bargained prices in as many days. As the man was leaving, the door swung open and Czar bounded into the room. When the wolfhound spied her, he sprinted forward, almost knocking her over in his excitement. Tears welled in her eyes.

When she rose he bounded around her, barking in

excitement, and the children gathered round at the sight of the beautiful dog. She glanced around, sure Hawke had brought him, but he was nowhere in sight. With a procession of children following, she walked to the main entrance door and opened it to see Hawke leaning against his coach.

How could he have ignored her impassioned plea? She opened her mouth to tell him exactly what she thought of this latest ploy when he smiled, as though he had not seen her note, and his dazzling smile threw out an invisible line to capture her and slowly pull her to him.

"I have Wildfire and Warrior at the town house. It's a nice crisp day and I thought a gallop through Hyde Park might be enjoyable."

"Wildfire's here?"

"Yes, and the head groom informs me Wildfire has been quite listless since you left. Remember, Shawny, you rode him nearly every day for six years, until two and a half months ago. Now he's not only lost you, but because he won't allow anyone else to ride him, he's not getting the runs he's used to. Perhaps if you visit with him for a while, he'll perk up."

"Oh, my poor Wildfire. Hawke, you know I couldn't bring him or Czar with me. I had almost no money, and I didn't know how I could care for them in the city."

"You change into your riding habit and we'll give him the ride of his life."

"I'll get the children and be right back."

"That's probably not a good idea today. Wildfire's going to be spirited and excited to see you after so long. You know he's high-strung. I'll keep him in London for you, and anytime you and the children want to visit him, you can. But let him get adjusted first."

"Yes, of course," she agreed, and hurried off to change.

Sometime later Hawke and Shawnalese were trotting along the equestrian trails of Hyde Park. Not an eye missed the passing of the duke of Foxridge astride Warrior. He trotted beside *her* on her spirited Arabian stallion, whose glistening coat of fire accentuated every rippling muscle in the animal's perfect conformation.

Wildfire's thick mane shone and his arched tail dragged the ground. Shawnalese's long hair whipped in the breeze, and with each hoofbeat her cares slipped farther away.

After a while, Hawke lifted Shawny to the ground, and they walked beside their winded stallions. She told him about going ahead with plans to erect the second story now that the building belonged to Childhaven.

"Shawny, you have to get licensing and government sanction. You're fortunate you haven't been shut down already."

"I will not have Childhaven operated in the disgraceful manner of the county orphanages, or the charity and poorhouses, where children little more than babies are sent out to the workhouses as cheap labor to die like flies or become crippled and stunted. I won't allow anyone but Grizzly, Nadine, or me to manage Childhaven. First I will hire the unemployed men of Spitalfields and arm them with muskets, and England will have to bring in her highly esteemed army and navy to take all those unfortunate children from me."

"Darling, calm yourself. Allow me to handle the matter for you."

He had called her darling. Never had he called her darling. She forced the fantasies from her mind and commanded her heart to stop thudding. "You would do that for me?"

He wanted to tell her he would do anything for her, but it was not the right time, so instead he replied, "I will do that for you."

"I'll be able to operate Childhaven exactly as I do now, with a homelike atmosphere and with foster mothers?"

"Exactly as you do now."

"Oh, Hawke, I—"

He wanted to still her with his lips, but he knew the folly of that, so he pressed warm fingers there.

A sweet and gentle breeze rippled her hair, for spring wafted in the air. The grass, kissed by the morning dew of the Thames, grew green and lush. Evergreens and hedges abounded among the many bare-limbed oaks and beeches. Birds chirped and sang their glorious songs.

Whether her weakness, or his strength, drew them to the cold ground, she did not know.

Hawke sat with booted feet pulled back, his arms resting on his raised knees, his hands clasped together. "By this time you know that I'm not a man with pretty words." At her astonished look, he grinned and added, "At least when I mean them I'm not." After that, with a most sober countenance, he said, "I love you, Shawny." At her slow intake of breath, he continued, "Although what I'm about to say are not my words, I wish they were, for they come from my heart." He reached out and turned her face to his. With his gaze locked to hers, with her face cupped between large hands, he murmured, "I loved you yesterday, I love you today, I will love only you through all of my tomorrows. My eyes have never seen any but you." He paused at the brilliant shimmer in her eyes, then added, "You see, Shawny, you don't live merely in my heart. You live in my soul. Will you marry me?"

Heedless of the couples who strolled in the distance, of the equestrians who might ride by, Hawke pulled her into his arms. At her silence he advised her, "I've only asked two other women to marry me. The first one ran off minutes before the ceremony, and the second said she wouldn't marry me if I were the last man on this earth. Say yes this time, Shawny, so we can finally have all this pain and agony behind us."

After so many years of living for, dreaming of, this

moment, it emerged bittersweet. "You know I can't, Hawke. It's too late for us now. You are titled, wealthy, and have the responsibilities of a dukedom. I am ignoble, poor, and have the responsibilities of the foundlings of London. You cannot give up your dukedom to live in my world, and I can no longer give up my life, my children, to live in yours. The months since I came to London have created a chasm between us that can never be bridged."

"Do you love me, Shawny?"

"Love you?" She reached up and brushed the curl from his brow, then allowed her hand to slide caressingly down his cheek. "There has never been any but you. There will never be. But you see, Gayhawke, I'm no longer the same person. I have another fire that burns within me, other than the one that burns for you." She dropped her hand from his face. "You once said to me, 'There is no room in your life for me, because there is no room in mine for you.' That's truer now than before, since the founder of Childhaven can't also be the duchess of Foxridge. So now I must also say those same words to you." She blinked back bitter tears. "God forgive me for saying it, for wanting it, but if it wouldn't be the slow death of my love for you, I'd become your mistress. Please don't spoil the beauty of this day by asking me to be." She rose to her feet and said softly, "Please take me home."

He leaped to his feet, and pulled her into his arms. Wordlessly they clung to each other, unable to move close enough, unable to linger long enough.

The following day Shawnalese sat absently staring off into space, her heart squeezed in anguish. The door opened and a coachman, liveried in the maroon and gray of Foxridge, approached her, doffed his hat, handed her a note, bowed, then turned and left. She glanced up, but there was no sign of Hawke. She broke the wax seal to read:

Tutto a te mi guida, mio destino.
"Everything leads me to thee, my destiny."

She pressed the note to her breast before she glanced up to see Hawke leaning against the portal, watching her.

Her heart replied, *Tutto a te mi guida, mio destino.*

As though moving of their own volition, as though to obey his silent command, her feet raced toward him and his outstretched arms.

Time hung motionless, held in a fleeting eternity, while they clung together; her heart pounded wildly against the hardness of his chest, his hammered violently against the softness of hers.

Hawke buried his face in the silky fragrance of her hair. "Ahh, Shawny, I didn't think you were going to come." After a time, he set her from him. "We need to talk."

"Oh, Hawke, what is there to talk about?"

"Building bridges. There has to be a way. Will you come?"

"I'll come, but not to your town house."

Well he knew the folly of that. "No, not to the town house. How about Hyde Park? We can't get into too much trouble there, and we'll give the scandal mongers more fodder." He smiled and added, "I understand the *ton's* all aghast over our behavior there yesterday."

On the way to Hyde Park, the coachman stopped, made a quick purchase, and they were on their way again. Shortly they were strolling across a meadow large enough to allow them to forget they walked in the center of London. The grass, a velvety green carpet, stretched in every direction, including that of the small Serpentine Lake—awash with ducks—toward which they walked. With a flamboyant swirl, Hawke swept off his cloak and flung it to the bench beside the lake for Shawny to sit upon. He opened the burlap bag he'd retrieved from the coachman and offered it to her.

"Oh, Hawke," she squealed, dipping her hand in to grab a handful of seeds. Soon they were surrounded by ducks and birds.

Hawke began by explaining why he'd never told her the truth of who her father was and apologized for having hurt her. Then he asked, "What must I do so that you will marry me?"

"You know it's impossible."

"I know anything is possible if you want it badly enough."

"I don't know where to start."

"Let's start by trying to narrow the chasm between us and then building bridges." He dipped his hand into the bag and scattered more seed. Birds flocked to the ground to squabble with the ducks for the delicacy. "You tell me everything you can't live without, then list everything you want, then I'll do the same. We'll whittle away one obstacle at a time."

"You're truly serious. You want to marry me?"

"I'm going to tell you something, Shawny, and I don't want you to forget it. Nothing I could ever do, ever hope to do, would be as meaningful as being married to you. No title, no accolade, no honor. Nothing. That is what you mean to me."

She stared at him, perplexed. In the space of two days he had said all she'd dreamed of hearing him say, and not only didn't she understand it, but she suspected the truth of it. If indeed he did love her, did want to marry her, why had he said none of these things in the time between their betrothal and their marriage? However, this time she felt certain that Rutger was not involved. Which left only two motives for his actions: either he still sought to make her his mistress by allowing her to believe he would marry her, or—God, let it be so—he actually loved her enough to marry her. Angry with herself that she couldn't accept his words at face value, couldn't completely trust him, she nevertheless needed to know the truth. Even though she could think of no possibility of their coming to an agreement with which they could both live, in order to marry—if indeed he really did want to marry her—she could think of only one way to learn the truth: approach the unsurmountable barriers and put him to the test. That she did now. "I will not give up my three children."

"I wouldn't expect you to. Timothy, Lawrence Richard, and Margaret will be my children, too."

"I will not give up Childhaven. That is my lifetime project."

"It will be your lifetime project. What's next?"

She inhaled deeply, then plunged head on. "I would insist that you contribute ten percent of your annual income to Childhaven."

"Agreed."

Shawnalese cast a suspicious eye at him. "I have your word?"

"You have my word."

"And I want you to lend me your consequence in fund-raising. Those last three noblemen who made such generous contributions refused to see me when I called on them before."

The shanty town urchin of New Orleans not only bargained with the duke of Foxridge—one of the wealthiest and most powerful men in all of England—before she would accept his proposal and his dukedom, but she also boldly set stipulations. God, she was magnificent! He smiled inwardly and said, "Shawny, I'm a little disappointed that the woman who helped lead the revolution in France is willing to settle for so little."

"What do you mean?"

"I'm not making light of your outstanding achievement, of the enormous contribution you've already made with Childhaven. But do you realize that the children of Whitechapel and Clerkenwell are as pathetic as those in Spitalfields? And that the homeless children in St. Giles live on gin—because it's cheaper than food, it keeps them warm in winter, and for a time it lets them forget they're alive? And the children of Lambeth would be a challenge even to you, for they're accomplished pickpockets and thieves, living in fear, for when they're caught they're placed in vermin-infested reform schools and prisons, forced to so many hours a day on the treadwheel and other horrors that defy the imagination. Some are even hanged."

"How would I ever take on such a monumental campaign?"

"As the duchess of Foxridge, with a husband of immense wealth and considerable consequence, how would a woman of your intelligence, cunning, and passion for causes accomplish such a task? Surely you jest." He grinned, brushed away the curling tendrils that blew across her face, and teased, "It should be a small feat for the *vainqueuse de la Bastille* to become the *vainqueuse de les enfants.* To begin, you might climb up on a table—say, here in Hyde Park—let your hair down, and pin a cockade in those golden tresses—as you did in the Palais Royal."

At the sparkle in his eyes, she whispered, "You know about that?"

He bent and gave her a brief kiss before he took the bag of seed from her, walked a short distance away, and flung it across the green lawns to the lake. They had important affairs to resolve that now left no time for ducks and birds. "I know about that," he replied, and returned to sit beside her again.

"How?"

"Later."

"All right, later. But, Hawke, don't tease me. You would lend me your consequence, your influence, to accomplish all you just said?"

"I could be persuaded."

"How?"

"If you marry me."

"You would do all of that only so I will marry you?"

Chapter 37

DID SHAWNY NOT REALIZE HE WOULD DO ANY-thing so that she would marry him? "Yes, I would do all of that only so you will marry me."

"Why?"

He started to reply, "That should be obvious." But then he remembered what had happened the last time he'd answered so, and he also recalled Laurel's sage advice. Instead he answered simply, but from the heart, "Because I love you and want to spend my life with you, to grow old with you."

"Oh, Hawke," she cried out, and threw her arms around his neck, then smothered his face with sweet kisses while his arms enveloped her.

"The most ignorant thing I've done in my life," he murmured into her ear while she still clung to him, "was to send you to Paris. The most intelligent was to bring you back." When she released him he asked, "Does it seem there are an inordinately large number of people strolling by this secluded corner of the park?"

She glanced around at the dowager who looked at them through her quizzing glass, and she flushed cherry red. "I've disgraced you again. I'm sorry."

"Sorry? I rather hoped you'd do it again. The gossip because my bride fled at the last minute has fairly well died down by now, although admittedly our many trips to Vauxhall with the children must have caused quite a stir. Perhaps I should roll you to your back on this bench.

"But before this conversation and I get beyond my control, Shawny, allow me to make a proposal to you and have this matter out of the way. We aren't leaving the park until everything is resolved between us. My coachman is prepared to bring us food and drink, even bedding and a tent, if necessary," he teased her affectionately, then his countenance sobered. "I am a much wiser man than the one who charged with fire in his eyes to Paris after you. I never again want to live through the misfortunes and misunderstandings that occurred after that, through all the misery of that year and a half. I only recently learned what could have prevented it all. You talk. You discuss. With that comes understanding, and then you compromise.

"If you marry me, I'll devote one-third of my time to all of your benevolent causes. I'll give ten percent of my income to those same causes, I'll accept your three children as my own, if you will devote one-third of your time to my life. That means, at times, traveling with me, on those business ventures that require it, for I want no more separations between us."

"And the other third?"

"That is the most important. That third is for us and our family."

"How could I not agree?"

He heaved a sigh. "Then you will marry me?"

She hesitated, her heart pounding with hope, pounding with fear. Would what she was about to say be the ultimate barrier? The issue about which there could be no compromise—for either of them?

"What is it, Shawny? We don't leave here until we've resolved everything."

"I'm afraid, Hawke, this cannot be resolved."

Fear shot through his heart. "Unless you want to

spend the night in Hyde Park, you had best say it. The sun is setting."

"If I marry you, we must have an agreement about the children we would have together. It's a matter about which, despite your generosity, I am adamant and cannot compromise." When he made no response, she sighed and continued, "I strongly and unequivocally believe that mere accident of birth does not entitle a person to ignore the rest of humanity and live blindly in his or her own world of pleasures. If my children are your children, they will know that their accident of birth into wealth, privilege, and a title carries with it noblesse oblige."

She beseeched *him* to allow her to give him the greatest gift a wife could give her husband, the gift of children of worth, children with mettle, children of merit—as she was herself. Choked, he could not speak. He stared down at her angelic face, her almond-shaped, emerald-green eyes that sparkled with the beauty of the most dazzling gem, a halo of tresses that shimmered like spun gold in the setting sun.

Now all the beauty of Shawny's face faded into nothingness and Hawke saw only the luster of her heart, the brilliance of her soul, and that little bit of heaven outdazzled all else.

He kissed her with all of his love, then finally spoke. "I'd like for us to marry as soon as possible. Is that all right?"

"You agree? About the children, I mean."

"I agree, and you have my word on it. Now will you marry me, *mio destino*?"

At his last words, his note sang through her heart. "Everything leads me to thee, my destiny."

She knew if she said a word, she would cry, so she simply nodded, and his lips again found hers. How long it was before they caught fire, she didn't know. Pulling free, she murmured, "I'm extremely tired, Gayhawke. Do you know of a place nearby where I might rest? Someplace private."

He swallowed hard. He would not again do the wrong thing. When he spoke his voice was husky. "I'll take you back to Childhaven."

"But there's no privacy there, and I had hoped you might also wish to rest."

Fire flashed through his loins. After a time he managed to say, "I would throw my cloak over both of us right here and now if I could rest with you, Shawny, but I will not make yet one more mistake with you."

"What if you were to say 'I love you' and I were to say 'P-l-e-a-s-e, G-a-y-h-a-w-k-e'?"

He groaned.

"Please, Gayhawke," she whispered.

"I love you, Shawny . . . I love you."

A short time later Shawnalese accepted Hawke's hand down from the coach. In record time they stood in his bedroom. Only one long taper had been lit when she inquired, "If I ask you one question, will you answer me?"

"Of course."

"When did you, of your own volition, with no coercion from anyone, decide to marry me?"

He grinned, looked rather sheepish, and replied, "Before I came to France to bring you home."

She gasped. "Before the duchesse de Vordeaux's ball, before the duel?"

"You said one question."

"Answer me, Gayhawke. Before *that* trip to France?"

"Yes."

Her eyes widened, then narrowed. "You have put me through hell, Carrington, and I will have some explanations."

"Yes, well, I have many regrets, and you will have your explanations. But unless I misunderstood, we didn't come here to talk. Shawny, have a little mercy and let us talk later."

Her eyes took on a wicked gleam. "I will have a bit

of my own back, and you have just named your punishment."

He reached out to pull her into his arms.

"Don't touch me, Hawke," she threatened, and undid the front buttons of her faded muslin gown.

"Shawny, if you want to talk, we'll talk."

"No, I don't want us to discuss anything now. Or at least I don't want you to speak now, and I don't want you to touch me. Please stand where you are and listen." She continued to unbutton her gown. "Do you know how hurt, how devastated, I was during the two years after you sent me to France? You never wrote me so much as a word."

Her gown was open to her waist, and he saw her lacy silk chemise, saw the mounds of creamy flesh above. "I'm really—"

"Please, Carrington. You are to say nothing. As you said, we can talk later. However, I have something I wish to say."

Her fingers kept undoing the fastenings of her gown, and she was down to her navel. The dress gaped open; he swallowed hard and fought the urgings of his body craving hers.

She shrugged one shoulder out of her gown. "Do you know how rejected, how unwanted, how abandoned, I felt each time Heather came to see me in Paris and you didn't? I knew, everyone knew, you were also in Paris each time she arrived."

She shrugged the other shoulder out of her dress, hesitated, then allowed it to fall to her hips. Hawke shifted uncomfortably to his other foot.

"I'd like you to think about all we might have shared these last three and a half years," she said, and pushed her gown to the floor.

"I have. Isn't that punishment enough?"

She stepped out of the dress. "Punishment enough? For a woman scorned?" She bent, giving him a full view of her cleavage, then reached up beneath her pet-

ticoat, untied the ribbon on her pantalettes, and
shoved them from her hips. "Can there ever be enough
revenge from a woman tossed aside"—she stepped out
of her drawers and flung them carelessly onto the
chair—"as casually as this?"

A deep sound came from his throat. He shifted his
stance and shoved his hands into his pockets.

She smiled and her fingers moved to the tapes of her
petticoat. It whispered down around her ankles, and
she saw the pained but hungry look on his face as she
stepped out of the garment and stood before him in
her chemise and silk stockings. "Are you sorry now,
Hawke?"

"I've been"—his voice cracked—"been sorry for
three and a half years."

With a deliberate taunting gesture of her shoulder,
she reached up and lowered first one strap, then the
other, and tugged her chemise down to her waist.

"Shawny . . ." Hawke's voice rasped, and his eyes
glimmered. Beads of perspiration broke out on his
brow and fire shot through his loins as he stared at her
heavy, pink-tipped breasts jutting toward him. He
reached out, and she danced out of his reach.
"Shawny—"

"Shush, Carrington. You deserve some punishment
for what you've put me through these many months.
Do you know you're really quite handsome,
Gayhawke? Actually quite the most handsome man
I've ever seen."

She turned her back and slowly raised her chemise
above her silk stockings gartered with lace and
rosettes, above the bare flesh of her thighs, above her
little, rounded derriere. Lust volleyed through his
loins, and a tormented groan escaped his lips.

She smiled inwardly. With her back to him, she slowly slipped her chemise over her head and tossed it aside.

Hawke watched as it floated to the floor, then fastened his gaze on the taunting curvature of her slender

body. The softness of her shoulders tapered to the tiniest waist, then swelled to the contours of her lushly curved hips and melded into graceful, shapely legs and slender ankles. She was a temptation from which no virile man should have to restrain himself. As though aware of that, she reached up and pulled the pins from her golden hair, and it cascaded like a glistening veil to below her hips.

She pulled her hair over her shoulders, and it tumbled across her breasts to below her hips and masked—almost—all she knew he wanted to gaze upon. At his swift intake of breath, she whirled to face him. She smiled at the bulge of his arousal straining at his breeches, a smile that lit her green eyes mischievously. "If you'd like me to leave, I will," she offered huskily. Rosy nipples peeked from beneath her silky hair.

"I'll manage," he croaked.

"I hoped you would," she murmured. "I really don't want to go." With a conscious teasing gesture she reached down and slipped the garter from one stocking, slowly peeled the sheer silk down her leg, and handed it to him. Then she bent low to remove the garter on her other leg, invitingly exposing her breasts beneath her golden veil. Seductively she slipped her other silk stocking down her leg and reached out to hand that one to him also.

His green gaze devoured her luscious body, in agony as she seduced him slowly, deliberately, coquettishly. "Shawny," he implored, to no avail, as she sidestepped his grasp.

All inhibitions gone now, Shawnalese grinned wickedly and tossed her hair to her back. He approached her and she stepped aside deftly, smiling alluringly at his eyes glazed with desire, at his rapid breathing.

The candlelight cast soft golden hues across the naked flesh of the goddess of perfection who stood before him. He reached out a hand, and again she avoided him, dancing on tiptoe, swinging her hips like a gypsy dancer. He could bear no more, and cornering her, he crushed her to him, ablaze with desire. He lowered his head to capture her lips in a burning kiss that kindled them both. Then she began the slow torment that drove him to the brink of insanity.

Slowly she removed his jacket and trailed butterfly kisses across his adored face, while his hands freely roamed her naked body. She unbuttoned his waistcoat unhurriedly pressed delicate, tortuous kisses on his ear, then searched for and found his anxious lips, pushing his hands aside as he attempted to help her undo the buttons.

"Patience, my love," she whispered as she removed the cursed garment and her breasts burned through his shirt to his heaving chest. Refusing his help, she leisurely unbuttoned his shirt and tortured him further by tickling his ear with the tip of her tongue, which elicited a groan from him. "Have I told you how much I missed you, my darling?" she murmured in his ear, spreading his shirt open to press her soft, warm breasts to his furry chest.

"Shawny . . ."

"Shush, my darling. You have not yet suffered enough," she teased, and raised on tiptoe to kiss him passionately. Her tongue curled around his sensuously as she removed his shirt and trailed her fingernails down his muscular back, gratified at his quaking muscles.

"I love you, Hawke, to a depth no other man has ever known," she whispered, and he smothered her with kisses that sent desire splintering through her body. She tried to ignore her own passion, as her fingers lightly, unhurriedly, moved from around his back toward his buckle, a slow, deliberate torture she felt sure would drive him to distraction. She pushed his hands away as he attempted to assist her in unbuckling the cursed thing, and a throaty laugh escaped her lips.

"Shawny, my love," he murmured huskily, and her lips stilled his protest as she continued to fumble with his buckle. Ever so slowly, she unbuckled his belt, then smothered his chest with warm, moist kisses that tortured his soul, working haltingly on the buttons of his breeches.

"Have I told you how many times I've relived our night on the beach?" she queried softly, and slipped her hand inside his breeches to shove them, inch by inch, to the floor, ignoring his quick intake of breath. She caressed his lean stomach, then moved her hands down his sinewy thighs and up to the manliness that took her to such rapturous heights.

His body trembled from head to toe, and he gasped at her intimate touch, excruciatingly aware of his blood rising thick. No more! He tugged off his boots, stepped from his breeches, and swept her into his arms.

"Your fun is over, my love. And now mine begins." He grinned as he tenderly placed on the bed.

He smothered her with sweet, gentle kisses, and his hands caressed her body, sending shivers of longing through her. "Have I told you"—his voice broke—"of the anguish I suffered, thinking your childish love had vanished with a puff of smoke?"

"But, Hawke, I—"

He stilled her with a kiss of such passion that it left her weak with wanting, and his hands began to work their spellbinding magic on her skin, leaving nothing but quivering flesh beneath his expert fingers. She murmured his name, his lips captured her soft, eager mouth in a kiss that torched them both with its intensity, and his hand trailed provocatively to caress her breast. He stimulated the pink peak to tautness and sent splendorous sensations crashing through her body. His lips moved to the pulse at her throat, to her temple, his tongue tormenting her ear while his fingers gently massaged as they slid over her abdomen and descended to her inner thigh to send a path of fire blazing through her.

"Did I ever tell you how many nights I went without sleep thinking you'd lain with man after man?" Hawke quizzed, then tasted her salty tears. He clasped her to him and kissed away each tear, hating himself that he'd hurt her, not meaning to, her pain—his pain.

"Have I ever told you, Shawny, that I love you to a depth no other woman has ever known?" He looked deeply into her eyes before his head lowered to hers. Their lips met gently, tenderly, to seal his vow, and he kissed her with a gentleness that slowly turned to fire.

She began a deliberate exploration of his virile body, her hands moving softly down his buttocks, over his thighs. She felt him tremble beneath her touch as she caressed him brazenly, moving ever closer to his flame. She yearned to appease the smoldering sensations that blazed within her, hungered for the only man who could drive her to insane passions of wild abandon.

"Have I never warned you about what happens to angels who fly too close to the ground?"

"Show me, Carrington."

He smiled at the echo of her sigh, happy that he aroused in her the same fires that she did in him. He seared a path of kisses down her throat to her breast, her wildly beating heart, in tempo with his, music to his ears.

She clutched him to her, and the world faded away as he entered her, as he plunged deep inside, as he fueled the flame that burned its way to her core. He whispered words of love, everything she wanted to hear. His love spiraled her into a world of erotic pleasure that words were inadequate to describe. Naught existed but this moment as they soared to the heights of rapture.

"I love you, Shawny. I love you, I love you, I love you. . . . " His words were a litany that sang through her heart.

Time hung suspended as they streaked a blazing path, reveling in a consummation of love and passion that transcended anything mortal, to a firmament where the awesome melding of two kindred souls became one.

For all time.

* * *

When Shawnalese awoke, Hawke, stirringly naked, was sitting on the edge of the bed.

"I think this time I had better give this to you before our wedding. It was specially designed for you." He handed her a small box wrapped in soft velvet.

Inside were two bands of gold, entwined together into one ring. A note—which had obviously been in the box for quite some time, for it had taken on the shape of the lid—was enclosed. She opened it to read:

> Shawny,
>   My love is as enduring as this band of gold. As long as you wear this ring, my life is entwined with yours, as these two bands of gold are inseparably encircled, with no beginning, no end, only forever.
>
>   Gayhawke

With tear-filled eyes, she looked at the misshapen note and frowned. "When did you have this ring designed?"

"In September when I purchased the diamond."

The enormity of what she had done to him overwhelmed her. Last September, the nobleman had proudly presented her with an extravagant diamond and nonchalantly proclaimed, "A ring befitting the duchess of Foxridge." Yet all the while the vulnerable boy within the man, who couldn't say pretty words, had forced himself to write the beautiful prose he could not express aloud. That same vulnerable boy had saved that gold ring, the gift of his heart, and his stirring note, to give to the bride who wouldn't betray him, who wouldn't abandon him as he'd believed one other woman had.

And she had not only betrayed him by abandoning him, but by abandoning him in the most humiliating manner possible. After all of that, the arrogantly proud duke of Foxridge had still come for her. She

had done as she'd once vowed: she had brought him
to his knees; that knowledge was a searing agony of
such intensity, it became almost unbearable. No deed
could undo the pain she must have caused him, no
words were adequate to express her regret. Tears
streamed down her cheeks, and she lifted pain-glazed
eyes to implore, "Forgive me."

He knew that he could forgive her anything. There
was nothing she could do for which he wouldn't forgive her. Nothing. "I forgive you, Shawny. Forgive me."

His mouth covered hers in such an exquisitely tender kiss of forgiveness, of love, that it flowed into her
soul. It was a kiss that spoke of something far deeper
than passion, a kiss that eclipsed all things of this
earth and promised a love eternal.

Two weeks later the clergyman stood on the dais at
the head of the cathedral. Hawke, handsome and aristo-
cratic in pearl gray formal attire, stood next to Chadwick
and looked down the aisle of the domed church for a
glimpse of Shawny. Organ music echoed throughout the
beautiful cathedral, rising to the high-vaulted ceiling.
Behind him white candles of every size and shape flickered softly in the pulpit. Bowers of white flowers
abounded everywhere, spilling their fragrance. Two
billing white doves, anxious to fly to their own destiny,
awaited their freedom in a gilded cage near the altar.

In the pews of the nearly empty church sat relatives
and loved ones—Rutger, Leif, Wilhelmina, Nadine,
Auguste, Timothy, Lawrence Richard, Margaret, Mrs.
Kendall, Thaddeus, Addison, Laurel, and Lord
Edmund Spencer—for no invitations had been extend-
ed to this wedding.

The organ music paused momentarily, then melded
into the processional. Heather, elegantly gowned in
maroon trimmed with gray, drifted down the long aisle.

"Ye're prettier than a speckled pup," Grizzly said in

a hushed tone to Shawnalese as she slipped her hand through his arm and looked up at him with misty eyes. The music soared into a crescendo, and they started down the aisle.

Then Hawke glimpsed her and inhaled sharply, his heart beating wildly at the angelic apparition in yards and yards of flowing creamy lace, silk taffeta, and tulle, her beauty unequaled. Mesmerized, he stared as she glided down the aisle on Grizzly's arm. Her silken golden tresses spilled in natural curls over her breasts to her slender hips. Her alençon lace skirts, embroidered with seven thousand seed pearls, billowed majestically from her tiny waist as she floated toward him, the sixteen-foot train of her gown and veils trailing elegantly behind. A diamond-studded pearl tiara held her three-tiered, lace-edged veil in regal splendor. She was ethereal.

Her gaze captured his and locked, all the words of love they'd whispered to each other mirrored there. As she approached him, he unconsciously held out his arms to embrace her. She smiled that smile for which he would gladly walk through fire, reached out, and took his hand to walk with him, side by side, to the altar.

The vicar began, "Dearly beloved, we are gathered here in the presence of God to join this man and this woman . . ."

A short time later Hawke and Shawny turned to face each other, and joined hands to repeat their vows.

The clergyman instructed quietly, "Repeat after me. I, Gayhawke Lawrence Richard Carrington, take thee, Shawnalese Lynelle Grenville, to my wedded wife, and do promise and covenant before God and these witnesses . . ."

"I, Gayhawke Lawrence Richard Carrington, take thee, Shawnalese Lynelle Grenville, to my wedded wife, and do promise and covenant before God and these witnesses . . ."

"To love, honor, and cherish you, keeping myself only for thee," the vicar enunciated.

"To love, honor, and cherish you, keeping myself only for thee," Hawke vowed, gazing deeply into his Shawny's eyes.

"In plenty and in want, in joy and in sorrow, in sickness and in health," the clergyman said.

"In plenty and in want, in joy and in sorrow, in sickness and in health," Hawke pledged, his eyes echoing his promise.

"Until death do us part," the vicar intoned.

"Through all eternity, Shawny. Through all eternity."

BRENNA BRAXTON-BARSHON attended the University of Ohio in Akron and the University of California at Santa Barbara. A former financial controller and accountant, she now writes full-time. She currently lives in Las Vegas, Nevada, with her husband and daughter. This is her second novel.

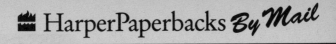

YESTERDAY'S SHADOWS
by Marianne Willman

Bettany Howard was a young orphan traveling west searching for the father who left her years ago. Wolf Star was a Cheyenne brave who longed to know who abandoned him—a white child with a jeweled talisman. Fate decreed they'd meet and try to seize the passion promised. 0-06-104044-4

MIDNIGHT ROSE by Patricia Hagan

From the rolling plantations of Richmond to the underground slave movement of Philadelphia, Erin Sterling and Ryan Youngblood would pursue their wild, breathless passion and finally surrender to the promise of a bold and unexpected love. 0-06-104023-1

WINTER TAPESTRY
by Kathy Lynn Emerson

Cordell vows to revenge the murder of her father. Roger Allington is honor bound to protect his friend's daughter but has no liking for her reckless ways. Yet his heart tells him he must pursue this beauty through a maze of plots to win her love and ignite their smoldering passion. 0-06-100220-8